THE POWDER MONKEY

I hope you enjoy my novel. Best Wishes!

George J. [illegible]

08/04/01

THE POWDER MONKEY

by
George J. Galloway

ISBN: 0-75960-477-0

This book is printed on acid free paper.

1stBooks - rev. 12/26/00

For Cathy, Connor, Patrick, and Mary Kate.

ACKNOWLEDGEMENTS

This novel was seven years in the making before a final edit. "I thank God and not my strength for it." He gave me the means, in Cathy, who recognized my need to write. In my sons and daughter, who patiently endured the many trips we took in our camper to visit yet another historical site as I did research. And in my dad and mom, brothers and sisters, who gave me every encouragement.

I also want to thank Jennifer Durkin, Harry Leib, Karen Diaz, Kara Balcum, and my brother, Brian, for their help in editing. Thanks also to Cathy's cousin, Anna, Uncle Charlie, and to Janet and Sharon from St. Martin of Tours for their kind suggestions.

To the many people who helped with advice and instruction over the course of years of camping in Maryland, New York, Ontario, and New England, I send my gratitude. Special thanks go to the staff of the Admiral Nimitz Library at the United States Naval Academy, the folks at the Maryland Historical Society, and to the crew of the *"H.M.S. Rose"* for helping me get my sea legs.

To the wonderful people of Baltimore and, especially, Fells Point and St. Patrick's Church, past and present, I am humbled by your inspiration.

George J. Galloway

Prologue: Baltimore, sometime before the Civil War.

The September rain was both a blessing and a bother. It matted the sawdust on the floor of the cooperage so that one could breathe easier, and an increase in the humidity seemingly made the hoops more pliable, readily softened under a pounding mallet, so that they could be wrapped around staved barrels and hooked into place. But the rain also laid an invisible film of stickiness onto everything in the workroom including the old man and the boy. Clumps of sawdust stuck to the soles of their boots, and shirts and trousers stuck to their damp, gritty skin even though the work was easy going.

Still, despite clammy skin and stickiness, it was the best time of the year for a cooper. Soon, everything, every imaginable commodity the earth and sea could give birth to, and man could harvest, would be barreled. The Dooley family cooperage had, for several generations now, made barrels for the world. Barrels for butter and cheese for the German dairy farmers of Lancaster, Pennsylvania. Barrels that were barged down the mighty Susquehanna, and then carted over the rutted roads of Maryland. Barrels for wheat flour from mills powered by the rapids of Jones Falls in Baltimore. Barrels for tobacco, the quintessential cash crop below the Mason-Dixon. And barrels for export to transport West Indian rum, English ale, German beer, Irish whiskey, and Spanish wine. Barrels for fish, oysters, crabs, and for salted beef and pork, the staple of seamen across the world. Barrels that were stowed into ships' holds plying the oceans and seas from Halifax to Polynesia.

There couldn't be a better place for a cooperage than right here, adjacent to the wharves of Fells Point, Baltimore, Maryland. The old man, who worked here his entire life, whose father and uncle started the business after the Revolution, gazed upon the young boy with pride. Tears welled in his eyes. The boy caught his grandfather's stare, put aside his mallet, and sat upon a pile of staves. His hands worked back and forth against each other, rubbing the dust and grit and stickiness in anticipation of his grandfather's words. The boy had been patiently waiting for this moment since he was six years old, when he first heard of the code from his father. References to the code were woven into adult conversations throughout his life: in times of danger and success, whenever there was a decision of import, always after birth or death. But, he was not permitted to know. That was a privilege of manhood or womanhood, and not yet for him. The code was given to one on the occasion of their thirteenth birthday by the senior member of the family; a tradition dating back to the Dooley clan in Ireland, centuries before. The passing on of the code - the telling of it - was a cherished thing, always reminisced with a smile.

Now, the grandfather grinned, knowingly. He too, laid aside his mallet and wrung his hands. His smile turned down so he could show a more serious attitude towards his duty; but it was hard for him, for he was enjoying himself too much. Nevertheless, he thought, this was more the boy's moment than his own and he must proceed with all proper decorum.

"Daniel Patrick Dooley," he stated, stiffly, as if he was reading from a muster roll, "son of Thomas Ignatious Dooley and Mary Margaret Callahan." He nodded to the boy who nodded back at the mention of his parents' names. "What I am about to tell you has been passed down to me from my grandpa, and to him from countless generations of Dooleys."

Daniel's eyes rounded as he inhaled. Every breath he took was timed to the cadence of his grandfather's words and gestures. The old man glanced about the workroom, obviously searching for a seat from which to deliver his discourse, a throne among the sawdust and stickiness. He picked a barrel directly opposite the boy and set it upright with the bunghole up. Reaching into his trousers, he pulled out a short, clay pipe, fished for his tobacco pouch, stuffed his pipe, lit it, and filled the room with the sweet smell of good Carolina tobacco. He drew on it and let the curling smoke exit his nose and the sides of his mouth, and said:

"Relax, son, I can't tell you the wisdom that is the code without tellin' you a story. I'm not bein' coy with ya Daniel. I know you're anxious for me to tell you the secret; but I've been thinkin' on the best way to do that and I can't separate the story of my father from the code itself. For me, they're one and the same. For sure, the code is something to build on, but ya gottta understand how it works as well as what it is. It's more than words etched into the Dooley mind. It's - it's a way of life. A way of helpin' you make choices - the thousands of choices you're gonna make throughout your lifetime. And from here on in, you're gonna change because of this simple code. I know I was changed because of it; but, I'm gettin' ahead of the story and that won't do."

It wouldn't do at all. Daniel had heard his father speak of Daniel's grandfather and great-grandfather, and some mention of adventures before, of course, and he had pleaded with him to tell him more. But, the answer was always the same: wait, wait until you're given the code. Now, it was time, time to hear the whole story and Daniel didn't mind it a bit.

"Tell me everything, grandpa. There's no more work for today. I want to hear everything." Daniel propelled himself from the pile of staves, sat down with his legs crossed on the damp floor, and attentively gazed up at his grandfather.

"Much obliged, Daniel," said the old man as he switched his pipe around to the other side of his mouth, clamped the stem with what was left of his teeth, and began his discourse again. "Why is it that man can remember who wronged him in the past, but can't recall why? Does everybody forget the two wars we fought with England and why we fought those wars? Why, this very city, in the Second War for Independence, was attacked and defended from crack lobsterbacks and the greatest navy in the world. And why do you think they came after us - us here in Baltimore after all? Because we hurt their pride, boy, that's why. The English are a proud people, and sly ones, too. Why, they know how to pull off a ruse better than anyone. Division is always their goal: in Ireland, America, anywhere a people claim to stand as one. Always schemin' to lift the hand of Cain against Abel. In the first war too, I can attest to that, heard it from my pa, who was one of the old fellows. And now there's talk of secession again. It's not the first time, I can tell you, no sir. There was talk of secession back then, too, in the year 14. And right in the middle of the war!

"People! Shortsighted, envious, selfish people talkin' about secession; of a separate peace with the British, despite the fact - the holy fact - that men were dyin' for their country. I've seen 'em, Daniel. Seen as much as any man would want to see of war. Folks who haven't seen a battle are the ones always talkin' for it. Folks who have seen it don't talk much about it, because they try to put it out of their heads so they can sleep at night. But, I've got to talk on it now, boy, so you'll get the full treatment. Only don't go tellin' your dear ma. She knows you're supposed to be getting the code, of course, but she might not appreciate me tellin' you about the war and all."

Daniel promised and then quickly crossed his heart with his index finger to show solidarity with his grandfather's sentiments.

"For me and Jessica, your grandma, the story begins right here on the Point. Together, we sailed across the Atlantic and back again on the glorious *Chasseur* with mighty Tom Boyle. And then onto New York City, all the way up the Hudson to a skinny stretch of lake called Champlain. That's where we served with him: Macdonough, though his name was, originally, McDonnough. Sure, he was Irish through and through, though a left hander, if you know what I mean. Dear Lord, I'll never forget. It's funny how some things come back to you as you get older: the smells and tastes and feelin's you had deep inside. Jessica tells me that women forget the pain they go through in childbirth; but I wonder if they really forget. The women talk so much about it when they get together, down to the smallest detail. Anyway, I know I won't - can't - forget the feelin' of it all - the pain as well as the glory.

"In the end we were lucky, me and Jessica and my pa, if you give any credence to luck. We lived and went right on livin'. For my part, Daniel, I don't believe in luck or chance. I'll stake my life on what Father John and my pa and Uncle Bob passed onto me through the code. The code that has guided my life ever since then, and will con the life of my children and theirs long after I've moved on to the better life with no pain." Just then, the old man paused with his mouth open and his eyes gazing upward - his mind borne back to another time.

Slowly, he brought his head down and stared at Daniel with a blank look on his face, forgetting, momentarily, where he was in his discourse.

"Ahhh," he sighed, "so much happened, before and after September, 1814. If it wasn't for the code, Captain Ken, Father John, Uncle Bob, and Jessica, of course, I don't know where I'd be or even if I be. And if it wasn't for Macdonough, there wouldn't be a United States of America for anybody to secede from, I can tell ya that right now. Awe, Daniel, if I laced my grog too thick I'd be cryin'. But everythin' seems so clear to me now. So, I'll stow my tears for the moment and let them git lose a little later. 'Bout the last thing we need in here is more wet. But, I don't mind tellin' ya, Daniel, I wept a good deal back then. Was blue for a long stretch of time. Especially after my ma died. She was the one that insisted everybody call me Michael. That was how they could tell us apart - me and my pa. They called him Mike, and they called me Michael - Michael Dooley Jr."

Chapter 1

June, 1812

TERESA'S HOME

There was something stirring him from sleep. It was something mingling with the warm, June breeze coming through his bedroom window. It was his mother. It was the scent of lilac from the soap his mother had always used in her bath. It roused him to semi-consciousness and he stretched and squirmed on the soft, eiderdown mattress while his mind reconciled the lilac with something else in the pit of his stomach: his mother was dead. Dead from the ravages of "The Fever" that had swept the Point toward the end of last summer, when the marshes surrounding the Point stagnated and provided a stench singular to tidewater areas. But, this sweet, flowery odor was comforting to Michael Dooley, Jr. As he opened his eyes, it quelled the sinking feeling in his stomach and brought a smile to his lips.

The peal of St. Patrick's burst into his ears and welcomed the new day. It was exactly six o'clock and time to pray. Ever since the 25th of March, the Annunciation, old Archbishop Carroll had requested the people of Baltimore to pray the Angelus. Years before, when the country first broke free from England, Bishop Carroll had declared the United States under the protection of the Blessed Virgin; and now, the aging shepherd, sensing conflict with England again, was reminding Our Lady of the special compact. Father John Francis Moranvillé, the French-born pastor of St. Patrick's, gave particular instructions at last

Sunday's Mass that the Angelus would be said fervently throughout the Point. He was looking directly at Michael when he had given those instructions from the pulpit. Michael plopped onto his knees.

"The angel of the Lord declared unto Mary..."

It wasn't the hard, cool planks of his bedroom floor against his skinny, knobby knees that turned his attention away from the prayer his lips were forming, but the prospects of the day. First, breakfast. Before his mother died, Father John had sent a young girl to help with domestic chores in the Dooley house. She would arrive shortly after lifting her knobby, thirteen-year-old knees off the hardwood floor of St. Patrick's Free School, where, as an orphan, she had lived since losing her parents to an earlier fever epidemic. Her name is Jessica Farmer. Her father was a caulker and her mother a seamstress. Father John had taken care of her ever since with the help of a strident group of women known as the St. Patrick's Benevolent Society. The society, in which Michael's mother, Teresa, was prominent, raised funds for the orphanage and free school.

Jessica, along with having a quick mind for study, also had quick feet. Michael heard her enter the unlatched door into the house and scamper across the living room into the kitchen, and then out the back door to the chicken coop. An abrupt cackle signaled that she had succeeded in pushing over a hen's bottom to snatch two warm, fresh eggs underneath. Jessica had prayed her Angelus fervently for she was a mature, serious girl. Then she had run the five blocks from the orphanage on Apple Alley to the Dooley house on Thames Street before Michael had even finished his morning devotion. But, Michael was still organizing the day's schedule in his head, while shifting his weight from one knee to the other in an attempt at preempting the sharp pang he received from spending too much time thinking on the day's events and not enough time being fervent.

"We ask this through Christ, our Lord, Amen," he said out loud, pushing the conclusion.

He slipped out of his nightshirt, revealing a scrawny, lithe body. He made his bed, or rather, completed his version of bed making, and while dressing in a light, white flaxen shirt, worn, gray britches, and black, buckled shoes, rounded out the day to his satisfaction.

"Now, after breakfast, I've got to run up to the center of town with my wagon," he said aloud again, "and cart a bale of newspapers - no, two bales. Business is picking up what with talk of war out of congress, then make my way over to Market Street and hawk papers before school starts at nine." A thought struck him and he stuck his head out the window to assess the weather. Rainfall had debilitating affects on newspaper sales. He sniffed the morning air in order to gauge dampness, a precursor to Fells Point thunderstorms this time of year. To Michael's satisfaction there were no smells or signs of rain, just the typical dewyness of dawn. He continued planning the day our loud. "After school, I'll pick up some milk and cheese from the Market - mmm, maybe ole' Sally's got some spicy blue claws today. Then, run down to the cooperage - see how Uncle Bob has managed to bungle the orders this time - examine the books, review the orders and, Jeez!" he shook his spinning head, "everything's got so busy since pa left."

Busy, indeed. Mike Dooley Sr. had made the decision to go to sea, sailing as a carpenter on the brig, *Mary Lynn*, some months before. The Dooley family cooperage, run by Mike Dooley and his rambunctious brother Bob, had seen better times. With the interruption of trade due to the resumption of the war between France and Britain, business at the cooperage had dropped off significantly. To keep food on the table and maintain their fine red, brick house on Thames Street, Michael's father had signed onto the merchant ship. He left Uncle Bob to run the business, Michael to keep the books and keep an eye on Uncle Bob, and Father John and Jessica to watch over Michael.

A basin of water, chilled from the night air, stood before an oak trimmed mirror across from his bed. Michael splashed the water on his face and rubbed it vigorously into his dark, curly hair. Blindly, he reached out for a soft, cotton towel, wiped his face, and took an ivory comb to his matted head. He tilted himself back and combed his long hair away from his face and over the tips of his ears. Then, he pulled a piece of blue ribbon from his top drawer and, after clubbing his hair in a seaworthy fashion, tied the ribbon in a bow at the end of his pigtail, which laid against his back, just below the shoulders. He stood in front of the mirror, admiring this dashing new style: thoroughly a Jack-tar, seen the world, old salt look, and he thought of Desiree. She would approve of this new fashion, even though Michael's father, who insisted upon hair cut short to the scalp in a modest, republican manner, would not. Michael was almost lost in his admiration for this young master posing in the glass before him when he smelled bacon.

To Michael, bacon signified a stack of flapjacks, oozing with melted butter, and covered with sugar, or better yet, enveloped with maple syrup; just the kind of breakfast his mother would have prepared for him. But, somehow, this thought didn't depress him. He remembered the lilac, and poked his head into his parents' room. There was her nightstand and mirror, with her brushes and combs that used to sweep over her long, gray-black hair before she would tie it up in a neat, rounded bun. Her only vanity would be to let just a wisp of a few locks dangle and curl across her forehead, above her dark brows and brilliant blue eyes. It was this insignificant touch that caught hold of Mike Dooley's heart and never let go. In their first intimate moment, Mike confessed the subtle attraction and Teresa made it a permanent part of her daily grooming.

"Practical and perfect," his father used to say. Practical, because of her personal sense of economy, nothing wasted, everything used for a purpose, everything done for a purpose. Practical, not in a stingy way, for she spared nothing to please her husband and son. She had good horse sense, the kind Uncle Bob didn't have, although, she loved and doted on Bob, and did her utmost to console Mike Dooley when his older brother was drinking and philandering. Perfect, because that's simply how she seemed to them; not that she would ever condone such a divine description. Teresa Dooley had a strong commitment to family by virtue of the fact that she had had none herself. Her father, who she rarely saw because of his almost constant life at sea, was drowned off the Outer Banks in a squall, and her mother died in childbirth - her birth. Orphaned at twelve, she was sent by her priest to work as a servant girl for a group of nine Sulpician Fathers at St. Mary's Seminary in Old Baltimore Town.

The Sulpicians were newly arrived from Paris. They were forced to leave after the French National Assembly instituted the Civil Constitution of the Clergy, an anticlerical edict. The priests were without a homeland and Teresa without a home. At the seminary, she learned the arts of cooking, cleaning, and diplomacy, the latter a must when living with Frenchmen. In time, she was introduced to a newly arrived cleric, an émigré priest, born in France and ordained at the Seminary Du Esprit, who joined the community at St. Mary's after escaping from Cayenne, the capital of French Guyana. The priest was Father John Francis Moranvillé, and he and Teresa worked out a wonderful arrangement: she would teach him English, and he would teach her everything else.

Since that time, Teresa was dedicated to the education and care of the orphans of the Point, and also to Father John, her confessor and confidant. It was Father John who searched Baltimore for a respectable, responsible, and loving husband for Teresa. The Frenchman had a keen eye, but there was little in the line of responsible romantics along the wharves of the Point, with its drunkards and prostitutes. Still, Teresa had become very much like a daughter to him, and he was determined to see her happy.

In answer to a prayer, Bishop Carroll introduced him to an industrious, tithing Irishman, one Sunday at St. Peter's. He was a Hibernian and a sober, self educated, veteran of the War for Independence, who had fought with Washington and Lafayette at Yorktown. He was Mike Dooley of County Cork, a particular disciple of Thomas Aquinas. After a respectable courtship, they were married at the new St. Patrick's church by Father John, now the pastor of the French-Irish-English community of Fells Point.

Michael bounded downstairs heading toward the delicious aroma of frying bacon. Jessica had already laid out the table with Teresa's everyday wooden dishes, lit a crackling fire, and sliced a fresh loaf of bread. Like Teresa, Father John had put Jessica to work. And, like Teresa, she had been used to cooking for ten grown men at the seminary, before being transferred to the Dooley's, so laying out a table and preparing breakfast for one twelve year old boy was hardly a bother. Besides, she was fond of Michael and it pleased her to cook his favorite dishes. Unfortunately, Michael took little notice of Jessica's affectionate care. He treated her civilly, like a sister; a sister who's job it was to cook and clean. But, his eye could not see the tenderness in her work: the sprig of posies on the table and the fact that she was wearing his mother's blue apron.

Surely, he should have noticed that, two days ago, she had spent hours preparing to do the baking for the week: brown wheat bread, large corn muffins (which he liked split with melted butter and warmed by the fire), sugar and cinnamon scones, and soft molasses cookies. She had left everything to rise overnight, in baskets and bowels, and baked all the next day. Michael eyes noticed nothing, but his nostrils took in everything the kitchen could offer. This was, at least, a small sign of gratitude, and she contented herself with the fact that, even if he did not see she was trying to please him, he at least smelt it. Jessica motioned for Michael to sit. He took a chair and smiled at the prospects of enjoying his breakfast. He looked at her, then stared longingly at the sweet, frying bacon, and then looked at her again. Jessica, realizing that his sense of smell was certainly not good enough for her this time, bit her lower lip as tears filled her eyes. She fidgeted with the bottom of her apron, turned her back toward him and went to the fire so he couldn't see her emotions.

Next to the coffee pot which hung on a crane bolted onto the back of a brick fireplace, swung a large skillet popping with steaming bacon, an inch thick, and four frying eggs. Jessica controlled herself, deftly lifted the coffee and skillet off the crane, and swept them down onto the table.

"Eat," she said directly, "I promised your mother." He looked up at her with her hands buried into the apron and was about to say something like "thank you," but she seemed to be staring beyond him, at something she must busy herself with out in the back of the house. Is today laundry day? Michael asked himself. Shrugging off the question, completely irrelevant to him anyway, he dug into his breakfast: sopping up yellow yolks with a large slice of wheat bread, covered with white, sweet butter; filling his stomach with juicy bacon, and downing two cups of fresh coffee and cream.

With a "see ya at school, Jess," he swung off the chair, grabbed his schoolbooks from the sitting room, and scooted out the front door. She quickly glanced toward the door and just caught sight of his pigtail and ribbon, bouncing out onto Thames Street. Alone and melancholy, she sat at the table on the edge of a chair. She always sat on the edge of a chair. Her tiny body would look foolish sitting back with her dainty feet lifted off the ground and her short, willowy frame set to far away from the table to reach her food. But being small and thin didn't necessarily follow that she was frail. On the contrary, she was strong in body, and stronger, still, in mind and spirit. It was because of her strong intellect that Father John had not placed her in servitude to one of the wealthier families of Baltimore. Many children were signed over to labor in service and, ofttimes, apprenticeship, to families and businesses throughout the city.

Yet, Father John, who saw the need for indentured servitude, could not bring himself to contract Jessica out in the world beyond St. Patrick's Free School. When he saw Jessica, he saw Teresa. And as the French cleric had combed the city, looking for a match for Teresa, he was determined to see to it that Jessica marry the right kind of man.

Despite her intelligence, Jessica did not see the big picture. She was only thirteen, and at that age smaller portraits prevail. Sure, she had her friends at school and at the orphanage, and she was kept busy from dawn till dusk, cooking, cleaning, and studying. But, she could only see her daily life in terms of days - not as invisible blocks of time. Time to build character, mold the mind, strengthen faith, and ensure salvation, the way Father John envisioned it. And, although her time was spent under supervised and constructive care - always industrious, never idle - her time, at least under the law, was her own. Had she been indentured, she would have been bound to servitude night and day for many years, with no hope of an education and poor prospects for a chosen marriage, home, and family. Eventually, she would have been released, of course, but not until her ebony hair grayed, her white teeth blackened, and her pink skin paled.

Jessica rose from the table and with the most correct, school girl posture, walked into the sitting room and closed the heavy, polished mahogany door with the bright, brass handle that Michael had absent mindedly left ajar.

"What's wrong with me?" she asked the empty room. From the closet beneath the steps, she drew out a cornbroom, a pail, and a feather duster. As usual, she started to clean the house from the top down, starting in Michael's room. Jessica smiled as she entered his small, comfortable bedroom and shook her head at the ruffled attempt Michael had made at bed making. She quickly undid, and then redid, the still warm cotton sheet and quilt, and spread them neatly over his mattress.

Dusting was the first and lightest housekeeping chore, and she always began her dusting with a song. She sang softly, mimicking, as Teresa had, the soft tones of the square piano at St. Patrick's Church. Teresa's music was light and as soothing as a lullaby, and Jessica, who had no memory of her own mother's voice, and who was exposed at too young an age to the harsh, crude sea songs of the Point, adopted Teresa's melodies into her heart. She sang as she dusted over the few furnishings. Michael's bed, which sat underneath a small window bordered by blue curtains, overlooked the cobblestones of narrow Thames Street. The room also contained a small chest of drawers, a writing desk with a quill pen, ink stand, and a little glass lantern, a shelf for his school books, and an engraved tin plate, hanging opposite his bed on a plastered wall, depicting the Battle of Yorktown.

The chamber pot was empty (it always was). Michael refused to use it ever since Jessica started working for the Dooleys. She hung the damp towel out the window, whisked her broom across the pinewood floor, and emptied the water from Michael's basin into the pail. Working up a lather with the bar of soap in the pail, she scrubbed the floor with a stiff brush. Running downstairs and out the backdoor, she grabbed a large bucket and walked in a quickstep to the public well, with its great 15-foot well sweep, at the end of Thames Street. Strong as she was, the bucket was heavy - heavy even without water in it. Nevertheless, she attached the bucket to a chain and let it drop, filled it to the brim and, with bent frame and callused palms, returned to the house walking sideways in order to lessen the pain in the small of her back.

She bore her load to the backdoor, placing the bucket there for a variety of uses throughout the day, and fetched another light pail from the closet. Filling that halfway, she tossed in a rag that was used to rinse off the soap from the flooring. After Michael's room was finished, she tiptoed into Mr. and Mrs. Dooley's room.

Everything there was as if Teresa had never died. The room was about twice the size as Michael's with a large four-posted bed made of shiny lacquered pine and, covering the feather mattress, a white quilt with a border of pink roses and blue forget-me-nots. Two fluffy pillows were propped up at the top of the bed: one with a soft, pink pillow case, the other a manly blue. A mirror, trimmed in dark oak reflected the setting sun that shown through a pink curtained window and faced the back of the two-storied brick house. Jessica carefully dusted Teresa's nightstand, a large chest of drawers, and a roll top desk with its quills, inkstand, and a three-wicked whale oil lamp. Standing on the stool from the desk, she scattered the dust off a thick shelf made from old oak staves that stretched the entire length of one wall, and carried accounts and ledgers from the family cooperage. She peeked reverently into the closet which contained the few plain dresses Teresa wore: two light cotton for hot weather; two woolen dresses for cold; a simple, red shawl that hung on a hook and, opposite that, Mr. Dooley's black Sunday suit. A small commode with a chamber pot was tucked neatly in one corner of the room, and, adjacent to it, stood a dainty ebony table with a white porcelain pitcher, a bowl the shape of a sea shell, and a clean, blue cotton towel. Since Mr. Dooley had not been home these past few months, the room needed only to be dusted and Jessica closed the door gently behind her.

Her spirits lifted by the memory of Teresa and the physical labor on a house she had come to love, Jessica descended the stairs attended by her retinue of cleaning devices as if royal escorts were her company. Centered in the sitting room, between two fireside chairs, sat an engraved wedding chest. The chest was made in Pennsylvania by German artisans, and it was a wedding present from the St. Patrick's Benevolent Society. It featured two large hearts etched on the lid with the names "Michael" and "Teresa" engraved in the hearts. It was where Teresa kept her linen tablecloth and napkins, her fine pewter and serving ware, and the family Bible. Upon the mantle above the fireplace sat two engraved pewter plates: one of Jesus, the other of his Blessed Mother. Anchoring the mantle, at each end, were a pair of silver candlesticks; and, in the middle, a Pillar and Scroll shelf clock from Plymouth, Connecticut. The sun was shining brightly now through the front window accented with Irish lace and a light, white cotton scarf trimmed with gingham. The warm, June rays fell softly on a simple ladder backed chair facing Teresa's spinning wheel. It was a small room that was easy to clean, yet with the carefully selected furnishings, though few in number, it made one feel comfortable and had a look of simple distinction. It was Teresa: "practical and perfect."

After Jessica finished cleaning the sitting room she washed the breakfast dishes and the black, iron skillet in a tub out in the back of the house, and thoroughly scrubbed the kitchen floor. In a kitchen, organization is everything, and she made sure that Teresa's kitchen was a model of efficiency. When she was finished, she sat at the table, on the corner of a chair, and let out a satisfied sigh. Everything was as it should be. The large, brick fireplace with its oven for baking and a swinging crane hinged to the side wall and from which hung an iron pot for soups and stews were all swept clean and scoured. Hanging beneath the pots was a griddle for making flat cakes, and positioned on each side of the crane were the "fire-dogs," to hold logs and support the long spit used for roasting meat and fowl. Stacked neatly next to the hearth was a trivet, a triangular three-legged stand used to hold pots and pans over the hot coals, a gridiron for broiling meat and fish, and a coffee grinder. Organization held sway above the fireplace as well where there neatly hung a collection of copper ladles, wooden spatulas, and brass forks.

The six foot pine table, where Jessica sat, with its wicker backed chairs was neatly centered in the room beneath a polished brass candelabra. The back of the room was dominated by a Dutch door, painted in hunter green, and a glass window with green curtains, tied and pinned on each end. Across the perimeter of the room, within arms reach, were hung straw, wicker, and wood baskets of every shape and size. Nearer to the Dutch door sat a butter churn, and adjacent to it hung scoops for removing the butter from the churn, and wooden paddles, called "workers," to work or remove the moisture from the butter.

Jessica gazed with awe at this, Teresa's home - Teresa's universe. This house was alive with the fidelity of family, faith, love, and work. It was simple and yet refined. It was organized and civilized, but touched by a romantic hand. Jessica worked hard to keep that spirit alive and it now breathed in her. She walked into the sitting room and sat crosslegged on the floor in front of the wedding chest. Opening the lid, the semi-sweet odor of cedar encompassed the room while she played her hand over the fine linen. She removed the Holy Bible and kissed it. She knew what she wanted. She knew her vocation. Staring at the engraved hearts, she reached out and ran her fingers around the one that read, "Michael."

Chapter 2

THE *AMERICAN*

Sailing from the West Indies with a hold full of sugar cane, molasses, and rum, and setting a northwest course at Cape Henry, Virginia, a schooner's captain would behold the great Chesapeake. Changing course north by west, a quarter north, would present the city of Norfolk just fine on his bow. Steering nearly due north now, and off to larboard, the ship would slide past the James, the York, and the Rappahannock rivers. Farther northwest, between Smith Point and Point Lookout, lay the mouth of the Potomac; and then, up and up farther, past the Patuxent river, and then Taylor Island, the elbow of Dorchester County, Maryland, just starboard on the bow. Still farther, and again off to starboard, Little Choptank, Trippe Bay, and ahead, Blackwalnut Point, dwarfish Poplar Island, and, opposite Kent Island, the port city of Annapolis, where the peace was signed by congress ending the Revolutionary War.

Gently now, past Sandy Point, north northeast, and then north by east, the stretches of coast line break like crabs' claws. Swinging the ship round northwest into the Patapsco, the ship would pass Federal Hill, and come into the Northwest Branch, to the docks of Fells Point, Baltimore. Home to a fine, safe anchorage with its finger like wharves stretching out into the river. Home to distinctive sailing vessels, schooners, with their raked-backed masts and low sleek hulls that would bring fame to Baltimore. Home, also, to an amazing array of sloops, frigates, brigs, ketches, barks, barges, gunboats, dinghies, rafts and river craft of every description. Home to mammoth shipyards, long rope walks, up and down saw mills, and spacious warehouses. And on the docks, brimming with activity, bawdy taverns and boarding houses with their proprietors and prostitutes. And, just off the docks, the stable, pious, and fervent flock of Father John. Home. Michael's home.

Michael ran. Ran with his wagon the whole mile and a quarter up Market Street to the Gay street offices of the *Baltimore American and Daily Advertiser*, or, to the folks on the Point, the *American*. The hot, tidewater sun had kept the dirt roadbed dry so his run wasn't as bad as all that, not for a lad of twelve years. But rain, any kind of late spring or early summer rain, would have made Market Street into a sinking, smelling, impassable mess. Still, a mess is what he saw the moment he opened the door to the office. Clerks were frantically dashing around the office. The printers, black with ink, nervously trying to put together columns of type, fumbled with their quoins. Everything was in a tizzy, and yet, everyone looked excited - harried, but almost jubilant. Michael stood in the middle of the office, frowning.

A clerk with a quill pen in his mouth and cradling a ream of papers was coming Michael's way fast. The clerk tried frantically to dodge Michael and get out the front door. Michael panicked and parried with him, first to the right and then to the left, to avoid a collision. But the clerk was too wide and his weight carried too much momentum. With a solid thump the clerk ran right into him. A tall, portly man, the clerk hit Michael squarely in the face with his chest. Papers flew through the air as Michael careened off the man and slid back on his bottom, smacking his head against the oak door. Michael shook himself and stared apologetically at the clerk. But the clerk was undaunted. He picked himself off the ground with surprising agility, gathered his papers, and glared at Michael, who was blocking the doorway. He then grabbed Michael by the shirt, and was about to toss him aside when Michael, in desperation, shouted "Sir! What is this business?"

The clerk, quill still set firmly between his teeth, could say nothing. Instead, he stuffed one of the papers inside Michael's shirt and then pushed the startled boy down on the floor and made his escape out the door. Michael sat up and removed the paper from his shirt. His mouth dropped as he stared at today's front page of the *American* and read the large, black headline: **"CONGRESS DECLARES WAR!"**

Michael looked up when he heard the editor's voice blasting across the office. The editor of the *American* was William Pechin. He was also Desiree's father. And sitting next to the irate Mr. Pechin was Desiree in a pretty, lavender dress. Pechin was a diehard supporter of the Republican agenda. His paper had been calling for war with Britain for some time and it made him a very popular man on the Point. Ever since the Peace of Amiens was broken and the European war resumed, both France and England had hurt Baltimore commerce. Without regard to a neutral flag, both France and England confiscated American ships and cargo. But, the one, keen difference was that Britain also confiscated men. Nearly a thousand Baltimore sailors, most of them from the Point, had been impressed by the British navy to serve on the King's men o' war, and it was the taking of men, not cargo, that stirred the ire of the people of the Point. A man impressed to slave on a British ship might never be seen again, and the brutal practice destroyed families who depended on a sailor's income for survival. But what really hurt, what threw the people of the Point into a deep resentment, even hatred, of Britain, was the attitude that the King's government and navy displayed towards the problem. They simply ignored it, pretended it didn't exist, said they were only taking back British seamen who had shirked their duty and illegally shipped on American merchant ships, even on ships of the United States Navy.

Everyone knew British seamen did, indeed, try to escape the evil treatment they received at the hands of the King's navy; but the fact was that the British knew they were impressing Americans as well as their own countrymen and they deliberately lied about it. But the people of Fells Point and other seafaring towns knew the truth. The truth that was written on the faces of abandoned wives and children of nearly every sea community in the country. Time and again, the United States tried to negotiate a resolution to the problem with the King's government, and time and again their words fell on deaf ears, or were thrown back in their faces with arrogant nonchalance and implausible denials.

Ever since Nelson defeated the combined French and Spanish fleets at Trafalgar in 1805, Britain ruled the seas. That rule led not only to a standoff in their war against Napoleon, but to an increase in the insolence of British naval officers and a total disregard for the rights of nonbelligerents from the government in London. Almost five years ago, to this very day, the U.S.S. *Chesapeake*, a frigate of 38 guns, was fired upon by H.M.S. *Leopard*, a 52-gun frigate, right off of Cape Henry. The British pounded three broadsides into the unprepared American vessel killing three of her crew and wounding 21. The British boarded and forcibly removed four seamen, but only one of these was a British deserter. Despite protestations, the King's government ignored the incident. Just a year ago, the British 38-gun frigate *Guerriere* took another American Navy seaman by force off of Sandy Hook. President Madison listed impressment as a primary cause in his request for a state of war between the United States and Great Britain, and Pechin had that portion of the president's message boldly reprinted in this morning's edition.

"Sir, we've already doubled our riders to and from Washington City. We're getting the latest reports from the White House and the Congress," an anxious Ned Haggerty, the man in charge of the messenger service for the newspaper, explained to his editor.

"Listen to me, Haggerty," Mr. Pechin shot back at him, "I want constant, do you hear me, constant and up-to-date information around the clock, and I don't care if your Irish rump gets so sore you can't sit down for a month!"

Mr. Pechin dismissed Haggerty with a wave of his hand and yelled "Bartlet!" for his Head Clerk. "Where is that damned Bartlet!"

Bartlet's tiny, sheepish frame appeared from the printing room where he was helping line up the columns for a second edition. His apron was smudged with ink, even his face and the lens of his spectacles were smeared black. Mr. Pechin, a tall, stately looking man, with a large, wrinkled face, and elegant, gray hair, towered over Bartlet from behind his desk. Pechin was wealthy and it showed in his regal bearing and impeccable clothing.

The editor walked from behind his desk with his hands clasped behind him and his head bent low in thought, like a captain traversing his quarterdeck. Bartlet blinked nervously, as his bespekled eyes followed his editor's steps, back and forth. "This is vitally important," Pechin said to the floor, concentrating on his words and the effect he was trying to make upon his assistant. "We must get the information out first, before... Desiree, dear, what are you still doing here?" he asked, as he noticed his daughter's shoes and lifted his head. "You're supposed to be at home. Your tutor will be expecting you."

Desiree raised her eyebrows in astonishment. "Honestly father, one would think you didn't have a daughter at all." But Mr. Pechin was all too aware of his daughter. Ever since his wife passed away in childbirth, he had doted on his daughter every extravagance his wealth could bestow. He stood looking sympathetically down at her, shaking his head. Poor child, he thought to himself, she's not even aware of what's going on. Mr. Pechin always attributed his daughter's ignorance - haughtiness really - to the fact that she didn't have a mother. His newspaper, his politics, his Republican ideals, all were his lifelong interests; but Desiree was his passion, and hence his downfall, for he could refuse her nothing. Desiree, of course, knew this, as any child would, and at an early age succeeded in manipulating her father with all the skills of a marionette.

"Father, I told you this morning that I couldn't bear that tutor one more day. He's positively insulting, asking - demanding - that I put to memory the Declaration of Independence - or the preamble of the Constitution- or some such nonsense. Can you imagine such impertinence? A girl of my station staying up all night memorizing something I could simply read from a book if I needed to, and I can't for all love think of why I would need to anyway."

"Very well, dear," Mr. Pechin said, surrendering immediately. "Just go home and - wait, here is a little money, take a carriage and go to that shoppe in Old Town where you saw that bonnet you took to the other day."

"Oh, father, you are a dear," she exclaimed, taking the money. "Just make sure you send word to dismiss that horrible tutor and I will make certain that cook will have your dinner ready for you when you arrive at home this evening. Oh, and father," she pleaded and demanded at the same time, "promise me you won't work till all hours, even if there is a war on?"

The editor made the concession and Desiree left with a wry smile on her otherwise pouting mouth. She cast a glance at Michael, who was busy collecting his papers into a bundle. Michael, forgetting that he had gussied himself up this morning with his new hairstyle just to please her, gave her a quick smile, raising his eyebrows in recognition, and proceeded to go back to work. Not liking this reaction, Desiree walked over to him.

"Is that all the attention I get Mr. Dooley," she quipped as she stamped her feet. "I admire industry in a gentleman, but I require at least a 'good morning' from someone I planned to invite to tea." Michael stopped bundling his papers and stood before her in humility. For a moment, he forgot about the headlines. The haste with which he had gone about his work in an attempt at involving himself in the war came to an abrupt halt. All his attention was transferred to the picture of perfection before him.

Desiree was blessed with chestnut colored eyes, just a shade darker than her light, auburn hair that was carefully stretched over slight shoulders in large ringlets. She pouted her full lips (like wet cherries, Michael thought) to achieve the effect she had managed with her father. Desiree was quickly approaching her fourteenth birthday, and yet she had all the attributes of Venus: a white, swan-like neck, pert breasts, small waist, and hidden beneath the layers of her dress, long, silky legs ending in dainty feet. Surely, her beauty would, and did, attract attention, but it was her flirtatiouness that drew men to her like sailors to the song of the Sirens. Michael's naïve heart, open as it was to the wiles of the world, lay at her feet.

"T-t-t-tea? Well, I-I, when?" Michael stammered.

"Why, this afternoon, of course."

"Mistress Pechin. I-I thank you for the invitation, but please, I can't. I've got to attend to the business, especially now. Mistress, don't you see?" Michael explained respectfully, "there's a war on."

"Oh, the war again, is it? Very well, Mr. Dooley, I withdraw the offer if the war means so much to you." With that, Desiree swung round, swishing her dress, her nose pointed towards the ceiling, and made her exit. Suspecting that she had achieved a moral victory, and with her back to Michael all the way out the door, the wry smile reappeared on her cherry-like lips. Michael was devastated.

"Dooley!" Mr. Pechin's voice thundered from his office. Michael, shaking off the blow from Desiree, raced into the editor's office. Bartlet was still there, wiping the ink from his spectacles. He squinted at Michael as the boy entered the room.

"Dooley, I'm writing a note to Father Moranvillé, asking him to excuse you from school today. I desperately need you to sell as many of these papers as possible this morning, there's no time to waste." Mr. Pechin sat down at his desk and wrote a brief note. When he was finished he banged his fist on the desk in agitation. Surprised at the tremendous thump that filled the small office, both Michael and Bartlet took one step backwards.

"Damn it Barlet! I want this whole town covered, top to bottom. Dooley, I want you to load up your wagon and saturate the Point. All of it! Bartlet, you set somebody up in charge of Jones Town, and you, yourself are responsible for Old Baltimore Town: from Saratoga to Liberty to the Basin, right up to the top of Federal Hill, every last little hovel. You got that!"

Mr. Pechin rose from his desk, intensity pouring from his eyes; the veins of his neck stretching his starched collar. "I tell you gentlemen this is no time to shirk our duty." Desiree could have lived a thousand miles away, now, as far as Michael was concerned. For when Mr. Pechin addressed Barlet and Michael as "gentlemen" and spoke to them of "duty" they soaked in the words as if they were soldiers receiving the order to charge from their commander-in-the-field.

"If that damned Federalist Hanson gets his side out to the people before we do there will be hell to pay. Make no mistake, gentlemen, this isn't just a war we wage against England. No, no, this is a war for ideas! The're going to throw everything against us, everything they've got, and if they won't hold back, we can't either. Bartlet, I want a man stationed outside the offices of the *Federal Republican*. I want to know what their up to. By God I'll have Hanson run out of town. Ha! He'll be tarred and feathered before I'm through. Well, damn it, Bartlet. Move! Dooley, you've got to get down to the market before Hanson's boy. Now go!"

For the last ten years, the Federalist Party was trying to infiltrate Baltimore. But it was men like Pechin who held them at bay, and championed Jefferson and Madison. Now, with war declared, the *Federal Republican* would try to use the war as a bully pulpit for a change in the Administration. Pechin *had* to be the provider of information - Republican information – for fear the Federalists might score big in the presidential election in November.

In the 1808 election, the Federalists managed to swing voters along the Potomac and in Anne Arundel County to their position. With the exception of John Adams, every president of the United States was a southerner, and worse, a Virginian. The Federalists saw their base dwindling as the country expanded to the west. Now, it was men like Henry Clay of Kentucky dictating policy that caused Federalists to became frustrated and alienated. But Clay saw an opportunity: with England struggling, virtually alone in her opposition to France, and with Napoleon on the verge of complete success on the continent, here was the chance for America to sweep into Canada and put and end to British tyranny once and for all. With an American gun pointed at England from one end of the Atlantic and a French gun at the other, Clay envisioned the end of impressment, the openings of new lands in the west, maybe even Canada itself, and American ships trading freely and safely around the globe.

The Federalists saw only futility and, possibly, annihilation, in declaring war against the sovereign of the world's seas. New England Federalists had fought their war with England and had bested her once. But, now, cautious, patient policy with Britain was the only prudent course. Yes, England was arrogant. Her men-of-war afforded her that luxury. But was she any more callous than the Corsican Emperor? After all, Napoleon's monarchy was a betrayal to the French Revolution, a revolt styled after America's, although turning embarrassingly and foolishly bloody. War with England, the greatest military machine on water, could only lead to the ruination of everything New England's sons had died for. The United States had no army, no navy, and Bonaparte had yet to take Russia. But the Federalist arguments were becoming old and confining to a new nation itching to stretch its young body, feast on new opportunities, redress old scores, and make England pay for the impressment of a free people.

Baltimore remained a staunch Republican town. Many identified the Federalists with aristocratic money and power, and much too sympathetic towards the English. But Pechin couldn't take any chances, especially now that war had been declared, a war against the greatest sea power in the world. Pechin knew there would be setbacks for an America that was horribly unprepared to go into battle on land or sea. He also knew the Federalists would blame Madison if the war went badly, and it was his newspaper that had to tell the story, right from the beginning. The readership war was waged, and Pechin was determined to win.

Michael made the turn onto Market Street with his wagon loaded to the brim with newspapers, determined not to let Mr Pechin and the Republicans down. Flooding the Point with the *American*, he thought, wasn't going to be very difficult to do. The thing was timing. Everyone on the Point did their shopping on Market Street. His plan was simple: he would haul his papers down the street, right down the middle of the street, and shout at the top of his lungs. "But," he worried aloud, "can I get there first?" His wagon was heavy but his spirit was flying with the thoughts of duty and of being the Point's messenger. He passed Dulaney Street, and then Smith and German streets. If he shouted out now, he would be late getting to the crowds below St. Patrick's, at Market and Bank Streets. No, he thought, I must wait. I must hold it in until I pass the church. His goal now was to get to the crowd at the busiest place, which was five blocks past St. Patrick's Church where the crowd was always the thickest, and this he must do before the boy selling the *Federal Republican* got there.

Michael could hardly stand it. Persperation soaked his forehead and the nape of his neck, trickling down his new, blue-ribboned tail. He could feel his heart thumping, pumping adrenaline through every vein. Slowly, past the church at Bank Street, his hands badly callused, then past Alifanna Street. He could see the crowds now, up at Shakespeare Alley. He saw the blackened chimney sweeps, the house slaves of the wealthy few of the Point, and the array of street vendors: tin peddlers, milkmaids, and flower girls, and now the butcher and baker shoppes. Finally, the roadbed changed from hardened dirt to bumpy cobblestones. He panicked when the cart nearly overturned as he darted in and out of the throng of the marketplace, desperately hunting the best location to hawk his headline. "At last!" he gasped, and no sign of the *Federal Republican*. Positioning himself in the center of the fray, right in the middle of Market Street, grabbing a bail of papers and jumping onto his wagon, his eyes wide with anticipation, he let out a wild scream above the din of the shoppers: "Waaaaaaar!"

Chapter 3

THE COOPERAGE

"Huzzah! Huzzah! Huzzah!" Through Old Baltimore Town, Jones Town, and now, Fells Point, three cheers and church bells were heard echoing around the city. Perhaps no where else throughout the entire young nation was the news of war more welcomed, cheered, and celebrated than on the Point. The crowds at the marketplace enveloped Michael. Everyone was hungry for the latest dispatches from Washington, and hungry, too, for the taste of war.

The people's resentment against England had hardened with each impressment, each slap at an already turned cheek. They had endured the sting of injustice. But now, instantaneously, their feeling of persecution was forgotten, and changed to retribution. Had the *Federal Republican* newsboy shown up now to hawk Hanson's diatribe against the Administration, the poor boy would have been lucky to escape with his life, and Hanson would have become a hunted man.

"Praise God and Jamie Madison!" ole' Sally gasped, as she took Michael into her arms, her large bosom pressing the air out of his lungs.

Michael sat in his wagon, the last of his newspapers sold, distributed really, the money tossed into his wagon as he passed out the *American* to the outstretched hands of the crowd. Fatigued from the morning's events, he just sat there, collecting his coins and thoughts, as well as his breath. He looked about him at the spectacle he had created and felt pride at being the first to deliver the news. Shoppers and shopkeepers, slaves and servants, sailors and stevedores all embraced, and chanted the much anticipated, often-infectious cry of "War!"

He cupped his hand over his eyes and peered up at the sun, nearing its peak. Towing his now empty wagon, he made his way down to the wharf. A growl from his stomach told him it was time for supper, but the crowd at Ole' Sally's Tavern was too much for even Michael to squeeze into and he decided to check on Uncle Bob. At the corner of Thames and Fells Streets, he spotted a group of his school chums lined up with broom handles, going through the motions of a military drill. Father John must have let school out early for it was not yet noon. Michael wondered if Mr. Pechin's note had been delivered to the school, or else, he knew, Father John, who didn't countenance unexcused absence, would come looking for him. Tough Gilly Morrison, Michael's best friend, was waving to him to come over and join in their parade down Fells Street, but Michael pointed to his wagon and then darted his finger in the direction of his house on Thames Street.

He opened the gate in the back of the house and poked his head in the top of the green, Dutch door, hoping Jessica would be there. "Hey, Jess. Didja hear the news?"

She was sitting at the table, on the corner of a chair, doing figures from her schoolbook. She smiled brightly at the sound of his voice.

"Michael! Yes, Father John declared a holiday. I told him you were probably busy with your newspapers but he said he would check on you anyway. Michael, you know how he is." Michael frowned.

"Mr. Pechin wrote a note, I saw him Jess. Must have given it to that damned Bartlet." Normally, Jessica would have balked at the use of any swear words, but she knew - everyone knew - that was how Mr. Pechin referred to his assistant; it was always damned Bartlet this or damned Bartlet that, it wasn't meant to be demeaning, even though it was. "Jess," Michael continued, "could you rouse up some supper and bring it over to the cooperage? Ole' Sally's was packed to the rafters, what with the war and all, and I'm powerful hungry."

She would have checked to make sure he'd stopped to get a bite anyway, that was the very next thought in her mind. But the offhanded way in which he asked her irritated an already bruised ego.

"I should have thought as much," Jessica retorted, her temper up. "It wasn't to bid me the time of day that you happened by. No sir. It was your stomach complaining again, and, naturally, when your stomach complains you think of me." She tossed her head back and gave him a sharp look: her left, scant brow hooked up into her wide, lightly furrowed forehead. But it was the color of her eyes that Michael took note of, even before his wits noticed her obvious tone of distemper. Her eyes, usually pale blue, like the color of a cloudless sky when the sun is full up, now changed to a decidedly deeper hue. They were like sapphires under a lamp, all the more brighter and bluer because they were surrounded by her pink complexion, dark brows and eyelashes, and her jet-black hair.

"But, Jess, I-I-I asked if you'd heard the news. 'Sides, I had t'bring the wagon home anyways and I thought, since the door was open and all, you might be here and, well..." Michael, his defense withering under the fiery-blue stare, just stood there, speechless. Jessica rose promptly, elegantly, from the corner of her chair. She quickly sliced two pieces of wheat bread and smothered them with butter and strawberry jam. At arms length from the door with her head still held back, her brow still hooked, and her eyes still beaming sapphires, she thrust the bread towards him defiantly.

"I promised your *mother*," she stated affectingly, as if that were the only reason she indulged him with food. Now, Michael knew she said the very same thing to him this morning. In fact, she said it quite often, but she had never said it like this before. She had never raised her voice to him. Nobody, outside of Father John, had raised their voice to him since his mother passed away. And this side of Jessica, that Michael had never seen, or rather noticed before, startled him.

Michael took the offering and retreated a step back from the door. "Jeez Louise, Jess, I'm awful sorry if I hurt your fee.." But before he had finished his apology, genuine though it was, the top of the green, Dutch door swung round in a flash and slammed shut in front of him. This was the second time in one day that Michael had incurred the wrath of a girl, and he hadn't the slightest idea why.

****

Michael didn't find Uncle Bob at the cooperage that day, but he did find Father John. He was waiting for him opposite the docks, where the family cooperage was located, and he was standing underneath a simple, wooden sign, chained to a weathered beam, that swayed to and fro in the wind reading, simply, "Dooley - Cooper." The business was centrally located to both sea and land transport, and to the myriad of structures, for business and pleasure, along the wharf on the Point. It was here where ships would dock and load and unload their holds with the commerce of the globe. Great warehouses stood beside taverns and boarding houses for sailors from every nautical nation. The wharves stood out into the Northwest branch of the Patapsco and were home to a variety of tradesmen vital to the shipping industry: blacksmiths, shipwrights, gunsmiths, map makers, caulkers, sail makers, and men working cordage for the rigging of ships in the long rope walks. There were shoppes and merchants too: wheelwrights, livery stables, hat makers, glassblowers, confectioneries, apothecaries, basket and broom makers, shoemakers, tanneries, tinsmiths, clock and instrument makers, candle makers, even a tortoise shell works.

On both sides of the long series of wharves were the great shipyards of Baltimore with their carpenters, lumberyards, up and down saw mills, black slaves and itinerant laborers. Goods were brought to the wharves by giant Conestoga wagons from Pennsylvania, and sturdy spring wagons from across Maryland and Virginia. Joining the wagons and rolling over the docks were the carriages of Baltimore's gentry, the buggies of the business class, delicate chaises with collapsible hoods for the city's ladies, passenger coaches with established routes to distant cities, and, of course, the horse flesh that powered them all and provided the constant backdrop of clip-clop that one was accustomed to.

Father John was obviously disturbed. He was no more than five feet tall and couldn't have weighed eight stone. Even Michael, for all his skin and bones, was a good two stone heavier and two heads taller. Still, height is only important to a man when he is conscious of it. Father John may have lacked height and weight but he was completely unaware of physical stature, his or anyone else's. One actually thought of him, when one thought of him, and one did a great deal on the Point, as being larger than most men. That notion was stamped on the brain because of Father John's piety, his personal sense of sincerity and humility, his courage and moral strength, and, most especially, because he had a fearful temper: one that could lash out with an acute and biting wit. It was too much even for an Irishman to stand up to.

"Good day, Father," Michael said with a wide grin. "I'm sorry you didn't get Mr. Pechin's note, Jessica told me. We're not open yet I see." There were no signs of Uncle Bob.

"Bonjour, Michael," Father John's French accent was more than noticeable, but his command of the English language was formidable. "No, I didn't receive any correspondence from the esteemed editor, nor have I yet seen your infamous uncle, but I shall see him presently, that I can promise you." The priest's subdued reply proved that Michael had nothing to do with Father John's troubled expression and that Uncle Bob had everything to do with it.

Father John pursed his lips and narrowed his eyes as he peered down the wharf. The war celebration was now in full swing amongst the patrons of the numerous taverns that dotted the docks. Crowds of sailors, laborers, and teamsters spilled out onto the wharf. The revelry of music, dancing and singing, as well as the annoying guffaws of mens' laughter and the irritating, high pitched giggles of the women who plied their trade in and out of the bordellos, burned in Father John's ears and showed red on his gaunt cheeks.

Suddenly, a vibrant, bellowing voice filled the air: "We'll show dem bloody black hearted King's sons of bitches what justice is! Ta Jamie Madison, God bless his Republican soul!"

Cries of "Jamie! Jamie! Jamie!" echoed the roaring sentiment and followed the singular, unmistakable, and booming Irish brogue of Bob Dooley. Michael looked warily at Father John and rolled his eyes.

"There should be more people in the churches on the day war is declared, praying to God for his mercy, and less people in the taverns with tankards in their hands winning battles that have yet to be fought," the cleric said, stoically. His dead gaze was fixed on the increasing mobs of men and whores gathering outside the taverns. He seemed to shake this off and looked at Michael, kindness coming back into his eyes.

"Open your shoppe, Michael, and make preparations for a great increase in your business. The war is going to keep you very busy." He placed his hand on the boy's shoulder and pointed to the ships along the quay: "Every one of these ships is going to go to sea with blood and glory on the minds of each captain and crew. And every one of these ships, and hundreds more like them that will soon be built, will require barrels. Dooley barrels, or someone else's if you're not prepared. God only knows how many of these laughing fools will return. Say a prayer for them, Michael, and for your father as well, he is at sea in a defenseless ship in a time of war and needs the grace of Christ to come home to you."

Michael, alarmed, looked upon the priest with sudden consternation in his eyes. In all the clamor and confusion, all the celebration and chaos of the morning, he hadn't once thought about what war would mean to his father. He knew his father was due home shortly, and that the *Mary Lynn* was built for speed, to outrun a threat, not with cannon to face one; but it was true, she was defenseless, and the thought betrayed fear in his eyes. Father John sensed his anxiety.

"Pardon. I did not say that to disturb you, mon ami, only to consider the fact that, at least for the Dooley's, this might not be the time for celebration. A fact I shall be delighted to put to your uncle." He peered down the wharf once more, and then raised his eyes to heaven and shrugged his shoulders. "'Hunanum est errare.' To err is human, oui? I shall be patient with him - understanding no, but patient with him for your sake. Au revoir, Michael, I will light a candle in front of the Blessed Virgin for your father's safe return."

Michael looked after Father John for a time as he made his way down the wharf, his black cassock and red sash playing with a fresh sea breeze in the hot June sun, and his silver crucifix bouncing lightly off of his slight chest. As he walked, the priest darted his graying head back and forth, scanning the taverns and inns, searching for the booming brogue. Father John had an elegant, royal bearing, which befitted his clerical garb, and the busy traffic, horse and man, yielded the right-of-way. Michael could just barely make out the features of his face: permanent arched brows; deep brown, burning eyes; high, prominent cheek bones; and an upturned nose that bespoke his zeal and seemed to help sniff out his prey. Father John turned into one of the taverns and disappeared from sight. Michael turned a key in the lock of the door and stepped into the cooperage.

Making barrels from wooden staves has been an art form that has existed before the birth of Christ. Now, in the early ninteenth century, the apex of this trade saw barrels transporting much of what was shipped, whether by land or sea. Up until a few years ago, the Dooleys were prosperous tradesmen, making full use of the ancient skills that had been taught to them by their father in the seafaring town of Cork, along the southern coast of Ireland. They set up shop here, in the new, united colonies after the War for Independence, but not together, at least at first. Both Mike and Bob Dooley had fought in that war, but it was the younger brother, Mike, who, after falling in love with the young, still virgin nation, decided to settle down and practice the trade of his forefathers. Bob, as rambuctious then as he was now, opted to seek his adventure on a privateer and make his fortune before England quit the war. He sailed with the incomparable Joshua Barney, a Baltimore native and a rougue of merchant ships on the high seas. That was how both brothers found their way to Baltimore after their enlistments were up serving in the Continental Army, after Washington's victory over Lord Cornwalis at Yorktown, Virginia. One brother dreaming of a dependable and responsible living on land, the other of quick wealth, danger, and excitement, with the pleasure of exacting a high cost to the British on the water.

Baltimore seemed a logical place to go for two young men who were far away from home, a home that was, for a Catholic, a conquered place ruled by a foreign government. Ireland: impoverished, dependent, forever a British colony ruled by an aristocratic ascendency. No, to go back was to be blind to the chance for economic opportunity and the refreshing aura of political freedom. And Baltimore was, it seemed, a friendly oasis in a Protestant dominated United States. After all, Maryland was the home of Charles Carroll of Carrollton, a Catholic family whose integrity and patriotism could not be denied. If the Carrolls could make a go of it, the young Dooleys thought, why couldn't they? Mike did succeed in establishing a business in Fells Point, but even though Baltimore was growing, at a faster rate than any other city in the country, competition among tradesmen was keen, even dangerous. If one decided to start a business on the Point, one would have to have connections, start up money, and protection. Mike had some money, enough to get started, but connections in the business community and knowing the right kind of people to protect your interests were things that an immigrant Irishman had to do without. And Mike Dooley wasn't the only Irishman who lacked these resources. Hence, the Irish formed an organization to help their own.

It was called the Hibernian Society of Baltimore, a non-sectarian, non-political association "...to advise, assist, redress and protect every native of Ireland or decendants of such." This was common among immigrants across the United States, and in Baltimore the Hibernians were joined by the Society of St. George for the English, the St. Andrew's Society for the Scots, and, even earilier, the German Society.

But, Hiberninans or no, Mike Dooley still found it hard to compete by himself. After the war, Bob came to roost on the Point with his brother. And although Bob was completely useless when it came to physical labor, he did provide the right kind of seafaring connections from his association with ship captains, who valued his fighting ability, and he stayed to work the business with Mike. The result, stemming from Mike's financial acumen and Bob's salemanship, was a prosperous cooperage, now one of the best known on the Point.

Michael closed the door hesitantly. He wanted to hear the ruckus that was sure to break out when Father John confronted his uncle, but, more than that, he suddenly needed some time by himself, to think on what the priest had just told him. The planks on the flooring of the dark room squeaked under his weight as he tread, cautiously, inside the dark room. "Pa," he whispered, and then blessed himself quickly. He was in the anteroom, where a counter with a swinging gate separated the front from a larger, workroom in back. Taking an apron from a hook underneath the counter, he placed it slowly over his head, and softly, began to sob. He felt for a stool behind the counter, and, finding it, he sat with his face buried into his knees. Tears pushed through his eyes and ran swiftly down his cheeks, dripping and dropping onto the unswept floor, caked with sawdust, and sounding like matches being puffed out in quick succession.

Pictures, too real for even a precocious and responsible young man like Michael to withstand, appeared before his tightly shut and soaking eyes. There he saw his mother: her hair tied up neatly in a bun with just a whisp of a few curls dangling across her forehead, wearing a chocolate-stained blue apron. A birthday cake with twelve candles filled her hands, and smiling, brilliant, blue eyes gazed upon him and told him how proud she was... There was his father: lanky and strong, leaning over the shaving horse, gently teaching him how to pin and shave a stave just so, pushing his wavy, brown hair from his understanding, brown eyes, patting Michael on the head with a great, callused-hardened hand, telling him how proud he was...

His sobs broke into convulsions now, quiet, but deep spasms, shaking his chest and stomach. His abdomen forced a contorted whimper out of his wet nose and mouth. "No, ma, please no, make pa come back, please, please - Oh, dear Lady, please." And then it stopped, as suddenly as it had started. "I haven't gotten the code yet. Pa'll come home to give me the code. He has to." Comforted with that thought he brought the apron up to his face, wiped his eyes and mouth, and blew his nose into it heartily, before stripping it off and tossing it angrily into a bucket under the counter. His eyes, blurred as they were from tears, had adjusted to the darkness of the room.

"The business? What Business! Look at this place! Pa'll kill me if he sees it like this. Damn you Uncle Bob." This last he said in a whisper; he didn't really want Uncle Bob or anybody else damned for that matter. It sounded different when Mr. Pechin said it and he was ashamed for having invoked his uncle to a speedy demise in hell. But the workroom was in chaos. He had filled an order, just yesterday: fifteen dry barrels for nails and two hogsheads for whiskey shipping on the *Dominic* returning to New York. He had swept the place clean, putting everything back in its proper place.

"What in the hell happened here?" he asked the dark room, for the shutters were locked tight and he had not yet lit a lamp. Promptly, carefully, he struck a match to a candle and stepped cautiously across the work room toward the windows, for the wood worked with in here had been sawed, planed, moistened, heated, shaped, shaved, and dried, and only a fool would allow a candle to burn without being wary of the consequences.

"Only a fool wouldn't sweep up so much sawdust off this floor," Michael thought as he unlocked and opened the shutters, splashing sunlight, piecemeal, over the breadth of the room. "Well I'll be a Federalist," he said aloud, the golden light showing, ingloriously, the mess before him. There was no mystery here, however. To Michael, who saw the empty bottles of Maderia strewn across the floor, and whose unclogged nostriles now picked up the scent of spent wine, the evidence required an easy verdict: "Uncle Bob was here last night all right," he said to himself, propping his fists against his protruding hips. "Probably late last night. He came in here to finish the churns and pails for the ship chandlery. He must have been a stinkin' wreck when he got here and even more stinkin' when he left. God only knows how the place didn't burn down, except for the fact that he knows more about fires than anybody else."

Michael couldn't quite understand. Uncle Bob was Foreman of the Deptford Hundred, the Point's volunteer fire brigade and a wiser man on the nature of fires and how to fight them than could be found anywhere. "But that should have been the one thing, even in his state of mind, to tell him not to work at night with a belly full of..." Michael stopped in mid-sentence, his mind replacing it with one more urgent. "Augh! What if pa does come back today? What if he comes back now!"

Covering for Uncle Bob, was something that Bob Dooley had taken pains to cultivate not only in his nephew, but in many other trusting and naive souls on the Point. It was important for a man not imbued with a work ethic to induce others to labor for him. Michael went quickly to work: sweeping the floor, tossing out the tell tale evidence of empty Madeira bottles, and putting all the tools back where they belonged. It was an untidy job, but good enough to demonstrate to the outside observer, as he hoped his pa would be after months at sea, that this was a working establishment. Having it too clean, well, that wouldn't do either. He sat back on the stool and stared into the workroom with a satisfied air of accomplishment. The froes, mauls, adzes, crozes, howels, sun planes, scorpers, bung augers, heading swifts, and sun planes were all stacked on shelves in a semi-disorganized fashion, to show that they were being used at least intermittently. The shaving horse bench with its variety of drawknives was placed in one corner of the room, while the jointer, a long upturned plane to edge staves for a nice, compact fit, was stationed nearer to the windows, where additional light would be needed for the close work. In the middle of the room, away from shavings and other incendiaries, stood the cresset: an iron basket where wood was placed and burned on the inside and over which an opened barrel would sit so that the heat and steam could soften it for bending.

Michael got up, opened the door, and stood underneath the wooden sign. From one of the taverns, a chorus of drunken voices, repeatedly missing notes, struggled with *Yankee Doodle*. The wind had shifted to a warmer, southwest land breeze. Soon hordes of mosquitoes would follow the stench of the breakwater, gorging themselves with the human blood of the Point. Michael, associating the stench with the disease, wondered if the fever would come back again this summer. Come back to claim the life of someone else he loved. "No matter now," he thought, "what with pa gone, and me with a war on my hands." The breeze blew in a stronger gust, a little more north than west as the tide began to come in. "Okay, Pa. This here wind is good enough to be right on your quarter, all the way up the Chesapeake." It was also good enough to swing the wooden sign, squeaking in its rusted chains, directly over him. He drew his head up and smiled, recalling the booming brogue. "Bring on the war you bloody black hearted King's sons of bitches. The Dooley's are open for business."

Chapter 4

YANKEE DOODLE

Michael hadn't seen Desiree for a week and his heart ached for a glimpse of her. But there was simply no time: with only a week remaining in the school term and examinations to cram for; with orders pouring in for new barrels and working late into the night at the cooperage; with hawking, now, three bundles of newspapers every morning, and, alas, having to arrive and depart the offices of the *American* well before Mr. Pechin and his daughter; and with his adrenaline from the first news of war now nearly pumped dry, Michael found himself completely exhausted. Study, staving, and selling papers had taken their toll, and Uncle Bob was no help.

Now, sitting at his desk at school, Michael found it difficult to keep awake. Father John was posing a problem on a slate that his students were supposed to be copying, and, dutifully, all the students were copying and working the problem - all save one. Father John had noticed the glaze in Michael's eyes when he came into class, late as usual from selling his papers. But, the good Moranvillé felt that he was partly to blame. The priest had never found Bob Dooley the day news of war had reached the Point and had not the time to hunt for him since and admonish him for his failings. Judiciously, he allowed Michael to drift off and rest his eyes, pretending not to notice.

That was indeed Uncle Bob's brogue they had heard that day on the wharf, but the Irishman was as cleaver as he was boisterous. He had put into effect a warning system he had planned for just this sort of occasion: whenever the priest was spotted on the wharf, a message was filtered through the taverns by way of an upside down cap upon the head of any sailor. To the mariners of the Point, whose keen eyes could detect the slightest thing amiss upon the person or uniforms of the liberty men who frolicked continuously in the smokey, seedy flophouses on the docks, this bold stroke against the forces of Christendom was a thing of innate genius. And, as soon as Father John put his sacred foot upon the wharf that day, headgear went topsy-turvy.

This was no small thing. Father John had been a holy terror to every sailor who claimed the right of Baptism. When a ship's company was paid off after a long voyage, and had just settled in for a nice toss off at a local haunt, there he was, himself: black robes, red sash, silver crucifix, and a three foot shillelagh. A crozier really, made of polished mahogany and as heavy on a tar's back as any boatswain's cane. What lashing he neglected to do with his sharp tongue, he made up for with his stick. One couldn't blame Father John for these outbursts, of course. He had heard the same sin in the private sanctity of the confession box for over two decades, since his arrival on the Point: "Father forgive me. It's been six months at sea since my last confession. I've spent all my ship's pay on spirits and wantonness." And the fury building up in the little priest from hearing fifteen years of status quo sinning, unchecked, and therefore, ostensibly unrepentant, unleashed itself upon unsuspecting seamen in every brothel and alehouse on the Point. So that, for the last five years, any Catholic salt would have taken his life in his hands if he didn't at least go home and give his pay to his wife first, keeping a little sewn into his sail cloth trousers for a glass with his mates later. And for five years now, the confessor has rarely heard anything damning, save foreign port sins.

Leave it the likes of Bob Dooley to bring the sinners home again: "No more of his tongue and war club!" he promised the Point's drunken sailors. The priest didn't have a chance, for the strict discipline in which the seamen obeyed this maneuver was accomplished with the speed and precision of a man-o'-war's gun crew beat to quarters. The "all clear" was even easier: one round of *Yankee Doodle*.

But then Michael snored. A loud snore very much like a pig's snort. This, Father John could not overlook for his reputation as a disciplinarian would be jeopardized, and for a teacher there is nothing more essential than discipline. But not, necessarily, of the corporal kind, which was used sparingly being a distraction to the mind if used indiscriminately. Rather, Father John preached and taught discipline of the intellect: the practice of mastering one's thoughts, words, and deeds through the art of selfcontrol. Only when that art was considered a futile endeavor, as in the case of sailors with money in their pockets and temptations on the quay after months and months of loneliness at sea, was a whack with a stick more apropos.

At Saint Patrick's Free School on Apple Alley, discipline was exercised in 90 minute classes, twice weekly, in Latin, arithmetic, geography, French, English, and religion; and once a week, on Friday's only: in navigation, spelling, and marching in a line up to the church, to celebrate the weekly school mass. Father John taught French, Latin, and navigation, which he had mastered in his voyage from France to the West Indies.

After school, which was finished by 12:30, the students would have supper and then proceed to their employers for work. The boys to their family businesses or at positions found for them by Father John, and the girls to the homes of mothers around the Point where they assisted in chores about the house, and in the arts of cooking, gardening, spinning, weaving, and sewing. Father John insisted that the girls of St. Patrick's receive the same rigorous academic and religious training as the boys, something the parents of the Point privately scoffed at. He believed this, he said, because "...practical work disciplines the body to do the work in the home; academics disciplines the mind to do the work in the head; and religion disciplines the disciplines to do everything first from the heart, and that is what civilization is all about, oui?"

But there was nothing civilized about the guttural sounds of Michael's sinuses. Father John put down his slate and walked slowly in Michael's direction with his hands tucked into the opposite sleeves of his cassock, sporting a dramatically raised left eyebrow.

"Monsieur Dooley!"

Michael, who was dreaming contentedly about Desiree in her lovely, lavender dress, raised his head, which had been cradled into his crossed arms atop the desk, and gazed at the blurry black figure before him. The vision of Desiree did not completely vanish from his mind, and it caused him to wear a sleepy, sheepish grin.

"Mr. Dooley, you are with us, no?" In a second, Michael was reoriented to the classroom.

"Yes, Father?"

"Welcome back Monsieur Dooley. Did you have a pleasant dream?" With this, the other children burst into laughter, a laughter that died quickly when Father John glanced sternly across the room.

"We were discussing the examination, Monsieur, the one on navigation, which doubtless, you remember?"

"Oh, yes Father, I've been studying."

"Good, then you'll recall, Monsieur, our discussion of Nathaniel Bowditch's *New American Practical Navigator*?"

"Indeed I do, Father."

"And, you will recall how Monsieur Bowditch, with no formal education and through great perseverance and self discipline, reworked John Hamilton Moore's tables and proved him wrong in many calculations?"

"Yes, Father." All the reading, with burning eyes, Michael had accomplished this week was coming back to him and confidence crept into his complexion. "As a matter of fact," he ventured, "the whole world was shocked that an American bested the Englishman, Morre, at his own game."

"Very good, Monsieur," the priest said slyly, for Michael had been playing Father John's game and fell right into his trap. "Then, seeing how you are so familiar with Monsieur Bowditch, pray, tell us how he worked his new lunar reading." Michael's mouth opened, but no words came forth.

Father John smiled innocently. "Come, Monsieur Dooley, we were just working the problem on the slate. Surely, you remember his method."

"Of course you do Michael," Jessica, who was sitting opposite Michael in the next row, chimed in. "We were just discussing it last night, after you came in late from working at the cooperage." She turned her head up to the priest, her eyes full of sincerity. "Father, for the life of me, I couldn't understand Bowditch's method until Michael explained to me how it was easier to calculate the angle of three stars to the position of the moon, than to wait for the moon to occult a star. Remember, Michael?"

"Yes, Jess, I do." He didn't, of course, but Jessica had given him enough to go on. "Father," his confidence returning now, "the difficulty lay in the fact that lunars taken before Bowditch's discovery were inconsistent, as well as inconvenient. Why wait for the moon to occult a star when the reading can be taken with great accuracy by measuring the angle of three separate stars?"

"Oui, oui, Monsieur Dooley, why wait for all navigational love? Bowditch was indeed a man who was very much awakened to the possibilities around him, as I'm certain you will be one day." Beaten by Jessica's timely interruption and the obvious fact that Michael had studied, despite his snoring demonstration in class, Father John decided on a tactical retreat. He looked down upon both Michael and Jessica, and supressed a smile, recalling a conversation with Teresa before her death.

"We will see if we are all awake enough to perceive the wisdom of God that surrounds us. The answers are there. They always were. For God is perfect and so is the universe he created. We each see but a small portion, which is wise if we see it in terms of the whole, but mere selfish stupidity if we only see what is in front of our faces, oui?" He chuckled, and went back to his position in front of the classroom. "Ha! The world, the stars, the sun, the moon, the planets, they all move for a purpose, you see? And what about you my children, do you move for a purpose? " He saw the complacent faces in front of him, soothed by his words of instruction, but utterly lost by them too. "Ha! Ha! Ha! You will," he said, musically, shaking his finger in warning, "you will." With that the bell at St. Patrick's rang to call the faithful to Friday's Mass.

The church was the pride of the Point. It measured one hundred and six feet by sixty-four feet. Its exterior was plain, in a colonial fashion, but with enough ornamentation to lend charm to its presence. It featured tall doors which were highlighted on either side with two plain columns surmounted by a narrow cornice topped by a gilded cross. Over the unstained windows, fronting Market Street, were two marble slabs etched with quotations from Scripture. On the left it read: "In this place I will give peace, saith the Lord of hosts"; on the other was written, "Blessed are they that dwell in Thy house, O Lord."

Uniformly, the children filed out of the school and formed a procession. With their pastor leading them the two blocks from Apple Alley to Market and Bank Streets, they sang out a favorite hymn of Father John's who led the singing in a spirited, monastic tenor:

'Praise the Lord! ye heav'ns adore him;
Praise him angels, in the height;
Sun and moon, rejoice before him;
Praise him, all ye stars of light.
Praise the Lord! for he has spoken;
Worlds his mighty voice obeyed;
Laws which never shall be broken
For their guidance he has made.'

****

July brought a hot summer sun to the Point and the collective imaginations of its residents was on fire with the prospect of prize money. Whole fortunes could be made in a single cruise by a daring seawolf sweeping up merchant vessels of the enemy caught, in mid-cruise, unaware of the declaration of war. Ships' husbands and captains competed for seamen and lubbers alike. Privateers needed to fill an exhaustive list of trained crewmen: able seamen, caulkers, cooks, sailmakers, carpenters, surgeons, sailing masters, gunners, boatswains, clerks, gunner's mates, ship stewards, boatswain's mates, carpenter's mates, quartermasters, armourers, marines, and even boys. In the heat of battle, the boys were as essential as any member of the crew - probably even more so. Because it was the boys who were fast enough, agile enough, to slip from the gun crews and fetch fresh cartridges from the gunroom below deck. It has always been true that in order to cause confusion of the enemy, the best target for a sharpshooter was an officer. But, ofttimes, whether the battle is on land or at sea, it is just as advantageous to pick off the boys first. If you kill the powder monkeys, you stop cartridges from reaching guns, and if you can silence the cannons of your opponents, then officers be damned, the battle is yours.

Because of its close proximity to Washington City, the privateers of Baltimore received their commissions from the Secretary of the Navy in quick order. Already, many ships that had received their commissions, or were expecting them in the pouches of a galloping courier, were getting ready for sea. When so many ships in a harbor make preparations to lift anchor at the same time, needing the same armory, bedding, pitch and tar, cordage, spars, sails and blocks, and above all, the same barrels, smaller fortunes could be realized from the tradesmen who outfit the ships. Father John was right when he told Michael to get ready for an increase in the business. But he was wrong not to have found and chastised Bob Dooley, because Michael was trying to do too much and the strain was showing on him.

The priest knew that the seamen were being alerted in some fashion to his appearance on the docks. He knew that, mysteriously, he couldn't find Bob Dooley and he remembered the promise to look after Michael and the Dooley business in Mike's absence. He also knew many respectable and sober people who worked amongst the throng of the inebriated and who rubbed shoulders with the proprietors of the many grogshops on the Point. He chose a humble churchgoer, Moses Pike, a shipwright who had sworn off the bottle for the past decade, but whose daily constitution included stuffing a bowl of tobacco and having a leisurely smoke in Gilhooley's Tavern at the end of the day. Pike, although having confessed his sins years ago, still felt the pang of guilt over wasting so many years of his life married to the drink and ignoring the needs of his wife and children. At Father John's request, Pike readily agreed to watch closely the actions of Bob Dooley, a regular at Gilhooley's, when the priest ventured onto the wharf. After a stroll down to bless the *Rossie*, Joshua Barney's new ship launched on July third, Father John waited for Pike in the rectory across the street from St. Patrick's. Pike observed the perfect simplicity of Bob Dooley's masterful deception, and he and Father John formulated a carefully laid plan to bag the Irishman on the nation's 36th birthday.

Independence Day, 1812, was a banner day on the Point. The Deptford Hundred Fire Brigade led a parade up Market Street with their Foreman, Bob Dooley at the head. As they approached St. Patrick's, Bob ducked behind the pride and joy of the brigade, their recently purchased, shiny red Gooseneck Engine, in order to avoid any contact with Father John, who was sitting in a chair in front of the church, holding an umbrella under the steady Maryland sun. At the church the parade would reform, just in time for a little refreshment. One of the best features of the Gooseneck (this, Bob Dooley's idea) was a small cask of rum affixed to the housing of the pump and painted a brilliant, cherry red. Marching in quick step, the parade would go down Market Street and end at Fells Street, where the participants were in easy range to a variety of taverns ready to welcome the parading patriots with rum, wine, beer, and women. With their cask drained, the Deptford, to a man, made their way to Gilhooley's following, again, the lead of their now swaggering foreman.

Father John waited an hour before sending for Moses Pike. "Let them get comfortable," he mused. Pike met Father John in front of the well on Thames Street as they had arranged the day before. As the priest greeted busy Fells Point mothers filling their buckets, he waited patiently for Pike to get situated and fulfill his side of the coup. Bob Dooley was a braggart and a bully. Nip him in the tuck, thought the priest smiling to the industrious women, and I'll have them all singing psalms instead of sea shantys.

Meanwhile, Pike had secured an advantageous position at the corner of the bar, nearest to the front door. With the silver jingling in his pockets that Father John had given him at the well, Pike proceeded to act the good patriot and bought the courageous men of the Deptford a round. This magnanimity instantly caught the attention of the foreman and he saluted the sober shipwright for his thoughtfulness. Pike saw him, staggering between the crowded patrons seated at tables and chairs, patting backs and toasting Jamie Madison and Henry Clay. He was nearly six and half feet tall, a lumbering, colossus of a man, twenty stone at least. His big, ruddy face was topped with bright, curly red hair over a massive head. Alcohol had fashioned a fine, bulbous nose that closely resembled the color of his hair. With his white uniform trimmed in blue with brass buttons, and with his tall brigade hat snug tightly over his red curls and secured under his granite like chin by a wide leather strap, he looked completely comical, though no one would dare tell him the hat was too small.

"Pike, me boyo. Ah, Moses Pike," he bellowed affectionately as he jostled the man standing next to Pike at the bar. With a hand the size of Pike's own head, he shoved the man out of the way while belching awkwardly, "pardon me, mister," for both the long burp and the sudden shove. "Take a glass with me Pike, good man dat you are, and not a better shipwright dis side of Cork," he said with a full smile showing that half of his teeth were gone, not from any man's fist, but from stumbling when drunk over a chair or table or down a flight of steps and knocking them out himself.

"Sorry, Bob, I've sworn an oath on the Holy Book that I'd never enjoy myself again. I have to content myself with this 'ere pipe and sweets from the confectioneries to take the place of the flask I was married to. But I'm in a gay mood. Such a wondrous occasion, this our day of independence. You'll have a glass for me surely, to toast the general's memory, was you that fought with him, side by side in the trenches in the siege of Cornwallis."

"Friend, dat I will," Bob said sadly, tears coming into his eyes, rubbing the back of his powerful hand over his leaking, big, red nose, and sniffing. Pike knew the very mention of General Washington was enough to make Bob Dooley sentimental, and whenever the Irishman was sentimental, and full of rum, he started to cry.

"Barkeep!" Dooley rasped angrily, "a tankard of rum fer meself and your best tobackee fer himself here." Gilhooley, not half the size of his best customer, jumped at Bob's command. Swinging round to the crowd of Deptford men and slamming his hand against the top of the bar to gain their attention, Bob solemnly raised his tankard. "Gen'lemen, I give you his majesty Gen'ral George Wash'ton." With that he tipped his head back and drained the West Indian rum into his gaping mouth as did every man in the room, save Moses Pike. Suddenly, a sailor burst in through the door, his cap upside down. Bob, his wits and eyesight dulled by the rum, took a full second to register the signal.

"Barkies! Up with ya now! It's da priest!" Everywhere men scattered: out the back way and into a skiff tied to the wharf, underneath the bar, up into the loft, and Bob Dooley, his place of hiding safely assigned only to him, into an empty hogshead of whiskey on the far side of the room. Minutes later, Father John poked his upturned nose into the door.

"Monsieur Pike, good afternoon." he said loudly, for all to hear. About half of Gilhooley's patrons had vacated or were stuffed into their hiding places. Those that remained were either strangers or, more likely, single men from the Deptford, who did not yet have to fear the indomitable Moranvillé, for they had no wives who would sob to the priest in the confessional, begging him to put the fear of God into their husbands.

"Well, good to see you, Father. Can I help you with something?" Pike asked innocently.

"Pray, Mr. Pike, have you seen the cooper, Bob Dooley, at all today?"

"Why, no Father, not I, have you checked at the firehouse? I heard some of the Deptford boys saying that was his destination."

"An excellent suggestion, Monsiour, I will take that advice. Good day to you, and a blessed Independence Day."

But Father John didn't go to the firehouse. He simply took two steps to his right so as not to be seen from the doorway and stayed there, desperately trying not to laugh.

"Here! Here! A glorious Independence Day. Mr. Gilhooley, another round on me for every one of these gallant lads from the Deptford!" Pike yelled across the bar. The young men swarmed around him, patting him on the back, and whooping it up over their good fortune for this generous shipwright. Pike got behind the bar and helped Gilhooley serve the tankards of grog and rum, and then whispered into the ear of one of the drunkest: "here's your rum, lad, now give us a song, *Yankee Doodle* if you please."

The young man staggered to the nearest table, jumped on top, nearly falling off and breaking his head, and let out in a fine tenor: "Yankee Doodle went to London just to ride a pony, stuck his feather in his cap and called it macaroni..." They all chimed in with the chorus, it being the Fourth of July, and every man there a patriot, forgetting, of course, that this was the "all clear." Bob was the first to come out, having to tip the hogshead over to allow himself to crawl out. Standing over top of him, waiting for him to get up, wearing a fixed upturned eyebrow and brandishing a "war club" was the victorious Pastor of St. Patrick's Church. Bob, merrily working his way out of the whiskey barrel, singing the chorus as he did so, stood up to find the little priest blocking his way to the bar.

"Jaysus, Mary, and Joseph!" Bob gasped.

"Not quite," retorted Father John. "But you will be invoking the Holy Trinity as well as the Holy Family by the time I'm done with you." With that the priest took both hands to his stick and promptly smashed it into Dooley's massive frame. Bob took the blow with the back of his shoulders, but it was swung with such force that it knocked him down onto the barrel which burst its hoops and sent splintered staves across the room.

When Bob woke up, his head splitting from rum, his back swelling from the blow of the "war club," he saw the priest sitting casually at the table in front of him, enjoying a cup of tea. Everyone else, Gilhooley included, had left the scene upon hearing the crash of the barrel. Father John delicately put down his cup of tea into its saucer. "Well, Robert, what do you have to say for yourself. You should be ashamed, *Yankee Doodle* indeed! And what do I tell you're brother when he comes home? If he comes home!"

Chapter 5

MIGHTY TOM BOYLE

Suddenly, everything changed.

"It is God's great irony," Father John had told Michael. " 'The fear of the Lord is the beginning of wisdom.' Indeed, it is. It takes man both fear and love to seek true repentance. Your uncle is quite capable of both. It is inside of him, you see. But he holds it there, deep inside, unwilling to let go, the difference between your uncle and your father. Yet, oftentimes, the greatest sinners make the greatest saints. We shall see. For now, at least, things will be easier on you. So, no more of the snores while I teach on the miracle of the stars, oui Michael?"

"Oui, Father," Michael had promised.

Father John was right. Uncle Bob seemed like a different man, at least in his business dealings. That night at Gilhooley's, Father John had extracted a promise from the Irishman to do right by the boy until his father came home. The promise came after the priest had stirred the memory of Teresa in Bob's mind. If he was anything, Bob Dooley was a loyal man. He was also pragmatic. The scene in the tavern would only repeat itself until Bob gave in to Father John's demands. Would he be quick enough, next time, to take the blow of the "war club" on the back of his shoulders? No, he thought, better there not be a next time, besides Mike would be home soon and a little discretionary industry now, would pay off dividends at a later date.

The agreement between Father John and Uncle Bob had three components: to stay out of the taverns until Mike returned; to conduct business during normal business hours, relieving the young Dooley from much of the labors of filling the orders; and never to expose Michael to the Irishman's indecent habit of associating with wanton women.

"One of these days, I will have you in my confessional, or some other poor priest will, and you will really change, Robert. No more guilt, no more shame, or whatever it is that pulls you to your debauchery and thus the ruin of your soul." Father John had warned him.

"Aye, Fadder," is all Bob could reply.

With examinations completed and the school term finished, Michael arrived at the cooperage one morning to find a clerk in the anteroom and two laborers busy in the workroom.

"I didn't t'ink you'd mind, Michael darlin', dat I hired dese boys ta help wit' da extra orders. Even wit' you here durin' da day, da work keeps pilin' up an' dese here ship captains are on fire ta set dere ships ta sea. Look here, an order for da *Highflyer*. Da first mate dropped it off dis mornin'. He said she would be haulin' anchor in a week, her commission secured."

Michael's skeptical air turned to one of confusion. He noticed that Uncle Bob was sober and that the *Highflyer's* order called for twenty water barrels. He looked at the clerk, a young man, possibly in his twenties, but with his spectacles on and his neat, white blouse he appeared to be serious about the books he was studying. The two laborers in the workroom were strong, capable looking men, again, in their twenties, both swinging mallets and providing a steady beat to, what was certainly, a thriving, industrious cooperage. At once, Michael saw the sense in this new arrangement, but what he didn't comprehend was how Uncle Bob saw the sense in it. After all, Uncle Bob had no business sense. He looked at his uncle with questioning eyes.

"Now, look here, Michael me boyo. You show Samuel, da new clerk, da ropes as far as keepin' da books. He's a Quaker from a good family in Elizabeth Town who's come ta Baltee'more ta make his fortune. Da boys in da back had a go tobakee farmin' before dey came ta dere senses. Dere da Smith brodders. When dey heard about da war, dey sold dere farm an' came here searchin' fer a trade. From da looks of dem, I'd say dey were raised wit' mallets instead of rattles in dere mitts. All in all, a fine lot I'd wager."

Bob whacked Michael on the back, proud of the accomplishments of the morning, and walked outside to have a pipe. Michael, feeling a newfound confidence in his uncle, followed him out the door. It was just ten o'clock, but the bright Baltimore sun, gleaming off the broken chop of the Patapsco, beat hard on their hatless heads and shoulders. They had to shield their eyes with their hands to view the intense activity on the quay. Privateers and commissioned traders, like the schooners the *Comet* and *Highflyer*, and brigs *Charles* and *Baltimore*, were frantically trying to put to sea. The wharf was mobbed with men, wagons, and horses. Screaming gulls competed with the bawls of officers directing the work crews provisioning the ships, loading holds, repairing rigging, sewing sails, and scrapping clean the copper from their bottoms. Added to the mix of sailors and stevedores were a variety of men from all different walks of life who had quickly formed syndicates in order to finance a venture. Lawyers and doctors, bakers and butchers risked capitol against their fever for prize money. They hired ship's husbands and captains, and petitioned Washington for a commission as either a letter-of-marque trader or a privateer. The traders were true to their name, because they were ships that filled their holds with goods to be delivered to harbors along the coast of the United States, or for ports in Spain or the West Indies.

The only differences between a commissioned and a noncommissioned trader were the amount of armament it carried and a letter from the country of its origin allowing it to plunder the shipping of an antagonist nation, that was their letter-of-marquee or their commission. Privateers, on the other hand, had nothing to trade. Their holds were empty when they first weighed anchor. But their ships were full of men. Men to reef and furl, of course, but an overwhelming number of men and boys to do one thing and one thing only: fight. A privateer was commissioned by the government to do as much damage to the enemy's commerce as possible. Unlike a letter-of-marquee or a noncommissioned trader, the privateer's crew, officers and men alike, was paid only by what they captured and could manage to a friendly port. But if they were successful, their cut of the take was more than enough to compensate for the risk. The men who sank their fortunes in the syndicates knew this; the old salts who plied the seas in merchant vessels knew this; the land lubbers who never set foot on deck before, knew this; and the recruiting agents, who, for a bounty, were hired by owners to man ships, and who doubled as business agents for the seamen selling prize tickets knew this better than anyone. Grocers, tavern owners, boarding house proprietors, lawyers, innkeepers, anyone who could scrape up some money did so and gave it over to seamen in exchange for a prize ticket: a percentage of an individual seaman's take from the sale of the prize ships and cargoes that would, hopefully, be captured during any one voyage.

The "King" of Fells Point recruiting agents was a swarthy, fat, and grumpy tar, years past his prime, by the name of Fitz King. No longer able to make a living at sea, King acted as a recruiting agent for a number of ship owners, husbands, and captains along the Point. His tactics were, at the very least, unethical. Before war was declared against Britain, King would stalk the taverns of the Point, buying round after round for unfamiliar sailors returning from long voyages, until they became blind drunk. Then, working in tandem with the owner of the tavern and a couple of cronies, he would have the seamen thrown on board an outbound vessel. Since the vessel would be from another port, preferably a foreign one, nobody would be the wiser, and King would feel comfortable in his retirement with new silver in his pocket. But now that there was a war, he cleaned up his practice to the point where he would just get any sailor or lubber drunk, convince him of the fortune to be made on a particular ship, sign him up on its crew, and purchase a portion of his prize ticket at a discount price. King would then make sure the sailor wouldn't renege on the contract by keeping him full of liquor, boarding and feeding him, and loaning him money, all against the security of the ticket or at a substantial rate of interest. This King would continue to do until the ship sailed, for if the sailor succeeded in skipping out of the agreement, all of King's efforts would have been to nought. Once, however, a sailor under King's guise was put on board a ship weighing anchor, King would receive a fat sum from the owner, husband, or captain. And if the voyage of the commissioned ship was successful, and the sailor returned home alive, it was King who collected most of the seaman's share of the money. To many of likeminded businessmen on the Point, war was the opportunity of a lifetime.

"What's the King up to these day's I wonder?" Michael asked.

"No good, lad, I'm t'inkin'. He's tryin' ta steal prize tickets from da boys on da *Comet*. He'll have no luck dere, praise be. T'ose are Boyle's men an' won't be had by da likes of King. But, if I were you, Michael, I'd get a piece of da *Comet's* tickets before dey ship out. Tom Boyle's an extr'ordinary captain, he's got money written all over his kind face an' a heart of gold. I've got t'ings under control here. Go on with ya. You've got a little money ta venture on t'ose lads, don'tcha? I'm tellin' ya right now you'll not regret it. I'd get a piece of da action meself, only I put everythin' I have inta da *Rossie*, it bein' himself, ole' Joshua Barney at da helm. I sailed wit' him during da last war. Ah, t'ose were da days. Was in charge of his marines, ya know." Michael shook his head, glancing up at his uncle's red curls. Locks that were still bright red, despite the fact that Bob Dooley was past fifty. But Michael wasn't aware of his uncle's escapades at sea. The only thing his father had told him was that they had fought at Yorktown.

"Sure, St. Patrick himself has laid a blessin' on Captain Barney, an' gave him da t'ree t'ings necessary fer a captain of a privateer: courage, brains, an' luck. Da captain an' I hit it sh'traight off. He sailed da ship an' I did most of da boardin' an' da fightin', singlehanded." With this last comment, Uncle Bob coughed loudly, cleared his throat, and quickly looked around making sure no one else was in hearing distance.

Captain Tom Boyle had a fine reputation on the Point and the *Comet* was a fast looking schooner. Michael did have some money saved up from selling his papers; enough to buy a percentage on some man-jack's ticket. It wasn't like Michael to gamble money he had earned, but his uncle had captured his imagination, and suddenly, Michael felt the same feverish anticipation of quick fortune that had seized all of Baltimore. "All right, Uncle Bob, if you think it's best."

He walked along the wharf towards the *Comet*, looking for a sturdy fellow to invest in. There was a sailor who caught his eye working on the rigging of the foremast. What attracted Michael's eye to the sailor was the seaman's agility: running up the ratlines into the foretop and then along the footropes, making his way, lightly, between the stirrups, attending to the yard in some fashion. Michael stood there for some time admiring this barefooted topman with his sailcloth pants, striped shirt, and jaunty hat. The sailor noticed the boy as well and smiled. He gracefully descended the mast and quickly came over the side.

" 'Arold George is the name, mate, though me shipmates call me 'Appy, and who might you be?" the topman said, smiling, showing a healthy set of teeth.

"Michael Dooley Jr., sir," he replied, extending his hand and smiling back at this tall sailor's contagious grin.

"Well, Michael Dooley Jr., ‘at's a fine tail ya have there, and would ya look at the blue ribbon, now. At's a sharp one ‘at is. Betcha the girls think so," he said, with a wink from one of his merry, green eyes.

"I - well, I hoped she would, but I couldn't go to tea and it's been ages since I saw her last."

"Tea! Well, ya run with a rich breed then, mate. You're father must be a squire at least."

"My father's a cooper," Michael giggled. Owns the shoppe right down there. Although he's at sea as a carpenter on the *Mary Lynn* now."

"Why 'es a warrant officer, then. As good as any bo'sun or gunner and entitled to a salute from such as me, rated able I am."

Michael pointed to the top of the foremast. "I knew you were an able seaman when I saw you practically dancing on the yard. Did it take you long to learn?"

"Long? Not likely. I began my service as a boy, third class, mind ya, but it only took me a year t'make seaman, and another t'be rated able. 'At was in the King's navy, Michael," Happy whispered, not wanting anyone to pick up this part of their conversation. "I been shippin' out of Philly'delphia ever since. 'At's where my wife, Peggy, and the young ones is. 'Appy as a clam, what with no cane or cat t'touch my back. My mates picked up on 'at, called me 'Appy they did, and it suits me just fine." He cocked his head back and examined Michael from head to foot. "Say, I bet you've got the makin's of an able topman yourself, Michael. 'Ave ya thought about signin' on t'this 'ere ship?" Happy asked, daring his thumb back to the *Comet.*

"Why no, Happy, I-I - well, I do dream of it sometimes. Of going to different countries around the world, I mean, meeting different sorts of people. But, my mother's just passed away and my pa's at sea, and there's Uncle Bob to look after, and my papers, and, well, someday Happy, someday I might."

"Sounds as though ya 'ave a 'ead on your shoulders, mate. School's the ticket for you. Brains is what ya got. Officers material, 'at's what."

"School term's just over, Happy, but I am interested in another kind of ticket, if you please, sir," Michael said hopefully.

"So 'at's your line," Happy beamed, getting Michael's train of thought. "You were a'ppeerin' at the top, scopin' out ole' 'Appy, what was workin' pretty as ya please and, ya says to yourself, now, there's a bloke what knows what 'es up to. There's somebody whats goin' out for 'es fortune and whats likely, 'e'll come home again. Safe as a baby in 'es mum's arms, ya might say. Well, Michael Dooley Jr., this 'eres your lucky day. I was just sayin' to myself: now there's a sharp lookin' bloke wit' a pretty ribbon on 'es tail. An' ole' 'Appy should be trimmed up proper, what with goin' t'plunder 'es ole' King's ships, riskin' a rope from a yardarm in the bargain. A mate deserves a ribbon on 'es tail if 'es riskin' 'es bloody neck. And a couple of bobs in 'es purse to buy it wit'. So, lad, out wit' your silver and we'll see if we can make a fair and honest deal of it."

Michael fished into his pocket, producing a small purse tied up with a drawstring. He undid the string and put six dollars in coins into the sailor's strong hand. This represented the bulk of Michael's life savings. Happy removed his cap and produced a bit of a pencil and a scrap of paper that was stuffed into the seam.

"Now, an able man like myself, what you call a First Class seaman, is entitled t'two shares on this 'ere ship. The Articles of Agreement, ‘at every man-jack aboard is signed, totals ninety-four and a quarter shares, leavin' five and three quarters for awardin' t'whoever first sights a sail or boards a ship in a fight. And I'm the bloke wit' the sharpest green eyes on this ship, Michael. So, I'm aimin' for an extra share or two t'use in my old age. But, between you and me, mate," he whispered again, “Appy won't be the first t'board anyone's ship in a fight. Not with a price on my head and a family in Philly'delphia. Why, if I got myself killed, my Peggy would kill me all over agin'. When I'd meet 'er at St. Peter's gate, ‘at is.

"Now, its six dollars you're puttin' up against, what could be, four shares. Let's see," he figured, with his eyes directed up to the sky, "’at'll make your investment an even two and a ‘alf percent." Michael concentrated on what two and a half percent would mean, but he didn't have the faintest idea. This bothered his good business sense. After all, six dollars was just about all the money he had in the world, accumulated over three years of hard work selling papers. Happy noticed the boy's confusion.

"Now, I think it's a fair offer, Michael, but I can see 'Appy's dealin' wit' a man of business. So, for the son of an officer and a cooper to boot, I'll give ya five percent, but ‘at’s my limit, not a farthing more."

"It's a deal," Michael said, smiling with the satisfaction of having conducted a profitable enterprise, and extended his hand to shake on the contract.

"You drive a 'ard bargain, Michael." They shook hands, vigorously. "Which I hope t'make it a king's ransom by the time I get back." Happy wrote on the back of the scrap of paper: "FOR SIX DOLLARS COIN. SOLD TO MICHAEL DOOLEY JUNIOR FIVE PERCENT OF MY SHARES. CHASSEUR – CAPTAIN BOYLE. JULY 1812. HAROLD GEORGE. FIRST CLASS SEAMAN." Michael stared at the little paper, wondering how much five percent would bring. He looked up, wanting to say something to Happy, but the sailor had already gone over the bulwark and up the ratlines to his top. Michael waved the paper at him. Happy swung his arm around a back stay, cupped his hands over his mouth, and shouted down to him, "which my Peggy taught me t'read and write like a gentleman. Ain't it 'rit nice, Michael?"

Walking away from the ship, back toward the cooperage, Michael spied a glimpse of white out on the water. He climbed to the top of a pile of water casks that were waiting to be loaded into the hold of the *Comet.* The sun was full up and, again, he put his hand to his forehead to narrow the glare and peered out where he, momentarily, caught a flash of white. His hopes told him it was a billowing topsail in the southwest wind. Baltimore sails were whiter than most, and they could easily be identified as the sail of a friendly ship at sea. Nearby, a tall, flamboyantly dressed man, sporting a thin mustache, was leading a convoy of men in business attire along the dock. The men were the syndicate sponsoring the *Comet's* voyage. They were all wealthy merchants: Andrew Clopper, Levi Hollingsworth, Peter Arnold Karthaus, and Jeremiah Sullivan. The man leading the group stopped when he noticed Michael, ten feet above them on the casks, peering, like a statue, his body rigidly pointed to the sea. The tall stranger whipped back his cape and pointed his walking stick up at Michael.

"You see gentlemen. That's what all of Baltimore is doin' right now. All of America! Looking to the sea! My dear Irish mother would call him an omen of good fortune. Look at him, gentlemen. Do you know what he sees so expectantly?" The businessmen gathered around the tall figure that spoke so eloquently, so deeply, in a very slight, southern drawl, and they all looked up at Michael. "By God, suhs, he sees a crop ready for harvest. Come gentlemen! Put aside your differences and put me to sea. There's a crop to reap and not a moment to lose."

The syndicate held the American Commission No. 4, issued by the collector of customs. They decided to place this valuable commission in the capable hands of one Thomas Boyle. Originally from Marblehead, Massachusetts, Boyle traveled south at the age of nineteen with his new bride. He had a queer mix of culture: his parents were Irish; he grew up in New England; and, he has spent his entire adult life in the South. This accounted for his drawl, which sometimes intermingled with a Massachusetts twang and an Irish brogue. The ship he was commanding was constructed by the premier Baltimore ship builder, Thomas Kemp. As Michael had guessed, it was fast - faster than anything in the harbor. In the right hands she could outrun or run down anything afloat, and Thomas Boyle was the man with the right hands.

Boyle motioned, regally, for the contingent to follow him, but stopped, when he saw the boy look down in dejection. Michael had seen a gull alit on driftwood, not a white, cotton duck topsail from the *Mary Lynn*.

"Ahoy! Boy! No sail ho? Come to me in the *Comet* and put those sharp eyes of yours to work on the crosstrees of my mainm'st. Spy sails there boy, and you and I will be rich beyond even your young imagination can dream." With this, Boyle turned, filling his cape with the wind, and tore away with the businessmen running behind his quick step.

Michael climbed down from the pile of casks and walked, with his head down, toward the cooperage. Fragmants of thoughts whisked into and out of his mind: he was worried about his father - wondering about the code he was supposed to receive soon - and curious about the strange man with the black cape and the deep, beckoning voice.

Chapter 6

"ONCE AN ENGLISHMAN"

"Why dat was himself you were talkin' ta," Uncle Bob explained. Michael had asked Bob who the tall man was, with the thin mustache and black cape. "Tom Boyle. As fine a captain of a schooner dat ever sailed out of Baltee'more. An' ya say he was askin' ya ta come wit' him on his ship as a lookout, didja? Well, Michael, don't it git yer blood up? T'ink on it boyo. What an adventure it would be!"

Michael had thought of it, of course. Every young boy, and an enterprising girl or two, had thought about it - going to sea.

"Why, every time I see a sail round da Point, haulin' her wind an' comin' inta da quay, I wonder where she's been An' every time I hear da boys at da capstan', singin' dere songs while dey up anchor, an' climin' da masts, unfurlin' da sails, me imaginations gets da better of me. Where for da love of Jaysus are dey goin' dis time? Ta what far off place? Is it ta plunder ships fer gold an' specie? Maybe it's ta reprovision at some wild, south sea island where dére's no priest an' no conscience. Where da sea is blue an' da fish pop out of da water inta yer hands. Where dey lie on da white, sandy beaches an' have da dark skinned girls pour co-co-nut milk down dere t'irsty t'roats. Girls who wear nothin' but a grass skirt an' a smile. T'ink of da romance of it all."

The two of them, uncle and nephew, were sitting atop newly made barrels, smiling at the picture Bob had just painted for them in their minds. But, they weren't the only ones dreaming on like that. The new clerk, Samuel, and the Smith boys in the back room had heard Bob Dooley's meandering as well. For the first time since the new hirings started at the cooperage, the constant pounding and sawing of the Smith brothers, and the scratching of the Samuel's pen, had stopped with this vision of romance and adventure and money. They sighed, collectively.

Uncle Bob coughed. "Enough of dis now. Dere's work ta be done!" he bellowed, as if it was their fault he had gone on like that. He turned to Michael and his massive face took on a contorted, painful expression. "Oh, fer da love of Mary, Michael, I forgot."

"Forgot?"

"Aye, dere was a messenger come fer ya dis mornin' an' dropped dis off." He reached far down into his trowsers and pulled out a note. Bringing it up to his veiny, red nose, he sniffed. "From a lass, I'm t'inkin'."

Michael took the note, raising his eyebrows at the heavy smell of roses emanating from the paper. His brows were still raised after he had finished reading. Uncle Bob stood staring down at the boy, waiting for some clue as to the contents of the message. But, Michael made no comment. He was motionless, breathless. This transfixion got the best of Uncle Bob's curiosity.

"Now, Michael me lad, I swore an oath ta yer fadder ta watch over an' protect ya. An' if dere's one t'ing a man needs protectin' from it's - it's a scented woman." But, Michael's mind was on something or someone else and he made no reply. "Come lad, wake up! Has dis vixen put a curse on yer head?"

Michael's complexion flushed with embarrassment. "Who? What's a vixen? No, this is from Desiree, Mr. Pechin's daughter. She's would like my company at tea this afternoon."

Uncle Bob's heavy jaw dropped a good six inches. "Tea is it? An' when did dis all start! Why, under me very own nose you've been playin' under da table wit' da editor's daughter. No wonder you've clubbed yer hair an' fixed yerself up like ya was da bloody prince of all Ireland."

Michael was confused. The last time he had seen his uncle with a woman, she was sitting on his shoulders, with her bare legs wrapped underneath his arms, while he danced a jig at Gilhooley's. And Michael had never once been alone with Desiree. "Uncle, I've only talked with her from time to time.

She's a nice girl from a good, respectable family. And when a lady asks a gentleman to tea it's only for some pleasant conversation, honest."

Uncle Bob was nearly distraught. "A gentle..." But Bob Dooley couldn't get out the word. He brought his great hands to his head and rubbed his curly hair back. "Michael, Michael, Michael," he said, taking the boy by the shoulder and sitting him down on a barrel. "It's time you were told da truth about women. Dis here girl, dis Dezzera..."

"Desiree," Michael corrected him.

"Shut up." Uncle Bob scolded. Then, with a change of attitude, "all right, den, dis *Desiree*," he said with a wide smile. "She's, well, she's - you're da son of a workin' man, Michael. A man who, wit' his own two hands, built a life out of nothin'. Who married a fine, hardworkin' woman an' together dey made somthin' out of dere lives. But, dis *lady*, she's been givin' everythin' fer nothin'. She doesn't know what it is ta scrape an' claw. She made herself inta a statue, lad. Sometin' you look at an' admire, but not good fer anythin' but standin' dere lookin' as pretty as ya please."

Michael looked puzzled. Why would Uncle Bob say things like that about Desiree, he thought. Desiree was beautiful. Yes, as beautiful as a statue, and smart and lovely, always lovely. "You don't even know her!" Michael shot back. "She's a fine lady. A lady, uncle! Not the kind of girl that-that-that you meet in Gilhooley's." There, it was out; and it was too late to take back. Michael immediately felt low.

Uncle Bob reeled around. He hung his head in shame and spoke softly. "You're right, boyo. I'm no one ta be talkin'. I've failed ya lad, an' yer fadder, too. Da priest was right. I'm no good fer ya, Michael. If only yer fadder was here. Him dat's followed da code. Not me. And yer ta be receivin' da words at yer birthday, an' himself away. I - I can't even remember dem. Da words - da code, I mean. It's been so long since me da sat me down an'..." But Bob could go no further. He heaved his bear like shoulders and sobbed.

"Uncle Bob. Dear uncle, please. I didn't mean to hurt..." But Bob was gone through the door, staggering in self-realization down the quay. Michael went to the door and stood under the creaking sign. He had hurt Jessica when he spoke the truth about the fact that he was hungry. He didn't mean to think she was only good for fixing a meal. He hurt Uncle Bob because he spoke the truth. Desiree was different from the women on the Point who for drink or money bared their legs for the drunken men in the taverns. Bared their legs and who knows what else, Michael thought. But, he didn't want to know what else. And what about the code, he thought. If for some reason, unthinkable reason, his father wasn't home to give it to him, who would? Uncle Bob doesn't even remember the words. He glanced down at the perfumed paper and wondered.

Michael left the cooperage in the dependable hands of Samuel, the clerk, and the Smith boys, busy as usual, in the back room. Before going uptown to Desiree's house, he stopped off at his home on Thames street to wash up and put on his best clothes.

Tomorrow was baking day and Jessica was busy kneading dough in the kitchen. Michael poked his head in and said hello, trying to determine if Jessica was still hurt by his words. It is true that she had gotten him out of a tough spot, throwing him a line on lunar readings. But Michael was taking no chances.

"Why, hello yourself Michael. You're home early. Everything all right at the cooperage?" Jessica asked with a pleasant smile, her tanning face and hands speckled white with flour.

"Oh, fine, yea." Michael said dejectedly, his mind still picturing Uncle Bob's shoulders shuddering from his tears. But Michael needed to hide that part from Jessica's searching eyes and he quickly added, "Samuel, the new clerk? He's a marvel, Jess. Does everything that needs done, and the Smith boys never stop until the job's finished." Jessica wasn't fooled. There was genuine sadness in Michael's eyes. But, she didn't know what to say. She continued with her kneading, hoping he would open his mind to her. He didn't. "I'm goin' up stairs to wash up Jess," and with that, he dashed away.

As he dressed into white cotton trousers, a fresh white scarf, and dark blue vest, he began to anticipate tea at Desiree's. Uncle Bob was wrong to have said those things. Desiree was a lady, no doubt, he said to himself. And he was the son of a successfull businessman, albeit a tradesman. Maybe he wasn't rich, but he was responsible and respectable. Why shouldn't a pretty girl invite him to tea? And why, for all love, shouldn't he accept?

By the time he had cleaned up and returned to the kitchen, Jessica had already finished her preparations. Across the table lie bowls and baskets partly filled with the dough for her bread and cakes. Tonight they would rise and tomorrow she would bake. Michael came into the kitchen with a changed mood.

"My goodness, Michael. What's the occasion? This isn't a Holy Day is it?" Jessica said, half in jest, half inquisitively.

"Go on with ya, Jess," Michael replied, repeating word for word what his father would say to Teresa when she needled him. "Now, don't laugh, or be shocked, like Uncle Bob, but I've been invited to tea this afternoon."

"Tea?"

"Yea, tea. You know, when a lady invites a young gentleman over for afternoon tea. You've heard of that haven't you?"

Jessica felt a weakness, starting in her knees. She balanced herself by placing a hand on the back of a chair. "*Yesss*," she retorted dramatically, "I haven't grown up in a cellar. I've heard of afternoon tea. As a matter of fact," she sounded as if she was completely at ease, "I've attended many teas in my spare time. Who may I ask is the inviter?"

"Well, let's see." Michael fished for the note, finding it in a vest pocket. "A Mistress Desiree Pechin, madame, daughter of Mr. William Pechin, the esteemed editor." Jessica smelled roses. The weakness turned to something like fear as it travelled up from her knees to her stomach. Somehow, she still managed her composure.

"How delightful. Well, now, a man of the world. Ms. Pechin will be pleased with her choice."

"Thank you madame. And now, if you will give me your leave, I shall go to tea."

Michael gave her a formal bow and Jessica, now gripping the chair, performed her best curtsey.

Tea at Desiree's was served promptly at three. Michael had never been to tea before, but he remembered his mother having people over for tea: Father John, and the women from the St. Patrick's Benevolent Society. But, this was different from the few times Teresa had given tea, he thought. Desiree had, certainly, invited him over for more than just tea. They would sip from dainty cups, of course, but then they would have precious seconds to stare into each other's eyes. Maybe, even inadvertently touch each other's hands as they reached for the same sweet cake. Sure, the only way a lady and gentleman could spend some time with each other was over a civilized cup of tea.

He found himself sitting in a finely appointed room. It was a quiet place, off to one side of the huge town house on Baltimore Street. It wasn't like Teresa's sitting room at all. It was fancier, busier. There were silk draperies and a thick, soft carpet. He appreciated the two symmetrical fireside chairs, and he planned to impress Desiree when he would casually note that they were indeed symmetrical. The servant who escorted him to the sitting room had asked for his hat and gloves, and he was embarrassed to say he wasn't carrying any. In fact he never possessed such things. In time, he mused, he would purchase a fine tall hat and white, silk gloves, and a respectable cloth coat as well. Maybe even a cape, like Captain Boyle's. Desiree would never have invited him to tea if she didn't see him, not too long from now, as a successful businessman.

Just then Desiree came flying into the room in a frenzied state. "Oh, Mr. Dooley, how good of you to come. I apologize for keepin' you. I know you are a busy man. A man of business should never, ever be kept waitin'." She spoke with more of a southern drawl than usual, but Michael didn't seem to mind. "I would have been ready hours ago if Susie, mah girl, hadn't been so stupid with mah seam. Of course, I had to correct her. I beg you, Mr. Dooley, to unda'stand mah position?"

"Oh, Mistress Pechin, of course. As a matter of fact I have plans to hire an indentured servant myself." Michael almost cut himself short, he had no such plans and he didn't know why he just lied like that.

"Well when you do, Mr. Dooley, oh, may I call you Michael, Mr. Dooley?"

"Why, yes. Yes, Desiree, please do."

"Well, when you do take on a servant, it's vital, vital to show firmness at all times."

"Yes, well it's just my father and I now in the house. Father John has been good enough to send over a girl to cook and clean. But with two men in the house it's hard to manage and we really should take on someone else to attend us." I did it again, he thought, and he didn't even know what exactly a servant would do when attending to someone's dress. Suddenly, he thought of Jessica helping him on with his clothes, and he blushed. No, it would be a man or a boy. And as he comforted himself with this thought a maid came into the room with a platter of tea and cakes. Desiree gently lifted up the tiny cups from their dainty saucers and poured. Michael nervously waited for her to drink from her cup first, it seemed like a gentlemanly thing to do. After an appropriate, silent pause, Desiree sighed. She gingerly picked up her cup, gently blew on the hot tea with her cherry, red lips, and sipped. Michael followed her example, but decided against blowing on his tea. Not manly, he thought. The tea was hot, very hot, and it burned his tongue and scorched his throat.

She reached for a cake, and Michael, wanting to put something cool into his mouth, reached down at the same moment. He accidently touched her hand. To his surprise, Desiree left her hand on top of the cake. She didn't try to draw it away like he thought she would. At that moment, the doorbell rang. Michael, still with his hand upon Desiree's took no note of the ringing, he thought it was in his head. Suddenly, Desiree snatched her hand away and rose to greet someone else who was entering the room.

"Henry! Come in! Do sit down. How wonderful of you to come," exclaimed Desiree, with joy in her voice. Henry looked down with a blank stare on his handsome face and barely took notice of Michael. "Corey, take Mr. Hampton's hat and gloves," Desiree instructed the servant. Henry Hampton was almost six feet tall with an athletic build. He must have been twenty years old, Michael imagined. "Mr. Hampton, may I introduce Mr. Dooley." They shook hands, each cracking a polite smile. Then they turned to face Desiree, each with a look of puzzlement in their eyes. Desiree drew in her breath and pouted her cherry lips.

"Oh, dear, this is all mah fault, gentlemen. Truly, all mah fault. Imagine inviting two gentlemen to tea on the same afternoon. Why, it's awful. But, please," she pleaded sweetly, a smile on her lips once more, "forgive me. My calendar is completely full and I have no head foh scheduling. Oh, dear, it's been so busy, what with the war on." This last she said looking at Michael.

Michael and Henry said they both understood that a girl in her position had so many commitments. Henry, Michael found out, has been appointed a midshipman in the navy and was soon to leave Baltimore and join his ship in Boston. Desiree made it a point to tell Henry that Michael was the son of a cooper, but Michael missed the intended slight.

It was all over by four o'clock. Michael, knowing he possessed neither hat nor gloves, decided to take his leave first, before Desiree rang for the servant to bring Henry's things. Desiree extended her hand. As Michael took it, she tugged his hand and squeezed it firmly and stared, briefly, knowingly, into his eyes. His heart leapt. As he walked down Baltimore Street, he convinced himself that Desiree had preferred him to the handsome midshipman. She must have, he said to himself, recalling the tug of her soft hand and the stare of her chestnut eyes. "Oh, how I love her," he whispered.

After Michael had left Jessica in the kitchen of Teresa's home on Thames Street, the young girl had poured out her tears over the rising dough on the table. Everything she had dreamed for so long was shattered and, suddenly, she despised the home whose spirit she had enjoined and believed in. She ran from the house. With Teresa's blue apron covering her face she ran right past Father John, who was making his way back to the rectory after visiting an elderly parishioner on Fells Street. She ran all the way to the dormitory at St. Patrick's Free School. The rest of the girls were at dinner or cooking for their respective host families across the Point. For once, the dormitory would be quiet; for once she could have a little privacy without the constant buzz of gossip and questions from the other girls. She threw herself onto her cot and sobbed.

Father John found her there. Her head buried into a pillow. "Mademoiselle," he said directly, but softly. "Shouldn't you be attending the Dooley home?" She quickly collected herself and pretended to straighten her bedding, while wiping the tears that had streaked down her face. The priest pretended too. He pretended not to notice her swollen eyes as he walked casually over to a window on the opposite side of the large room. He clasped his hands behind his back in a thoroughly clerical fashion.

"Are you happy here, Mademoiselle?" Father John asked the window. Jessica turned to see his back. She sat down on the edge of her bed.

"Father," she said nervously, "yes, I-I-I was. Happy that is." And now the tears came back, flooding her already soaking apron. "Oh, Father," the nervousness had gone, replaced by honesty, "I'm worried about the future. About what I will do. I loved Teresa Dooley, but she is gone now. Couldn't I be reassigned to another house? The Dooley business is as busy as it ever was. They'll have plenty of money to hire a girl. I could be indentured to a businesswoman in town. You know, at one of the shoppes where they have the latest fashions. I'm a good seamstress, Father, and you know I'm good at figures. I will be much happier knowing about the future. Even if I'm contracted for the next ten years, at least I'll know."

Father John turned from the window with a smile that stretched his drooping, wrinkled cheeks. "The roses were late in blooming this year, did you notice?"

This turn in the conversation left Jessica unbalanced. Her otherwise sharp intellect left her completely and she sat there on the corner of the bed feeling stupid. The tears had gone now. She thought she had been reasonable, but the priest's question and his disarming smile halted her train of thought. She just shook her head.

"But it was a harsh winter," Father John continued, as if there were no other conversation. "And a late spring. So, they waited until this late in the season, and now they are in a rush to bloom. They were so anxious to see the sun, but it was not meant to be. Not until now." He walked over and sat beside her on the bed. "I was a fool. I was afraid they would not bloom at all."

For a time neither of them said anything. Father John rose and went back to the window. " 'Ask and you shall receive', He said. But He did not say right away. The world is full of dreams and prayers, Mademoiselle. Let the Master do His work. Give Him time. I thought the roses would not bloom this year. But there they are," he said with a gentle chuckle, "there they are."

Michael didn't go home right away. He wanted to savor the feelings in his heart. The heat of the day was gradually subsiding with the descent of the sun and a fresh breeze was blowing in from the southeast. A good quartering wind for ships climbing up the Chesapeake. Still, despite the cooling effects of wind and setting sun, Michael had had an altogether warm day. Besides, he wasn't hungry, and Jessica would leave him something to eat for dinner later. He decided to walk to the western side of the Point and dip his feet into the rising tide of the cool Patapsco. And there he sat, trousers pulled up to his knees, sitting back with his feet playing in the water and his mind playing over and over again the tug of Desiree's hand.

It was getting dark now. Michael leisurely strode back to Thames Street. Before he opened the door he heard voices. One was a familiar voice that he hadn't heard for quite some time. He opened the door, slowly, and listened.

"They just took him!" the familiar voice squeaked loudly. "He pleaded with their cap'n. Said he had a boy who just lost his mother from the fever. But the rascal just stood there, with his hands behind his back as if it was his own quarterdeck. I'm tellin' ya Bob the man was an ass, an arrogant English ass! He said to our cap'n: 'Once an Englishman, always an Englishman."

Michael walked slowly across the now dark sitting room. He knew the familiar voice was that of Captain Ken. He knew the old man was talking about his father. Michael saw them all at the kitchen table: Uncle Bob with his hands covering his face; Father John muttering a silent prayer; Jessica, her eyes still red and swollen from this afternoon, now filled with new tears; and old Captain Ken, just in from the *Mary Lynn*.

Michael appeared at the doorway, stunned. The knife had already pierced his heart. But the pain was too great to allow feeling. His eyes were dead. He was numb. Just then, they all noticed him.

"Michael, boyo. Come in, lad. We've got – I mean – dere's sometin' we got ta say ta ya."

George J. Galloway

Chapter 7

THE CODE

The southeast wind that had brought such a fresh breeze now blew in gale force. Black clouds rushed in from the sea full of rain. Rain tore down upon the heated cobblestones and slapped the hardened brown dirt of Market Street. Dirt that, with the busy traffic of hoofs, spoked wheels, and hurried boots, quickly turned to mud. The mud thickened. At first it was just an unpleasantness to be scraped off at one's door. But, as torrents of water fell from the sky, the mud deepened into a mire. It thickened with the constant clap of rolling thunder, and gleamed momentarily off speedy bolts of lightening.

Michael sat, stone faced, as Captain Ken described in detail how Mike Dooley had been impressed. It was just after they first put to sea, off North Carolina. The *Mary Lynn* was making her way down the coast with a hold full of tobacco, Irish whiskey, and flour. The tobacco and flour were Maryland export staples, but the whiskey, originally from Dublin, was aged for ten years in barrels at a warehouse in New York. When the owners of the *Mary Lynn* had heard of a shortage of whiskey in the West Indies from the scuttlebutt of sailors whose traders plied those waters, they immediately sent dispatchers to Philadelphia, New York and Boston in search of a substantial quantity. Finding more than 100 barrels available in New York, they quickly outfitted the *Mary Lynn*. It was the whiskey that seamen, Irish seamen worldwide, craved for that would ensure the ship's owners a successful year.

Leaving Fells Point in the spring of the year, the *Mary Lynn*, with Mike Dooley and Captain Ken aboard, rounded Cape Henry and headed due north. After loading the whiskey they cleared New York for the Caribbean. Late in May, well before President

Madison sent his war message to Congress, the *Mary Lynn* was hailed by British frigate *Cleo* en route from Jamaica and returning to her station in Halifax. The frigate carried 44 guns and the helpless *Mary Lynn* had no choice but to back her topsails. The British captain, who was rowed over in a calm sea, quickly went to work, probing the officers and crew of the *Mary Lynn* about their nationality. Mike Dooley was an easy target. He was fairhaired and fair skinned, but what was worse, he had a brogue. It was not as pronounced as Uncle Bob's, but there was no mistaking its genesis. Mike Dooley, regardless of the fact that his proof of citizenship was valid, was the only crewmember taken off the ship. He didn't go without a fight. Not a physical demonstration, that was useless, but a heartfelt appeal to the British commander.

"Captain," Mike Dooley had begun, "Are you a father?"

"Yes, man, what of it?" the captain snapped.

"Then from one father to another, sir, I beg you not to do this. It isn't for me that I'm askin' ya. My boy, goin' on thirteen he is. His dear ma dyin' with the fever just months ago. I'm all he has, really. If I don't return, if I go aboard your ship, then you know I'll be away from him for years and years, if ever I see him again. It's not right, sir. Not before God nor man. My certificate is genuine, sir, just like everyone else's aboard this ship. I left Ireland when I was a boy. I've owned and operated a cooperage in Fells Point for over twenty years, and I only sailed this voyage for a little extra money. Captain, one poor cooper can do nothing for the king. But this poor cooper is the whole world to one poor boy."

The captain listened patiently to Dooley. Perhaps he listened because Dooley first asked him if he was a father; perhaps he listened because Mike Dooley's soft brogue, combined with his honest face and passionate words unmasked the captain's stoic bearing. But, as it turned out, it was for none of those reasons.

"Well done sir! Well done, indeed! I've haven't heard a performance like that since the theater in London. You might have been the best one yet, I dare say. I will repeat your plea when next I dine in the wardroom for the education of my officers and I hope to do justice by it. But I'll be honest with you man, I care nothing for you colonists telling his majesty which country you like to swear your allegiance to now. As if you were choosing a wench from a French bordello. No, sir. Once an Englishman always an Englishman. Now, off with him sergeant, have the bosun take the cat to his back if he gives you any trouble."

"They just took him then?" Jessica asked, lighting a second lamp and putting it on the kitchen table.

"Aye, girl," Captain Ken sighed, "they just took him."

Uncle Bob could bear no more. The whole time, before and after, Michael entered the room, he sat at the table with his head in his hands. Mike Dooley was, after all, his little brother. Bob suddenly rose and kicked the chair out from under him.

"T'ose bastards! T'ose bloody red bastards!

"Robert!" Father John shouted.

"I'll take it out on dere heads. Dey did it ta me fadder, an' now Mike. I won't stand fer it d'ye hear! I'll take it out on every last one of 'em!" With that he stomped out of the house, banging the front door behind him.

Father John looked around the kitchen. In panic he fled from the table to the sitting room and then quickly upstairs. He returned, breathless.

"Michael is gone. I cannot guess where, but he must be found. He is in a daze, oui? The mind plays tricks. He is vulnerable and may do harm to himself. Do not concern yourselves with Bob. He will find his solace in a bottle. Jessica, run up to the firehouse and tell the wardens to begin a search. Captain, you know the ways of the seamen, those who are plagued with evil desire. Anything could happen to a young boy who has lost his senses. You know who preys on such unfortunate creatures. Please, go and see Michael does not meet with such a fate. I will go first to the man they call the "King" and then to every other seaman's agent on the Point. No one must take advantage. After that I will be at the church. An angel might guide him there. Now, we go."

Going anywhere in Fells Point was very difficult. Torrents of rain blinded horses drawing their carriages, and people made their way either in the mud, now ankle deep, or along slippery cobblestones with trepidation. Father John made certain that Michael wouldn't fall prey to a dishonest agent, who could have easily filled the boy with strong drink and promises of revenge to get him to sign aboard an outbound vessel. Captain Ken passed the word along the docks that anyone who spotted the boy was to restrain him and bring him to the Dooley home under guard until the captain could talk to him. Jessica ran quickly to the firehouse of the Deptford Hundred. The wardens, who weren't going to make their rounds of the streets and alleys of the Point until after the storm had cleared, volunteered to brave the howling wind and driving rain because the boy was a Dooley.

But Michael, although in disbelief that his father was impressed, wasn't about to do anything foolish. He was, after all, his father's son, so he tried to reason the problem out in his mind. But it's hard to think a thing out thoroughly when the heart is needled with pain. It's different with physical pain which ebbs and flows allowing the mind brief moments of clarity. Emotional pain is constant. It burns, deeply, unremittingly. Burning without charring, at least on the outside, like the perpetual fires of hell.

"Who could know," Michael chanted over and over, his head bent low, making his way up Market Street. He trudged on in the mud, one step at a time, the wind and rain beating at his back. On and on he went, trying to think of someone who would know what to do. Michael didn't want to accept the fact that his father was gone. He wanted to do something. To make a plan. But the deadness that he felt inside him, the cold and constant pang of loneliness, overcame all judgement. The windswept rain had pelted against him so hard that his back was sore. He straightened up, only to find himself at the door to the offices of the *American*.

"Mr. Pechin! Mr. Pechin will know!"

The storm had caught William Pechin unaware, and he decided to ride it out in the comfort of his office before going home. He sat up in his chair and laid down his quill as Michael dragged himself in the door. Michael was also unaware. His trek up Market Street had taken its toll: mud sloshed out of his shoes and across the floor of the *American*; his trousers and shirt, even his face showed splatterings of mud; his hair was matted and dripping. He made an attempt at wiping his eyes, but it was like wiping his face with a sponge full of water. Pechin recoiled from the boy's appearance and the deadness in his eyes.

"What's this? What's happened?"

Michael wanted to start reasonably, to clearly state the facts as Captain Ken had explained them. But he couldn't find the words.

"Here, Michael, here, sit in my chair. Tell me what's gone wrong. I'll do my best to help you."

Mr. Pechin's charity helped bring some of Michael's good sense back again. His determination to act and think responsibly made one final attempt to usurp the pain.

"It's my father, Mr. Pechin. I need your help."

"Has the *Mary Lynn* come back then? Damned Bartlett! I should have been informed at once." The comings and goings of vessels were important to the nautical and commercial interests of Baltimoreans, and Mr. Pechin noted them in his newspaper.

"She's in Mr. Pechin. But without my pa. He's been impressed."

"Impressed, you say?" Michael nodded. They were both silent as Mr. Pechin worked this over in his mind. He began strolling, back and forth, across the breadth of the room.

"And you want to know what you can do about it?" the editor asked, matter of factly, still walking with his head to the floor. Michael nodded, again. Mr. Pechin didn't need to see this.

"All right, Michael. It's a journalist's job to look at the facts. Look at them blindly. Unless you're working against the Federalists, and then one must grant certain liberties. But, generally, we have an obligation to our readers to present the cold, hard facts. Do you get me boy?"

Michael found his voice again. "Yes sir, one should write a news piece differently than an essay. Ahmm, objectively instead of subjectively."

"Right! There's a time for opinion, to say what you think; there's a time for emotion, within reason, of course, to say what you feel; and there's a time for stating the facts as they are - not how we would like them to be. Are you still with me, son?"

"I'm with you sir."

This is what Michael was searching for: to deal with this situation objectively. It was only through a clear and unemotional mind that he could find the answers to his questions. He admired Mr. Pechin's intellect and perked up at his every word. Mr. Pechin knew this. He knew Michael was in shock, or very close to it. He also knew the boy to be industrious and responsible. He wanted to bring Michael back from his pain into the reality of reason that had championed the age. The editor smiled when he noted a working brain behind Michael's deep, round, brown eyes.

"Very well, then. Let's begin with the impressment itself. I take it this all happened before war was declared?"

"Why, yes sir. But how did you know?"

"Son, the ship has returned. She would be an English prize right now if she were taken on her return voyage. So, she was boarded before war was declared or possibly before the English ship was aware there was a war on."

"That's right, sir. I-I mean the former. It was the frigate *Cleo* sir, 44 guns. The *Mary Lynn* was off Cape Hatteras, making her way down to the West Indies. Captain Ken says she's returned with molasses, sugar, and rum. The British frigate was on her way from Jamaica to Halifax."

Mr. Pechin hurried to a cupboard and drew out a large map. He hurried because he knew Michael came here needing to act on this tragedy. Pechin cleared his desk with a sweep of his hand, sending everything on the desk off onto the floor with a crash. He spread the map out and the two of them stood bending before it in earnest.

"Right, now show me Cape Hatteras, Michael."

"That's it - there sir!"

"Good. Now hold your finger on that spot, no, a little out further. They would have stood out from the cape, in case of a storm, you see. Now, show me Jamaica."

"There sir."

Mr. Pechin kicked through the items on the floor until he found a straight edge. He drew a line from Jamaica, through Cuba, and up to Cape Hatteras where Michael held his finger.

"Well it's not unreasonable that the British frigate would have taken this course. Yes, around Cuba and then back on line. The Florida Stream runs strong up the coast here and the British would have been too far south to take advantage of the westerlies. Still, if I were setting a course from Jamaica to Halifax, I would have weighed anchor in Bermuda, which the British might have done already, only that information never reached Captain Ken. The point is they certainly would not have gone back to Bermuda when they were north of her off the cape. Now, that's important, Michael, because we must be firm in our opinion of where your father is now. If we can say, and I think we can with justification, that your father is in Halifax, then we can notify the State Department of that fact and they can relay that information to Mr. Beasley in London."

"Mr. Beasley, sir?"

"Yes, Mr. Beasley was the seamen's agent for our nation in England before the war. It was his job to provide the names of impressed Americans to the Admiralty, supposedly so they could look into the matter. And that's exactly what we're going to do, but that's not all. We have to also determine what your father is likely to do."

"Does he have a choice?"

Mr. Pechin thought momentarily before answering this question.

"Yes, actually he does, Michael. You see, your father was impressed before war was declared. At first he had no choice but to serve on the British frigate. But now that war is declared, he - ah - well, he could refuse, you see."

Michael became adamant. "Of course he would refuse. My pa fought with Washington at Yorktown. He would never serve on a British ship while England was at war with our country."

The editor smiled broadly at the boy's insistence. "Easy, son, easy. Nobody's challenging your father's patriotism. But we must think as if we were in your father's position. If he refuses further service in his majesty's ships what would happen to him? Remember, he isn't regarded as an American, but as an Englishman; he wasn't taken after war had been declared, but before it. So, he saw some service already in the King's navy. To refuse to serve now would mean severe consequences."

A crackle of thunder reinforced the fear that showed on Michael's face as he digested Mr. Pechin's words. They made sense. His father had a choice: to serve in the king's navy or be hanged. He could fight against his country or never see his son again. Mr. Pechin saw the obvious conclusion developing behind Michael's brown eyes.

"No son, no. No one would hold it against your father for serving in the British navy. But I've heard bits and pieces about your father over the years, Michael. I don't know him personally, but I know of him. Apparently, he is a smart man, a sober thinker, and a hard worker. The question is what will he do? My thinking is that he will try to figure out a way to get as close to home as possible. He has skills as a carpenter and as a cooper. That makes him a commodity."

"Commodity?"

"A valuable person in Halifax. He could remain on this frigate and be stationed right off of our very own coastline; or he could be assigned to work in the dockyards of Halifax, wherever the British need him most. Be certain of this, Michael, your father is thinking - just as we are doing - of a way to get back."

"But, Mr. Pechin, what about our State Department and Mr. Beasley in London?"

"Unfortunately, Michael, Mr. Beasley, although a very thorough man, has always been hamstrung by the British Admiralty in being of service to our impressed seamen. When he provided a name of an impressed American, they would tell him that the sailor was dead, or that he married an Englishwoman and has babies to feed, or he is on a foreign station and there is nothing they can do. All lies. And now that there is a war, well, everything gets worse from here on in. Mr. Beasley will still keep on at his post in London, but his skills will be used to negotiate for the exchange of prisoners. Circumstances being what they are, your father is not a prisoner but an English sailor. Still, we have to at least try to obtain your father's release. We will communicate with Mr. Beasely and seek his opinions. But, we must accept the reality of the situation and know that it will probably be the outcome of this war that decides your father's fate, after all."

Michael couldn't accept this. "But, I'll write to President Madison and tell him of my pa's service. I'll write to Mr. Clay!"

"Michael, I'm going to tell you the truth: it would be a waste of time. Mr. Madison is doing all he can right now. It's why he asked for a declaration of war in the first place. You remember the Lewis boys who were impressed out of a merchant ship in February? It was on our front page."

Michael nodded.

"That was February; this is July. Nothing has been heard from them, and they are great nephews of George Washington. No, Michael, we will go through proper channels and ask the State Department to do its job. We have a leg up on the situation because we are pretty sure that your father is in Halifax. But really, everything is up to your father. It's his wits I'm banking on. Son, you know your father. Trust him now. Think of what he would expect of you."

****

The 27th of July was a memorable one for everyone in Baltimore, especially for Alexander Contee Hanson, the owner and editor of the *Federal Republican*. Bob Dooley would have had a memorable day as well, save for the fact that he was drunk for a solid week after hearing the news about his brother. For seven straight days he drank and cursed and beat up anyone who even looked like a Federalist. Mr. Hanson, to his misfortune, decided to publish his newspaper and put it on the streets of Fells Point where it met the angry, blurred vision of Uncle Bob.

Bob had taken Moranvillè's instructions to heart and he didn't find his bottle in one of the seedy taverns on the Point. Instead, he held court in the firehouse, passing out next to his precious Gooseneck Engine, between bouts of drinking. The Gooseneck's keg of brandy was emptied by Bob on the first night and was replenished with rum and then Irish whiskey. The whiskey somehow managed to make its way from New York to the West Indies to the Point aboard the *Mary Lynn*. To this day, the crew has sworn that the ship's clerk simply miscounted.

Uncle Bob had called an emergency meeting of the Deptford Hundred. All the volunteer firemen assembled at the firehouse and spilled out into the street to hear Bob Dooley speak. He stood upon the missing barrel of whiskey and cleared his throat before beginning his oratory.

"Gen'elmen. Reprub'ican brodders all an' fello' volin'teers. Tonight we have work for us ta do. I'm sure you've all read Ha'son's lies in da paper today. And fer t'ose of you too stupid ta read, I'll read it fer ya. Where's da damned paper?" He shuffled around atop the barrel, his weight straining and creaking the staves, and peered about the room for the newspaper. "Dere it is on the back of da 'ingine. Joe Durkin! Will ya fetch me da paper, Durkin darlin'?"

Durkin was the Assistant Foreman of the Deptford Hundred and a prosperous shipwright. He was a full two feet shorter than Bob Dooley. When he handed the newspaper up to his foreman, Bob nearly toppled onto him trying to reach it. Luckily, Joe Durkin had been swinging a hammer for forty years in his trade, and this had made his right forearm twice the size of his left and twice as strong. After handing Bob the paper, Durkin steadied his foreman with his one huge arm.

"Thankee Joe. Now, dis here Ha'son seys dat ar Pres'dent, dear Jamie, is..." Bob drew the paper close to his bulbous nose, "...nothin' but a dupe of Irish imma - immer - imm'grants.' Kin ya bereeve dat? Nothin' but a dupe of poor, stupid Irish imm'grants."

Bob's mouth drew down in a tremendous frown. "Dupe! he seys! Ar pres'dent, da Commander-in-Chief of ar army and nabee. An' dis here Has'on seys 'es a dupe."

Bob stood there, teetering on the barrel, shaking his massive head. As usual when he'd been drinking and thinking about presidents or like things, he became sentimental. Tears appeared in his blood shot eyes.

"Lads, 'es not right. Why, when ar armies are in da field, bleedin' an' fightin' da Tories an' Brits'. 'Es not right. I say we pay a small visit ta Mr. Has'on an' teach him ta have a li'l' respec' fer da con'try. What da ye seys lads, are ya wit' me!"

To a man the Deptford shouted support for their foreman.

"All right, 'den. Joe, be a dear and go down to da pubs and pick out sum' fightin' men. Make 'em Irish, Joe." The shipwright ran out the door, making his way down to the wharf to fetch more men. Uncle Bob, his oratory complete, promptly fell off the barrel.

Armed with pikes and knives, sticks and rocks, Durkin's band of Irish seamen and Uncle Bob's firemen met on South Charles Street to plan their assault. Hanson, himself a capable fighter, had heard about the mob's presence and had gotten ready for them. His group of men, armed with swords and muskets, barricaded themselves in the offices of the *Federal Republican*. One of his men, a friend from Virginia, was the old revolutionary war soldier "Light-Horse Harry" Lee. For two hours the mob outside the office taunted the Federalists and cursed them as traitors. Bob Dooley led in a chant:

"We'll feather and tar every damned British Tory / And this for American glory."

"Come out from your fortress and fight like men!" Bob screamed. "Come out Ha'son! You English lovin' ass!" But the barricaded men knew better than to show themselves. Their aim was simply to ride out the night, and hopefully, disperse the mob through the mob's own impatience.

Citizens from across Baltimore descended on South Charles Street. The situation grew more dangerous with each new bottle that was passed around. Twice, now, Uncle Bob and the men of the Deptford prevented torches from being hurled upon the roof of the building. Suddenly, a shot rang out from the downstairs window and Joe Durkin fell to his knees. Within moments he was dead, the ball had severed a major artery. Now, the mob was out of control, even the men from the Deptford joined the chant to smoke out the Federalists villains.

A company of militia arrived just in time to prevent a rush of men, Bob Dooley in the lead, with a battering ram to knock down the front door. The colonel of the militia persuaded Bob to back off while the officers of the militia negotiated with Hanson's men. Bob agreed when he learned that General Lee was among Hanson's supporters. It was General Lee who delivered George Washinton's eulogy. Lee knew that Hanson's situation was hopeless. There were only ten men inside the office and well over two hundred outside. He convinced Hanson that they would be better off under the protection of the militia. The company of musket bearing soldiers surrounded Hanson's men as they made their way into the street. They were escorted to the city's jail just a block away and kept under lock and key until it was determined who fired the shot that killed Joe Durkin.

But Durkin was a popular man and to the men who made up Bob Dooley's mob the enemy of their nation was inside that jail. A group of men from the Deptford persuaded Bob that "Light Horse" Harry Lee or not, the men in the jail should pay for the death of the beloved shipwright and for the fact that they dared oppose a war which was already in progress. It didn't take much persuading. "Are we gonna let dem aristocrats get away wit' killin' Joe Durkin?!" Bob shouted to the men.

"Death to the monarchists!" the crowd chanted over and over until the battering ram appeared once more. Bob led a group of men towards the jail. The militia fired volleys into the air but did not take aim. At the sound of the report from the muskets the mob scattered. All except Bob and six other determined men. Bob met the colonel of the militia at the door of the jail and pushed by him, knocking him to the ground as if he wasn't there at all. The militiamen refused to fire on their fellow citizens and backed away at the sight of the fire in Bob's eyes and the size of his hulk barrelling into the jailhouse.

In minutes it was over. Bob Dooley and the six men who followed him into the jail met the now disarmed Hanson men and beat them to a pulp. Hanson was badly mauled, but he survived. James Lingan, another veteran of the War for Independence, and a friend of Hanson's did not. By the time Bob and his small band were finished, everyone of the Federalists lie on the ground: eyes gouged out, teeth gone, scars everywhere. The war had come to Baltimore, but not one red coat was yet to be seen. Mr. Pechin was right. This was a war for ideas. Ideas that took the lives of Durkin and Lingan and would take many, many more.

****

The weeks passed quickly now for Michael, who was no longer waiting for his father's homecoming. Michael distanced himself from everyone, keeping himself busy at the cooperage and following the war's progress in the newspapers. Uncle Bob, sober now from the affects of both his brother's impressment and the death of Joe Durkin, returned to work at the cooperage. Bob's guilt over his actions with the mob caused him to work on a plan to do right by Michael. He decided to put Michael's name up for membership in the Deptford Hundred. To some extent the plan worked. Michael actually smiled when he heard he was to be made in the Point's fire department. Gilly Morrison and Michael's other young friends on the Point were jealous of Michael's nomination. It was an honor to be a volunteer fireman. Every man of prominence in Baltimore, indeed in every city in the country, was enlisted on the rolls as volunteer firefighters.

Membership meant that one was a patriot and a civic minded individual. But it also meant that one could extract certain political and financial favors from these, ofttimes, elite and powerful organizations. Even George Washington had been a volunteer fireman. But for young men, the advantage to fire service was in its influence upon young women. Handsomely dressed in their uniforms, young symbols of virtue, upward mobility, and authority, the girls of the Point would think themselves proud to take the arm of a firefighter. Michael knew that Desiree would appreciate his nomination. He engulfed himself in the business of fighting fires and Uncle Bob couldn't have been more pleased.

It was close to three o'clock in the morning when Michael sat up from bed with a start to the familiar and enticing sound of a rattle. The fire wardens with their long staffs and loud rattles that cranked awake the men of the Deptford were running up and down Thames Street shouting, "Fire! Fire! Fire at Gillhooley's!" Michael jumped into his clothes and dashed out to the firehouse on Fells Street.

Uncle Bob was already there with, perhaps, forty men. The doors to the firehouse were swung open wide and the lanterns of the engines could be seen from a block away. Michael's job was to act as a lantern boy. He would lead the men pulling the engines down the dark streets and alleys of Fells Point. This was no easy task. The men ran hard and the weight of the engines propelled them dangerously along the cobblestoned roadbed. If Michael, running precariously just ahead of the engines, slipped on a wet stone, the men would not be able to halt their engines in time and would crush the lantern boy.

The Deptford Hundred was the fourth fire company organized in Baltimore and the first for Fells Point. Gillhooley's was obviously within their jurisdiction. However, the Deptford competed with other companies in fighting fires close to Jones Falls and even Old Baltimore Town. The competition was keen. Insurance companies paid a bonus to the first company who could tap the water supply with their hoses. In Baltimore, the Deptford was always a favorite to get the bonus. That was because of the strength, agility, and bulbous nose of Bob Dooley. His strength was legendary, sometimes pulling the engine so fast that the other men couldn't keep up. And his sense of smell was so acute he could detect the scent of smoke at great distances and would rouse his men to their engines before the competition even heard the rattle of the warden's cranking machines. But his biggest asset to the Deptford was his willingness to cheat. If the competition were ahead of him to the water source, Bob would nonchalantly clip their hoses. This he would never do, of course, during a house fire, when human lives weighed in the balance; but if the fire occurred in a warehouse, then all was fair game to Dooley.

The Deptford had two engines to fight fires. The first was an old Newsham that couldn't pivot its wheels, so that the firemen had to lift the engine off the ground when rounding a corner. It also had to be picked up to point the nozzle in the direction of the fire. The second was a brand new Gooseneck that could both cut corners and swivel its nozzle in any direction. The Gooseneck carried two hundred feet of leather hose on a reel in front of the air chamber housing. It was colorfully painted and all of its fittings were of polished brass. Its major innovation, the source of pride in Baltimore firefighting circles, was the keg that Uncle Bob had installed in the front of the rig. "To ease da boys' pain t'rough da long, cold nights," he had explained to the company's executive board.

Each engine was decorated (on parade day and other important occasions) with paintings that were positioned on removable placards. These paintings were another source of competition for the different fire companies and their respective communities. The Deptford's engines were decorated with paintings of strong, busty, nude women: one blond, in the front; two brunettes at the sides; and a redhead in back. Like the figureheads of ships, these were thought to bring good fortune to sailors and firefighters in a stormy tempest. The Gooseneck's brakes or pump handles were mounted on the sides and required fourteen men to work the handles up and down. To pull it down the street required a good many more men.

The distance from the firehouse to Gillhooley's was only four blocks. Still, by the time the engines had arrived, the tavern was all aflame. The men went to work pumping water from the Patapsco onto the buildings astride the tavern, for Gillhooley's was a total loss and the rest of the wharf had to be saved. Axe men chopped at the frames of the adjacent buildings as well, tossing everything into the river. By the time it was over, old Gillhooley and Bob were in tears over the demise of the structure that had meant so much to them.

Michael was tired. He had helped at the pumps all night long. The dawn was just now rising over the Chesapeake. His arms ached and all Michael thought about was a quick wash, to remove the soot covering him head to toe, and the comfort of his eider down mattress.

In the back of his home on Thames Street, Michael stripped his clothes and poured a bucket of cold water over his head. With a brush and a bit of soap he worked up a lather, scrubbed his body clean, and then rinsed with another bucket of water. Wearing a towel he walked into the house only to hear a knock at the front door. "Oh my goodness," Michael panicked, "Jessica!" But then he realized that this was Sunday, and Jessica's day off. He opened the door and peeked at his visitor.

"Good morning, Father."

"Happy birthday, to you Michael!"

Michael stood before the opened door, grasping the towel around his waist. He had forgotten. This seemed incredulous. How could he have forgotten his own birthday? Father John stepped in and closed the door behind him.

"I have heard of the fire. Gillhooley's is lost, what a shame," the priest said with a grin.

"Yes, Father. We were at it all night. I was just going to get a little sleep before Mass."

"Then I will give you something to think on while you slumber. Before your father left he asked me to do something of great importance, in case he could not return to perform it himself."

At once, Michael knew exactly what he was referring to and he was tired no more.

"It should fall upon your uncle to do this service, according to the dictates of your family custom, but your father knew that your uncle could not be of use in this matter. Michael I am pleased to give you the code of your ancestors. The code that has guided the lives of Dooleys for generations. What I am about to tell you will - if you let it, if you, yourself, decide to follow its sacred maxims - change your life, forever."

Michael was almost crying now. This was something he had been waiting for, dreaming about, wondering on, since he was a small boy.

"I'm ready, Father."

"Good. The code is from the great and gifted St. Thomas Aquinas. It is from his *Two Precepts of Charity*, written in the year of our Lord 1273:

'Three things are necessary for the salvation of man: to know what he ought to believe; to know what he ought to desire; and to know what he ought to do.'"

George J. Galloway

Chapter 8

CALVARY

With every victory and every defeat, Michael's young heart soared and dived like the ever-present flight of the gulls off the docks of the Point. It was almost Christmas, but since June, the war, at least on land, had not gone well at all. First, it was the Dearborn massacre and General Hull's surrender of Detroit. The whole northwest was lost, needlessly, when the general gave his sword over to an inferior force. General Hull was outwitted by the British commander, General Brock, who marched the same red coats, continuously, in front Hull's fort pretending to command a mighty army. Brock also allowed one of his couriers to be captured. The messenger carried a letter in his leather bag from Brock to the Royal Governor that foretold of thousands of Indians sweeping down from the north to join the British assault on Detroit. The letter was a skillfully played ruse. Even with his Indian allies, Brock's forces were still inferior in number, and any assault on Detroit would have been too costly. Finally, Brock wrote to Hull and informed him that the British would not be able to control their Indians should a battle commence. General Hull, possibly fearing a bloody massacre of the women and children under his care, including his own family, possibly because he had lost his nerve, despite his courageous service in the Revolution, finally capitulated.

But American hearts and hopes were buoyed with news of another Hull whose imaginative and daring exploits outrunning a British squadron off the coast of New Jersey was hailed as if it was a great victory. Captain Isaac Hull, of the USS *Constitution*, General Hull's nephew and adopted son, had used ingenious sailing ability in avoiding capture while being pursued by four British frigates. In a calm sea with no wind to propel their ships, the British captains signaled each other and decided to act in concert. Three ships provided Captain Broke, in HMS *Shannon,* their crews and boats to pull the *Shannon* close within range of the *Constitution.* Meanwhile, Hull's crew wearily worked their own oars in a desperate attempt to escape the superior British force. But the *Shannon*, with all the additional boats and oarsmen, was gaining fast. Hull took the advice of one of his seasoned lieutenants and signaled to one of his cutters to stow their oars and come along side. The American crew strained to bring up a two hundred-pound kedge anchor from below and quickly set it into the cutter. Connecting lengths of cable and rope and attaching these to the kedge anchor, the cutter's crew returned to their oars and rowed ahead of the *Constitution.* On board the *Constitution*, the officers directed the men to connect the long, makeshift cable to the capstan and assembled the crew to make ready, as if they were going to weigh anchor. At an appropriate distance, the cutter dropped the kedge over the side. Immediately, the order was given to push the bars around the capstan and every available man joined in the attempt. The *Constitution* edged forward. Hull had a second cutter and a second kedge fitted out on the opposite side of the ship. In this way, and old trick, really, known to American coastal vessels as "kedging," the *Constitution* was able to stay out of range of British cannons and make her escape.

When the news came that an American skipper had out sailed and out thought the British navy, even Federalists cheered openly. Later, when dispatches arrived containing the accounts of the first American-British frigate duel, the American war effort was given another needed boost.

After provisioning the *Constitution* in Boston, Hull took his ship about 750 miles off the coast, laying a plot to Bermuda, hoping to meet a convoy of West Indiamen on their way back to England. Instead, Hull met the esteemed frigate, HMS *Guerrière*. As the *Constitution* approached, the British ship fired one of her long guns. It was a direct hit, but the cannon ball that slammed into the *Constitution's* side bounced, harmlessly, off of her pine planking to the surprise and delight of the American crew. Captain Hull maneuvered the *Constitution* across her opponent's bows and poured on a raking fire, sweeping grapeshot clear across the *Guerrière's* upper deck. Down came the *Guerrière's* mizzenmast. Hull quickly came about and raked the British a second time. Within minutes the *Guerrière's* two remaining masts were blasted into the sea and the engagement was finished. The British captain, James Dacres, had no choice but to lower his flag.

The world was stunned. In twenty years of fighting Napoleon and his minions, England had lost only five battles at sea out of over two hundred engagements. The story of the cannon ball that bounced off the *Constitution's* side and plopped into the sea became instant legend. From then on, the ship was nicknamed "Ironsides."

And so it went, defeat on land and victory on water. And with every victory over the British at sea, Fells Point went mad with celebration: USS *United States* vs. HMS *Macedonian*; *Wasp* vs. *Frolic*; *Constitution* vs. *Java*. All victories. All amazing victories. America became dizzy with successes at sea. Successes that, on paper, meant nothing. The American navy could never take the seas from the British; numerically, that was impossible. What they could and did do, was to damage their opponent’s ego and bolster the self-esteem of a nation whose people were deeply divided on the war issue.

And that was only half the story. Millions, hundreds of millions of dollars worth of British merchant shipping was being taken by American privateers. Now, this did more than bruise English pride. It lashed out at the heart of the British economy: her commerce at sea. For an imperial island nation, such as England, whose existence depends upon uninterrupted and safe avenues across the world's oceans, American privateering became an acute and immediate problem.

"Don't surprise me none at all," Captain Ken stated emphatically to the group assembled at the Dooley Cooperage. "We did it before, in the Revolution. You were there, Bob. You sailed with Barney, after Yorktown. Lord, how we hammered those bastards. Drove the insurance rates up somethin' awful. But it was the private navy that did it. So, we're doin' it agin'. Only nows we got more ships and more money to build new ships. But, if we had just one more naval squadron or two to really make the Britishers nervous. Ah, damn, if we had just built a fleet. I mean a real fleet of ships of the line, instead of these stupid little gunboats that Jefferson insisted on..."

"Whoa! Dat's Federalist talk, Captain. Don't ya know it's dangerous ta be talkin' like a Federalist. An' wit' poor Jamie up ta his bloody neck wit' New England Britishers," Bob warned, shaking his finger at Captain Ken.

"Don't you scold me young feller." Ken was at least twenty years older than Uncle Bob. He had fought with Wolfe on the Plains of Abraham against the French. He had fought with General Arnold in the siege of Quebec, and commanded a sloop in Arnold's fleet on Lake Champlain. He was more than seventy years old, but how much more nobody knew. Yet, he had a quick step and even quicker blue eyes. He was short, almost as small in height as Father John. But, unlike the priest, Captain Ken had a thick chest and arms, and squatty, powerful legs. He moved as if selfpropelled with his arms acting like pumps to an internal engine. He could beat any man on the Point at arm wrestling, and did so nearly every time a new ship came into port. Age had whitened and thinned his hair, but he still managed a respectable tail that was always well greased and neatly tied. He was bespectacled now, and his glasses made his blue, searching eyes only bluer and more searching. There was no getting around his eyes which showed the vitality of his heart as well as the speed and intuitive logic of his mind. Above all, he was a fine seaman and respected on the Point as well as any captain, although for the past ten years or so he sailed as a master or offered his services to pilot ships coming up the Chesapeake.

"I know what I'm talkin' 'bout. Sure I'm a Republican through and through, and I know that what's good fer the Republicans is good fer the country; but I also know we should'a builded a stronger fleet. At least strong 'nough to make them English think twice before they boarded one of our ships and impressed our mates the way they been doin' these past ten years. So, I disagree with Jefferson, so what? And I always had a likin' fer ole' Johnny Adams, so what? The fact is, we shoulda been buildin' up our army and navy ever since the last war with that damned English King. Iffin' we had, maybe Michael's father wouldn't be in the predic'ment he's in right now."

Bob frowned back at Captain Ken, but he couldn't say a word. Since the Republicans took power, the army and navy were scaled back. Something the Federalists had been complaining about for years. The captain was right, and everybody in the room, Bob included, went back to reading the *American*. As they finished reading a particular item they passed on the newspaper to the person sitting on the next barrel to them. In this way they were able to share the reading of the latest news and comment upon it at the same time. This "group reading", as Michael called it, had become a daily ritual.

Even the Smith brothers, the laborers Uncle Bob had hired, and Samuel, the Quaker clerk, were welcomed at these morning news discussions. They all sat around, and close up to, the Franklin stove in the middle of the anteroom. There was a cold sea breeze that wooden doors and shutters could not halt. It was essential, however, that the Smith brothers sit next to Samuel, because he had just started teaching them how to read and they could digest very little of the news on their own. Still, the Smiths sat upright on their barrels and looked at the newspapers with the appearance of discerning eyes and flashes of concern and amusement darting across their faces. Every once in a while voicing an appropriate and judicial "umph" at the mysterious columns of print before them.

"Says here that Napoleon's retreating from Russia, is that true?" Michael asked, innocently.

Uncle Bob peered over the top of his paper, revealing a knitted brow. "True? Jaysus, Michael I'm surprised at ya.

Would Mr. Pechin print anythin' dat wasn't da whole God's truth?"

Michael thought for a second and then shook his head in the negative. "No, only maybe when it concerns Federalists."

"Dat's right, boyo. An' only 'cause dey be lyin' first an' Mr. Pechin, good man dat he is, has ta come up wit' a better one ta put dem in dere proper place. Oh, tis certin, a Federalist kin lie like an Englishmen, when he has a mind ta."

"If it weren't for the Federalists, we be sitting in Halifax right now telling the British what port to land all of the seamen they took from us, and to put a couple of coins in their pockets to boot," Captain Ken chimed in with his high pitched voice. He put his head back into the newspaper. "Listen to this:

> On all three fronts, at Detroit, Niagara, and in the fiasco that was supposed to be the march on Montreal, state militiamen refused to cross the border into Canada. The invasion of Canada cannot hoped to be accomplished without the support of the militia, and why is it that the militia marches in glory right up to the national boundary and refuses to go one step further? Because of incompetent generalship and Federalist determination not to engage in fighting unless it is to defend their states.

Ha! Ha! Ha!" Captain Ken laughed heartily. Everyone joined him. It was so incredulous they had to laugh. The object of the American war effort was to take Canada and then sue for peace. Nothing would be gained fighting a defensive campaign.

Uncle Bob laughed so hard he had to get up and bend over, stomping the floorboards with his heavy foot as he did so. Everyone laughed at the sight of Uncle Bob's uncontrolled fit. The Smith bothers laughed so much they cried.

"Ahhh... Tis good ta laugh when t'ings are goin' so bad."

They all shook their heads at Bob's remark and, breathing in much needed air, the room quieted and papers were once again hoisted in front of noses. But Bob Dooley didn't sit back down. He became melancholy and walked quietly out the door. They all put down their newspapers and watched him. Suddenly, they all became melancholy. It was nice to be able to laugh at the mistakes and the near treason of the American war effort on land thus far into the war. But they couldn't extend their mirth for more than a few minutes. The irony of lost opportunity wouldn't allow it. The Smith brothers returned to the back room, and soon the pounding of mallets filled the cooperage. Samuel had already gotten behind his desk and busied himself with replacing the tip on his quill pen. Michael and Captain Ken joined Uncle Bob outside.

The stiff, frigid breeze off the river forced Bob Dooley to stow his pipe back into his trousers. "Gettin' cold," he said to the others, aimlessly. And then, "How long we gonna put up wit' dis war, Captain?" All three of them stood beneath the creaking sign of the cooperage staring out at the white caps on the Patapsco, feeling the cold sink down into their bones.

"I'm goin' out," Ken answered nonchalantly. "Out with Boyle as soon as the *Comet* gits back. Should be any day now, I think."

Bob nodded his head. "No use us sittin' here when dere's a fight on. Damn, our people shoulda been in Montreal, at least, by now. Quicker we head out da better. Boyle's a good man. I woulda preferred Captain Barny but da word is he's goin' back inta da service. Always was a navy man, Joshua was, God bless his salty soul."

"I gotta go anyway, Bob. I'm gittin' old. Need sometin' to put myself up with in my old age. Boyle's the man allright. If we live we can sit out the rest of this here war and beyond in lux'ry, or head up to the North and show them militia how to cross a border."

"Boyle it is," Bob agreed. "Let me know when *Comet* comes in an' make da arrangements. I gotta go down ta da firehouse an' have some poor slob take me place as Foreman since - since Joe Durkin's gone, God rest him." With that, Bob Dooley turned and walked toward the Point. He reared his head back and looked at Michael. "Ya see now, don'tcha boyo? Me an' da Captain's gotta go."

"You gotta go because we can't just sit here and laugh at those militia anymore," Michael said, tears welling into his eyes, his voice thick with emotion. "You gotta go because there's money to be made and Britishers to kill, don'tcha? You gotta go because nobody is doin' anything to win this war and get my pa back home. And you're not comin' home again until it's all over. That's right isn't it Uncle?"

Bob stood there staring at him for a few, long seconds. "Dat's right boyo. Dat's right." The big Irishman turned his head away, his curly red locks blowing across his face, and tromped down the quay with his huge shoulders jerked up against his thick neck, an icy wind whipping against his lonesome back.

Michael shivered and looked at his uncle's mammoth frame trudging up to Fells Street. He cupped his hands and blew warm breath in them. "Know what to believe. Know what to desire. Know what to do."

"What's that ye say, boy?"

"I know what to do, Captain," Michael said, turning to the old man, conviction filling his voice. "I know exactly what to do."

****

The *Comet* sailed into Fells Point ten days before Christmas. Everyone knew her cruise had been a great success, but no one, except the ship's owners, fully realized the profit that was to be realized from the *Comet's* voyage. Three ships loaded with goods that Captain Boyle had seized made their way back into Baltimore. These ships were adjudicated in the prize court and then auctioned off. Their cargoes were auctioned off too, and the money from just these three captures was enough for Michael to have made a nice return on his piece of Happy's prize ticket. But Boyle had captured a total of eighteen prizes. Three of these were sent to Baltimore, four to Charleston, two to New York, and one each to Boston and Portland. The rest of the Ships were either sank by Boyle or were recaptured by the British. Happy couldn't be truer to his nickname. He stuck his head in the cooperage's door, flashed his white teeth in a quick smile, and winked a jubilant green eye.

"Happy! Why, Happy! It's you!" Michael screamed from behind the counter, where he was going over the ledger with Samuel.

"And who else might it be, mate. Just the best topm'n this side of Liverpool ‘at's what." Michael ran out from behind the counter and took Happy's hand. "'Ere, let me take a good look'it you. Why you must'a grown out of your trowsers since the last time I saw you, mate. And you're still sportin' ‘at lovely tail, I see."

They stood there staring at each other for a few moments. Happy grinning down at him while Michael gazed up into his eyes, not knowing quite what to say.

"The *Comet's* just in?" Michael said, finally, nervously. Happy shook his head up and down and kept on shaking it. His eyes got bigger and brighter and greener with each shake. And with each shake of the sailor's head, Michael's own grin widened, anticipation at its breaking point.

"You got the extra share, didn't you," Michael ventured.

Happy cocked his head up like a rooster, loosing his smile and presenting a false frown. "Why, Michael. I'm ashamed ‘at's what. 'Ere Appy logs over three thousand miles from Newfoundland to Haiti and back agin just to see your face and it's all you can do 'es think on an extra share or two."

Michael became ecstatic. "Two? Two? Two! Oh Happy, two extra shares, it's - it's wonderful!" They took each other's hands and danced round the room. The Smith brothers ran out to see what the commotion was. "Did you hear that Samuel! Boys! Didja hear? Happy's come back with two extra shares!"

"Huzzah!" They shouted.

Suddenly, Happy became businesslike and drew his cap off his head. He pulled up a barrel and felt in his cap, revealing a scrap of paper and the remnants of a charcoal pencil.

"Now, what was ar agreement? Oh, yes, ole 'Appy 'es encumbered upon you for five percent of my shares in this 'ere expee'dition. Now, five percent of what's already been adjudee'cated ... less double duty for ole Jamie Madison ... Owner's share 'es 'alf the take ... and then, 'Appy receives two shares of the venture and two additional shares for spyin the masts of good prizes ... and they'll bring in a prime price of let's say ... Umm, Michael, I figur' my prize money to be about - steady mate," Michael had his hands in front of his face as if he were praying, his eyes shut tight awaiting the tally.

"'At's right. Ole 'Appy is two thousand treasury notes richer than 'e was just a few short months ago. Isn't America a fine country t'work for. And won't my Peggy be pleased. Just wait till I tell her 'at her beloved spouse is..."

But Michael couldn't wait. He quickly did the calculation in his head. "A hundred dollars! Samuel! Boys! I've got a hundred dollars!"

They all, finally, calmed down, but Michael was wearing a permanent smile. "Well, Michael, 'at's a good deal of money for a young bachee'lor likes yourself. What are your plans, mate?"

"I know exactly what I plan to do," Michael answered, the smile dropping from his face and a queer intensity forming in his eyes. "Is the *Comet* shipping out again soon?"

"The *Comet*? Why, no - 'ere, 'ere, what's you up to behind 'em brown eyes?"

"You said yourself, I'd make a good topman."

"By the King - er, by 'es majesty Jamie Madison, 'at I did, Michael. So, as much as a hundred don't fill your sails, hey? You're figurin' on gettin' into the business yourself, then. Well, 'at's a tall order. Cap'n Boyle didn't lose one man on this 'ere voyage, not a one. But the scuttle is 'at the *Comet's* to be sold. Cap'n Boyle wants a bigger ship. They say 'es lookin' over the big new schooner, *Chasseur*. They say Tom Kemp's built her and 'at's she's faster than anything afloat - faster even than the *Comet.* Somebody says she a clip, no, a clipper, because she runs at such a clip."

"Please, Happy," Michael pleaded, the sincerity burning in his eyes. "I'm very satisfied with a hundred dollars, believe me. It's - it's not the money. It's something I have to do. Something I know I have to do."

"Ah, well, 'at's different ain't it, mate," Happy said, turning from Michael and curling his brows in confusion. "Well, let's see. You say you've got something to do - and it's as important as all 'at, huh?" Happy slowly swung round again to Michael, placing his hand on the boy's shoulders. "Something 'at might 'ave to do with - Michael, lad, where's your father?"

"He never came home, Happy. Last I heard, he was in the king's navy."

"Well now, pressed before the war?"

"Yes, before."

"You figur' you won't see 'im til this business is over and done with, don't you lad."

"That's right, Happy. According to the newspapers, the war's in the west or up north. But I think it's also being fought right here, specially right here. I mean really fought. This is the offensive. This is the front. Every ship you take from the king's merchants helps to hurt England. There's no other way to hurt England, Happy, not for me... Oh! I-I-I'm sorry," Michael put his hand to his mouth, "I didn't mean you, Happy. I'd never want to hurt you. It's not the English people you see..."

"Don't give 'er another thought, Michael. 'Appy knows zactly what you're up to. Do the same myself if'n I were in your shoes. Well, Michael, the *Chasseur's* a fine, big ship. She'll have no need for more sailors, like myself, but boys are always in need, I suppose. In a fight, it always seems the boys get it first. But, we didn't lose a one this trip. Captain Boyle's got luck on 'es side, 'at's what. And a captain with luck is what a sailor prays for. All right, Michael, I'll put in a good word for you."

Michael jumped up with joy. "Now, hold on, mate. I don't walk the quarter. I'm only 'Appy, remember? But I'll talk to Mr. Hollingsworth, 'es the Super Cargoe. But the word is we ship out right quick. Captain Boyle's brought news back 'at this 'ere port's gonna be blockaded, and right soon, too."

Happy rubbed Michael's head for luck and left wondering if he was right in his decision to speak on the boy's behalf. Michael noticed that Samuel and the Smith boys were looking at each other with questioning glances.

"Samuel, do you think you can run the cooperage while I'm gone?"

"Why, yes, Master Dooley. As long as the Smith boys stay on."

The Smith brothers nodded to each other in agreement. "We got no plans, suh. But we was wonderin', if'n yer sailin' on that ship, would ya consider sellin' us a piece of yer ticket?"

No, Father John did not understand. They were outside the back of the church, standing before Calvary. Father John had a miniature Calvary built last summer to honor those who would not come home from the war. A pleasant, southwest wind and a sparkling December sun made for a warm day beneath woolen winter clothing. Their discussion was also getting warm.

"Michael, you do not understand your family's code at all. It makes no sense to follow your uncle to sea. In fact, everything about your code suggests not to follow anything your uncle does. Pass me that little cross there, the white one."

Michael reached down and picked up a cross from a barrel at the foot of the small hill. Father John had two hundred crosses made for the deaths he expected to hear of from engagements at sea.

"Merci. Now, please be so kind as to hand me the trowel." The priest climbed to the foot of the large cross in the center and began to dig with the trowel and his little hands. "This is the second. The first is that one over there. That is Joseph Durkin's. This is Moses Pike's". Father John blessed himself and said a short prayer. Moses Pike had signed aboard the privateer *Dolphin*, of just twelve guns. On November 20th, the *Dolphin* sighted the 550-ton, sixteen-gun ship, *John Hamilton*, bound for London from Honduras. The next morning a battle ensued between the little privateer and the mammoth merchant ship. Moses Pike was hit with a musket ball while repairing damage to the *Dolphin's* hull sustained from an unexpected broadside. The next day, *John Hamilton's* captain struck his colors after several of his men lie wounded on deck. Moses Pike was forced to undergo an amputation of his right leg, just below the knee, before the surrender. But it was a running sea and the operation took far too long. Tourniquet or no, he simply bled to death.

Father John descended the mound and stood before Michael wiping the black dirt off of his hands. His face was sour, his cheeks pale. "They were both good men. They both had wives and children. You knew them both, Michael. Are you in so much of a hurry to join them?"

"But, Father, Captain Boyle didn't lose a man on his voyage. Most of the merchant ships surrender without firing a shot."

"Moses Pike wasn't just aboard a ship, Michael. He was involved in a war, as you wish to be. In a war people die. People *always* die in a war!" Now, the priest's cheeks turned red and there was a fire building in his eyes. "Your place is here. It's where your father expects you to be. He has lost his wife, his love, his all - save for the fruit of that love: you, mon ami. And now you want me to condone your decision to go to sea in wartime! Think, Michael, think! I've taught you the value of using your mind and thinking a problem out carefully, deliberately. You are not using your mind, that is to say your logical mind. You are not using your heart, either. You are acting on emotion only. In this case anguish. Anguish over your mother's death and your father's impressment. We, all of us, have feelings, Michael. But how we act on those feelings, ahhh, therein lie the snares of the devil. To alleviate the anguish you feel, you are going to inflict pain on your enemy. Is your enemy the English?"

"Why, no, not the English people..."

"So, why do you want to destroy them?"

Michael wasn't backing down. "No, Father. My enemy is not the English. My enemy is the *war*! I want it to end. I can't just sit around and read about it in the newspaper anymore. I have been thinking about this, Father. And I have been using my mind and my heart. Know what to believe. Know what to desire. Know what to do. I believe the war to be evil. I desire to end it. I know that to do so, I must go and destroy the enemy's commerce, or travel north and join the army. The war goes on and on. Canada's not taken. It goes on because no one is winning anything. And neither our government nor Great Britain is going to sue for peace unless and until something is won. Isn't that so, Father?"

Father John blinked and stared at the ground. The boy made sense. He had been thinking, quite clearly and rationally. Still, there was something missing in his logic.

"You are right, Michael. Wars do not end unless somebody wins. They might stop for a period, like the Peace of Amiens. But nothing was decided, not conclusively, and so the swords are unsheathed once more. And, this country of your birth and my adoption has never won its independence from the English. They still treat America as if it were a colony. The War for Independence was never over, oui?"

"Oui, Father."

"But you are wrong about two things. The enemy is not the war. It is pride. Pride is like fire. It can be good if used cautiously, discriminately. As you would feel after a good day's work. Bad, if left to its base nature, and that is to burn and keep on burning, indiscriminately. Burning everything in its path. Not caring what it burns. The pride of Napoleon, daring to call himself an emperor, the pride of arrogant English sea captains, and of aristocrats who treat humanity below their status as if they were cattle - less than cattle. Wars stem from such as these. And you are wrong about the code. Aquinas said: 'Know what you *ought* to believe. Know what you *ought* to desire. Know what you *ought* to do.' You have forgotten the full quote and therefore have misinterpreted the full meaning. You sound as if Aquinas meant that you should follow your own dictates: if you say this is what I want, this what I desire, therefore, this is what I shall do, then, you go and do it, without logic, without compassion. No, Michael, no. He meant duty. He meant an obligation, a personal obligation. Since it is personal, I cannot tell you what to do. It becomes a matter of conscience. Each conscience speaks differently. This is the voice of the angels. And what is your duty, Michael? What does your angel tell you to do? Think on your obligations: you have a duty to your God; duty to your church; duty to your country; duty to your father; duty to your mother, deceased or not; duty to a great many things, even people you don't even know and will never see. Think on all of these and listen to the truth that will be revealed inside your soul. Pray on it. Pray to your guardian, your personal angel. You cannot do this alone. Pray on it and grace will be given to you by the Christ. Then, you will need only to cooperate with that grace. You are a good boy, Michael. You have always been a good boy. Now, go and pray. I will pray also. Then come back to me and I will give you my blessing no matter what decision you come to."

Michael nodded in agreement and walked to the church. Father John looked after him with concern in his drooping eyes. "Duty. Oui. We each have a duty," he whispered. "Do not worry, Teresa. Moranvillé did not forget the promise." He glanced at the middle cross atop his Calvary, and then up farther, beyond the snow-white clouds. "But, you may not appreciate how I will keep that promise."

Chapter 9

THE LONG GOODBYE

The *Chasseur* had a full contingent. Most of the *Comets* who realized their fortune with Tom Boyle were anxious to put to sea and increase it by who knows how much more. Happy was right in saying that Boyle had luck on his side and seamen and lubbers alike sought to sail with him. The duty of a captain of a privateer was to capture prizes and bring them safely into a friendly port. Luck alone can't explain the surprising rapidity with which American privateers accomplished this duty, and Tom Boyle, lucky or not, had the fortunate combination of skill and daring that exceeded the records of the best of America's private ships of war.

To capture the enemy's merchant ships, a captain was charged with frightening the enemy with destruction while refraining from opening up his guns. Privateers were expensive to build and maintain, and the owners frowned upon a captain who resorted to too much violence in a confrontation at sea. Moreover, the prizes that a privateer sought to capture were poor prospects to regain a home or neutral port if they were shot to pieces by the attacker. Early in the war, most of the prizes taken were poorly armored and the sight of a fast Baltimore schooner with its raked masts and low charging hull full of men and cannon was enough to bring down the flag of most merchant vessels. But now that hundreds of hungry privateers and tens of thousands of men armed with musket and pike prowled the seas, merchantmen took steps to defend their vessels from attack by carrying more cannon and shipping in convoys. These convoys were guarded by a ship of the king's navy and sailed in mass with the thinking that there was indeed, safety in numbers. Daring, then, or something akin to it, was necessary for

American privateers to continue their assault on the British at sea. Tom Boyle knew that if he assumed an audacious manner with regard to seeking his prey, his men would follow his lead.

"So, what we will do is change our tactics," Captain Boyle told Captain Ken. "You know as well as I do, Captain Russell, that if we dog a fleet of fat merchantmen long enough, one or two will lose their way, like sheep in a fold. Especially in bad weather. These ships are built for capacity, suh, not speed. Anyway, I'm holdin' onto my orders until we set sail. I don't mind pickin' up a partner once we've hauled anchor, but I'll be damned if all of Baltimore knows where we're goin' before we get there."

"Everyone wants to work in pairs, at least pairs, nowadays," Captain Ken mused.

"And pairs are just fine. There isn't a better way to tactically approach an escorted convoy. I unda'stand that. But, for the safety of this ship I'll keep the nature of our cruisin' grounds a secret until we are well away. Then, by God, we'll hit them. And, if we come across a worthy Yankee captain that appreciates the unsubtle aspects of our profession, why we'll make a fine pair."

"Aye, sir. On another matter, I understand that you've given permission for a young man - name of Dooley - to ship out with us," Captain Ken stated, a smile forming across his lips.

"Why, yes. Mr. Hollingsworth mentioned him just yesterday. He said one of our topman, ah, Happy George, had given him fine praise. But, that smile of yours tells me there's more in this than meets the eye. All right, Ken, what's on your mind?"

"Tom, the boy is the son of Mike Dooley, the cooper?"

"I thought there was a resemblance. I remember Mike well. And of course, Bob Dooley, his brother. I never in my life saw anyone drink as much as that man. But that Irishmen will be worth his weight in gold, literally, in a fight. That's why I made him Captain of my Marines. He's not afraid of anythin', no suh. By the way, wasn't Mike Dooley impressed, early in the year?"

"That's what I was a gettin' around to, Tom. I want the boy to stick close to me. I'll keep him busy and out of the way. The priest over at Saint Patrick's asked me to take him by the hand so that his father isn't hit with bad news when he comes home, whenever that may be."

"No, Ken. You didn't even have to ask me for that favor. You're my sailing master as well as being a reputable ship captain, yourself. There's something more behind that Dutch grin of yours. Besides, the Dooley boy is a competent cooper, although I'll only sign him on as a boy, I've got all the skilled tradesman I need right now. Of course, he'd come in handy to make up one of your prize ship crews. You assign him to one of the gun crews as a powder monkey. Now, out with it Ken, what are you up to."

"Norwegian-Irish, if you please, Tom."

"What? Oh. Funny, I always thought of you as Dutch. Pardon me, suh. Still it's the Irish that I must have liked about you." They were both smiling now. Tom Boyle rang a small bell that sat atop his chart table and a servant appeared at the door to his cabin. "David, the Portuguese wine I had you bring aboard." And then, turning to Captain Ken, "this calls for a glass, doesn't it?"

"Well, Tom, I guess you know me better'n I thought. I need you to do me this favor. It's a whopper, Tom, but you've known me these many years and you know I'd never be askin' you this, less I had a reason." David, Captain Boyle's cabin boy rapped quietly on the door before entering. Every time he left the Captain's cabin and before he reentered, he knocked on the door. The captain's privacy was solemnly acknowledged and adhered to. David had a towel draped across his left arm, a bottle and two glasses filled his hands. He placed a glass before Captain Boyle and adeptly removed the cork from the bottle. He filled Boyle's glass half way and awaited a response.

"Mmmm, wait till you taste this Ken, it is so subtle, yet it is quite remarkable, truly."

Captain Ken waited for his glass to be poured, then raising his glass to Boyle, as if he was about to give a toast, he smiled broadly. "And so is what I'm about to tell you..."

Michael waited for the last possible minute, figuring that if he were not meant to sail on the privateer, Happy would not be able to convince Mr. Hollingsworth of his value. As far as Michael was concerned, all of this was kept a tight secret. In truth, however, just about everybody knew. When Happy asked Mr. Hollingsworth if the *Chasseur* needed another boy, and told the super cargoe his name, Mr. Hollingsworth immediately told his friend, Captain Ken, since it was well known that Ken Russell and the Dooleys were good friends. Captain Ken, of course, had spoken about it to Uncle Bob, who went to the extraordinary feat of knocking on the door of St. Patrick's Rectory, to see if the priest could talk Michael out of his plans. Father John, then, had informed Uncle Bob of his discussions with Michael and suggested that a council of war between all parties concerned (all except Michael) would be the best way to come up with proper stratagems to deal with the situation. So, the highly unlikely, yet necessary, meeting between the good Moranvillè, Uncle Bob, Captain Ken, Happy George, Samuel, Mr. Hollingsworth, and the esteemed editor, Mr. Pechin met at the rectory.

Michael didn't want Captain Ken or Uncle Bob to have any knowledge of his plans because of the arguments that each of them, he was sure, would proffer. But even if he could convince them to see the merits of his position, and even if they would agree to help him, he didn't want their assistance either. No, Michael thought, this was between God and himself, as Father John had instructed, and Samuel and the Smith boys who wanted to purchase a piece of his ticket.

His answer came rather quickly. Happy told him to sign aboard as soon as possible. Captain Boyle was afraid that the British would bottle up the Chesapeake with their blockade and he was in a hurry to weigh anchor. But, there were two things that Michael knew he had to do: he had to tell Jessica, but not until it was all finalized; and he had to tell Desiree, and he wanted to make certain that she would wait for him. He knew exactly how he would deal with Desiree: a quick, but romantic farewell. Jessica, on the other hand was something of a problem. "No long goodbyes, it's better that way," Michael thought, and he avoided Jessica's searching eyes as much as he could.

"If you are quite certain, Michael, then I will not stand in your way. Do you know what you *ought* to do?" Father John asked.

"Yes, Father. I ought to sail with my uncle and Captain Ken. I do this out of good conscience."

"Then, God be with you, mon ami. A happy and safe voyage. I will see you when you return." Michael was quite pleased with Father John's attitude about the whole thing. He said he would grant him a blessing and he did so, without fanfare or argumentation. This also pleased Michael very much, and now he was becoming more excited as each hour brought him nearer to his adventure.

But he had little time to prepare. The cooperage was in safe hands, Samuel had displayed both loyalty and industry, and the Smith brothers were working harder than ever to fill the increasing amount of orders that came into the cooperage. Besides, Father John had promised to keep an eye on the business, without Michael even asking him. Thanks to Happy, Michael was fitted out with clothing for both the winter and the coming spring, he had forgotten all about sea clothes. With his hundred dollar windfall from the *Comet's* cruise and Happy's sharp, green eyes, he bought Treasury bonds that Mr. Pechin suggested would help finance the war, but not before giving his tithe to the church. He visited the cemetery, bringing a lunch that Jessica had prepared for him, and said goodbye to his mother and asked for her blessing, as well.

Happy brought him on board the ship on the eve of their departure. Every crewmember had to sign the Articles of Agreement before shipping out. Mr. Hollingsworth, the super cargoe, brought him to the captain's cabin. Slipping off his cap, and holding it tightly with both hands, Michael waited, patiently, as Hollingsworth rapped on the door.

"Enter."

"Mr. Lieb's watch, if you please, sir, and he sent me down with the new boy," Hollingsworth said as they entered the cabin. Few schooner captains, least of all privateers, could speak of such luxury as was evident in Tom Boyle's cabin. It was finely appointed with dark mahogany furnishings, silk drapes across the stern windows, red, velvet pillows lying on a plush blue, velvet sofa, even a small, square piano and a polished, black bench. This could only be topped by the man himself. Tom Boyle dressed like a dandy. He appreciated and revelled in the finer things in life including the clothes he wore: tailored broad cloth coat; white, silk shirt with ruffles; pants that hugged tightly to his bottom and athletic thighs; black, leather boots that hugged his calves. Boyle rose when Michael entered the room, something that surprised Hollingsworth. Captains don't rise when common ship's boys sign aboard.

"Well, so this is young Dooley! Welcome aboard, suh. Your family's reputation has preceded you," Boyle exclaimed as he waved Michael to the sofa. Hollingsworth was beside himself. The captain was actually allowing this lad to sit down right in front of him, sit down even before the captain did. "Remarkable," Hollingsworth whispered. Michael was dazed. This was even better than Desiree's sitting room. He glanced at the far side of the cabin with its magnificent bookshelves and great brown leather chair, and he followed Boyle's steps to his large, chart table with its maps and instruments. He wondered if Captain Boyle had read *The New American Practical Navigator*, and if he knew how to do lunar readings from the angle of three separate stars. Boyle fished into his table drawer and produced a scroll. He laid it, elaborately, on the chart table and unrolled it. The scroll unravelled quickly over the span of the table and down onto the planking on the floor, all the way to Michael's feet as he sat on the sofa. It must have been six feet long.

"There, my young friend. The *Chasseur's* Articles of Agreement. Please note that everyone on board this ship has signed it, including myself."

Michael stood up and approached the table. "May I read it, sir?"

"Ha, ha, ha, Boyle chuckled, I heard you were an educated boy, of course you may read it, only don't take too long, it has many very detailed clauses. May I suggest you concern yourself to clauses, er, let's see now... Yes, clauses six, seven, and - no, not that one, that has to do with female prisoners, I take it we'll have no problem with you there - and number fifteen. Michael read quickly:

> 6th. That whoever first spies a prize or sail, that proves worth 100 dollars a share, shall receive an additional share from the nett sum; and if orders are given for boarding, the first man on the deck on the Enemy shall receive an additional share from the nett proceedings...
>
> 7th. That if any one of the said Company shall in time of action lose an eye or a joint, he shall receive Fifty Dollars, and if he lose a leg or an arm, he shall receive Three Hundred Dollars to be deducted out of the Gross sum of Prize-money.
>
> 15th. That One Half of the Nett proceeds of all prizes taken by the said Vessel which is appropriated to the Vessel's Company shall be divided among them in the following manner (viz) To the Captain sixteen Shares and all such privileges and freedoms as are allowed to the Captains of Private armed Vessels of War from this port. To the First Lieutenant nine shares. To the 2nd and 3rd Lieutenants and Surgeon eight Shares each. Prize masters and Mater's Mate and Captain of Marines six Shares each; Carpenter, Boatswain and Gunner four Shares each. The residue to be divided among the Company in equal Shares excepting

> Landsmen or raw hands who draw one and one half shares each, and boys who draw one Share each. Ten Shares to be reserved to the order of the Captain to be distributed by him to such as he may deem deserving among the Vessel's Company.

"I am to receive at least one share, sir?"

"Listen, Mr. Hollingsworth, the boy's an optimist. An educated optimist. That's right, suh. By God, it'll be at lest one share! Now, if the Articles of Agreement agree with your most discerning eye," Boyle said bowing, drawing a quill pen from the drawer and flourishing it before him, "may we have your signature - ahmm - at the end of the scroll if you please." Michael took the pen, bowed, and knelt on the floor to sign at the very end of the scroll.

"Mr. Hollingsworth, it appears we have room for one more, and only one more signature, and that I expect shortly, so please to escort young Mr. Dooley here off the ship and instruct him to rejoin this crew tomorrow morning. We sail with the tide, and God willing, bad weather."

Michael had taken care of everything - everything except Jessica. He had left a note for Mr. Pechin, telling him of his plans; had left an additional note for Desiree, asking her to meet him at the docks. The one thing he couldn't manage was Jessica. She was no where to be found. Time was running out and he simply couldn't find her.

At last, he ran into Father John at the orphanage and asked him to say his goodbyes to Jessica. "I am so sorry, Michael, I have sent Jessica on an errand. But, do not worry, mon ami, I will relate your sentiments. Now, go. The tide is turning and Captain Boyle will be most anxious to leave port."

"Thanks, Father. Tell Jess I'll miss her and I hope she understands that I gotta go with Captain Boyle on the tide or he'll ship without me."

"Then go. By all means, go. But please do not forget what I have taught you. Remember Aquinas and what he really meant.

Do not put yourself in danger unless it is necessary, and most of all do not forget that your father is thinking about you right now and will attempt to rejoin you at the most convenient moment. Escape is on his mind, Michael, he will try to come home to you. How, I do not know. Ask Captain Ken. He will tell you how such things are possible. Live your code, Michael, and God be with you and your father. Oh, and a very, merry Christmas!"

At dawn the *Chasseur* prepared to weigh anchor on a storm-threatening Christmas Eve. Father John was there to bless the ship and its crew, Samuel and the Smith brothers were there to purchase as many prize tickets as there meager savings would allow, and Desiree was there to say goodbye. As Michael had wanted, their farewell was quick and romantic. He met her before boarding. She wore the lavender dress that she knew he was fond of and played the parting scene with all the theatrics she could muster.

"Oh, suh," she began, descending from her chaise, "I want to wish you the best of fortune on your cruise." As Michael approached her, she held out her hand. He stooped to kiss it, and the array of sailors and officers of the *Chasseur* who did not have families to say goodbye to, Uncle Bob and Captain Ken included, broke out into a sudden guffaw. But, Michael didn't notice. He saw and heard only one thing before him. The crew's reaction to the performance attracted the attention of their captain. Boyle grinned at the young couple below him from his position of the quarterdeck.

"Desiree, thank you for coming to see me off. Please, accept this..." Michael unravelled the blue ribbon from his tail and placed it into her hand "...as a token of my esteem." Desiree broke out into tears. She had always fantasized a romantic parting with a sailor, not knowing when or if he would return. Her heart stirred at the simpleness of Michael's gesture. Desiree dabbed her eyes with a pink, silk handkerchief and put the scented cloth into Michael's hands. He tied the handkerchief around his neck, bowed, and picking up his sea bag turned to the ship. Applause was heard from the marines while the sailors, busy on the yards and rigging, gave out a robust cheer. As amusing as this was to Captain Boyle, however, this was a ship of war, albeit a private ship of war, and he could not condone the distraction. He pointed his cane at the boatswain.

"Mr. Lugger, stop that racket this instant!"

"Aye, sir. Silence on deck, there!"

Boyle then turned to his first lieutenant. "Mr. Leib, foretops'l, if you please."

"Foretops'l, it is, cap'n"

"Mr. Davis, hands ready at the braces."

"Ready at the braces, sir."

"Mr. Conner, pass the word for Captain Russell."

"Aye, sir, Captain Russell to the con!"

"Mr. Lugger, perpare to cast loose."

"Preparing to cast loose, aye, sir."

As the *Chasseur* made her way down the Patapsco, Desiree shouted, repeatedly, from the quay, "Bon Voyage! Adieu! Adieu!" This gently tugged the hearts of every seamen and landsmen aboard, except Uncle Bob, who thought it nauseating. Father John watched the process from underneath the creaking sign of the Dooley cooperage. He prayed he would not have to use his trowel for anyone aboard the *Chasseur*.

****

Tom Boyle was bent over his charts in his cabin when Captain Ken rapped at the door. "Enter."

"You sent fer me, cap'n?"

"Oh, yes, sir. Please close the door and come in." Ken joined him at the table. "This will be a cold night, Ken. Help yourself to the coffee." Ken rubbed his aged hands vigorously before pouring himself a cup. "We'll have all hands ready for action until we're clear of the bay," the captain said, sipping the hot brew from a delicate cup of china decorated with a blue sea, yellow sun, and a brown Chinese junk.

"You're expectin' the blockade, then?"

"Yes, at least the frigates, anyway. I hope to God this weather picks up. What do you think of her, so far?"

"I've never seen or felt anythin' like her, Tom. She handles like a gelding, a champion gelding. Everythin's set perfickly. She responds to the wheel better'n anything I've ever sailed. I bet she's quicker'n the *Comet*."

"That'll take some doing, suh. But I believe you. She's singing in this wind. I can't wait to test her. All right, this is what we'll do." Boyle refilled his cup and sipped, longingly. "We'll take her up north to Newfoundland, word is there's still fine pickings to be had up there. Depending upon our luck, we'll stay in those waters for a bit. We'll have to send our prizes to New England. The blockade is to be in place along the coast, from the Carolinas to the Chesapeake. The British are leaving the New England coast alone, at least for the moment. They're telling New England that they were right in opposing the war, so their commerce isn't going to be punished. Britain also needs New England ships to send wheat to Wellington's army in Spain. They're giving a special license to New England ships to get to Spain safely. Can you believe it! Our own ships are supplying the English with wheat! This is insane! But, it figures, those Yankees will do anything for money. But, then again," he said with a smile, "so will we. But it's getting tougher and tougher to send a prize back safely. Those fat Merchantmen are slow, dangerously slow, and they're being recaptured by the score. Still the cartel wishes me to try and get a few back safely, but to transfer anything of real value into our hold first. If their recaptured we still can boast a strong profit." Captain Ken nodded in agreement. "I don't want to ship you out too soon, Ken. You're the best master I have. I'll save you till the last, probably when we hit the Indies, after a time in the Channel." Boyle slapped his hands together gleefully. "It's my favorite spot," he said, grinning.

In the *Comet*, Captain Boyle had much of his success in the English Channel and the Irish Sea. It was, indeed, his favorite spot, but it was also the most dangerous for obvious reasons.

Still, the thrill of sailing in waters so close to your enemy was something that Boyle, and many American privateer captains, lived for. "Just think on it, Ken. With this ship, with all its speed, think what we can accomplish."

"I could use a nice, little nest for my retirement years, Tom."

"Why, you old coot! The day Ken Russell retires from the sea is the day the good Lord stops making salt water. Oh, how'd everything go with the boy yesterday?"

"I don't know. I will when he finds out, though. I've got my mate holed up in my cabin. Tell me, didja see that beauty the Dooley boy was a'sayin goodbye to on the dock?"

"As fine a filly as I ever seen in Baltimore. That was Bill Pechin's daughter wasn't it?"

"Yup. She sure put on a fancy show. Actin' as if the boy were the crown prince. But she's a looker, a real looker. I don't know, Tom. I don't know iffin this plan kin work like the padre wants."

"Come, Captain Russell, you been at sea long enough to know that anything can happen, and often does. Now, we should be at the end of the bay. Pass the word to clear for action, no drummer, if you please."

As the deck was cleared, the powder monkeys were assembled behind their gun crews with a fresh cartridge. Michael was positioned at the bow chaser. The *Chasseur* carried fourteen long nines, and two long toms, one each in the bow and stern. Captain Boyle preferred this armament to the short carronades that many ships used. He despised cutting up a prize with the carronades, and then having to repair all the damage twenty four-pound round balls and grapeshot could do. The long nines fitted his style, his moxie, in threatening his prey from a distance and then boarding her with his marines if any attempt at a fight was made. Still, it was carronades that the men longed for as the *Chasseur* slipped quietly over the water nearing the end of the bay. Carronades that could pound a sloop-of-war and give the schooner at least some hope of survival in a close contest with no sea room to maneuver.

Boyle joined Captain Ken on deck. The weather had been turning for the past half-hour. The wind had come up from the northwest and white clouds had, momentarily, brought a specter of dangerous light to the bay. But then the snow started. Tiny flakes that flew every which way in front of faces that now felt the bitter gusts of wind. Ken was positioned on the lee foreshrouds, steadily conning the ship, relaying orders to the helm by way of a master's mate. The mate was quick in making the distance between his master and the wheel, and he was so small that no one seemed to notice him. Michael was frozen. He had been at his station for over an hour and despite the warm clothing Happy had procured for him, the lack of movement made the cold feel twice as bad. Now, the snow curled up into his nose and down underneath his chin. He shifted up the collar of his coat and yawned. He had little sleep the night before his voyage and little again the first night at sea. He was just too excited to sleep and he regretted that now. It was going on three o'clock in the morning. The ship had plied down the bay with amazing speed and at this point the chop grew stronger and Michael was doused with icy cold water that swept up over the bow from the ship's momentum and the rising sea. Captain Boyle ordered all lights out. The darkness added to the cold. They were fifty miles past Tangier Island and had only another five to go before the safety and room of the Atlantic.

"Excuse me, sir!" the master's mate said excitedly, running up to Captain Boyle at the wheel, "but, Captain Ken says he can't see the light off of Cape Henry anymore because of the snow, but that we're on course and have plenty of sea room. He proposes that you alter course for the Atlantic."

"Thank you boy, but you'll address him as Captain Russell, not Captain Ken. Give Captain Russell my compliments and tell him we'll port our helm directly. Oh, and good work, boy. What's your name again?"

"Henry, sir. Jeremiah Henry, master's mate," Henry said, saluting the captain with his knuckles.

"Well, good job, Henry."

"Thank you, sir!"

Michael took notice of a shadow on his right in back of him.

"Captain Russell? The captain's compliments, sir. He said they'll port the helm directly, sir - and that I was doing a good job."

"So you are Mr. Henry. And a job that's well over, too, I believe. But please to keep yer voice down," Ken said, quitely. The old man jerked his thumb foreward. "No man aboard is permitted to talk above a whisper when we're cleared for action. Only the captain of the ship and the lookout should be heard clearly. Now you might as well go below. With this snow I can't see much of anything and..." Captain Ken's old, clear blue eyes widened. He jumped up into the shrouds as fast as any twenty-year old topman and climbed up, quickly, into the masthead. "On deck! On deck! Sail ho!"

"Where away!" Captain Boyle shouted from the wheel.

"Fine off the port bow!"

Boyle ran to the lee side and peered into the snow. He could make out several lanterns in between gusts of wind. "What is she Captain Ken? Can you make her out?"

"She's a brig - no! I believe it to be a frigate, sir, and bearing down on us."

Michael could hardly believe it. They were so close to making it. And that voice he heard a moment ago bothered him - that Mr. Henry. He sounded just like... Michael turned behind him.

"My Lord! For the love of Mary, it's you!" Michael's voice could be heard across the ship.

"You there, boy! Face your gun and shut your mouth!" Mr. Lugger, the boatswain, shouted. Michael did so, immediately. The slight form of the shadow standing behind him whispered, desperately, into his ear and then disappeared below deck. Mr. Lugger saw the master's mate, Mr. Henry, say something to Michael before running below.

"Don't get us into trouble, Michael. As far as you're concerned, my name is Mr. Henry. And for God's sake don't get hurt. I'll explain everything later," Jessica had said.

Chapter 10

MASTER'S MATE

"She's a frigate, sir," said Captain Ken, intensely, "I'd say *Lively* class, 38 guns."

"She hasn't seen us yet, but she will any moment now, and then she'll blow us to pieces. Praise God for this dirty weather. We still have a chance if we ship rig and let this blow take us out to the open sea." Boyle had insisted that the *Chasseur* be built to be able to function as both a fore and aft and a brig rigged vessel. This gave the privateer a distinct advantage over other schooners in that she could utilize square sails when running before the wind by setting a fore course and topsail, and a main topsail. With the wind blowing hard from the west, right on her stern, the *Chasseur* could fly out of the Chesapeake and into the Atlantic. The British frigate would have her chance, however, because the *Chasseur* would have to pass her in order to reach the sea.

Michael heard the commotion behind him but dared not turn around for fear of the boatswain's cane. He had heard stories all his life about the beatings applied by an angry warrant officer and although Boyle's reputation was one of fairness toward his seamen, Michael was taking no chances. As a powder monkey to the long tom in the bow, his job was to fetch fresh cartridges from the magazine below deck. After receiving a new cartridge, Michael would place it into a metal canister to shield it from any flying sparks on the main deck. The cartridges had to be brought up one at a time. This was the only way to deal with exposed gunpowder on a wooden ship where explosions, and consequently, fire, meant certain death. Michael could see the silhouette of the frigate ahead of him as the *Chasseur* dipped down in the trough of a wave. The snow was whipping at his back and, conversely, luckily, into the eyes of the middle watch on the frigate. They were well within firing range, but despite their proximity the towering frigate had not yet seen the schooner. The British were now on the starboard tack, working to windward, beating into the Chesapeake tack after tack.

There were five men in position at Michael's cannon. The captain of the gun crew was a tall, skinny black man who stood, crouching in front of Michael at the breech of the gun. The cannon was loaded; Boyle always had his guns loaded, whether there was a threat or not. The black man was whispering orders to the gun crew. Every eye of the crew was on the black man, and as he whispered an additional order, the men used crowbars and handspikes to adjust the aim of the cannon. This was done repeatedly, for the motion of the ship, rolling in the stormy water, constantly shifted the muzzle of the gun away from its target before them. Michael, who had never been to sea before, desperately tried to maintain his balance, for he too was shifted to and fro by the rolling deck. Every time the ship would slip into a trough of a wave, Michael would be propelled forward, into the back of the black man. Each time Michael hit the gun captain's back, the man would shove him aft with his massive hand, but after awhile the black man gave him a stern look and said quietly, but directly, "Kneel down, boy, fah God's sake, kneel down."

Michael noticed that the men had stopped adjusting the gun with their handspikes. The black man was no longer whispering, but soft noises could be heard from the larboard side of the ship. The seven gun crews there were now leveraging their cannon and Michael could hear the soft, but agitated whispers of their gun captains. With the creaking of planking and rigging, the swishing of the ship as it plied into a trough, and the flap of square sails catching the wind, Michael couldn't make out what the gun captains were saying. He only heard a jumbled, constant, and eerie sound of high pitched s's. As the ship rose on the next crest, Michael peered over the bow. The frigate was not there. She had tacked and was sailing close-hauled off the *Chasseur's* larboard side. The frigate was sailing right for them.

The sound of a cannon was heard a second before the sound of a drum, and then, a second after that, a splash of water, a foot in front of the bow sprayed Michael with cold water. He didn't feel it. The British had finally spied the privateer and everyone on board the *Chasseur* knew their life was in danger. Strangely, this thought warmed them.

"Augh!" Michael screamed as he hit the deck. Uncle Bob, who was below with all the other Marines until now, came running up from behind him and pushed him down with one of his great paws.

"Stay down, boyo! Only get up when da Captain of da cannon gives ya da word." Michael gazed up at his uncle in horror. Bob Dooley was green, as green as a leaf on a tree. He was sweating profusely and bent over Michael with a sword in one hand, while gripping his stomach with the other. "Oh, Jaysus," he moaned, and went quickly to the rail, vomiting into the water. Suddenly, Michael realized that his uncle was seasick, deathly seasick. But there was no time to dwell on why his uncle was sick and he was not - not in the slightest way at all - for at that moment the *Chasseur* became alive.

The marines came through the main hatch and swarmed in the waist of the ship, a dozen sharpshooters carried their rifles up to the tops as the *Chasseur's* drummer beat to action. Technically, the *Chasseur* was already cleared for action, had been these past two hours, but the sight and sound of the marines was welcomed by the sailors manning the cannons anyway. The silence had been broken, their ruse discovered, and it felt good to see burly men, seasick or not, brandishing tomahawks and to hear the clatter of swords and scabbards.

"Mr. Leib! Let go the larboard guns as she bears!" Boyle shouted, his black cape whipping over his shoulders.

"Aye, sir. Larboard guns! Fire as she bears!"

Boyle jumped from the railing and ran to Captain Ken, now at the wheel, putting the new schooner to the test to see if the *Chasseur* would get more speed having the wind almost on her stern.

"For God's sake, Ken, can you get more out of her?" Boyle's voice was excited and breathless, but controlled. Captain Boyle had seen a great deal of fighting in his life. He was not daunted by battle. Still, he knew the *Chasseur* would have to take at least one broadside, and one broadside from a 38-gun frigate could destroy his ship.

"It's too rough, Tom, I'll break her if I put any more sail on her! But she's quick! Lord, she's quick." They both stared at the raked back masts and the weather sails, and then, quickly, at the oncoming frigate. The snow poured down so heavy it was difficult to make her out.

"You're right. By God the British know it too. They'll not follow us out. We're too quick for them. Bless you, Thomas Kemp!" Boyle laughed as Captain Ken took everything he could from the wind and discovered the schooner's best point of sailing. The *Chasseur* seemed to lift right out of the water. "You have her flying, sir! Now she'll neither follow us nor get behind and rake us, not in this blizzard, not without daylight, she won't be able to see us. She has no choice but to wear and give us a spanking. There she goes, Ken! They're porting her helm now."

The English captain stood on his quarterdeck, awed by the shadow of the graceful vessel before him. He couldn't run down this privateer. This schooner was the fastest vessel he had ever seen. He couldn't get in back of her and rake her, as Tom Boyle had surmised, the snow was too thick and blinding. He could only give her one broadside and hope that his gunnery would knock away a mast or damage her rudder.

But as the frigate came about, Lieutenant Leib had the *Chasseur's* gun captains ready. The *Chasseur* had the best gun crews in Baltimore and Boyle intended to give back as much as he expected to receive. It was the schooner that fired first. Leib had his cannon fire in quick succession from bow to stern. He waited until the ship was in the bottom of the trough, for if the balls fell short of their target they could still skip on the water and strike the frigate's hull. As each shot hit the British ship of war the idle starboard gun crews let out a wild cheer. But then the frigate belched with smoke and the roar of the British broadside sent chills of dreaded expectation up and down every American spine. The first few balls wafted through the foretopsail harmlessly, but then a crash on the main mast sent hands up to cover heads. And then more crashes, jolting the ship everywhere, followed by screams and blood. Michael was on the ground, face down. He felt the timbers of the ship reverberate as the British carronade smashed into the *Chasseur*. He felt tremors throughout his entire body, as if he were part of the planking on the deck. A sudden thud about his head was mixed with a flash of white. And then he felt nothing.

Jessica was mopping the blood off Michael's face when Captain Ken grabbed her arm and pulled her away. "Don't act like a nurse. It's all right. I'll take care of him," Ken whispered in her ear. Michael was below deck, lashed to a table. The surgeon had his back to the table and was busy sewing up a leg wound sustained by one of the marines. Captain Ken was alarmed when he came down to check on Michael and found Jessica tending to him with a little too much compassion. Jessica's sex was a secret. It had to be. She was on a crowded ship about 100 feet long with over 150 men. She would be on that ship for months, presumably, without ever leaving it. It's true that she looked just like a boy, with her hair cut short and her figure, slight as it was, hidden beneath bulky clothing. But if she was a boy, she was a handsome one. She still could not hide her bright blue eyes or her dark brows and long lashes. She tried hard to act like a young man and she applied some grease to her hands and face for effect. But the correct, schoolgirl posture was still there and she still sat, daintily, on the edge of a chair. Captain Ken sent Jessica to his cabin.

It was the black gun captain, James Darymple, who picked Michael off the deck and brought him below, lashing him to a table during the storm, until the surgeon could see him.

"Rather a close one wasn't it Captain Russell," Doctor Williams said, almost nonchalantly, as he turned from the marine and attended to Michael.

"The boy er the frigate?"

"Both."

"Well as fer the boy, you tell me doctor. The frigate was very close. Too close. But things like that happen at sea. One day there's not another ship 'round fer a hundred miles, the next day, it seems, you start bumpin' into everything that floats. But we were lucky. That frigate coulda tore us to bits. Thank God Boyle had the sense to have the schooner ship rigged. But even with all our speed it was the snow that saved us. A lovely Christmas present, don'tcha think? One I'm sure this boy won't forget too soon."

"The boy is fine. Just a slight wound above the ear, here. Whatever hit him must have been blunt, the wound is superficial, you see? But the blow was enough to render him unconscious." Captain Ken studied the wound while the doctor cleaned it.

"Well, it was pro'bly a block. The arm on the mainm'st is shot to pieces. Is there any permin't damage, I mean to the skull?"

"I don't believe so. But there's no telling with these kinds of things. He could be out for a few minutes more or he could take a few days, maybe a week, to revive. The body takes its time to heal, especially with a head injury. Simply keep him quiet and watch for any changes." Ken was relieved by the doctor's prognosis. Doctor Williams was Boyle's personal physician and was well respected on board. He had sailed with Boyle, and consequently, with most of the *Chasseur's* crew, off and on for more than twenty years. A good surgeon was an enticement for sailors to sign aboard a ship, especially a privateer. Seamen took comfort in the fact that a capable pair of hands was around to remove a musket ball, sew up a sword slash, even amputate a limb when necessary. The surgeon was entitled to eight shares of the prize money, and since the war began, Doctor Williams had become quite wealthy from his shares.

"What's the rest of the damage down here, doctor?"

"Please inform the captain that all is well. I have a shattered femur from one of your topman, Happy George, that will keep him off duty for five or six weeks, and half a dozen nasty splinter wounds, nothing life threatening, just a great deal of blood." Ken glanced over at Happy, who was lying on the floor, his leg in a splint. Somehow he managed to smile at Captain Ken and wink one of his green eyes. "The rest of the men down here are simply sea sick landlubbers. Speaking of lubbers, here comes the worst of them now." Uncle Bob trudged to the table with his body bent low, both from the constant pain in his stomach and the fact that there was only a six-foot clearance below deck.

"It was all my fault," he moaned, "I told da boy ta lay down. I t'ought it would be safer. But den da damned Britishers fired dere cannon an' one hit da mainm'st and one of t'ose, whatchamacallits? Da t'ings you use fer hoistin'..."

"Block and tackle," Ken said.

"Yea, it was da block dat hit him in da head. James, da gunner, brought him below. Tell me now, doctor darlin', is he in bad shape? Why don't he move? His fadder's goin' ta kill me; his mudder will haunt me da rest of me days"

"He's fine Captain Dooley. I've pulled plenty of balls from the chests of powder monkeys in my day. Believe me I've seen worse, much worse. He does have a concussion. However, there is very little swelling so there is no need to operate to relieve the pressure. To be sure, he's out cold, but his respiration is normal. The human body is amazing, gentlemen. As I was just telling Captain Ken, the body takes its time to heal, but the boy is strong. He'll survive, but I'm not so sure about you. Why did you take this voyage? Had you any idea that you were so given to sea sickness?" Bob studied the doctor for a minute. Doctor Williams was close to sixty. He carried a small frame and a thin and studied face. His spectacles mirrored the lamp swinging over the table and caused Bob to blink several times before answering.

"Whaddaya mean dis voyage? Why I've sailed wit' Joshua Barney in da rebellion. Dis is nothin'. Back den it was a lot worse."

"Captain Dooley, in my twenty years at sea I've never seen a man so green."

"Look doc, you pay tention ta boyo, here, an' never mind bout me. I'll be fine in a couple of days." Doctor Williams bent down over Michael once more and opened the boy's eyelids, observing the cornea's reaction to the swinging lantern.

"Very well, Captain Dooley. But I shall be available even for old salts like yourself if you need me. Good day to you sir," Doctor Williams said, bowing to Uncle Bob. "Captain Russell, your servant, sir." And he bowed again.

"Nice feller. Very formal though," Captain Ken said after the doctor had left. He brought his face closer to the big Dooley and squinted his eyes. "By gimminy, you are a sight, Bob, even for old, sore eyes like mine. Never seen anythin' like it. Look after the boy while I go report to the cap'n, and keep Mr. Henry astern, in my cabin. I don't want him nursin' the boy, if you git my meanin' "

"Are we out of danger, den?"

Captain Ken had started for the gangway, his arms propelling his body along like the pumps of the ship. He swiveled his thick body around at Bob's question. "Fer the time bein', Bob. Do you know what that there frigate coulda done to us, iffin we didn't have the snow to hide behind?"

"Yea. But don't be tellin' me, I don't wanna know."

Bob sat down beside Happy as Captain Ken climbed the gangway and went up through the main hatch. It was nearing dawn, with the storm passing to the north. The *Chasseur* was heading due west, but would soon alter course and make for the coast off Newfoundland. Happy would be out of action the whole time the *Chasseur* feasted on those waters.

"This 'ere leg is goin' to tie me up until we reach the Channel. Thank goodness my Peggy taught me my letters. Looks like I'm going to be reading and thinking like a bloody pheeloseepher, Captain Dooley." Bob paid him little heed. He was too sick and too worried about his nephew, who lay on the table, motionless. "Oh, by the by sir, can I call you Bob like I did at the reverend's meeting we 'ad before we shipped off and I found out 'at you was the captain of the guard? I'm getting a little confused with this 'ere captains business. We 'ave a captain of the ship, Captain Boyle, and the sailing master, Captain Ken, though some call 'im Captain Russell. We got the Captain of the Marines, ‘at'd be you, sir. And we got the bloody captain of the guns, one for each and every gun on this 'ere ship. And your's truly is the captain of the top - it's very confusing, sir." But Bob couldn't or wouldn't acknowledge the sailor. To him, Happy George was an Englishman, and Bob Dooley hated Englishman.

"Shut your trap an’ watch da boy. I'm goin' ta sleep."

"Aye, Captain."

It wasn't until New Year's Day that Michael opened his eyes and said hello to Happy in a weak voice. And it was two days after that before Doctor Williams allowed him to be bundled up and carried on deck. The sky was a bright, pale blue and the sun shown down and brilliantly lit up the slight chop on the Atlantic.

"Thank you, uncle. But I can't open up my eyes, the light is too bright."

"You'll get used ta dat in a little while, boyo."

"Are you still green?"

"Am I what?"

"Are you still green? uncle. The last time I saw you - after you knocked me down - I remember you being terribly green."

"Well, now. No I'm meself ag'in. And I'm sorry fer knockin' you over, but I can't forget' da stories I heard of da powder monkeys who stand behind dere cannon an’ get picked off like so many apples from a tree." Uncle Bob placed Michael down in the bow of the ship and sat down beside him. "Are you warm enough, boyo?"

"Oh, yes. And I can breathe again. The air below is horrible, and the constant snoring."

"Dat's because dere's always men sleepin' below. Dere's too many men an' not enough hours in a day to bunk dem all. By the way, I never did get ta wish ya a blessed Christmas an' a joyful New Year." Michael smiled and peeked at his uncle through squinting eyes.

"Blessed Christmas, uncle, and a joyous New Year to you, too."

Jessica left Captain Ken at the wheel when she saw Uncle Bob carrying Michael on deck and made her way forward, trying to act disinterested.

Good morning, Captain Dooley."

"Ah, Mr. Henry. A good day ta you, lad. Do you know our patient here, Michael Dooley?" Jessica prevented the smile that was breaking out on her face from exploding with delight.

"Why, no, I don't believe I had the pleasure. How do you do Michael?"

"I'm just fine - ah - Henry, thanks."

"Mr. Henry, Michael. Address him as Mr. Henry," Uncle Bob corrected Michael.

"Why do I have to call him Mr. Henry! For the love of God, uncle, somebody had better start explaining to me why I have call her Mr..." But Bob Dooley clamped Michael's mouth shut before he could say another word.

"Quiet, boyo. Mr. Henry, I'm goin' ta stand in front of you two while you explain ta da boy what you're doin' here, but be quick about it because a master's mate an' a powder monkey shouldn't be takin' liberties ta have da decency ta talk ta each other." As the tall and wide hulk of Bob Dooley surveyed the deck aft, Jessica slipped in behind the Captain of the Marine and sat next to Michael.

"Don't make this harder than it already is, Michael," she began, with pleading blue eyes. "Now, Father John desperately needed some work done on the roof of the orphanage. You know as well as I do, it leaks terribly." Michael nodded, the roof did leak, it always had. "Well, since you were going to sea on Captain Boyle's ship, I suggested to Father John that I go along and finance the repair of the roof from my share of the prize money."

"That's ridiculous! I had to pray all night long to search my heart before Father John would allow me to sail. Father John would never let you go to sea on a privateer, never, do you hear me!"

"Keep it down, boyo, you'll have da whole ship's company knowin' da secret wit' your blabberin'. "

"He's right, Michael, no one must know that I'm a girl."

"Why not? Plenty of women go to sea. What do you think I am, daffy?"

"Plenty of women, but not girls, Michael. Besides, Captain Boyle doesn't allow females on his ship."

"You mean the captain doesn't know either?"

"No, Michael, Captain Boyle knows because Captain Ken asked him to do this as a favor after Father John had asked Captain Ken to do this as a favor to Father John, understand?" Michael didn't. He was beginning to wonder if the blow he took on his head had affected his mind.

"Let me get this straight. You asked Father John to give you permission to sail on an armed ship during a war with the greatest naval force in history just because he needed his roof fixed. And then Father John, who's planting little white crosses on the Calvary in back of the church, says 'Oh, sure Jess, that's a capital idea, simply capital. Go on and here's my blessing but try not to get yourself killed so that I gotta plant one of these little white crosses on Calvary with your name on it.' " Jessica cocked her head up and stared furiously at him, her blue eyes turning to sapphires. "And Father John goes to Captain Ken and says 'Hey Captain why don't you do me this little favor by taking one of my orphans and making her a master's mate so she can give me money to fix my roof.' And Captain Ken strolls up to Captain Boyle and says 'Hey, captain, I know you've got this rule that says that no women, let alone girls, can sail with you, but the roof's gotta be fixed and, by the way, you have no choice in the matter.' " Jessica continued to stare down at him, her left brow arched up high.

"Zacly," Uncle Bob said. Someone was in the waist cocking his head up towards the bow, as if he was trying to see beyond Dooley's massive frame. It was Mr. Lugger, the boatswain. Uncle Bob stared at him hard and Lugger frowned and went below. "Jaysus, Mr. Henry, hurry up. Da bloody police are watchin' us."

"Of course, Michael, if you possessed an ounce of intelligence, you could see that it was Father John and I who hadn't any choice in the matter. The roof must be fixed or there will be no orphanage. He appealed to Archbishop Carrol, but the archbishop told him that collections were down. Without the roof being repaired, Father John was going to have to close the orphanage until funds could be found. Either that or contract out some of the girls of the orphanage into indentured service, and one of those girls was going to be me!" Michael was tongue-tied.

"Jeez Louise, Jess, I - I - I'm sorry. I - I didn't know that you would have to... Hey! How come you get to be a master's mate and I'm only a powder monkey? As a master's mate you're entitled to six shares! For the love of Mary, six shares Jess. Why, that could be a fortune. Only the captain of the ship, the lieutenants, and the surgeon receive more than that. And Captain Ken and Uncle Bob get six shares for being a prize master and captain of the marine. I know. I read that section in the Articles of Agreement that each man jack has signed. If the crew finds out that a girl is the master's mate and entitled to six shares, then you're gonna be in deep trouble."

"No one is going to find out. That's why I was made a master's mate in the first place. I do not have direct access to the crew, nor they to me. And how could I have been made a powder monkey? Do you think Father John would have said yes to this whole thing if I was assigned a place behind a gun?"

"Oh, no, of course not."

"There's only a few on board who know, and they're not going to give me away."

"Who are they? The more who know the worse it's going to be keeping this a secret."

"Well, there's you, of course, and your uncle, Captain Ken, Captain Boyle, and that seaman friend of yours, Happy George.

"Da limey," Uncle Bob said over his shoulder.

"Happy? Why does Happy Know?"

"Because he saw you and I together at the cooperage."

"He did?" Michael still didn't understand. "But a master's mate, Jess..."

"Why not a master's mate? Besides, who do you know at school who's better than me at navigation?"

"Well - er - nobody, Jess..."

"Astronomy?"

"Ah, you're pretty good at astronomy, I know, but for crying out loud, Jess you're a girl, and if .."

"Mathematics?"

"Alright, Jess, jeez, I get your point. Uncle Bob, you can take me back down now. I think I've had enough fresh air for one day." Jessica placed her hand inside Michael's blankets and squeezed his hand.

"I am glad you're feeling better, Michael. Truly. You scared me half to death. I don't know what I'd do if something happened to you." Jessica removed her hand and brushed a tear from her eye.

"Here, here, none of dat now. Stand up sh'traigt and act like a gentleman." Uncle Bob pushed Jessica aside and lifted Michael into his arms as if he picking up a toothpick. "Good day ta ya, Mr. Henry," he said gruffly.

"Good day, Captain Dooley. I hope you make a speedy recovery, Michael."

"Thank you - um - Mr. Henry.

Chapter 11

"SLING SHOT"

Michael had Uncle Bob carry him into the bow every day as the *Chasseur* made her way north towards Newfoundland. And every day Captain Boyle exercised his gun crews with targets made of empty barrels. But these were more than mere exercises. Boyle pitted his starboard and larboard gun crews against each other in a spirited competition, along with the long toms in the bow and stern. The sailors who manned the great guns looked to this target practice with salivating expectation, partly because it made sense to be able to rely on skilled gunnery when capturing fat prizes from the enemy. But, the immediate reward for their steady eye and ever-quickening rate of fire was an extra allowance of grog at supper. Nothing was more cherished in an old tar than his grog.

In the weeks that passed, even the inexperienced and, therefore, slowest of the gun crews quickly enjoined the art of gunnery with fascination and relish. It was always one of the primary topics of conversation amongst the crew, second only to the weather. For the captain, who dispensed the money for the large quantities of powder used in these exercises out of his own pocket, the expense was well justified. Sure the *Chasseur* was as well manned and as well armed as any American privateer. But when an enemy merchant's master was faced with the decision to fight or surrender, there was nothing as convincing as a well placed ball on the quarterdeck.

"Listen, boyo, you study James Darymple, da gun captain of da bow chaser, soes ya knows what ta do when it's your turn ta work da gun," Uncle Bob said, gently placing Michael down well behind the gun crew.

"But, uncle, I'm just the powder monkey. That's all I do is fetch cartridges from the gun room and run them up to the cannon."

"An' what would happen if one of dese here boys went down in a fight? Everyone assigned ta da cannon should know what everyone else's job is. Why, dat way, if one of da udder fellows fall, you can jump in an' take dere place. I'm goin' ta organize da marines an' set up our own competition."

"What competition?"

"Why, if da sailor boys can have a go at pickin' up an extra pint or two, for da love of God, why can't da marines be entitled ta da same booty? After all, boyo, da sailor boys just sit behind dere cannon an' peep out of dese little holes in da sides of da ship! It's us who climb up ta da yards an' risks our bloody necks sharpshootin' da enemy! An' who do ya t'inks does da boardin' an' da fightin'?"

"Why, you do, uncle. You told me you did it single handed for ole' Joshua Barney in the rebellion." Bob glanced around and let out a loud, congested cough.

"Now, we'll keep ole' Joshua's tactics ta ourselves, won't we lad. Wouldn't want valuable information like dat gettin' in da wrong hands. Now, back ta me competition. I says ta Captain Boyle, good man dat he is: 'Captain, da boys in da marines is gettin' pretty sore wit' dis business of extra grogs fer da gun crews dat hit da most barrels an' fire da quickest.'

'I am sorry ta here dat, Captain Dooley,' says he. 'An' how can I git dese boys ta forgit about how sore dey is?'

'Why, cap'n, you just leave dat ta me. I'm yer Captain of da Marine, ain't I?'

'An' one of da best in da country, sir.'

'Den I'll take full responsibility for da men under me command,' says I.

An' dat was all dere was of da conversation, boyo. Captain Boyle is dependin' on me ta get dese boys ready for action."

"But, exactly, how do you plan to do that, uncle? You can't just put an empty barrel out there in the water and take shots at it. How would you know that you hit anything?"

"Ha! You just leave dat ta me. Captain Boyle has givin' me full responsibility an' I can't let dese boys down. Da main t'ing is ta make sure da boys is got sometin' ta work for - a reason ta go beyond da call of duty - a little enticement."

"Extra grog does it for the sailors," Michael suggested, innocently.

"Dat's because t'ose sailor boys have been cooped up on a ship most of dere lives an' got no appreciation for da finer t'ings in life. No, da captain says I can take whatever steps necessary for da good of da ship, and dere's a fine, ole' cask of whiskey, Irish, no less, sittin' in da storeroom. Now, da storeroom is under guard an' lock an' key..."

"Uncle!" Michael sat straight up, a ringing in his ears and a sharp pain in the side of his head made him wince, "you're not going to break into the storeroom are you?"

"Break in? Who says I ever broke inta anythin'? Besides, dere's no need ta be breakin' down doors, boyo. Captain Boyle said I can have whatever I need ta fulfill da needs of me boys, didn't he?"

Michael put his head slowly back down, shaking it at the same time. "No, uncle, he said that you must take full responsibility."

"Dat's right, boyo. An' what dis ship needs is some real competition. An' ain't I da Captain of da Marine? Isn't it me who assigns a guard ta da storeroom? An' isn't it me who's in charge of da key?"

"Uncle, just be careful. Remember, Captain Boyle gave you full responsibility, and that means you're responsible if anything goes wrong."

Bob Dooley gently lifted Michael's head and propped it up on a pink, scented pillow that appeared from nowhere behind his massive form. "Here, boyo. I brought up a pillow for dat achin' head of yours. Now, you put your head on dat an' study da gun crew. If da boom of da cannon gets too much for ya, just call me name an' Uncle Bob will take ya back ta your berth. An' don't be worryin' so much. I'll take care of everythin' "

Uncle Bob went below to organize his brainchild of exercising the marines, and Michael, his head propped upon the soft, sweet smelling pillow, observed the gun crew of the bow chaser. James Daryrmple, the tall, lanky, black man, whose back Michael had repeatedly bumped into before the brief encounter with the English frigate, was busy, tenderly wiping the barrel of his gun. In bold but sloppy white letters on the top of the barrel was written "Sling Shot." The bow chaser was Tom Boyle's gun. Each of the officers was charged with supervising part of the ship's cannon. Mr. Leib, the first lieutenant, had the seven larboard guns. Mr. Davis, the ship's second lieutenant, was responsible for the seven starboard cannon; and Mr. Connor, the third lieutenant, controlled the long tom in the stern. But Captain Boyle rarely fired his gun in the bow. He usually left that to James, who was the best man to sight a gun on the ship, and James had developed a particular pride in that responsibility. This afternoon's exercise was announced after the noon sighting, and James and his gun crew were the first to arrive at their stations.

All of the guns were now properly manned and everyone had their eye upon Mr. Lugger as he stood, surveying the preparations, amidships. Boyle's competition fell into two parts. The first part of the exercise was speed. While targets were being rigged for the gunners to shoot at, the crews competed against each other to see which crew was fastest at firing, reloading, and firing again. This part of the competition simulated a desperate action against another ship, firing broadside upon broadside at close quarters. Hopefully, the men would never have to realize this scenario. Such a close and repeated fire meant unnecessary destruction for both the *Chaesseur* and the enemy she engaged. Captain Boyle and all other American privateering captains were under strict, ofttimes written, instructions not to engage the enemy when such destruction was avoidable. The destruction of ships, whether American or English, cost money and time to repair. And the purpose of privateering was to make money, not spend it. But, if a privateer was trapped into an engagement with, say, a British naval sloop, it was either blast away with everything she had as quickly as she could, or face surrender. The English were not gentle captors. Surrender meant harsh treatment and certain, often cruel imprisonment. On occasion, however, such as rushing in on the enemy in an attempt to board, with the deck swarming with men, a quick succession of broadsides, aimed high, was needed to cause as much confusion on the deck of the enemy as possible. Aiming high, up into the rigging of the enemy and not firing into the hull, would entail the least possible destruction of a prize ship.

This was the only time that James Darymple and the other gun captains anticipated the boatswain's crass voice: "Silence, fore and aft!"

While targets were being rigged off of starboard, Mr. Leib, on the larboard side, began the contest, starting with his foremost cannon. Since this gun was relatively close to Michael, he felt the blast shiver through the pine planking, and though the noise did give him a start, it didn't aggravate the sore wound above his ear. He remembered the last time he had felt the ship shake so, when the British volley had crashed into the privateer at the mouth of the Chesapeake. He remembered the screams of pain from the *Chasseur's* company as splinters from the yardarms were blasted off in chunks and hurled with great force down onto the deck tearing into flesh. He remembered a thud just before the flash of light.

One after one the larboard guns were fired, run in and reloaded, and run out and fired again. Each gun performing in the same manner with Mr. Lugger timing the crews and shouting their time to the ship's company in general, and to Captain Boyle in particular. In this way, everyone on board knew which crew had established the best time and a cheer echoed throughout the ship when that time was beaten by faster, more skillful men. The larboard side having completed it's routine, targets were rigged off of larboard while Mr. Davis started his guns, likewise, from bow to stern. In turn, Mr. Conner had the stern gun fired and their time was duly noted by Mr. Lugger. Now, it was James Darymple's chance. Michael watched with fascination as James put the crew through the drill. Since Michael was injured, another boy, David, the cabin boy, had taken his place behind the gun crew as their powder monkey.

"Cast loose the gun," James instructed and with that the muzzle lashing was tore off, and the quoit was pushed in so that the muzzle cleared the porthole. Meanwhile, the powder monkey ran off and returned with a lighted match from the match tub located amidships. James grabbed the match and put it to the touchhole. The gun exploded and reeled.

"Run out!" James roared, and the men quickly took hold of the gun tackle and brought the cannon back from the porthole. "Worm!" One of men picked up a long rod with a twisting end and shoved it into the muzzle ripping out pieces of spent cartridge. "Sponge!" A second man was ready with a wet sponge, again at the end of a long rod, and he rammed it down and twisted it around to extinguish the remnants of flame and spark. Simultaneously, the powder monkey removed a cartridge from his metal container and a third man grabbed it and, along with a wad of paper, sent it home into the chamber using a rammer, while James felt the cartridge reach the chamber by placing a priming wire in the touchhole. "Home!" cried James, and the rammer was quickly removed. A fourth man stood waiting with a ball and this he pushed into the cannon along with another wad of paper, and then the third man with the rammer jammed everything in with a grunt. As soon as this was accomplished, James pricked the cartridge with a long, sharp needle inserted into the vent. The gun crew glistened with sweat despite the cold January breeze as James poured gunpowder down the touchhole from a powder horn that hung round his neck. As soon as the powder was poured down the touchhole, and not before, a piece of wood with a lighted match was thrust into James' hand while the rest of the crew ran the cannon in using tackle and hand spikes. James placed the match to the touchhole and the sound of the explosion burst into Michael's ears.

Mr. Lugger, still looking at his timepiece, shouted across the deck "one minute, forty four seconds!" The entire ship's company, save the captain and the crew of the gun that performed at one minute fifty two seconds, let out a rousing cheer. James and the rest of his crew slapped each other on the back in congratulations. Michael couldn't believe the whole drill took less than two minutes. It seemed to him much longer.

"Well, boy, Ah see you still ain't found yo' sea legs yet," James said as he approached Michael, laughing.

"N - n- no sir, I, well, no sir."

"How's that head a yo's. Did *Sling Shot* hurt it some at all?"

"Oh, no sir, not at all. Is *Sling Shot* the name of your cannon, then?

"Sho' is. She was awful good to us today." James had a wide smile to compliment his broad face - a face that was disproportionate to his tall, skinny body. He shirt was opened and the sun gleamed off the sweat on his chest. Michael looked up at him in awe. James was taller that anyone he had ever seen before. Taller than Uncle Bob, Michael guessed, but it was hard to tell since James was bent over him with his hands propped against his knees.

"My name is Michael, sir. Michael Dooley, Jr."

James removed his right hand from his knee and held it out to Michael. "Pleasure meetin' you, Mike. Mah name's James Darymple."

"The pleasure is all mine, James," Michael said, placing his hand inside James' giant palm. "But, if you please, sir, it's Michael. My mother, God rest her, insisted that I be Michael cause my father's name is Mike. It made it easier on her, I guess."

James burst out in a gentle laugh, "You don't say. Ha, ha, well if that don't beat all. You know, mah mama said the same thing bout me? The 'zact same thing. Ever'time she called 'Jimmy,' from the house, foh this thing or that, mah pappy and Ah would both come a'runnin'. And one day she decided that 'nough was 'nough and sat us down and says to mah pappy, 'honey, you always been Jimmy since the day yo' mama named you, and Ah can't change that. But, boy,' she says to me, 'Ah'm your mama and I can call you anythin' Ah have a mind to. So, from this day on, you come runnin' only when you hear me callin' James. You got that, James?' Ha, ha, ha. Well, now, we got somthin' in common, you and me, Michael."

Michael laughed, too, for James' smile and deep chested chuckle were contagious. Just like Happy's smile, Michael thought. "We have two things in common, James. Our names and *Sling Shot*. I'm sorry for bumping into you like I did before I got hurt. I thought I was supposed to stand at attention behind the gun. I thought that if I didn't, I would be hit by the bosun."

"Ha, ha, ha, ha, Michael. This ain't no navy ship or nothin'. You don't have to stand up at attention, jest be in your proper place, is all. And don't you be frettin' bout Mr. Lugger. He's like a dog who makes a fuss, barkin' and yelpin', when he's in front a his mas'er. But when he's all by his self and nobody else around, why, you just have to look at him sideways and he'll go away with his tail between his legs, guarantee."

"Thank you, James. I'll remember that. Oh, and thank you for carrying me down to the surgeon after I got hit."

"Don't you go thankin' me foh that." James glanced at him sideways, his eyes bulging in earnest. "That's a duty foh every man jack aboard this ship. We takes care of our own. Man goes down, its our God given duty to help him up or carry him if that's what you got to do. No, suh. Like ol' Ben Franklin say, we all hang together or we all hang separately. Sides, Michael, we ship mates, now. Brothers of the sea. It's got to work that way if we're goin' to live together, peaceable, and fight together, like men. If anybody even think any other way, all a sudden you got trouble. Divisiveness, you unda'stand, boy. Deeevisiveness. It's a big word, but it jest mean makin' two out of one. The only one that got the right to do that is the Lord Almighty."

"Like when my ma died," Michael said, reflectively

" 'Scuse me?"

"I'm sorry. I was just thinking on what you were sayin'. When God took my ma, it was like my family was split apart."

"Nah, Michael, that ain't it!" James sat down and wrapped his sprawling arms around his tree like legs. "No, suh, that ain't it at all. The last time the good Lord split two to make one was with ol' Adam. And that wasn't devicesivness at all. That was unity. Yo' mama is always goin' to be one with yo' pappy and with you. Now, her body ain't hear no more, that true. But, her spirit is with the Lord and the Lord is with you. Nah, Michael, your family ain't in two, not by a long shot from the that cannon over there. You and yo' mama and yo' pappy is always one if that's the way each of ya'll want it to be. You got any brothers and sisters?"

"No, there's just me."

"Soes you got to bear this all by yo'self, huh? What about yo' pappy?"

"Well, my pa was impressed, just before the war."

"And you got nobody?"

"My uncle, he's the Captain of the Marine."

"Well, do you think yo' pappy thinks that yo' family is split up, Ah mean in here?" James pointed an elongated finger at his heart.

"No, not in there, never."

"Alright, nows you got it, boy. And do you think that jest because yo' mama don't have a body anymow that she thinks yo' not a family?"

"No, she - she would never think that."

"Not even because she's dead?"

"No, not even because she's dead."

"Well, now, why don't you git yo'self better then, and git back to me and *Sling Shot* and start fightin' this war soes you can see yo' pappy again." James sprang up and took long strides back to his cannon. Michael never took his eyes off James' beanpole frame.

"'Know what you ought to believe,'" Michael said to himself.

The target barrels were in place floating off both sides of the ship. Mr. Lugger was amidships with his hands on his hips. "Silence, for and aft!" In turn, starting from larboard, each gun crew was given their chance at the targets. There were several direct hits before the starboard cannon opened up but cheers for each hit were heard less as the targets floated farther away from the ship. Mr. Conner aimed the sights of his cannon and fired the stern gun. It was short but close enough to warrant applause. The *Chasseur* came about and James set his sights on a distant target bobbing just above the surface of the water. The crew intensely followed his instructions in traversing the gun with crowbars and handspikes. When James had the cannon elevated with the wedge to his satisfaction, he took the match from the powder monkey and put it to the touchhole. Everyone on board trained their eyes on the target, now just barely visible. *Sling Shot's* ball smashed into the barrel sending hoops and staves flying high into the sky. The *Chasseur's* deck exploded in cheers. Captain Boyle smiled. He knew that as long as James was onboard, he would never have to fire his gun again.

Bob Dooley had the carpenter and his mates fashion a large platform in the waist of the ship. It was buoyed by a series of barrels lashed around the edges. This platform and a boat were hoisted and lowered off starboard. When the boat had tugged the platform a hundred yards off, Dooley crawled onto the platform and erected a five-foot painted panel. The picture, painted by Bob himself, was of a British soldier in full uniform, but, instead of a face, it featured a large bull's eye. The sailors, crowding to starboard to see this presentation by the lubbers, cheered Bob's creation and offered to blow it out of the water. When Dooley returned to the ship, he directed his marines to the tops of the masts with muskets, balls, and powder. Even Captain Boyle joined in the fun and sent for his pistols.

"Well, Michael, have you ever seen shootin' like that befoh?" James had returned to Michael, who was attempting to lift himself up to see his uncle's invention.

"I couldn't see it hit the target, James, but I actually saw a piece of it fly into the air! It was a marvelous shot." James took Michael's arm and helped him up and over to starboard.

"That uncle of yo's has got some sense of humor. These ole boys haven't had so much fun since we cast off from the Point." They smiled at the poor attempts the marines made struggling to balance themselves in the tops as the ship rolled slowly over the water.

"James, why do you call your gun *Sling Shot*?"

"Samuel. First book. Chapter 17, verses 42-54." Michael had read Samuel, had read the entire Bible, cover to cover, but he couldn't quite recall chapter 17.

"It's the one bout David. You know, David befoh he was king. Goliath says he was goin' to give the boy's dead body foh the birds and the animals to eat. Curse him somethin' awful. But David had no fear. He jest took a nice, round stone from his pouch and put it in his sling and do what God born him to do. Now, this here England we's fightin' is a giant, jest like Goliath. They been cursin' us and laughin' at us cause we're so small and all. But's God's with us Michael. We's different than them countries with kings and queens and dukes and such. Bout the only thing we need to do is free the slaves."

"You ever been a slave, James?"

"Me, no, praise the Lord. Mah pappy was tho'. Mah family lives near Elizabethtown. Lot's of Quakers up there. They don't believe in slavery. They believe in hard work, tho'. They let mah pappy buy his freedom in the rebellion, on board a ship jest like this one. Sailed with Joshua Barney."

"Barney! My uncle sailed with Barney!"

"He did! Lord, Michael, he don't look that old."

"He's a big boy, James. But a boy all the same. That's what Jessica used to say."

"Jessica?"

"Ah, Jess - Jessica is the name of the girl who helps out at our house."

"She ain't a slave is she?"

"No, no, James. We don't have many slaves on the Point. Most of the rich people live in Old Baltimore Town. She's just an orphan that Father John sent to us. All the children at the orphanage do work for people on the Point. It's not for money. It's just Father John's way of - well, it's part of his educational philosophy."

"Mah! Mah! Mah! Ha, ha, ha. Y'alls educated ain't ya. Educationa...whew! Goin' on bout pheelosophee and all. And here Ah am teaching you bout the Good Book and such."

"Oh, no, James. That was interesting. You have a way of talking to people so that they'll understand your meaning. That's a gift, James. That's what Father John would say."

"Ah'd like to meet this Father John."

"And he'd like to meet you. He's always been good to us. My pa would like to meet you, too. You remind me of him, James. You understand 'what you ought to believe,' not what people tell you to believe, or feeling sorry for yourself and believing in something you shouldn't." Michael was silent for a moment, thinking about the code of his ancestors and how he could recognize a flaw in his behavior because of it. Only, he wished he could know more about how he could make the code work in his life. James broke the silence.

"That's a real nice thing to say, Michael. Thank you. Thank you, kindly. Now let's get back to this girl. How old's this Jessica, anyways."

"She's my age, I think. We go to school together."

"Is she pretty?" Michael jerked his head back at James, a scowl appearing on his face. "Sorry, Michael, I didn't mean to poke into things that way. I jest thought I'd ask. Boy yo' age starts to notice things like that." Michael thought on the question to himself for a moment. Was Jessica pretty? "To bad's she an orphan. Ah always feel sorry foh orphans."

Chapter 12

HALIFAX

In conning the ship Jessica had little to do, for the *Chasseur* was sailing on course with a free wind. Still, it was wise to have the master's mate take the con on just such an occasion, since the time could be spent paying particular attention to the compass and the ship's motion in relation to the water and the sky. That is to say, it was good practice. The ship was on a northwest course, and the officer of the forenoon watch, Mr. Leib, was responsible for getting the most out of the ship's sails. So, a sailing master or mate had only to keep the helmsman alerted to the assigned course. Besides, the seamen who sailed the privateer, and who all took their trick at the wheel, knew far better than the master's mate how the ship should be steered, or so they thought.

"Steer nor' nor'west," Jessica shouted from the weather shrouds in as manly a voice as possible. Cyrus Bently, one of the lookouts and an old salt who was at the helm, could plainly see both the compass and the sails. He smiled at the orders so voicefully given by the young Mr. Henry. But he was also a stubborn sea dog who saw nothing wrong in letting the ship veer a half a point now and again in order to take advantage of a freshening breeze. Bently was a curious old coot, too, who was more interested in the punishment that was openly talked of this morning than rigidly adhering to the ship's direction. Now, there was nothing wrong with any of these idiosyncrasies at the wheel. But the fact was that Mr. Henry was a bright mate with plenty of book knowledge and little practical experience. In short, Mr. Henry was an academic sailor. If the book said to sail by the compass, then Mr. Henry assumed the book should be taken literally.

"Nothing to westward!" Jessica shouted again. Bently checked the compass. It was a fraction off, indeed to westward, and he looked around to make sure none of his compatriots noticed Mr. Henry's correction. But by looking around and feeling embarrassed by this upstart master's mate, Bently again went off course.

"Steady a-starboard!" Jessica's voice could now be heard by most of the hands. If the anticipation of punishment had not captured the crew's attention, Bently would have been the laughing stock of the entire company. As it was, just a few of the men paid any mind to Bently's harmless error.

"Steady," Jessica said, as Bently put the helm a little to starboard and turned the ship to the right heading.

"Steady, it is, sir." Bently grumbled. He knew nothing of Mr. Henry except that the mate was just out of some lubbers' school, but he did not like his tone of voice, in fact, he didn't like him at all.

Captain Boyle always came on deck at the turn of the morning watch and today was no exception. But, instead of checking the course and the trim of the sails, he went directly to the quarterdeck and paced there for a half-hour before speaking. "Mr. Leib, assemble all hands."

"Aye sir, all hands. Mr. Lugger, all hands on deck!"

The morning watch that had gone below knew, as did everyone aboard ship, that the Captain of the Marine had gotten himself into trouble. They also knew that fighting on board ship was not uncommon, especially on a ship that carried ten times the men needed to sail her. Captain Boyle knew that, too. This was one of the hazards a privateer's captain had to accept since he needed that many men to man prize crews and overwhelm the enemy in a boarding. But, discipline was necessary to maintain, even more so in a crowded ship.

"Good morning, Captain Russell."

"Good mornin', sir."

"Please, pass the word for Mr. Lugger, and have the prisoners brought on deck."

The entire ship's company was assembled in front of Captain Boyle and his officers. Boyle had selected ten sailors, who had been with him most of his career, to take charge of the armory. They stood in back of him now, each carrying a loaded musket. Uncle Bob and the ten marines accused of fighting on deck during the last dog watch, were marched in irons up the forehatch. Bob stretched his head over the crowd to see if his nephew had been carried on deck. Satisfied that he was being spared that embarrassment, he proceeded forward. But Dooley wasn't quick enough for Mr. Lugger, who jabbed him in the ribs with the end of the cat. The Irishman stopped and gave him a hard stare. Lugger turned away and marched the prisoners up to the captain. Boyle motioned for Captain Ken to accompany him.

"Very well, then," Boyle began softly. "Mr. Lugger, read the charges against these men." Mr. Lugger saluted his captain and pointed an accusing finger at Uncle Bob.

"Sir, the Captain of the Marine broke into the storeroom early last night and made off with a cask of whiskey." As the wind was off the quarter, it blew the stale remanent of whiskey in the direction of the officers. Being not yet nine o'clock in the morning, the stench was particularly offensive. "They proceeded to get drunk and harass other members of the crew. Then they developed an argument amongst themselves over..."

"Yes, Mr. Lugger, continue."

"I hesitate to say, sir."

"Come, Mr. Lugger, I grow impatient enough. Argue over what!" Captain Boyle rarely lifted his voice in anger and the sailors who had known and served with him the longest cast uneasy glances at each other and bowed their heads.

"Their argument, sir, was over who could relieve himself, um, for the longest duration and the greatest distance." Except for the prisoners and the officers who stood before them, everyone on board broke into immediate guffaws. Boyle was not so humored. He was a gentleman of self-made breeding who led a civil and upright life, and who expected no less in others.

"Do the prisoners have anything to say on their defense?" Boyle asked the marines, directing the question to their captain.

Disheveled and dishonored, as he was, Bob Dooley stood straight, with his shoulders back and his powerful chest pushed out, nearly ripping his blouse. "No defense, sir. We are guilty as charged."

Boyle looked around and in back of them. "Is there anyone else who wishes to put in a word for these men before they are punished?"

Captain Ken cleared his throat and glanced at Boyle, it was obvious he wished to speak.

"Captain Russell, do wish to add anything to this investigation before I proceed with punishment?"

Ken could tell that Boyle, although a fair man, was in a distemper. It wasn't that the men had gotten drunk, or even that their late night party broke into a melee. It was the fact that he expected his officers, and that included the Captain of the Marine, to act as gentlemen - always, as gentlemen. It was the officers who had to set the standards for the rest of the crew. If their conduct was crass and crude, and disobedient, blatantly disobedient, then their punishment should be all the more severe.

Captain Ken didn't totally mind if Uncle Bob received a lashing. After all he deserved it. But, in a short period of time, it was Bob Dooley who would lead these men into battle. As Captain of the Marine, Bob would have to give the order that could mean certain death for some of his men. And if Captain Boyle relieved Dooley of command, then that would necessitate choosing another captain from the body of marines. In any other case, this would probably be the right thing to do. But, there was no one aboard who could best Bob Dooley in a fight. All the marines knew this from his reputation on the Point. They knew and admired his strength. They respected his courage. He was the only one that could lead them, and his office must be spared its dignity.

"Cap'n Dooley," Ken began, "a few partikalers as to the fight last night. Didja akchilly break inta the storeroom?"

"No sir, I used me key."

"As Cap'n of the Marine, then, you have a key to the storeroom?" Captain Ken raised his high pitched voice in addressing this question. It was important for the men to hear this.

"Aye, sir. We have no purser, as you well know, sir. I have keys ta both da storeroom an' da armory." Uncle Bob looked down in all humility and continued, "at least until last night, sir."

"Why didja take the cask a'whiskey, Cap'n Dooley?"

"As a prize for da men, sir. Da ones dat won da shootin' competition yesterday."

Captain Ken looked around at the faces of the ship's company. It was important for him to remain impartial, despite his long friendship with Uncle Bob. It was vital for the men to see that he was seeking truth and fairness, not creating it. "Come, Cap'n Dooley, the winners of the great gun compeetition were only rewarded with an extra ration a'grog. Iffin the sailors only got grog, why is it that you rewarded yer marines with a whole, bloody cask of whiskey?" Every man leaned a little closer to hear this answer clearly.

"Most of dese boys is Irish, sir, an' lubbers like meself. Whiskey, is mudder's milk ta dem, sir. I t'ought it would be a fine prize for da winners. And, if I may, sir, I and I alone, am responsible fer dis donnybrook. If it please your honor, I should take da entire punishment upon meself, since I am senior in command, sir." At this gesture, the men, marines and sailors alike, immediately took Uncle Bob's side. But Captain Ken could not let the issue rest. All animosity must be dealt with hear and now.

"Cap'n Boyle, the issue seems to be one a'quantity. Cap'n Dooley neither broke inta the storeroom nor was in error for rewardin' his men with whiskey. But, I submit, sir, he was in foul weather when he distributed such a mighty sum of aged Irish whiskey without thinkin' first, that he was akchilly denyin' this to the rightful owner's of that whiskey, the crew of the *Chasseur*, in its entirety. And if it pleases the Cap'n, I have one more question to ask Cap'n Dooley." Boyle had known Captain Ken a long time, almost as long as he had been to sea, but he had never heard such an artful defense.

"Proceed, Captain Russell."

"Very well, sir. Cap'n Dooley, please spare me the details of yer urinary contest. But when yer men performed this feat, did they, sir, squirt on or out of the ship?" Upon this answer, everyone knew, swayed the balance of punishment. Each man held his breath awaiting the answer.

"I'm happy to say, sir. We pissed outta da ship." Heads nodded across the deck and a collective sigh of relief was quite audible. Now, all eyes were fixed on Captain Boyle.

"Mr. Lugger." The boatswain stepped forward, his cat-o'-nine-tails dangling in his hands. "Dispose of the cat, we'll have no further need for that at the moment."

"It was on da tip of me tongue ta tell ya lad." Uncle Bob was carrying Michael up to the bow of the ship on a perfectly clear and cold Sunday morning. "I was goin' ta tell ya all along. But me duties is gettin' da better of me."

"Everyone on board was there except me and Happy. You can let me down now, thank you." Michael was dressed warmly in a woolen coat, mittens and a scarf. He stood and climbed, precariously, up the forehatch and into the bow. "I feel fine, uncle, the dizziness has gone completely. Now, tell me everything that happened."

"Michael, boyo, nothin' happened a'tall. It was strictly a formality."

"But what was your punishment. They told me Mr. Lugger was there with the cat!"

"Ah, don't worry your poor self. Ain't I still da Captain of da Marine? I simply explained da situation ta da captain an' he winked at me and told me not t'do it again."

"Then why did Captain Ken have to rise to your defense?"

"An' why shouldn't he back me up? Me who's been his friend dese many years? Enough of dis now." Uncle Bob bent down and whispered into Michael's ear, "Didja know dat Mr. Henry's been takin' da con of da ship?" Michael became even more irritated than he was before.

"As if I don't have enough to worry about," he stated softly, but emphatically. "How could Captain Ken do such a thing. She's - he's never sailed anything outside of a skiff in her - his life. I'm tellin' you uncle, the whole thing is rotten business. Just plain rotten. Do you know what would happen if anybody finds out? This whole ship would go crazy. I don't like it. And now I feel responsible for her being on board. Why, if I had never made the decision to sail, then this would have never happened. Are you sure Captain Ken knows what he's doing?"

They were leaning against the lee rail and staring out into the deep blue water that sparkled under a full sun. "Ah, Michael, just breathe dis delightful air. Forget about yer worryin', lad. Look up at da white sails, dere full of clean wind." Michael lifted his head and took in the spectacular spread of canvass on the two masted schooner. The wind had been fair these many days and the *Chasseur* flew over the water at twelve, thirteen, even fourteen knots. Michael and his uncle were both mesmerized by the sight.

"It's like we were bein' summoned by da sea ta Newfoundland. As if it knew our purpose an' was doin' everythin' she could ta speed us on our way."

"Jest wait till we hit the westerlies, then I'll have her faster than any ship afloat." The high pitched voice said with enthusiasm. Michael and Bob turned to see Captain Ken join them at the rail.

"Why it's me savior," Bob laughed.

"I shouldn't even be talkin' to ye, Bob. If I'da been captain of this schooner, I'd have ye flogged out of yer socks." Bob grimaced and put his hand behind and above Michael pointing downward, sending a signal to Captain Ken. "Oh, yes. Well I'll be pickled, look at him, Bob, don't he look the picture of vitalitee."

"Thank you, Captain Ken for defending my uncle. I hope Captain Boyle took the keys to the storeroom back." Captain Ken threw his hands up

"No use, Bob, he's as smart as his pa. Yes, Michael, and in addition, yer uncle and the others who stood guilty with him, are to forego their ration of grog until this cruise is over and done with."

"Or until I board da first prize ship," Uncle Bob said underneath his breath.

Something else was on Michael's mind and he thought this a good time to broach the subject. "You didn't leave Mr. Henry at the con again, didja captain?" Michael asked in earnest. Captain Ken looked around to make sure their conversation was private.

"Mr. Henry's quite a capable feller. I'll lay odds that at the end of this cruise I'll have him takin' us back up the ol' Cheseepeke." Michael leaned forward and grabbed Ken by the jacket.

"Please, captain, be careful."

"Well now. I've been trainin' young folk, seamen and officers alike, fer goin' on fifty years, and I never had anyone question my trainin' before. How is it that yer so concerned about Mr. Henry, Michael?" Michael let go of his jacket and put his hands back against the rail, adopting a casual stance.

"I - I'm not exactly concerned, captain. I do feel responsible for, um, him being on board. After all, if I had never sailed then this idea about," he whispered now, "the roof would never have come up, at least not for this voyage." Captain Ken and Uncle Bob smiled, discretely, at one another.

"So, tell me youngster, do ye feel as good as ye look?" Ken asked, taking a step back to scan Michael up and down.

"I could climb up to that mast head right now, " Michael replied, pointing up to the foremast.

"Well, I don't doubt it. Ha, ha, and if ye did, and we was another hundred miles on our course, ye know what ye would see?" Michael shook his head in the negative. "Nover Scotia, lad, Nover Scotia!" The mention of that place sent chills up Michael's spine.

"Captain Ken? Do you think my pa's in Halifax?" The old man put a wrinkled hand to his chin and scratched it with short, stubby fingers.

"As to that, I can't rightly say, boy. I been thinkin' on what Mike was up to these past few months, and I think I'm straight in my mind on what course he'd set. Iffin I were him, I wouldn't want to foul my hawser with unnecessary compleekations. Just think on it, now. He'd want to keep a low profile at first, ye know, watch his back and make no trouble until he was one of the crew. His skills as a cooper and carpenter will serve him well. There's need for his skills in Halifax and in the interior, on the lakes.

"Let me tell ye somethin', I was wit Arnold on the march to Quebec in '75. The Brits knew the only way to subdue Amereeka, was to cut her in two," Ken made a chopping motion with his hand. Bob and Michael saw the blue light in the old man's eyes grow in intensity as he remembered his service in the revolution. "Ye have to understand, this country's a big place. To control it takes more than blockadin' its seaboard. Unlike other countries, we don't have to rely on foreign commerce to survive. Bein' an island, England knows this. Why, we've got everythin' we want and more right in front of our eyes. This land is blessed with riches that England can only dream of. We've got good soil for growin' our own food and natural reesources to build the things we ain't got. Britain would have to put great armies on this continent to control us, more armies than she kin muster, even with mercenaries. Boys, she can't beat us. She knows that. The only thing she can and will do is to subvert us. She'll do the same thing to us as she tried to do in the rebellion. She's got to cut New England off from the rest of the country."

"Jaysus, yer right, Ken," Bob Dooley exclaimed, "Dey'll take Boston an' - an' - New York, an' roll right across da countryside. T'ose Federalists will help dem all da way, too."

"No, no Bob, ye got it all wrong. Sure, they could take one of our cities, two mebee, but the minute they step out into the interior, they're done fer. Every country boy in this nation has got a musket. And the British will die a slow death iffin they dare march an army through Massachusetts and New York."

Uncle Bob grinned, "Soes, how dey gonna split da country in two like ya says?"

"Ah, yer too young ta remember. Why ye didn't git yerself over here from Cork until it was all over."

Bob put his great hands on his hips and shook his head. "So, ya t'ink Yorktown was just a minor skirmish, den?"

Captain Ken waved his hand, dismissing Bob's comments. "The real fightin' had already taken place, I tell ye. The English held New York, but they didn't march from New York into the interior. They sent an army down the St. Lawrence! Canadee, ye big, stupid Irisher, Canadee! They went down the St. Lawrence and came down Champlain. Why, it was as clear to Arnold as it is, now, to Clay! That's why they both wanted to take Canadee in the first place. That, and it should a'been easy pickin's fer us anyway, iffin we knew how to cross a border."

Michael's head was swimming. "Wait a minute! What are you talking about, captain? What's all this have to do with my pa?"

"Yea, ya old sea bag!" Bob chimed in, "what about me brodder?"

"Iffin ye let a body finish, I'll tell ye!" Ken pulled out his pipe, but was too agitated to fill it. "Dang it! Where was I?"

"Splittin' us in two," Michael reminded him.

"That's it, boy. Don'tcha git it! England's goin' to take an army, when she can git one out a'Europe, and sail it down the St. Lawrence and then take control of Lake Champlain! That's their line of supply, the water, the interior waterway! Then they kin march till their hearts content and ain't nobody gonna stop them. Their gonna cut us in two, as I seys before. Then their gonna negotiate a separate peace with the New England States." Bob wanted to say something, but couldn't think of anything that would tarnish the validity of Ken's theory.

"And my pa, since he's a carpenter, he'll be needed to help build the ships to get the British army down Lake Champlain?"

"Yer pa will pull off any trick in the book ta do jest that! Why it's as plain as the nose on yer face. They don't need any carpenters or coopers in England, but, darned it all, iffin they don't need them on Champlain."

Bob was not quite convinced. He pointed a finger at the old man, was about to make a comment, and then forgot what he was going to say.

Michael, however, was lucid in his thinking. "But my pa's an impressed American seaman. Why would the English let him just stroll into New York?"

Bob repointed his finger. "Dat's what I was gonna say. Why, dey would put him in irons before dey let an American build British ships for an invasion of America."

Ken's red face and angry, blue eyes showed his frustration, but he demonstrated it better with swinging his arms in front of him, as if he were beating on a drum. "Don't ye know yer own brother! Don't ye think he'll try anythin' and do anythin' not to go to England er be shipped out on another man-of-war! He's no fool! He'll hear the scuttlebutt in Halifax. He'll watch and he'll wait. Why that frigate he was on needed more scrappin' and more refittin' then anythin' I ever saw. And the whole time, Mike will be a'workin' and a'plannin'. There's practical nothin' else he kin do. Think a'what ye would do in his place, Bob."

Uncle Bob was taken aback by Ken's thoughts and his direct question. He rubbed his hands through his curly, red hair. "Well, I'll be damned! Mike's always been an honest man, praise be, but he's a Dooley. If I was in his place, I'd be da bloody crown prince by now."

"Now, yer gettin' it!" The old man urged Bob Dooley on by doing a little jig in front of him.

"Why, I'd be buyin' more rum fer more information den ever in me life. I'd find out which ships were sailin' inta da St.

Lawrence and I'd make meself da most loyal Britisher son of a bitch dat ever was born ta St. Georgie!"

"That's it! That's it!" Ken screeched with delight.

"Why I'd be da best dammed carpenter dey ever did see. Or I'd offer me services ta da Admiralty or da foreign office boys and say dat I was da best spy dey could ever want, an' knew da North country betterin' any Injun scout dey could ever hire. I'd make up such a whopper of a lie dat dey would t'ink I was runnin' fer president on da Federalist ticket. I'd sneak behind dere lines an' cut dere hoses, aha! Ha! Ha! Ha!

Uncle Bob and Captain Ken laughed until they noticed that Michael hadn't joined them in their mirth. "Don't ya see, boyo, da Captain's got it right. Yer fadder was better at foolin' people den even I was, until he got da code an' amended his life, praise be."

Michael was incredulous. "But he's an American. How could he act that way. How would anybody trust him?"

"No, boy." Ken put his arm on Michael's shoulder. "He's not an American. He's a British sailor. He was taken before the war, remember?"

Slowly, Michael drew up a wizened smirk. He had always known his father to be good, and industrious, and honest; a man that couldn't lie. But, this was different. He was behind enemy lines, and by England's own reckoning, one of their own. "Yea," Michael said, seeing the sense to it all, "remember when they took him off the *Mary Lynn*? 'Always an Englishman,' that British officer said.

Chapter 13

GOOD HUNTING

It had been a month since the *Chasseur* left her berth at Fells Point. And by this time, everyone had become accustomed to the regularity of shipboard life. At the outset of the voyage, the men who sailed the ship were divided into the larboard and starboard watches. Everything on board ship revolved around this rotating division. The first watch is at eight o'clock in the evening and stretches for four hours until midnight. It is called the "first watch" because that was the time when hammocks were hung and the rest of the crew prepared to go to sleep, those working the ship at this time were the first one's to "watch." And watching is important on a ship at sea. It is the only way of warning the rest of the crew of possible dangers from a fire, a storm, another vessel, and the murky perils of seas be they charted or unknown.

But, this division constantly interrupts a sailor’s rest. For, at midnight, the second or "middle watch" rises to relieve the first. This lasts another four hours, until four in the morning, when it is relieved by men (formally of the first watch) who make up the "morning watch." At eight o'clock, the "forenoon watch" comes up, and then at noon, the "afternoon watch" works the ship until four in the afternoon.

This drudgery is changed once a day. From 4PM to 8PM, two "dog watches” are set up. In this way the larboard and starboard watches don't continually work the same hours. To measure the time on watch, each half-hour is noted with the clanging of the ship's bell. Happy was attempting to explain all this to Michael one Sunday afternoon. He had managed to hobble up from the sick bay, using Michael as a crutch.

"And then they knocks off and break out their mess kids till nine o'clock when they go back t'work. In the meantime, I does whatever drill or exercises the officers tell me t'do till I go to my top in the afternoon watch at 12 o'clock." Michael was beginning to understand - sort of.

"That's when the captain and the other officers perform the noon sighting."

All of the officers of the *Chasseur*, including Captain Ken and Mr. Henry, gathered at noon with their sextants to record the noon sighting. This was extremely important, when no charted land was in sight, because it gave the ship's latitude. By looking through the sextant's half mirror the observer can measure the angle between the horizon and the sun at its zenith. First, the sextant is leveled to bring in the horizon, then the sun is brought into focus. This angle is added to the sun's declination listed in the ship's almanac. Michael and Jessica had both learned to "shoot" the sun with a sextant at St. Patrick's Free School. Now, Jessica was getting the chance to take the measurement at sea, along with the other officers, and Michael found himself feeling a little jealous.

"I 'erd Mr. 'Enry's faster at 'es calculatin' than any of the other offeecers, includin' Captain Boyle. Everybody's talkin' 'bout how 'e kin figur' without usin' a slate."

"Why doesn't that surprise me," Michael moaned. "Forget about that, Happy, go on with the watches."

"Well, let's see. After I gets relieved at four o'clock, I goes and gets my supper till five. Then from five to six, I knock off t'do whatever ole 'Appy 'as a mind to till I'm called for the second dog watch, from six till eight. After 'at, hammocks is sent down, and 'Appy is sound asleep till they calls me at midnight. So, on the first day, I 'ad the first watch, but on the second day, I 'ad the middle watch. Now, what could be plainer then all 'at?"

"Since they already have the crew split into the larboard and starboard watches, why don't they just have one watch work during the daytime and one work at night? Wouldn't that be much simpler?"

"Well, now I never thought about 'at, mate. But if theys do 'at then ole' Jack would be fallin' off the yards as regular as a parson sayin' 'es prayers, especially when the weather is foul and it takes all your strength just to hang on. The more time a tar spends aloft, the bigger the chance 'e as an acceedent. 'Sides, mate, what would I do wit' all 'at time t'myself when I was off watch? Why I'd get drunk. Now, every man Jack is partial to 'es grog, Michael, I'd be the first t'admit. But too much grog and workin' in the top is askin' for a fall. And when a Jack falls 'e either hits the water or the deck. If 'e hits the water and they can fish 'im out, then all's well and good and 'e goes back to 'es top wit'out sayin' a word t'man nor Savior. But, if there's a runnin' sea, or if 'es got a line round 'es neck to weigh 'im down, or if the ship's runnin' large an' fast, well, most Jacks can't swim t'save their soul. And by the time a boat's been let out the man is gone. And if 'e hits the deck without fallin' inta the lovin' arms of a sail on the way down, then there's nothin' t'be done but to throw 'im over and say a prayer. Besides, mate, workin' twelve hour watches just ain't civilized. One watch would be forced t'work all days and the other all nights. Now, how fair is 'at, I ask ya?"

Michael sighed. It was obvious he was no sailor. "I understand, Happy, at least about the watches and all, but I don't think I'll ever quite enjoy the life of a seaman. It's sounds so exciting when you hear the sailor's stories and all, but to do the same thing day after day, I'd get bored."

"Why, don't you do the same thing day after day at the cooperage?"

"Yes, I do, but I see different people, and I eat different foods, and I get a good night's sleep. Life on ship is like living the same day, over and over."

Happy looked insulted. "Why, ya don't know what you're talkin' bout, mate. Don't ya see? 'At's the beauty of it all. I don't 'ave to make any decisions. Everythin', down to the smallest detail, is already taken care of for me. I don't 'ave to think on anythin', really. Just do my job and do it right. What better life can there be for a man? On Monday, we do our laundry. On Tuesday, we sew our clothes. On Wednesday, we air the bedding and wash the hammocks. On Thursday, more sewin' and mendin'. On Friday, we do our laundry again. On Saturday, we wash ourselves. And on Sunday, we read, or write letters to send home, or play the pipe, or just talk. And we appreciate the time we 'ave because it's not commonplace. If we 'ad more time, the days would drag on and on. It's because were so busy 'at we don't take notice. Ahh, I'll tell ya, mate, ya just can't get a better life then 'at."

Michael looked around him and saw the sailors at their leisure. They truly looked like they were enjoying themselves. Sunday was their day, without officers to harass them and bark at them to go about their duties. Some were leaning with their backs against the rails, chatting to their mates about their last voyage and how they fared in prize money. A few had their Bibles and were either reading to themselves or reading to small groups that encircled them. The marines, on the other hand, appeared to be bored and anxious. They walked about aimlessly or huddled about the waist, which was their turf on board ship. Unlike the sailors who got the most out of the time allotted to them, the marines, were cursing up a storm over their lack of privacy or taunting each other, enmity filling their voices.

Michael left Happy and walked down to the waist to see his uncle. Bob Dooley was walking amid the throng of marines, his head bent low. Michael assumed his uncle was still embarrassed by his silly contest and all the fuss it caused Captain Boyle and Captain Ken.

"Hello, uncle. May I have a word with you?"

Uncle Bob lifted his eyes and looked at his nephew, his head still bent low. Michael noticed that his uncle was sweating.

"Are you okay, uncle? You don't look well."

"Well? Of course I'm not well, boyo. I haven't had a drink dese many days. This is no time ta sober up. We'll be fallin' onta a ship any day now, any minute now, and I can't even hold me arm out straight." He lifted up his arm and held it out, momentarily. The long fingers of his powerful right hand were shaking badly. He curled them up into a fist and smacked his opposite hand with a loud crack.

"Why does your hand shake so, uncle?"

"Why? Oh boyo, please don't ever take up da drink. After awhile it owns yer soul. But that's me problem and I deserve every bit of it. But, Lord, if we should befall a ship, and me have ta lead da men in me condition. Why, I'd shoot meself in da foot."

Michael reached out for his uncle's sweaty hand and pulled him aside. "Go see Dr. Williams. Ask him to give you something to help you stop shaking". Michael peered into Bob Dooley's bloodshot eyes and noticed the black, heavy circles underneath them. "Uncle, when's the last time you slept?"

"Not fer a week."

"Then inform the doctor of that, too. He can help you. In the meantime, you've got to do something for your men."

"Me men? Whatta ya mean me men?"

"Look at them. They're like a keg of powder waiting to explode."

"But dat's 'xactly how I want dem ta be, lad. Why dere more ready fer a fight den I ever saw any group of men before."

"Ready to fight each other, maybe." Michael pointed at a group of sailors, busy with needles or stretching out on the deck beyond the foremast. "Look at them, uncle. Do you know why they appear to be so relaxed?"

"Because dere lazy, good for nothin' tars."

"No, because they are relaxed. The reason they're so relaxed is because they've been working hard all week. The week skipped by so fast for them, cause they haven't had time to think about anything but sailin' the ship. Now, look at your men. Their ready to pounce on each other the minute one of them says a cross word. You've got to get them organized into daily activity, you know, keep them busy or you'll have them at each other's throats." Bob withdrew his hand from the boy and brushed it through his matted red hair.

"Ah, Michael darlin', if only I had a nip ta straighten out me thoughts." The Irishman glanced down at his nephew and smiled. "All right, den, lad. Let's go and see what Captain Ken has ta say about all dis. Me poor head is twirlin' like one a t'ose hoops ya used ta play wit' up and down da bloody street all day."

Captain Ken was on the quarterdeck instructing Mr. Henry in navigation. Bob left Michael and approached Captain Russell. The quarterdeck was sacred turf, reserved for officers only, and Michael was not permitted to walk upon it. He felt a sudden gush of jealousy watching his friend, Captain Ken, lecturing Mr. Henry. They each had a copy of Bowditch's *The New American Practical Navigator* in their hands.

Why couldn't that have been him up there, he thought. Why couldn't he be learning the art of sailing from knowledgeable and practiced hands? Why did it have to be her? He should be jealous in any case, but why Jessica? Thank goodness Desiree had no knowledge of this. She would have been proud of him if he had been the master's mate, sailing the ship into battle, sailing the *Chasseur* right up the Chesapeake for everyone to see. Suddenly, Michael felt a pang of guilt. "Know what you *ought* to desire," he whispered.

Uncle Bob was talking to Captain Ken, pointing his finger in Michael's direction. The old man nodded in assent, but then put up a stubby finger under Bob's nose in warning. He must be telling him "no prizes," Michael mused. Mr. Henry cautiously lifted her blue eyes and peeked at Michael. Michael pretended not to notice Mr. Henry's glance, but out of the corner of his eye, he did notice Mr. Lugger. The boatswain was standing with his arms behind him aft the mainmast on the starboard side. The favorable wind that had taken the *Chasseur* so far north in so short a time stung Michael's face, but the fridgid stare of Mr. Lugger's eyes was colder still. Michael looked back at Mr. Henry, to see why Mr. Lugger was paying so much attention to the master's mate. Mr. Henry slowly picked her head up from her manual again, to get another look at Michael. Lugger followed Mr. Henry's gaze. For a brief moment, Lugger and Michael locked eyes. Michael remembered James, the gun captain, and his advice: "Jest look at him sideways." Michael knitted his brow and stared, severely, back at Lugger. The boson opened his mouth and was about to bark an order, when he suddenly broke eye contact and quickly moved forward.

"All right, boyo, Captain Ken says it's a good idea. 'Specially after I told him you t'ought of it."

For two weeks, the *Chasseur* sailed off of Newfoundland with no luck. Boyle was becoming impatient. Captain Ken was with Mr. Henry in the sailing master's cabin when they heard a knock at the door. For the sake of Jessica's privacy, Ken had hung a blanket that separated the small cabin in two. Upon hearing the knock, Mr. Henry grabbed the blanket, pulled it down, and untied and stowed the rope it hung on. Captain Ken waited for his mate to take a seat on her sea chest and pick up a book before he gave his permission for the knocker to enter. It was David, Captain Boyle's steward.

"Beg'n yer pardon, sirs. Cap'n Boyle's compliments. He was wonderin' if you've had yer breakfast yet."

"Good mornin', Davey ol' boy," Ken said from his cot. "Inform the cap'n that we would enjoy nothin' better so long as the coffee's hot."

David beamed, "Oh, it's hot, sir. You know the cap'n would have me clapped in irons if it wasn't." David was a robust youth of about fifteen years. His aim was to please Boyle at all times. This, because Thomas Boyle had found the boy, when he was only ten, begging in the streets of New York for an unscrupulous old thief who beat the boy if he didn't bring back enough money to suit him. Boyle had noticed the boy's black eyes and puffy jaw. He also noticed the boy's insistence in obtaining the alms he was pleading for. After a few discerning questions, Boyle was able to put the boy's history together and offered him a job on his ship. Since that time, David had taken pains to discover the elegant tastes of his captain, and the boy worked to keep his captain in fine, regal style.

David also paid a great deal of attention to his own personal grooming. This morning he was dressed in a white, ruffled blouse, a deep blue jacket, white knickers and stockings, and brass buckled shoes. His face was clean and displayed a handsome, chiseled chin, deep set, brown eyes, and light, blond hair that he had tied neatly in a queue that was set off with a blue ribbon to match his jacket. Captain Ken dismissed him. But, before David made his exit, he bowed, exquisitely, to Mr. Henry.

"My, he certainly knows his manners," Jessica remarked after the steward had gone.

"That he does miss - Mr. Henry - it's his job. The cap'n has fancy tastes and likes to be surrounded by fancy things. I ain't go no appetite fer that sort of thing. C'mon. Git yer coat. I've a feelin' the cap'n's got sometin' on his mind this mornin'."

"Enter." Captain Ken and Mr. Henry opened Captain Boyle's cabin door and took in the sweet scent of Brazilian coffee. "Ah, good morning, gentlemen. Please help yahselves to the coffee and take a seat." Dining with Captain Boyle was a rare treat. Not only was the food and drink at the captain's table of superb quality, but Boyle himself was delightful company. Yet, the captain of the *Chasseur* was for the most part, a private man, given to reading and letter writing to his wife, children, and friends. This was the first time this voyage he sent an invitation for anyone to dine with him. Jessica was anxious and excited. She drew in a sudden breath upon seeing the finely appointed cabin. Delight beamed from her blue eyes.

"I see you have an eye for the better things in life, Mr. Henry."

"Oh, I apologize, captain, I couldn't but help admire your taste in furnishings."

Captain Boyle waved his hand in the air, "Tut, tut, Mr. Henry, don't apologize, please. Many a man has entered this cabin and seen its comforts, but a lady's eye is more discerning and appreciative. It's true my little luxuries are, in part, a personal vanity. Ostentatious as it is, however, my wife actually decorated this cabin and, hence, being here brings me a little closer to her when I'm away." Captain Boyle drew a chair to the table and motioned for her to sit down. "Well, now, the hands are quite busy and despite the terrible reputation that ship life has for keeping a secret, I believe we can address each other as God intended. David, my steward, is the soul of discretion. He is aware that we have a woman on board, so do not bother to conceal the fact from him as he attends us." With that a gentle knock was heard on the door. "Enter."

Jessica saw David come in and place delicate trays upon the table full of cheese and pastries. She remembered the elaborate bow that the steward had given her this morning, and she knew now why he had given it. Still, she never really thought of herself as a woman. A girl, yes, a young lady, perhaps, but not as a woman. Not as a woman who would be at the receiving end of an elaborate bow from a gentlemen. It was the same bow Michael had practiced in front of her in the kitchen of the Dooley house, when he announced he was having tea at Desiree Pechin's. But that was silliness on Michael's part, heartbreaking silliness, and this was - was what? Besides, Michael never paid that kind of attention to her. In fact he rarely paid her any mind at all.

Jessica could feel David's presence as he attended to them at the table. When he was finished, he stood behind Captain Boyle's chair. Since Jessica sat directly opposite to Captain Boyle, she could not help but glance at him occasionally. David, although thoroughly attentive to his duties, could not help but do the same.

"Tell me Miss Farmer, for I am most curious, how does it feel to be master's mate on board my ship?"

"I'm enjoying it immensely, sir."

"It appears that you are. Captain Russell tells me you are comin' along nicely. He has complimented you on your sailing ability. Isn't that so, Ken?"

Captain Ken slurped from his cup and placed it on the table. David was quick to refill it. "I did indeed, Tom. A most prominsin' prospect if ever I saw one. Father John was right to recommend you, Jessica."

Jessica smiled, and not just for the praise from the two remarkable seamen, but from the fact that she was being addressed without deceit. It felt good not to pretend. It felt good to be herself again. She finished her cup and David was at her side, gently pouring more of the delicious brew. Suddenly, Jessica realized another joy from deep within herself: it felt good to be a woman. It felt good to be paid attention to.

"Thank you Captain Ken. That is most kind of you."

As they ate their breakfast, Captain Boyle and Jessica discussed the schooner's best points of sailing. But as they finished eating, Ken brought more serious matters into consideration.

"Listen Tom, we haven't had much luck in these waters. Isn't it about time we moved on?"

"You've known me too long, Ken. I've been thinking about that for the last couple of days. I'm yearning to sail east and play with the English in the channel, but the ships we take here we can send into American ports. Once we cross the Atlantic, it'll be a different story. Yes, there's good hunting over there, I know. But then we'll be obliged to send in our prizes to France, and you know how risky that can be. Besides, I'd hate to leave Canadian waters without having made my mark."

"You're mark has been made a dozen times over, Tom."

"Yes, but not in the *Chasseur*. If we leave now, the men will think me wanting in the allocation of the good Lord's blessings."

"You mean they'll think ye lost yer luck."

"It's not just them, Ken. Every sailor is born to superstition. We're no exception. Besides, the men are in good humor. They go about their business without complaint. It would be a pity to dampen that."

"It would be a pity to risk reprovisionin' the ship before we make the crossin', too. Now's the time to move on, Tom."

"I will give the matter more thought, suh. You know, it's a queer thing. I was raised in New England. It seems men think faster or act faster there than they do in the South."

"I believe that is because of the climate, sir," Jessica suggested.

"By God, I think that's true. In any event, I've been a Southerner these many years, and as such, I have the right to act..." Boyle leaned back searching for the right word. He refused to say "slowly."

"Deliberately," Jessica ventured. Both men laughed.

"Indeed! A captain's prerogative, my dear. By the way, Ken, how is the Irishman?"

"You'll be glad ta hear he's sober, sir. Only he's got the shakes so bad he kin hardly stand it."

"I suggested, captain," Jessica said to Boyle, "that he visit Dr. Williams."

"My goodness, Ken, are all the girls at St. Patrick's this intelligent and this charming?" Jessica dropped her head and blushed. She raised her eyes only to notice David admiring her, and blushed, again.

"It's not just the girls, Tom. Father John knows how to raise these youngins' with proper horse sense. Michael Dooley is as sharp a boy as I ever did know. He knows his uncle better'n anybody. He's already directed his uncle to the doctor. And, that's not all. The marines have become lazy and sour headed. But Michael's gettin' Bob Dooley to start drillin' them proper. Ah, if only you could'a knowed his mama. By God, she was a fine woman." Suddenly, Jessica felt a pang of guilt as the vision of Teresa took hold in her mind. Lately, she hadn't thought about Teresa at all. She had never been away from Fells Point before. It seemed like years since she had polished the hope chest with the two hearts. A loud rap at the door made the vision of the hope chest disappear.

"Enter."

It was Mr. Lugger. "Pardon me captain, Mr. Leib's watch, sir. He told me to tell you a sail's been sighted under our lee."

Everybody rose at once from the table. Captain Ken and Boyle darted out the door. Jessica saw that David was bowing to her as she left. She also saw Mr. Lugger's cold eyes. She had to pass by him to get out the door and follow the others. As she neared the door, he seemed to hover over her.

Jessica turned to the steward. "My compliments to you, David. What a pleasant breakfast." She turned quickly to the boson and met his stare, at once adopting the persona of Mr. Henry. "Come, Mr. Lugger, surely the captain will have need of us on deck."

Chapter 14

"BLOOD AND CRUSHED APPLES"

"Where away, Mr. Leib?" Captain Boyle shouted up the companionway. The fist officer turned to see his captain hurl himself onto the main deck. Boyle's eyes were bulging, his mouth agape. For a moment, Leib could swear he saw his commander salivating.

"The deck's just been hailed, sir." Leib cupped his hands and bellowed angrily at the direction of the lookout "On the forem'st! Where away!"

"Good God!" Boyle cried, "where's his eyes! Has she seen us?"

Leib's own eyes were straining forward, scanning what could be seen of the horizon from the disadvantage of being on the quarterdeck. But on the top of the foremast an inexperienced topman was busy counting. "On deck! - ten, no twelve - fifteen sail!"

Boyle swung round and barked up at the foremast. "Damn you!"

The marines crowded the waist as news of the sighting reached every corner of the schooner. Uncle Bob grabbed Michael by the back of the hips and lifted him, effortlessly, atop his shoulders.

"Does ya see anythin', boyo?" Michael cupped his hands around his eyes to shield them from the scrap of sun in the east. He shook his head. "Nothing, uncle. Nothing but sea."

Boyle's face became contorted with anger. "Damn your eyes! Where away?" Before the lookout could respond, Boyle jumped down into the waist from the quarterdeck. He ran forward. On the crowded deck, men scurried to get out of his way. They saw the fierceness in his eyes. The sailors, to a man, knew what was wrong.

"Poor, stupid boy, he'll learn the hard way" one old hand said to another. Boyle seized the ratlines and scurried up to the foremast.

"My glass, Mr. Leib. My glass!" his fading, but still deep, invective voice bellowed as he climbed up over the top. He vaulted the fighting top of the foremast and bumped into the lookout who staggered back and screamed out in dread. Boyle reached out and managed to fill his right hand with the man's shirt just before he fell. The lookout's feet had already left the platform; his eyes bespoke the fate of landing on the hard deck below.

"Jaysus!" Uncle Bob cried as the ship's company looked up to see the lookout's back and arms and legs sprawled out above them. A collective and raspy gasp wound round the main deck as the crew drew in its breath. But the lookout had his back to them, and what they couldn't see was the lacy cuff of Boyle's jacket and his mighty hand bring the lookout back onto the platform. It was as if the man moved vertically in mid air. They did, however, hear the crack of an open hand across the lookout's face.

"You infernal lubber! The helm said where away!" Boyle still had the lookout by the shirt, threatening to strike again. The man stretched his shaking finger two points off the leeward bow and Boyle let him fall to the platform.

David came into the top and Boyle yanked the glass out of his hands. In seconds, the captain's attitude changed as he raised his glass and caught sight of the convoy. The northeast horizon was full of sail, but the captain had no intention of counting them. He smiled at David and winked his eye.

"Good boy, Davey." Boyle jerked his head at the lookout, still lying on the platform.

"Now instruct this man down," he said, blinking an eye.

Boyle poked his head over the top and smiled at his first officer. "Take her inta the wind, Mr. Leib, and call all officers inta my cabin. We'll resume the hunt at a safe distance."

The lookout was Jhoel Rose, a new deck hand who had taken Happy's place as topman. He didn't quite look every bit of his seventeen years, and managed to be aboard only because his father was one of the members of the cartel that launched the *Chasseur*. To Boyle, the young Rose might as well have been his father. It wouldn't have mattered to the captain who he was. Boyle would strike anyone who risked the safety of his ship. It was vital to position the privateer on the windward gage of the convoy so as to be able to strike when the hunter wished to and not before. It was also important to tail behind the merchant ships, at a distance where the *Chasseur* could not be seen so as to gain the advantage of surprise. But before these things could happen it was necessary to know where the other ships were in relation to the *Chasseur*. Not only prize money was at stake here, but the very lives of everyone aboard ship. Those lives require the sharp eyes of a lookout and the sharp mind of the privateer's captain, or officer of the watch, to work in tandem, as if they were the eyes and mind of the same person. What Jhoel didn't understand was that it's the mind that tells the eyes what to do, and the mind demands an immediate visual response. But Jhoel had been too excited about the additional shares he would receive for sighting the convoy. He also wanted to be the one to report the wonderful sight of multiple sail to captain and crew.

On the way down the ratlines, David laid a gentle hand on the topman's arm and whispered, alternately, in his ear. "The captain's already forgotten about this incident... You should too...But learn from it...When he hails the lookout, answer sharply and honestly...Don't hesitate or try to think...Just answer the question that's been asked...They'll be another chance fer you...Don't feel ashamed...Feel like you've learned the best lesson of yer life." Before they came over the bulwark, Jhoel blinked back tears and stared into the compassionate, walnut colored eyes of the captain's steward. David smiled and nodded his head. Jhoel took a deep breath and nodded back.

Captain Boyle clapped his hands together and rubbed them in delight. All of the officers were crowded into his cabin, save for Mr. Leib who had the watch.

"Very well, Captain Russell, do you agree with my location?" Ken was pouring over the charts on the long table.

"Aye, sir, and the noon sightin' should bear us out, I think. The convoy's headin', as expectin', on the current, the most direct route this time of year." In the early part of the year, ships could sail by the most direct route from North America to England without fear of melting ice drifting south. Boyle turned to Jessica, bestowing on her a fatherly grin.

"First crossing, Mr. Henry?"

"Yes, sir. Are we sailing to England, then?" Jessica replied, innocently.

"England?" Boyle was seated at the head of the table full of charts and instruments. "Why, yes, in manner of speaking. But with God's help not all of us, Mr. Henry, not all of us." The seasoned officers exchanged knowing nods and chuckled at their captain's response.

"In a little while we'll start our pursuit of the convoy, who, I wager never saw a spar of the *Chasseur*, and follow their most deliciously, predictable path to jolly old England. But I can't see why we couldn't divert a few of them before they reach their destination."

"Excuse me, sir, but when would be the best time to divert them?" Jessica's honest face and sincere demeanor was the only reason the rest of the officers didn't burst out in laughter.

"The hunter must be patient, Mr. Henry," Boyle said with a smile.

"Likely the convoy's has an escort, cap'n." Ken interjected.

"Yes, Captain Ken, they were hull down, but I'd wager a small frigate was in attendance. And so, Mr. Henry, with a British man-of-war to guard their precious merchant ships, our plan will be to wait for a natural diversion."

Uncle Bob suddenly became aware of the gist of the conversation. "Captain, darlin', da clouds comin' in from da west, is dat da diversion your honor is waitin' fer?"

"Indeed, Captain Dooley. The glass is down and every seaman on board can smell a storm. A whopper I think. Captain Russell?"

"Aye, sir. My bones is hurtin' all over. We'll be down to practical no sail at all, scuttin' before this un comin' along."

"Quite right, Captain," Boyle agreed, "those fat merchantmen will scatter far and wide. Hopefully, we'll steer a safe course from their armored friend." Boyle clapped his hands and rubbed them again, utter joy beaming across his face.

"A glass of wine before the storm, gentlemen. David see to it." This was highly unusual. Boyle rarely entertained. His officers shared side glances and raised eyebrows. David rolled a cart into the cabin full of a variety of wines from all across Europe. In moments, the finest crystal glasses were clinking and toasting success around the table. Ken grabbed Uncle Bob's glass out of his hand and put it on the table, but Boyle picked it up and offered it back to the delight of the Irishman.

"Gentlemen, this is indeed most prodigious, so I'll suspend punishment in recognition of the occasion," Boyle said in earnest, taking the time to look at each one of them in the eyes. "God almighty, just think of our luck. A storm and a convoy!" Boyle stood and raised his glass. "To President James Madison." Chairs shuffled back as the rest of the table stood at attention and joined the toast.

"To President James Madison," they echoed. Bob Dooley made sure everyone had started to drink first before he brought his glass to his parched lips, closed his eyes, and let the entire contents of the glass pour down his throat.

****

Michael sat between two apple barrels with his knobby knees supporting a tablet upon which he was writing to Father

John. An inkstand stood on top of the barrel to his right. He precariously raised his arm, pen in hand, and dipped the quill tip into the purple-black ink.

"A sailor's life is not for me. Today, Mr Lugger had the crew paint and then repaint the long boats, even though everyone knew a storm was coming and the paint will just wash away. I don't know Father, but if I ran the cooperage like they run this ship, I'd be out of business in a month. Happy, a sailor friend of mine, says it's customary to keep the men on board a ship constantly busy, even if the work they are doing is senseless. He claims it keeps them from going mad on long voyages. Is that why you sometimes have us do the same problems over and over again on our slates? I wonder.

"Anyway, there is very little to report from the *Chasseur*. Every day seems so much like the rest. I've retaken my position as powder monkey on the bow chaser. The captain of the gun is a man named James, who I think you would like to meet." Michael puckered his lips and tapped his pen on the side of the barrel a few times before redipping it and continuing.

"I said I've retaken my position, because coming out of the bay I had a little accident. Don't worry, the wound has healed nicely and everyone else on board is in good health. As I said, there's a storm coming and the sea is a little rough so please forgive me if my writing is a little sloppy. Uncle Bob says the storm is a blessing, since we sighted a large convoy heading toward England and the storm is supposed to drive the ships apart. He says after the storm, we have a good chance to fall upon one of the merchant ships and take her as a prize. Provided, of course, that we sight a merchant ship and not a British frigate.

"Everybody is so excited about the situation. Even the marines are smiling and talking politely to each other. Everybody except Mr. Lugger. He's the boatswain and a strange sort of fellow. I'm worried about him with Jessica on board. I can't quite put it into words, but there's something wrong with Mr. Lugger. He's a sneak, of that I'm certain. I'm not making uncharitable judgments, Father. I've seen him spying on people. I've seen him looking at Jessica and I don't like it. James says to give Mr. Lugger a hard stare when he's looking at you for no good reason.

"Oh, while I'm on the subject of Jessica, Father, I must tell you that I don't understand what she's doing on this voyage. Should she 'ought' to be here?

"Anyway, if we take one of the merchantmen, I'll try to get this letter sent back home when the captain fits her out with a prize crew and sends her to a home port. It would be a blessing to get some of these people off this ship just so I could breathe in my hammock at night. And it's not only the crowded conditions that I find bothersome. It's the noise. Men are constantly coming in and out and up and down, because of their watches. Happy tried to explain the reasoning behind that to me as well, but I guess I'll always be a cooper's son and not a son of the sea.

"Father, please continue to pray for us. Pray especially for my father. Captain Ken says that my father is smart, and will try to make his way to Canada and the interior lakes. He says that will give him a fighting chance to escape to the American lines. It sounds like something worth doing. Even Uncle Bob thinks so..."

The *Chasseur* rolled heavily from stern to bow with heavy seas getting up behind her. Michael steadied the ink well and dipped his quill in one more time.

"I have to go now, Father. Don't worry, even if I am. I've been thinking about the code and am glad that I've followed it. We're going to take the merchant ships and make this war a costly one for King George. If we take enough ships, maybe, please God, we can force their hand and settle for peace. I hope that the spring brings triumph for our armies in the north. I pray my father will be there to greet them. And I pray for you and everyone back home. Give my best to Samuel and the Smith brothers. And please give my regards to Mr. Pechin. Tell his daughter, Desiree, that I shall write her soon, as well."

Michael capped the ink well and blew the ink dry on his letter. He gazed at the name he had just written: "Desiree." A smile came upon him. "She'll be so proud of me," he thought. "If we can get even one of these ships safely to port, it'll be worth six months work at the cooperage, maybe. She'll have to be impressed by that." He leaned back against the bulwark and closed his eyes. As he drifted off to sleep, another pang of guilt swept subtley over him, but he did not understand why.

The ship rolled up the crest from one wave and down into the trough of another with an accelerated rhythm. But to Michael, it was like being on the swing hanging from the strong branch of the old hickory in back of St. Patrick's Free School. He held onto the thought of Desiree in his mind, of her light auburn hair and her chestnut eyes. Before he fell asleep, his last conscious thought was of her squeezing his hand and giving him a knowing look.

The *Chasseur* was under double reefed foresail when the gale hit. At Boyle's instructions, Captain Ken directed a team of sailors in securing the guns by lashing the cannon across the portholes fore and aft and had all the ports closed and caulked. Lifelines were rigged on deck fore and aft to help sailors move about. These lines were the only things between them and being swept into the icy Atlantic. Anchors were held taunt with ring and shank painters. The caulkers were busy plugging leaks below and the carpenter had securely battened down the hatches. Only Boyle and Captain Ken were allowed to take the wheel, they being the most experienced hands, while a second helmsman was placed on the lee side of the wheel in order to prevent it from taking charge and spinning out of control.

Just experienced hands were permitted on deck, and that meant the marines were kept below where they would be out of the sailors way and where they could be organized into teams to work the pumps. A schooner - any ship - allows prodigious amounts of sea to swarm over her deck, even in the mildest of storms. And as the *Chasseur* dipped into ever deepening troughs and was emersed in seawater, there were audible and forbidding moans from the landsmen below deck.

"Cap'n Dooley!" screamed a shaken marine by the name of Donovan who was clinging to a mess table, "we're sure to go down in this tempest if we don't slow down! Why does da ship fly in da storm so?" The *Chasseur* was scudding before the storm, causing her to roll and yawl violently as she raced before the gale at some eight knots. Dooley had his huge arms clawed around another table and grimaced at the marine that was making all the fuss. Despite the storm, he was in fine spirits. As far as Bob Dooley was concerned, the ban against his imbibing alcohol was over, since Captain Boyle didn't actually specify how long punishment would be suspended. That meant he could look forward to a daily ration of grog, and whatever he could manage to sneak out of a prize ship that lay in the convoy a comfortable distance east of them. In addition, and quite to his surprise, he felt no seasickness.

"Don'tcha be worryin' about da *Chaser*, Dan Donovan. An' ta t'ink you were Irish. Behavin' like a schoolgirl at a time like dis. Ya t'ink you could do better takin' a trick at da wheel in dis hurricane! Why, ten of ya couldn't hold a wheel as steady as Ken Russell, even when he's a hundred years on dis ocean. Himself told me just dis afternoon, didn't he, dat he'll point da boat just off da waves so we don't have ta take da full brunt of it? An' you sit dere in a panic, as if we've been pooped. Get down to da pumps ya yella bellied son of a - hey! - " Bob's mouth went agape, "has anybody seen da boy?"

"He was makin' letters last time I saw him, cap'n," Henry Watson said, pointing aft, "down by the storeroom, only I think he dropped off after a bit and took hisself a nap." Watson was a stevedore, who joined Boyle's marines in Charleston where the *Comet* had refitted for a cruise.

Bob wrenched himself from the table and grabbed Watson by the back of his shirt, leading him forward. "Show me."

From the galley, whose stove was cold due the fact that ventilation was impossible during such high seas, they stumbled down to the storeroom. They both were hunched over, Bob's body bent almost perpendicular.

"He was right over there, cap'n," Watson said, pointing to where the apple barrels used to be. "Now if that don't beat all. He was squished between two barrels, writin' up a storm, but I don't even see where the barrels got to, now." Uncle Bob raised the lantern he was carrying and started for the opposite side of the storeroom. In place of what was supposed to be a locked compartment for the captain's stores was now a smashed in grating. Foodstuffs were scattered all over the floor. The smell of the room was thick with fresh apples.

"Michael! You in here?"

"Uncle, look out!" The voice came from above Bob's head and he lifted the lantern to it. But as he did so, and with the roll of the ship, he heard hundreds of apples tumbling over the floor planking toward him.

"Uncle, the barrel! Watch, its coming to you!"

In an instant, Bob realized the danger. Rolling over the apples was a sealed hundredweight barrel coming right toward him. He ran backwards, but being hunched over, he couldn't see Watson, who had followed him into the captain's storeroom. They both somersaulted over the planking and lay on the floor facing the oncoming barrel. Bob, instinctively, lunged for the barrel as it came toward them and caught it with his massive arms and hands. But not before it had bounced off his nose. Bob lay motionless on the floor, the barrel secure in his arms. The danger had passed and Uncle Bob had passed out.

"Michael, the lantern, quick!" Henry Watson shouted.

Michael jumped down from the shelf he had safely tucked himself into after being thrown across the room with the barrels when the gale hit the ship with full force. Fortunately, Michael hurled aft airborne, while the barrels simply rolled astern and crashed into the captain's storeroom. Michael acted quickly and saved the last two chickens for the captain's table before they were crushed in their coop. The open barrel unleashed its hold of apples everywhere. It was relatively simple for Michael to grab it and lash it down. The closed barrel, on the other hand, rolled with the ship, crashing into everything fore and aft with impunity. Until it met Bob Dooley's nose. Blood and crushed apples were everywhere.

Henry Watson looked down at the big Irishman. "Boy, fetch Doctor Williams."

Michael scampered up the ladder and aft to the doctor's cabin. Meanwhile, Watson was able to secure the sealed barrel with bundles of spent sail and had managed to jerk Bob's hands away from it. Doctor Williams brought a half dozen marines with him. But they couldn't lift Uncle Bob's massive frame out of the storeroom and up the ladder. A healthy Happy George mumbled something about incompetent land lubbers and sent for Captain Ken. Together they rigged a series of ropes and pulleys and lifted Uncle Bob, now on a litter, out of the storeroom and onto a galley table.

"Well," Doctor Williams breathed out after finishing a quick examination, "keep his head turned so he doesn't choke on his own blood." Watson carefully cradled Bob's immense skull and turned it sideways. Doctor Williams dabbed the small stream of blood that oozed from Dooley's nose. He looked at Michael who was still holding the lantern, and who stared down at his uncle with concern. "Don't fuss over him, son," the doctor said soothingly, "he'll recover nicely. It's not like the blow you took in the Chesapeake. But, upon my word, you Dooleys have a knack for falling out of consciousness. See," the doctor pointed at Uncle Bob, "he coming to now."

"Augh! Oh! Me poor nose. What was it doc, a whale dat hit me?" Bob Dooley gingerly got up from the table shaking his head. As he did so, his nose swung about like a door on hinges.

"Lie still, now Bob," Ken urged, but Bob brushed his hand away.

"Just let me be."

"Why you cantankerous Irisher. That barrel must'a weighed ten stone, mebee. You never in your life took a fist like that before," Ken chuckled. Bob looked confused.

"Barrel. What bloody barrel?"

"Don't you remember, uncle? You got hit with the apple barrel in the captain's storeroom. Or, you *hit it*," Michael said proudly. "I was writing a letter to Father John and I must have fallen asleep, when the ship lurched and threw me across the room. I was lucky to land before the barrel crushed me, and I jumped up on the top shelf with the last of the captain's chickens. But I couldn't get down, for fear of the barrel rolling with the ship and smashing everything in sight."

"It wasn't just the chickens what was saved down there," Henry Watson chimed in. "I want ta thank you, cap'n. I would'a been crushed if you hadn't gone for that barrel the way you did."

"I want to thank you, suhs, for saving my dinner." It was Captain Boyle, dripping in a tarpaulin jacket, smiling from ear to ear. "Mr. Conner's relieved us from the helm Captain Russell. I think the ship's out of danger now." Boyle examined Bob's face. "Well, rather a close one, hey Captain Dooley? Doctor Williams, I'll take your report," he said, still looking at Bob. The doctor gave his report while he dressed Uncle Bob's nose with a curious bandage that was wrapped around his head and that fastened his nose with a splint.

"I've cleared Harold George for active duty," the doctor began, "his leg has healed nicely. And, surprisingly, we took no major injuries so far in this storm. Now, as for this specimen, I think I can report your Captain of the Marine has a perfectly broken nose and an even more perfect sense of irony." Uncle Bob gave the doctor a stern glance.

"Whadda ya mean, doc? Why me senses have always been...hey!...who's an irony?" Doctor Williams couldn't help but smile.

"Come, come, Captain Dooley. You mistook my meaning, sir. But surely even you must see the humor in this situation?"

"Humor?" Boyle looked at his physician with questioning eyes.

"Yes, captain. The cooper being hit by his own barrel."

"Aha! Ha! Ha! Ha!" It was Captain Ken who laughed first, and then they all did, even big Bob Dooley.

"Just wait till my pa hears this one!" Michael chuckled.

Dawn the next day proved to be a glorious one. The sun rose off the shimmer of the North Atlantic revealing three unescorted merchant ships clumsily making their way in a stiff breeze. Captain Boyle clapped on as much sail as the schooner could handle. The little *Chasseur* skimmed across the water as lightly as the hearts of her sailors, who scurried up her windward rigging pointing with glee at their intended victims.

It was Jhoel on the foremast fighting top who had spotted sail at first light and answered, without hesitation: "broad off the starboard bow!" to Mr. Conner's question: "Where away!"

Michael's heart was light, too. He was in the waist with his mess kid munching on ship's biscuit and spooning hot, honey flavored oatmeal into his mouth. The rising sun, the prospect of a prize, and the oatmeal all offsetting the steady, but brisk, morning breeze. The *Chasseur* was flying down onto her prey. Jessica was at the helm with Captains Ken and Boyle, and Mr. Davis, who had the wheel. She looked down and spotted Michael and smiled. Then she glanced up at the foremast and saw David enter the top and shake hands with Jhoel. Captain Ken had told her about how Boyle often used his steward to calm the nerves of new recruits who had been scolded, or worse, for making mistakes as raw hands often do. The smile had left her face, but her eyes bespoke admiration as she watched David put his arms around Jhoel, who was chatting up a storm and gesturing at the horizon, obviously describing when he first caught sight of the merchant ships. She thought back at the way David had looked at her in the captain's cabin. She wondered if it would be improper for a master's mate to speak to the captain's steward.

As the storm finally blew out the night before, Captain Boyle had the *Chasseur* sail North by East in order to gain the weather gauge on the convoy. Having achieved this, there was little to do in the way of sailing other than pounce down on his targets, one by one. The headache here, for the captain, was purely administrative in nature.

"Captain Russell, as I said when we first shoved off, I don't want to lose you and your experience unless I can help it. I intend to bag all three of these fat prizes and send them into Maine - Bath probably. We have a decent agent there who can see to their adjudication. Does this sound reasonable to you suh?" This would have been unusual, for a captain of a ship to almost ask permission of a sailing master, but Boyle respected Captain Ken too much not to seek his opinion.

"Aye, captain, I've signed on for the duration. Remember my retirement. Might change ma mind though, iffin' you make this whole cruise as borin' as this mornin's' goin' to be. Man likes to feel a little fight from his catch now and again." Boyle showed his ivory white teeth and laughed.

"We've got them on the hook, Ken, but we still have to reel them in. Time to go to work. Pass the word for Mr. Leib." Leib came puffing up the starboard ladder to the quarterdeck. He was a bit pudgy and sported an expansive paunch owing to a weakness for German beer.

"Aye, sir,"

"We'll take the ship first, that big one, forward of the others. That'll convince the captains of the two brigs we mean business. But we're closing to fast. I don't want to shoot past her just yet. Reduce sail and beat to quarters." Leib gave his captain a knuckled salute.

"Aye, sir, reduce sail, beat to quarters." As the expected drum sounded, men scattered all over the ship making preparations. Marines gathered around Bob Dooley for instructions. The effects of the apple barrel had left Bob with two very black eyes and a swollen, red face. The white bandage circling his head and the splint supporting his nose gave the Captain of Marine a fierce look, much like an Indian warrior.

"Dis is it darlins'. If anybody fires a shot before I gives da word, I'll run 'em t'rough meself. Does ya feeble wits understand me? Good. Where's dat Dan Donovan wit' da weapons?" Donovan and a half dozen men made their way up the forehatch with the armament. The marines scurried to get the weapons that suited them best. "Sharpshooters ta da tops wit' rifles an' pistols. Careful now, lads, not ta step on da sailors toes, ya know how dat bodders dem. Tommyhawks, boardin' axes, pikes, an' steel ta da waisters. Go now boys, Patrick be wit' ya!"

Uncle Bob stuck pistols through his leather belt and clenched his long knife between his teeth as he tied a polka dotted handkerchief around the top of his monstrous head. Despite the knife, he grinned at the prospect of English blood.

Meanwhile, the *Chasseur* was alive with the grunting of men and the dull squeak of cannon being run out the ports. Smoke from matchboxes wafted over the deck as the gun crews readied themselves behind their cannon. Michael was at the bow, kneeling behind James, alternately poking his head up, peering over the bow to catch a glimpse of the merchant ship. The *Chasseur* had run up alongside the British ship almost within range of one of the long nines. Boyle looked, briefly, at his second mate.

"Mr. Davis."

"Aye, sir."

"Captain Russell will relieve you at the helm. Go to your starboard guns and put one close enough to her hull to demonstrate our intentions." Mr. Davis was in his late twenties and was a thorough seaman. But, he was also young and tended to get too excited under pressure.

"Mr. Davis!" The second mate came running back up to the quarterdeck.

"Aye, sir?"

"In your hurry to get to your guns, you neglected to provide Captain Russell here with the course." Davis quickly became red with embarrassment. No one, no one, was permitted to leave the wheel of a ship underway without first stating clearly and precisely what her course was. It might be considered useless information to the second mate, who knew the captain would change course in a few minutes anyway, and quite absurd to presume that Captain Ken wouldn't know what course to sail, but it was an institutional practice on any ship in the world and rigidly adhered to. A ship's heading can never be presumed, even in the middle of the Atlantic, where there was no danger from shoal or reef. Davis gave his Captain a knuckled salute and approached the wheel.

"Steer due East, Captain Russell." Ken smiled at the way Boyle handled his young officers. The rebuff not only reinforced a necessary practice, it showed the crew who was in charge, and being under unmistakable and competent authority when facing danger, any danger, has a calming effect on the nerves.

"Due East it is," replied Captain Ken.

"Pass the word for Mr. Lugger," the captain said over his shoulder as he walked to the lee railing. Lugger stepped up to the quarterdeck. Boyle stared deeply at the merchant ship wondering if she would put up a fight. He raised his glass to see if there was any activity on her deck. Without turning from the railing he addressed the boatswain. "Raise the colors, Mr. Lugger. Make sure they fly from the masthead before Mr. Davis' starboard gun fires."

"Stars and stripes, sir?"

"Yes, Mr. Lugger, look sharp now." Lugger raced to a chest on the lee side of the quarterdeck. At the top of the box was the flag of the United States, below that the flags of nine other nations, used alternately to disguise the true nature and nation of the *Chasseur*. Lugger hoisted the colors. As he was making the line fast, a starboard gun pierced the frigid morning air. Davis had set his sights well. The ball landed 50 yards off the merchant ship's weather quarter. Boyle lowered his glass and smiled.

"My apologies, Captain Russell. She's about to lower her flag. They'll be no fight this day. Mr. Lugger, get the gig ready."

"Aye, captain. The gig it is. Larboard watch prepare the captain's gig!

"As she heaves to, put us about, Captain Russell, if you please."

"Aye, captain, will take her inta the wind as she heaves to." Boyle turned toward the stern gun and pointed a finger at Mr. Davis.

"I don't want you to take all day, Mr. Davis. Timing is essential, do yuh get my meanin' mister?" Davis shook his head. "I want you to take a boarding party and secure that ship in fifteen minutes. That'll just give us enough time to get to the brigs before they think they can run away

"I'll be the prize master then, sir?"

Boyle had gone through a mental list of the *Chasseur's* officers and crew deciding on masters to sail the prizes to a home port. This was always a difficult decision since he needed capable sailors to take charge of the precious prizes and since, at the same time, the *Chasseur* would be depleting itself of talented men for the duration of their cruise.

"Yes, Mr. Davis. You'll do nicely if you pay attention to your duty and see the ship safely into Bath. Use your good judgment, suh. After I lay hold onta the brigs we'll rendezvous. Watch for the signal. I'll want to see the captain, ship's log, and a complete inventory of what's aboard. All specie is to be brought aboard the *Chasseur*. Any cargo that's valuable merchandise is to be transferred to our hold along with their crew. Is that unda'stood?"

"Yes, sir, all specie, valuable cargo, and crew to the *Chasseur* it is, sir." The ship had come about as did the *Chasseur*. The captain's gig was dropped over the side with an armed boarding crew. As soon as the ship was secured, Davis signaled Boyle and the chase for the brigs began. In two hours it was all over. Not a shot was fired. Hands were dismissed for dinner and Michael found Uncle Bob sitting in the waist and waving off the young Dooley's question.

"No! I'm not hungry."

"Well, I am, uncle. Taking prizes has made me powerful hungry. Why do you look so disappointed? Everything went so well today. And why are you wearing that thing on your head?" Uncle Bob reached up and snatched the polka dotted handkerchief from his head. His red curls hung down over his eyes.

"Dis is ta keep me sweat from gettin' in me eyes, or blood if I get a blow on da head." Bob glanced up at his nephew. "How can ya be hungry? We didn't even kill one Englishman? Jaysus, boyo, not even one little scrape. Dey just hauled down dere flag and surrendered wit' dere tail between dere legs like puppy dogs. Hah! Da mighty British Empire, indeed. A man can't work up an appetite when he's done no work atall."

Michael shrugged his shoulders and started for the galley. He turned back to his uncle. A question he had wanted to ask for months was now on the tip of his tongue.

"Why do you want to spill English blood so much?" Uncle Bob dropped his mouth in astonishment.

"An' wasn't it you, who requested ta be put ta sea soes ya could make da Britishers pay fer yer fadder's impressment? Whaddaya mean why do I want ta spill English blood? It's either dere's or ours, boyo."

"Yes, I know. But, uncle, these men who sail these merchant ships aren't the Royal Navy. They work hard, just like us, and try to raise families. You saw them as they came on board. They're like Happy. Why, Captain Boyle's having dinner with the masters of the prizes now, and in his own cabin. Is it their fault that their English? So, when we take three fat prizes in one day without spilling any blood, why, that's a good thing isn't it? It's hurting the commerce of England that's the point. That's why I went to sea. It's what I *ought* to..." Bob cut him short. His painful looking face wore an even more painful expression. He got up and walked toward the boy, towering over him.

"Listen ta me, boyo. Don't be lecturin' me on what I *ought* ta do an' what I *ought* not ta do."

For the first time in his life Michael was afraid of his uncle. Afraid of what he saw in his uncle's eyes. They were eyes without - without what? - he thought.

"Da code is not fer me. No, not fer me." He turned away from Michael and sat back down. "It can never be fer me." Bob raised his hands and opened his thick fingers. He sat there staring into his hands, his voice trailing off into a whisper. "I - I'm not like ya, Michael ... not like yer pa, neither ... I - I have no *ought* left in me ... I have no conscience." Michael waited for his uncle to continue speaking, but Bob Dooley's giant body sat motionless, except as it swayed with the motion of the ship. His eyes staring fixedly at his open hands.

Chapter 15

LESSONS LEARNED

The eight-gun ship *James* with hides, tallow, bark, and furs was sent into Maine along with brigs *Atlantic* and *Antelope*, which were carrying Havana sugar. As Boyle had instructed, all specie, which amounted to eleven thousand pounds, was taken aboard the *Chasseur*, as well as select furs, 47 prisoners, livestock, water casks, and as much Madeira wine as Bob Dooley could safely pilfer and stow away.

"With luck, Mr. Davis will reach Maine, all right." Boyle was sitting in his cabin with his fine, leather boots resting on a stool, and talking leisurely to Captain Ken. "Your retirement already looks pretty good, Ken."

"Ships and cargo worth a pretty penny, Tom. Knew yer luck would change. But the brigs are too slow. I'd venture they git no better than a fifty-fifty chance of making the coast. Makes ya laugh, though. The Britishers spend most of their time retaking their own merchant ships." Ken leaned back in his chair and put his hands behind his head. The two of them were silent. Years of sailing experience had taught them to pause now and again and listen to the creaking of masts and yards, and the groaning of cordage. Those sounds told them all they needed to know about wind and weather.

Ken broke the silence with a predictable question: "Where we haulin' ar wind ta now? What little there is of it." Boyle smiled - a sneaky, little smile.

"This is where the fun begins, my friend." Ken knew that smile. Something was up and he had the feeling the fun would begin immediately. "You don't mind if I play a little bit with that large Irish oaf of yours, do ya Ken?"

"I knew that you were up ta no good, Tom, but ah, what you got in mind?"

"David!" Boyle shouted. The door opened and David appeared, smartly dressed and groomed as always. "Pass the word for Captain Dooley."

"Yes, sir, Cap'n Dooley." After David left and was reasonably far enough out of hearing distance, Ken Russell leaned closer to Boyle.

"Okay, Tom, out with it."

"I unda'stood our prizes were outfitted with only the best Madeira, Captain Russell?"

"Aye, sir. Madeira they stocked up on before they left Europe, and rum, they picked up comin' in from South Ameriker," Ken answered, his stubby fingers playing with a few days growth of gray beard on his chin. "The Supercargoe, Mr. Hollingsworth, says the rum is all accounted for. No tellin' how much Madeira they had on board."

"And how much do ya think that Irishman has stowed away for his personal pleasure?"

"Now, Tom, give the devil his due, huh? Why he won't pull another stunt like he did befer, wit' that pissin' contest. The man is a swill, I know. Lord, how Teresa and Father John tried ta git him ta stop. But, he'll go plum crazy iffin' he don't take a drop out here wit' nuttin' ta do on the water. Why it's practical medicinal..."

"Easy, my friend," Boyle reached out and patted Ken on the knee. "I know that. I merely wish to have some amusement. In fact, I'm counting on his medicinal doses to create the proper sentiment I would like to affect." Captain Ken looked perplexed. "Ken, you know better than I, that this fellow wells up with emotion when matters of patriotism are addressed."

"Aye. He gets teary eyed when he's been drinkin' and talkin' of presidents and the like."

"Exactly. Some people feel that peculiar tinge up their spine more than others when matters of country and honor are discussed. And I'll wager that our Captain of the Marine will still have those same sentiments towards the country of his birth?"

"Why, he was very active in the Hibernians, back on the Point."

"Good. Then I think my plan will work." Bob Dooley knocked on the cabin door and, instinctively, stomped his feet, as if there were mud to be knocked off his boots in the middle of the Atlantic.

"Enter."

"You wish ta see me, yer honor?" Bob was still wearing the contraption around his bulbous nose that Doctor Williams had rigged up. The bandages were dirty now, smeared with black tar.

"I do indeed, Captain Dooley." Boyle kicked a chair in Bob's direction. "Here ya go, suh. Pull up a chair to the chart table, I want to show you something." All three captains sat close together around a formidable chart lying on the long oak slab that doubled as the captain's dining table.

"This is our approximate position, here," Boyle said, pointing to 50°N 30°W, about a thousand miles from the West Coast of Ireland. "My plan is to sail on this line," Boyle used his finger to draw an imaginary line across the chart, "and head for the Northwest coast of Ireland. My question to you Captain Dooley is this: In your judgment, where could we reasonably choose a safe harbor - an island harbor - to procure some fresh porter."

Up to this point, Uncle Bob had kept his mouth closed, for fear of letting out the smell of the Madeira he had secretly drank in the head. The head was the perfect place to sneak a drink. No one could smell anything but what is generally smelled in such places. So, the risk of uncorking a bottle in the presence of the sensitive noses of sober sailors was mitigated. But, more ingenious, to the minds of old sots like Uncle Bob, was the fact that he could dispose of the bottle simply by breaking it over the head and letting the glass slip into the sea. He couldn’t let the bottle drop into the head without breaking it first. Any sailor’s eye would spot an empty bottle bobbing on the surface of the water. But, when Bob heard the word "porter," he promptly dropped his jaw.

"Porter? Porter, is it? Captain, darlin', does ya have a particular love fer dat luscious brew?" Boyle and Ken turned their heads as the first waft of Madeira hit them at such close quarters.

"I do indeed, Captain," Boyle said, backing his chair to a safer distance. "I'm Irish, too, you know."

"An' a better one, praised be, never sailed a ship."

"Ah - thank you, Captain. But, I have an ulterior motive."

Ken, who had also backed away, was completely lost by Boyle's line of thought. He knew Boyle would never risk the *Chasseur* for anything as crack brained as a pint of porter, and that that was just having fun with Bob Dooley. In addition, the *Chasseur* was newly loaded with water and stores from the prizes; there was no need to put into port anywhere, let alone Ireland.

Uncle Bob, however, took the captain's notion, and his regard for black brew, very seriously. Boyle was about to explain his 'ulterior motive' when Uncle Bob interrupted.

"I once knew a pious man from home," he said, meaningfully, and 'home' meaning Ireland, not America, "who gave up his porter every forty days of Lent." He raised his thick forefinger as if to make a point. "He had no stomach for da whiskey, mind ya. All he loved was his glass of porter. He used ta cry himself ta sleep at nights, but not because he ached fer it as some do, but because he missed it so." Boyle cleared his throat. The look on his face suggested he doubted Uncle Bob's sanity.

"Be that as it may, my motive for finding safe harbor is to prove a point."

"A big one, I trust, sir." Ken wasn't too far from doubting Tom Boyle's state of mind, too.

"Yes, suh. I hope it will be. I had it in my mind after a discussion I had when *Comet* was in after my first cruise in her.

I had the opportunity to dine with Bill Pechin, sirs, the renowned editor?" Ken shook his head in acknowledgment.

"A fine, repubrican gen'elmen, but wit' a brat for a daughter, poor soul," Bob interjected.

"Yes... well, that may be but - but he put an idea in my mind that has taken shape on this voyage. I must impress upon you, gentlemen, that ideas, and the words that project ideas, are just as powerful a weapon as any army in the field or fleet in a line of battle."

"Yes, sir, the pen worse than the sword, isn't it?" Ken stated flatly, in agreement.

"Quite right, Captain Russell. 'Hinc quam sinc calamus saevior ense, patet.' From *Democritus to the Reader*, by Robert Burton, but I didn't know you for a scholar, Ken."

"Phooey! Scholars are folks with letters after their names. Better than a half a century at sea has left me time to read a library full of books, Tom. I was thinkin' on that book after we left the Point. Do ya remember the line "women wear the breeches...in a word, the world turned upside downward'?"

"Ah, yes. You were thinking of Mr. Henry, no doubt. Ha! Ha! Very good, suh, but to proceed. Burton knew, as Bill Pechin knows, that ideas are, perhaps, the most powerful tools of war. Now, follow me gentlemen. Pechin projects his ideas in the *American*. That's his vessel, if you will. I think it's time to project our ideas in our own vessel, the *Chasseur*." Ken leaned forward in his chair.

"What are you proposin', Tom? Do you wanna pass out some pamphlets ta the Irish? Git 'em to strike out at the British? I thought that was all through in '98?" In 1798 and again, in 1803, the United Irishmen broke out in rebellion, only to have the English crush the movement and hang its leaders.

"Pamphlets are no good," Bob said, remorsefully, "it's guns an' da French dey be needin', just like we did in America."

"No, no, gentlemen. Not pamphlets, although a proclamation might be in order, but not just yet. No, what I mean to accomplish won't help the Irish, unfortunately. The

Chasseur can do little for them, God help them. I'm talking about the blockade. The British claim, and their people believe, that the Royal Navy has blockaded the United States." Boyle grew red. "But, they have done no such thing. We still have an active coastal trade, to say nothing about hundreds of privateers and letters-of-marquee. They have the arrogance, and this is what bothers me most, to say that the Yankees are banished from the seven seas. That the oceans belong to them! As if God Almighty had declared it to be so!" Boyle thrust his hand down onto the table. "Let's show the world, especially the English people, that no such blockade exists! We'll take one of their islands, we'll tweak their beards with our proximity. We'll laugh at them! We'll blockade! Don't ya see? We'll turn the tables on them! Their newspapers will love it. One American ship blockading all of the United Kingdom."

Boyle looked at Uncle Bob, whose eyes were gaping wide, his forehead mopped with sweat, his enthusiasm and the Madeira pouring out of him. Captain Ken bent his head down low. He knew Uncle Bob had taken the bait. In fact, Ken, himself, had almost taken the bait. What a whopper, the old man thought. He held his face in his hands so that Bob couldn't see him trying not to laugh out loud.

"I'm wit' ya Captain!" Uncle Bob cried as he grabbed the chart. "Someplace safe...an island...northwest...no, no! Captain Boyle, sir, let's take a part of da island proper!"

"The island proper, suh? Why wouldn't that be - er - are you suggesting - just what are you suggesting Captain Dooley?" Uncle Bob pointed down to the chart. He was so excited his finger was shaking.

"There, sir! Donegal, sir. If yer honor wants ta let all Ireland know what we're up ta, we've got ta hit da island proper. If we take one of da little islands off da coast, who will know? T'ose people, poor souls, don't even know about America yet. Why dey only speak in da Irish. News would never get off an island like dat. Even if it did, nobody would believe dem. But if we start here, in Donegal, an' make some noise, why... an' den we can sail around da whole of Ireland an' take English prizes an' send some of dem back ta where dey came from spreadin' da news all over Ireland an' beyond, ta Scotland an' England itself. An' dis is safe, sir, scattered population, mountains here, sir."

Ken stopped laughing and picked his head up. Boyle stood up and scanned the chart in earnest.

"Me mudder's from a little village called Falcarragh, on da Northwest tip of da province of Ulster. She lived dere before me fadder, who sailed as a cooper, married her an' took her ta Cork. I spent many a summer day back in Falcarragh. Me mudder used ta get lonely fer her people, and she would take us boys ta visit me Uncle Liam.

"Dere are only t'ree ways ta get inta an' outta da place. We could bring some cannon wit' us an' hold 'em off fer a week, sir. Den sail outta dere pretty as ya please." Boyle swallowed hard. He glanced at Ken and motioned for him to stand with him and review the chart.

"He's right, Tom," Ken whispered. "By the Lord who made us, he's right. Arnold couldn't have thought of a more brilliant plan, not Washington neither, even John Paul Jones, by God."

"Do you really thing so, Ken? Can we pull it off? I love the daring in it, but..."

"Tom, he's right." Ken straightened his back and put his hands on his hips. "Cap'n Boyle, this will make history."

At that, Bob Dooley brought his fists to his eyes to wipe away his tears. Boyle had succeeded in making the Irishman sentimental and, at the same time, had come up with the most audacious plan of the war in the bargain.

"David!" Boyle roared. His steward poked his head through the cabin door. "Wine! The finest!" Boyle looked at Uncle Bob. The giant Irishman's eyes were still wet from the emotional twinge that screamed up his spine and seized his being. Boyle suddenly realized this was more than sentiment. It was inspiration. "My apologies, Captain Dooley. I'm sure the joke is on me. I've learned a lesson."

"Joke, sir?"

"Never mind, Captain Dooley." David came in with a tray full of tinkling bottles and crystal. The *Chasseur's* Captain had intended only to have some fun with Bob Dooley. Boyle's feelings about the blockade were expressed honestly enough; but the idea of taking an Irish island was just an amusing proposition meant to get the big Irishman excited. Now, all that silliness was erased by Uncle Bob's sincerity.

The cabin was suddenly filled with an intense aura. David noticed it when he came into the room and started filling glasses. All three captains wore deep, contemplative expressions. To them, the cruise was never just a financial expedition. Making money was primary, true enough. They owed that to the syndicate that sponsored them. But they each felt the national importance of privateering; they knew its value as a weapon of war. Now, that importance magnified. Each of them was cognizant of a higher gain. A reason for them to be together on a ship bound for adventure and glory. It is the unexplainable feeling of purpose - of personal destiny.

For a time each of them played with their wineglasses, basking in the joy of the moment. Even Uncle Bob hesitated to drink. An old, but comforting thought was making its way through his mind. He suddenly realized that this is exactly where he should be. That what he had proposed was what he *ought* to do. He hadn't had that feeling of certainty in decades. Not since he left Ireland. And now he was coming home. Coming home to the truth.

Tom Boyle raised his glass and broke the spell. Adventure was in his eyes. His teeth contrasting their whiteness to the manicured cut of his black mustache as he smiled, broadly. "To Ireland, then."

It was just past midnight. The wind had been backing off all day and now the *Chasseur* was just making headway. Captain Ken and Jessica were on the quarterdeck with their sextants. Ken was demonstrating Bowditch's method of taking lunars.

"I know the definition, Captain Russell, I mean I know what the books say, but I've never actually taken a lunar before."

"Don't worry about it, Mr. Henry, yer good with a sextant and speedy with yer slate. You'll be doin' lunars faster than anyone on ship befer long. Now, as I was a'sayin', we used ta shoot a bright star as it occults the moon. That is, as the moon passes it, right?" Jessica smiled as she thought back to a lesson in the schoolroom at St. Patrick's. It seemed so long ago.

"I remember. It had to be a very bright star so you could still see it as the moon passed it by."

"That's right," Ken said. He peered up into the clear black sky. "But the quarterdeck won't never do this evenin'. We need a better angle to do the new lunar. Let's walk for'd, beyond the for'mst in the bow, soes the sails don't git in the way."

The marines were all asleep and only the starboard watch was on deck, huddled into corners and trying to stay warm, though the air felt much warmer since the wind had abated. The waist was clear of both men and running rigging as the ship was carrying most of her sail and the lines were all made fast to their belaying pins on the rails. Jessica loved this time of night on the ship. She didn't have to be as careful, always looking down or away from the notice of the men. Playing the part of Mr. Henry had begun to agitate her. It was fun in the beginning, almost like a child's game of dress up. But Jessica had done some growing up since the *Chasseur* loosed her moors from the wharf at Fells Point. She was maturing quickly, in both mind and body.

There was another reason she enjoyed being on deck at night when most of the crew was fast asleep. David had gotten into the habit of attending to her and bringing her a cup of steaming, fresh coffee on nights like these. As she walked to the bow, Captain Ken behind her, she noticed someone standing in the bow, looking out to sea. She hoped it would be David.

"Good evening, Mr. Henry. Captain Russell."

"Well young feller, yer up past yer bedtime. What's the matter, can't sleep? Ha! A sailor's never got that problem. Kin sleep in a gale, soakin' wet. Done it myself many a time."

"I'm afraid I'm not much of a sailor, Captain Ken," Michael said truthfully. He crossed his arms and leaned against the railing, staring at them pensively. "I was thinking of Ireland, out there somewhere. About what must have happened to my uncle. About why he's so different than my father and me." Jessica put her hand on his arm.

"Are you all right, Michael?" He looked in her eyes. He could see her concern. For the first time he even felt it.

"Thanks Jess," he whispered. "I'm fine."

There was something different about Jessica that Michael suddenly took note of. He didn't know what exactly, but something did look different about her. Just then he saw the moon reflecting in her deep blue eyes. It reminded him of something. It was when he was thinking of his uncle and Ireland, and the code that his uncle had abandoned. He was staring at the moon mirrored on the calm, deep blue wavelets of the Atlantic. Her eyes were just like that, he thought.

Funny he hadn't noticed that before. The only thing he noticed about her eyes was when they suddenly turned to a sapphire blue when she was angry or excited; like the day the *American* carried news that Congress had declared war. He remembered the hunter green, Dutch door off the kitchen at his home on Thames Street, and how she had slammed it after giving him a sandwich. All at once it came to him why she had done that. How it came to him he didn't know. It was something in her eyes. She cared for him. She really cared. He felt foolish now about the way he had told her about Desiree's invitation to tea. He wanted to tell her that now, to apologize. "Know what you ought to believe," he said to himself, "know what you ought to desire, know what you ought to do."

"Different? I'd say yer uncle and yer father are bout as different as any two brothers I've ever known," Ken said indignantly. "Why, I don't know much about this so called code of yer family." Michael looked at Ken sharply. It was if the old man was reading his mind. "Oh, don't git riled, boy. I know it's a cherished custom in yer family. Yer father has spoken of it often enough. To other folks it doesn't carry much meanin', but that's only cause it isn't passed on ta them the way yer family does it."

Ken fiddled with his sextant and laughed. "In my family, the women folk pass on a ring - a big fancy ring that nobody wears. It jest gets put away in a drawer somewhere until one of the women wants ta show it off, and then gits put back again. Has sentimental value, as they say. Not much meanin' there at all. But yer family's got sometin' of real value. To bad Bob lost it somehow."

"At least you have a family to pass something onto," Jessica said, feeling awkward for having said it. Self-pity wasn't one of her failings. Michael looked at her again. He never talked to her about the code or her family before. Somehow it felt comfortable - even comforting. He was about to lay his hand on her shoulder when Ken became impatient.

"Nough of this now. Let's git ta work. Michael, you know anything about lunars?" Both Michael and Jessica laughed. They each recalled the last time Michael was asked that question.

"Yes, Father. According to Mousiour Bowditch, it's easier to take the angle of three stars to the position of the moon, than to wait for the moon to occult a star," Michael recited, pretending to have his hands clasped in front of him, as if he was sitting on the bench at school. Jessica laughed again. A bright feminine laugh. She assumed a school-like position too and giggled through the rest of Michael's answer to Father John. "Why wait for the moon to occult a star when the reading can be taken with great accuracy by measuring the angle of three separate stars? 'Why wait at all for all navigational love?' " Michael answered himself, mimicking Moranvillé's deep nasal tone. But Ken wasn't sharing in their mirth.

"Get your sextant up Mr. Henry. We haven't got all night."

After the reading had been taken, Jessica removed a piece of paper from her coat listing the numbers she had taken from the almanac in Ken's cabin. She drew up her slate and quickly went to work on her calculations. Michael watched her scratch furiously through the mathematics in the glow of the moonlight. He liked the way she worked: her passion for computations, the determination in her eyes, the way her tongue stuck out from her red lips whenever she was doing figures. He had seen all this at St. Patrick's Free School, of course, but he had never enjoyed it before. Jessica giggled and held the slate up for Ken to see.

"Well, a might farther than I thought we were." His patience had returned. He looked with pride upon his protege. "Not bad for a youngin' - heh, heh, - no not bad at all. The cap'n will be pleased to know our longitude. Iffin' I was you, Michael, I'd make sure I sat beside her when I was at school, heh, heh."

"Shhh." Jessica had her finger to her lips, turning her head round to make sure no one else was within listening distance. They all glanced aft, peering in the dark to make certain no one was there. They didn't see the shadow making its way from the main mast to the companionway, or that the lookout on the maintop had come half way down the lower shrouds to hear their conversation. But the shadow and the lookout saw each other.

Satisfied that no one else was listening, Ken looked back up at the countless stars in the black, moon-washed sky.

"Always seems you kin see more stars on a cold night. The winter's night chill must make 'em keener to the eye, I reckon," the old man mused. "Let's see how much Father John has taught ya with all that book learnin'. Where's the North Star?" Michael studied the sky.

"There it is, there. Only it's a little farther up than it is back home."

"That's cause we're farther North," Ken explained. "Sits 'bout 40 degrees North at the Point, but the further North ya are the further up in the sky Polaris sets. But that was too easy. How 'bout Cepheus?"

"There," Jessica pointed. "You can see the tip of his crown just above Polaris."

"And his wife?" Jessica and Michael looked at each other at the same time, both hoping one of them would know the answer.

"C'mon Jess, you know this stuff like I know the inside of a barrel."

"I know it in books, Michael, but out here it's - it's just not the same. I never saw so many stars before. I can't make out anything." But Ken wasn't going to let them give in just yet.

"Hold on youngins, there's an easy way ta figur' it all out. Now, ya see ol' King Cepheus of Ethiopia up there, right? Michael, are ya wit' me?"

"Yea. Where Jess said, just above the North Star."

"Okay. Now, I'm goin' to tell ye a story that'll help ye remember a piece of the sky." Ken put his foot up onto the railing and took out his pipe. "Listen ta this here story and you'll never ferget, I promise." He filled his pipe and lit a match to his bowl, puffing as he did so. "Don't look at the sky now, look at me."

Jessica and Michael both relaxed against the bulwark and stared at the old man whose scruff of a beard now matched his wispy, white hair. Ken Russell's youthful, bright blue eyes were dancing as he recalled the story.

"It's thousands of years old, from the ancients in Greece, or Egypt some say. Now, ol' King Cepheus had a wife, name of Cassiopea. She was pretty in her day. Was the envy of every woman in the kingdom of Ethiopia. But she was gettin' on in years, and the years kin be mighty hard on a woman's features. Long, deep grooves covered what was once the nice and tight skin on her face. Without her looks, she felt empty, ya know, like there was nothin' else fer her ta live fer. Vanity's like that. Seen some vain people do some awful silly things - both men and women.

"Anyway, this ol' Queen Cassiopea took notice one day that her daughter, Princess Andromeda, was comin' of age. The daughter appeared ta be turnin' inta a beautiful woman, herself. An' the ol' girl realized that, even though she had lost her looks, she could relive those days through the beauty of her daughter. Ya know, dress her up in the finest gowns, throw big parties and such.

"Now that's all well and good, known a lot of folks in my day who tried to live out the rest of their lives through their children. But this Queen Cassiopea went too far. Yes sir, too far fer any mama ta go when it comes ta braggin' rights.

"She started tellin' everybody who would listen, that her daughter was the prettiest thing in the universe. Now, that's a bold statement to make when ya figur' those ancients believed in not one, but a whole bunch of gods and goddesses, each of whom had a streak of vanity in 'em a league deep. Heh, heh, those gods and goddesses got wind of what Cassiopea was braggin' about and they didn't take ta kindly ta it. A whole crop of 'em, in partikaler, got so gosh darned mad they decided ta punish the ol' queen. They were the sea nymphs, ya know, and they had some acquaintance with one the most powerful god in the seven seas..."

"Poseidon?" Jessica ventured.

"Yup. Poseidon, the great god of the sea. Though the Romans called him Neptune. Sailors, even to this day, salute Neptune. Sailors bein' the most superstitious of creatures, ya understand. Well, the sea nymphs took Poseidon aside and told him all about their troubles with Queen Cassiopea. An' Poseidon took one look at all those beautiful sea nymphs an' agreed with 'em that Andromeda couldn't possibly be half as good lookin'.

"Poseidon was as angry as any rocky coast on a lee shore. He decided that Cassiopea had to be punished fer her braggin'. He rose from the depths of the ocean and called the wind and the rain and the waves ta pass the word fer the sea monster. Well, the sea monster came as ordered and Poseidon says ta him - "go and ravage the coast of Ethiopia as a punishment fer Queen Cassiopeia's braggin'. So, the sea monster, it was a big whale the size of a first rate, goes and starts tearin' up everythin' on the coast: ships, fishing boats, docks and harbors, everythin'.

"As ya kin imagine, the people of the sea fairin' towns of ol' Ethiopia were kinda mad that they had ta take all the blame fer the fact that Andromeda was the most beautiful woman in the whole universe. They didn't know the reason the sea monster had come was because of Queen Cassiopeia's braggin' and not the innocent beauty of her daughter. And they forced King Cepheus and the Queen ta do somethin' ta stop the great whale from destroyin' the whole coast." Ken's pipe had gone out and he struck another match to the bulwark and laid it against his pipe.

"The Queen started in on her husband bout how they shoulda never had a beautiful daughter, that this whole business was Andromeda's fault fer claiming to be the prettiest women in the universe. Mind ya, Andromeda was a sweet girl and not given ta vanity like her mama. No, she didn't have the slightest idea of her beauty at all. Women who have that quality are the fairest creatures on earth.

"But, the Queen got her way and placed all the blame on her innocent daughter. King Cepheus ordered his daughter to be chained to the rocks on the shore soes the sea monster could have her fer his supper and thus end the affair, neat as ya please. The ancient folks of Ethiopia figur'd that was fair 'nough, after all it was Andromeda's fault to begin with.

"Well, sir, they tied Andromeda up with chains and waited for the sea monster to come. The innocent Andromeda screamed fer help. She couldn't imagine why the gods had fated her that way. Luckily, a handsome young god with a good heart heard her pleas and went rushin' ta git the chains off her just before the whale had his supper. The young feller's name was Persius, and he had a winged horse named Pegasus that streaked out of the sky and went down and rescued Andromeda just in the nick of time. Persius gently pulled her on ta the back of Pegasus and away they flew up inta the sky. It wasn't long after that the two were married and flew off on Pegasus, lovin' each other ferever."

Captain Ken knocked the remnants of his pipe into the water and put it back into his coat pocket. Jessica sighed and Michael turned his face toward her. They were leaning on the railing and had, instinctively, moved closer to each other in the cold. He hadn't planned to say anything in particular, but somehow couldn't help himself.

"I know a girl like Cassiopea. And I know a girl like Andromeda, too."

"Look up at King Cepheus," Ken continued. "Now, follow a line due South and you'll see Cassiopea. Further South ya kin see Persius reachin' out ta the West, ta the outstretched hand of Andromeda. West of her, just past the great square, is Pegasus, on the Western horizon all saddled up and ready to take them away. And South of Pegasus, past the great square and the fishes, lies the sea monster: the great whale of the sky, ready to devour poor Andromeda. Come up here for, oh, three or four nights in a row and remember the story and you'll come to see all of these like ya was born ta the sea."

Captain Ken had finally finished his tale, but Michael and Jessica hadn't heard the last part of it at all. They had been staring into each other's eyes.

Captain Ken cleared his throat and shuffled his feet. "Gettin' mighty cold. I'm headin' below deck. Comin', Mr. Henry?" Before she left his side, Michael slid his hand into Jessica's coat and found her cold hand. He gave it a slight tug as she followed Captain Ken aft, and he gave her moon-reflecting eyes a knowing look.

"Thanks for the lesson in astronomy Captain Ken," he called after them. "I learned a lot."

The lookout watched Ken and Jessica walking toward the main hatch and grinned. The shadow scurried from the companionway and went below. There was a third figure lurking in the darkness that joined Michael in the bow after Captain Ken and Jessica went below.

"Good morning, Michael."

"Good to see you, David." Michael saw he was carefully carrying a cup of hot coffee. "Is that for me?" The Captain's steward looked somewhat embarrassed.

"No. Actually, it was for Mr. Henry. He's went below, I see."

"Just now. Say David, are you in the habit of bringing Mr. Henry a cup of coffee in the middle of the night?" David felt awkward. Five minutes before, he had come on deck and spotted the shadow and the lookout spying on the party in the bow. He had heard enough to know that Jessica's identity had been given away, and so he knew that the shadow and the lookout were now a threat. He had also seen Michael and Jessica staring into each other's eyes. Right now, he didn't like Michael too much. But his duty to his captain and his affection for Jessica were more important than his jealousy. He pretended to sip from the cup, but, instead, whispered in Michael's direction.

"Follow me down below. I need to talk to you on a most urgent matter. Jessica's safety is as important to me as it is to you."

Chapter 16

"TO DONEGAL, THEN, BOYS!"

Boyle took every precaution. He swung the *Chasseur* into the northeast, around Tory Island and then came into Tory Sound well off of Horn Head. Lying to, under the lee of Inishbofin, and flying a British flag, he sent his gig into the island to procure the services of a pilot. One has a great deal of respect for the Atlantic off the northwest coast of Ireland. Here the ocean constantly punishes the land. Forever beating the rocky shore for the effrontery of standing in her way. No captain would risk going in, with even the most up-to-date charts, without the assistance of a local pilot.

Because of his boyhood familiarity with the place, Bob Dooley was chosen to lead a party ashore. The east portion of the Isle of Inishbofin lies about five miles from Falcarragh, Donegal. Most of the fishing boats, the carraghs, were out, since it was still early in the morning. Boyle knew his sleek schooner would be a strange sight in these waters. It was vital to stay as far from the curious eyes of sailors and fishermen as possible. The element of surprise was in the balance, and Boyle needed surprise, and a little assistance from the right kind of Irishmen, in order to succeed with his plan.

Uncle Bob chose Dan Donovon, whose family fished Donegal Bay out of Killybegs. Donovon knew the ways of the fishing communities of Donegal and was much more familiar in the Irish tongue than Bob Dooley, who hadn't been to Falcarragh since he was a young boy. Donovon also knew the names of certain individuals who were prominent in the Uprisings of 1798 and 1803. It was in the former year that Donovon and all nine of his brothers fled Ireland to escape, at the most, hanging, or at least impressment in the Royal Navy for their activities as members of the United Irishmen.

The United Irishmen was the brainchild of Theobold Wolf Tone. Its membership was a secret and curious collection of Catholics and Protestants, aristocrats and peasants. The goal of the organization was to rid Ireland of the yolk of British tyranny. For the Catholics, tyranny was, of course, in the form of religious persecution. For both Catholics and Protestants, it was economic repression. Wolf Tone masterminded the formation of a hundred thousand men under a banner of freedom for all Irishmen, regardless of religion.

These men were organized into brigades and even battalions. They drilled and waited for the right time to rebel. The problem was weaponry. They hardly had any guns at all. What little they did have in the way of armament was constantly in danger of discovery, for the British were relentless in their searches. On top of that was the never-ending threat from an informer and the fact that the organization was rife with British spies.

The success of an Irish revolt hinged upon outside assistance. As in the case of the American Revolution, help from a foreign power was necessary. Wolf Tone attempted to persuade the French to invade Ireland, where there would be substantial and organized support from the island's natives.

Where Benjamin Franklin had succeeded in scoring an alliance between the American Colonies and France, Wolf Tone could manage little in the way of military support. Ireland would have fallen easily to a large invasion force. All Ireland, even the English government knew this.

While Wolf Tone was negotiating with the Directorate in Paris, England was busy trying to put a wedge in the ranks of the United Irishmen along religious lines. The Orange Order was created and religious differences were purposefully used to break all relationships between Catholic and Protestant Irishmen. Knowing Ireland would revolt, regardless of the schisms sent upon them, England deliberately forced the Irish to do so prematurely - before the French could send troops - so as to force the United Irishmen out in the open and kill the movement. This is precisely what happened in 1798 and again in 1803.

All hopes of an independent Ireland, free and united, were crushed forever. Wolf Tone was caught with a small French force off the coast of Donegal. The French officers were treated with dignity and respect, and later, paroled. Tone, who was captured wearing a French army officer's uniform, expected to be put to death. As a colonel in the French Army, he requested the right to die with honor, as a soldier. The request was denied, a rebellious Irishman had no rights. He committed suicide rather than face the ignominious death of hanging as a traitor. The United Irishmen dispersed, Protestant and Catholic never to be united again. England had won.

By 1813, Napoleon was on the run from Russia. There was no more hope for a French invasion. But Dan Donovon knew there were friends still to be found amongst the shattered cells of Wolf Tone's army.

"Be careful, now, Dan," Bob Dooley cautioned, "we don't want ta tip anybody off. Remember, we're from da brig *Antelope,* outta London from South America. We lost our mainm'st an' had ta come inta da nearest port fer repairs. Do ya t'ink anyone will remember da old password?" Donovon was seated in the bow of the boat alongside Uncle Bob.

"Aye. Unless dere all dead, the people of Inishbofin will remember."

Dan Donovon was a big man in his own right, even if it didn't appear so, huddled, as he was, so close to Uncle Bob. Unlike Dooley, Dan had wavy, black hair, which suited his thick, black eye brows and dark brown eyes. He had a young and reasonably intelligent face, especially now as it scanned the shoreline looking for a safe place to bring the boat in. He turned to his Captain of Marine and grinned, boyishly.

"I'll have your pilot an' da information you need in a hour." Bob returned his smile and laid his arm over Donovon's shoulders.

"Just the same, Dan, I'll be goin' wit' ya. When I was a child, I heard stories of you boys from da west enjoin' a local whiskey wit' your porter." Dan laughed.

"You've never had the poitín, then?"

"I was still clenchin' me mudder's skirts when last I was here, Dan Donovon, an' dat's da truth of it." Uncle Bob smiled again, this time from the memory of his mother. "But, I'd say dere was some of dat brew in dis pub we're goin' ta, isn't dat true *Lieutenant* Donovan?" Dan lifted his dark eyebrows in surprise.

"Me? Jaysus and Mary wait till da girls in Killybegs here dis!"

"We'll be long gone before dat happens, God willin'. But I need a man I can trust on dis mission, an' since no one's got da sense ta be from Cork, a Donegal man is only natural."

The boat crew stayed on the shore while Bob and Dan climbed over a stone wall and trudged down a worn path into a small village. Even though the sun was nearly full in the cloudless sky, the air, blowing in off the North Atlantic was still cold enough to keep the residents close to their peat fires. For a moment, the peculiar smell of burning peat stopped both men as it came wafting down the road. They inhaled, deeply, and then turned to each other exchanging the utter joy that leapt from their hearts to their eyes. It was the first time each of them felt the happiness of being back home.

There was no sign hanging over the pub just off the path in the center of the village. There didn't need to be, everyone knew where it was. Donovon entered first, Uncle Bob at his elbow. There were barrels for chairs and one long table facing the door. The pub was empty of patrons save for a group of very old men, who stood at the far end of a counter that served as a bar. What little conversation there was immediately ceased, and the newcomers were greeted with stares and silence.

Donovon led Uncle Bob around the long table to the opposite end of the bar. He turned his back to the group of old men and leaned his elbow against the counter, adopting a casual stance.

"Dere the old ones," he explained to Bob. "Too old ta work in da curraghs or in da fields, but dat's who we want t'talk to. Pretend dat you don't notice dere stares. We'll be meetin' dem soon enough."

The proprietor, who had been talking with the old men, nervously picked up a glass and pretended to clean it with a rag as he approached the newcomers from behind the counter. He stopped in front of Donovon and was about to address him, but then looked sternly at Uncle Bob until Dan broke the tension.

"Mary, Patrick, an' Bridget be wit' you."

"And you," the proprietor mumbled, gruffly. The proprietor was younger than the old men in the corner, but was bald, except for tufts of grey hair that stuck out from his temples. He was fat, too, owing to his occupation. Uncle Bob sensed that his lieutenant and the proprietor knew each other from the way they exchanged nervous glances, even though neither of them had acknowledged the acquaintance. But then Donovon spoke the password.

"*Croisini.*"

"What's that ya say?" the proprietor whispered, incredulously. "Cross, is it? What in the name of the Savior are ya doin' here? Nobody's used that password in years. An' who's your friend, here."

"He's from Cork," Donovon whispered back, "but now he's an American, like I am."

"That doesn't answer my question," the proprietor snapped back. "Whaddaya mean bringin' yourself, who's wanted for capital crimes, and this stranger inta my pub, an' riskin' everybody's neck? Have ya gone daft man, or turned King's informer?" Donovon raised a finger to his lips to quiet the redfaced proprietor.

"Do you want da story or da truth?"

"Both."

"I suppose you would. How do I know *you* didn't turn King's evidence? After all, it was me and me brothers who had t'flee. I noticed *you* haven't gone anywhere." At this, the proprietor's face grew even redder. Before, he was agitated, now, he was angry.

"Why, you son of a bitch. I'll tear your eyes out." The proprietor lunged for Donovon, but, in a second, Dan was lying on the floor, and the proprietor found himself dangling, by the throat, from the outstretched left arm of Bob Dooley.

"Nobody's goin' ta tear me lieutenant's eyes out. Except me. But right now, I'm on a mission fer da President of da United States, dear Jamie Madison. An' nothin', nor no man, is goin' ta keep me from servin' me president. Have we reached an understandin' Mr. barkeep?"

The proprietor, whose face was now more blue than red, tried to shake his head in understanding. Bob Dooley let him drop to the floor, and then leaned his massive head over the counter.

"An' when yer yerself again, it's customary manners ta ask a guest if he would like somethin' ta drink."

The old men in the corner were awe struck. One of them curled a faint smile on one side of his wrinkled face and stepped forward. He walked slowly, with his right hand gripping the railing of the counter. Despite the feebleness of his gait, his frame still boasted a strength that was legendary in his day. Years of pulling on the oars of his curragh had fashioned a wide back and shoulders of stone. It was the old man's rheumatism in his knees that now deprived him of the spry step of his youth. Decades of wind and weather marked his cleanshaven face with creases that only seemed to draw more attention to his bulging blue eyes. In his prime, he was known for the curling crop of red hair that dangled in his face and fell in ringlets to his shoulders. It had turned snow-white these past twenty years, and was now held taut and tied with a leather strap in back.

The old man glanced at Donovon, who was still lying on the floor. Then, the old man looked over the counter.

"You can git up now, Jimmy."

The proprietor lifted himself up, cursing under his breath, and straightened his clothing.

"Ah," the old man grunted, shaking his head in disappointment. "There's no hope for Ireland. Look at these boys. What have the generations done. Their too soft for a fight, God help us." He fixed a discerning gaze on Uncle Bob. These were not eyes you could lie to. "What's yer name?"

"Dooley. Bob Dooley."

"An' yer father's name?"

"Patrick, from Cork. Me mudder was Bridget. Bridget..."

"O'Brien. Yes, I know, dat's my name, too," the old man interjected. He turned to the group of men in the corner. "All right, lads, it's all right. Come an' meet me nephew." Bob's mouth dropped. He hit himself on the head and then crashed his fist down onto the counter.

"Uncle Liam! It's you! Jaysus! I can't believe me eyes."

"Of course it's me," the old man said in exasperation. "Where the hell have you been for the last fifty years, an' where's yer brother, Mike." Bob opened his mouth to explain, but there was too much explaining to do and nothing came out.

"Ferget about dat, you can be tellin' me about the family later. Now, what's all this about the President of the United States."

Glasses of porter and poitín were on the bar immediately and everyone listened intently to Bob explain how he and Donovan came to be in Inishbofin, and what Captain Boyle's plans were for the *Chasseur's* cruise in Irish waters. Jimmy and the old men looked to see what Liam's reaction would be to the American raid. For thirty years, Liam had been their Captain of the local Defenders. Irish Catholics had no rights under English laws enforced by the magistrates and constables. But the peasant farmers and fishermen lived under their own, secret, set of rules. Whenever an injustice was perpetrated by a constable or tyrannical landlord, Liam would see to it that some retribution was inflicted: a midnight fire in a manor house, an unfortunate accident befalling a constable. No one talked about such things openly. But they were as much a part of life as the poitín and potato.

"You can do what you like with Falcarragh, Bob," Liam said sipping a glass of Poitín, "but, no one can know dat we helped you in any way. In a week, you'll be gone. We're the ones who live here and have ta put up wit' those British bastards, although a few of the young ones will probably want to ship out wit' you when you leave. There's nothin' here for the young ones, not anymore, no hope atall. You didn't see what happened after the crackdown, Dan Donovan. T'ousnands died. Died outright, with a bullet in their head, or slow from the torture. Nothin' could satisfy their t'irst for Irish blood. Women...children...all Ireland was like - like hell." Liam stopped himself, before he lost his emotions.

"Now finish up yer drink. You say you got a privateer wit' cannon and powder? Well, the Britishers got nothin' here atall except the law - the police dat we pay taxes t'keep here. The more fuss we make the more police come an' the more we pay in taxes. They have it all figured out. But, they haven't got anything t'resist what you got on dat ship - not outside of Londonderry.

"We'll put men out at night. They'll take their curraghs and reach Londonderry by Lough Foyle and assess the naval strength of the enemy. We'll need a lookout on Horn Head," Liam nodded to one of the old men, "Jerry, that's you. Tonight we'll send messages to trusted friends in Dunfanaghy in the northwest, Creslough in the west, and Bunberg-Derryberg in the southeast. Mount Errigal protects the south, nothin' can come over the Derryveagh Mountains. We'll know if the bastards move a finger in our direction. In two days we'll have all the information you'll need on the strength of the enemy by land and water.

"We can show you where t'put your cannon and seal off the roads. Everyone will cooperate. You have my word on it. But we just won't look like we're cooperatin'." Liam turned to the group of old men.

"This can't make up for what we've been t'rough. But, as God is my judge, it's goin' to be the most fun we've ever had."

Smiles appeared on every old face, even Jimmy, the proprietor, seemed to warm to the idea and to Uncle Bob. He thrust a fresh glass under his chin.

"No more of dat, till the job is done," Liam shouted pulling the glass away and tossing its contents on the wall behind the bar. "No drink atall until the town is secured. Are you wit' me boys!"

Everyone shouted in agreement. "Then, let's be off. Spread the word by the old method - family by family. Let's go. The blessing on everyone." He grabbed Bob Dooley by the arm. "I've got t'talk to yer captain. I'll pilot the ship in meself."

Liam O'Brien, Uncle Bob, and Dan Donovan walked back down the path to the stone wall over which the boat crew was looking at them with curiosity. Instead of limping painfully on the path from the village, Liam positioned himself between Bob and Dan, and had them carry him. When the boat crew saw the marines panting and sweating from carrying the old man, they rigged a litter from the boat's oars and had Liam over the stone wall and into the boat before Uncle Bob and Dan Donovon had caught their breath. One of the sailors whispered something like "lubber" under his breath. Before the boat headed out, Liam leaned over and dipped his hand in the water.

"In God's name," he said, making the sign of the cross.

While the boat was making its way to the *Chasseur*, the group of old men from the pub were busy sending messages to every cottage on the island via a network of boys too young to man the curraghs or work the fields. In half an hour all of Inishbofin had the news and a boat had cast off for the mainland to alert a similar network in Falcarragh.

Mr. Leib was ready with a sling for Liam and sent word to the captain that the gig was alongside. Boyle made his way on deck interested to see if Uncle Bob had procured a pilot. Mr. Henry was there, as well, reviewing some figures. Michael and David took turns, as they had for the past two weeks, watching Mr. Henry whenever she left Captain Ken's cabin.

This was at Jessica's insistence. She pleaded with them not to tell Captain Boyle, or anyone else, that, at least, two crewmembers might know she was a girl. Her fear was that Captain Boyle would confine her to her cabin for the remainder of the cruise. Moreover, she enjoyed the work of a master's mate. Not the charade of playing Mr. Henry, but the business of sailing and navigating she had become so adept in. The boys, for the moment, agreed. Neither one wanted to risk losing her affection.

"Michael, boyo!" Uncle Bob shouted as he came over the railing. "I've got a surprise fer ya!" Uncle Bob stood Michael in front of Liam. The old man took a painful step towards the young Dooley.

"You don't have ta be tellin' me who this is," the old man said, his blue eyes sparkling like white caps on a turquoise sea. "This is Michael's boy. Praise be. I can see the sense in him. Just like his father, God bless 'em." Michael looked up at Uncle Bob like one would look up a tree standing beneath it. Uncle Bob looked down at the boy's quizzical expression.

"Don't ya see, boyo? This here is me Uncle Liam. Liam O'Brien, me mudder's brudder." Michael could smell the foul stench of spent whiskey on his uncle's breath, but he was too confused to mention anything about it.

"Your uncle? Uncle?"

"Dat's right, boyo. Me Uncle Liam! An' Uncle Liam is gonna help us raid da British, ain't dat nice?"

"Captain Dooley!" Boyle came down into the waist, impatience in his voice. "Is that my pilot?"

"In a manner of speakin', Captain darlin', it is."

"What's that supposed to mean?"

"Well, as heaven would have it, I bumped inta me uncle when Dan and I were ashore an'..." Boyle could smell the still potent alcohol emanating from his Captain of Marine. While Uncle Bob went into a hasty explanation of his time on the island, Boyle's patience was wearing thin. He had sent his Captain of Marine on an important expedition to enlist the assistance of a pilot, voluntarily or at the point of a dagger. Everything depended upon this. And now, he was hearing something about an uncle and a bar. He was about to lose his temper, but reminded himself that a Southern gentleman should be respectful of family reunions, even if they did occur on his deck an hour before he was going to raid enemy territory. "...an' everything is set fer us ta go in ta take da town, owin' ta da fact dat me uncle is head of da rebellion in dese parts, an' has da boys in his organization takin' care of everythin'"

Boyle shook his head, confusion replacing the remnants of his temper. He glanced at Liam and began to speak slowly, as if the old man couldn't understand the King's English.

"Are - you - or - are - you - not - the - pilot - I - sent - for?" Liam could sense that Boyle was confused about something, although he hadn't the faintest idea what his problem was and answered his question in the same slow manner.

"I - I - I - I a - m - m - m - m."

Captain Boyle breathed out a sigh of relief. He shook his head once more in an attempt at clearing his mind, hoping that the vision of the three generations before him would just disappear.

"In all my years at sea, and in all the engagements with the enemy, I've never experienced..." He stopped short of expressing his thoughts when he noticed the three generations staring at him, wondering what on earth could be wrong. But now wasn't the time to be confused about anything. He paced the breadth of the deck and regained control over his faculties.

"So, Captain Dooley, you're mission was a success after all. My congratulations." Uncle Bob came to attention, military fashion.

"T'ank ya sir, just doin' me job."

"And, this gentlemen," Boyle said walking over to Liam, "I don't believe we've been properly introduced, suh." Uncle Bob stepped in between them.

"My fault, sir. May I present Mr. Liam O'Brien of Donegal. Me uncle, sir." Boyle extended his hand in greeting.

"An honor, sir."

"T'ank ya, captain. Are ya ready ta take the town now, sir? Or would yer honor like ta take a little time ta t'ink t'ings over." Boyle smiled. Finally, he recognized the situation for what it was: a joint operation. O'Brien's Defenders and the United States Privateer *Chasseur*.

"I - well - yes, what do you propose, Mr. O'Brien?"

"Fill yer boats wit' as many men and guns as possible, and follow me. I'll take twenty men and seal of the roads to the town, nothin' will move in or out. You take a company of men, an' one of my boys will lead you to the magistrate's office. Then, we'll borrow some horses and proceed to go an' visit the home of every constable within ten miles. Falcarragh will be in American hands by sunset. An', by the way, Captain Boyle," Liam said, in all sincerity, "during this expedition, as I am Captain of the Defenders, you may refer to me using that title."

Boyle smiled, inwardly. He had no doubt as to who was in charge. "After all," he thought to himself, "it's his country." He took a step back so that the entire ship's company could see what he was going to do. He raised a knuckled salute to his forehead. "Your servant, Captain O'Brien."

Liam returned his salute. Uncle Bob and Michael smiled with pride.

Happy, on watch in the fighting top of the foremast, shook his head in disbelief. " 'Ere we go again. Another bloody captain."

Boyle ran up to the quarterdeck. "Mr. Leib! Get both boats ready. Stores, ammunition, muskets and broadswords. Prepare to raid the town."

"Aye, sir, prepare to raid the town." The *Chasseur* became alive, men swarming over her deck, orders from the mates barking in all directions. Boyle, enjoying now the taste of the coming fight, yelled down midships.

"Captain Dooley! Assemble your marines in the waist, arm them, and get them into the boats."

"Aye, sir, 'semblin' da marines."

"Captain O'Brien! Join me, suh, on the quarter!" Donovon had two marines carry Liam to the quarterdeck where Boyle was strapping on his two finest, pearl handled pistols. He shouted to the crew in his flamboyant, deep and resonant voice: "I declare the commencement of the invasion of the British Isles! To Donegal, then boys! To Donegal!

****

"It's the barkeep, Captain," Uncle Bob said as he spotted the grey tufts of hair running up to the boat that had just landed on the strand, a mile to the east of Falcarragh. Liam and his boat sailed a mile to the west, onto the headland that shelters the town from the mighty breakers of the Atlantic. The proprietor reached them, kicking up sand and out of breath.

"I closed up early...didn't want t'miss this... for anyt'ing in the world," he panted between gulps of air. The men were assembled on the beach, looking fierce with pistols and scabbards sticking out of their clothing. Uncle Bob had his polka dotted bandanna wrapped around his thick, red head. Boyle turned to Happy George, who, with Jhoel, was to take the boat back to the *Chasseur*.

"Tell Captain Russell, that Captain O'Brien will be joining him on the ship after he's secured the roads. He said it would take an hour - no more. By that time we would have taken the magistrate's office and the ship can be piloted into Falcarragh. He can anchor at his discretion and then see to the unloading of the cannon - three long nines will do the job. After the town is secured, I want the prisoners taken out of the hold and brought ashore. There must be a gaol someplace to put them in while we're here, and when we leave we'll just let them go."

The forty-seven prisoners taken from the prizes were a headache to Boyle. Not only did they have to be fed and given precious water from the ship's stores, they were also a threat. Many ships were taken in the dead of night by prisoners, no matter how well they were guarded.

Jimmy, the barkeep, led the party down the strand, keeping off the roads and out of sight. In twenty minutes they reached the small wharf in Falcarragh. The curraghs were all in and the wharf was busy with men unloading the days catch. Heads turned when the fishermen saw the armed band coming to them, but they had already gotten word of the raid and they pretended not to notice. Several fishermen dipped their hands in the water and blessed themselves as the Americans passed them. A hushed chorus of "in God's name" was heard on the wharf of Falcarragh.

Jimmy pointed to a road and made a motion with his hand signifying a left turn, and then hid himself in the middle of the raiding party so as not to be seen helping the Americans. Boyle took the lead, along with Uncle Bob. Pistols were drawn. Uncle Bob gripped two in his hands and clenched a knife between his teeth. Boyle waved his hand and the party climbed the rocks to the road above the wharf. As they reached the roadbed and could see the town, with its shoppes and pubs, a shot rang out.

"Pistol!" Bob Dooley said, flatly, pointing to the opposite end of town. "Uncle Liam's boys. Somebody must'a squealed. Damn, da dirty informin' bastard."

"C'mon boys!" Boyle screamed and he led them into the town making a left turn. A rider on a horse fired a pistol shot that caught Boyle's right arm, forcing him to drop his gun and sending blood down the lacy cuffs of his sleeve. The rider came right at them as the Americans filled the breadth of the road and the rider, probably someone sent to get reinforcements or alert the local militia, wore a determined look in his eyes to get through. The men scattered to the side of the road, but Uncle Bob, wearing his own look of desperate determination, knelt down on the road, in front of the charging mount, and fired both pistols into the breast of the animal. The horse came up on the rider and bellowed in agony, blood spurting from its chest onto Uncle Bob. But the rider had not been thrown. Uncle Bob sprang to his feet, pulled the knife from his mouth, seized the reins, and sliced the length of the animal's chestnut throat. The horse collapsed on its rider as it expired, instantly breaking the rider's leg.

Boyle had fashioned a tourniquet around his arm and had managed to pick up his pistol. The magistrate's office was about fifty yards forward of their position, sitting in the center of the road and encircled by the homes of the town's elite. The town's streets were deserted. It was painfully obvious that the law had been informed about the American raid, but the question running through Boyle's mind was when? An hour? "No, shorter," he said out loud, "they only now sent a rider for help."

"What's dat yer sayin', captain darlin'," Uncle Bob was at Boyle's side fidgeting with his tourniquet.

"I was thinking that the magistrate hasn't had time to call for help. Leave two or three men, here, tell them that nothing passes without my permission." He peered down to the magistrate's office. "David! My glass."

The captain's steward ran from the opposite side of the road, holding the glass out in his hands. Another shot, this one from the magistrate's office, pierced the cold air. It went clean through David's thigh, knocking his feet out from under him. He hit the road with a thud.

"Boy!" Boyle shouted, running to his steward. David was crying, his dusty face distorted with pain. He grabbed the boy's hand. "Captain Dooley! Have two of your men take him back to the ship, tell them to rig a stretcher." But, in a second, James Darymple was kneeling on the road beside the boy.

"I'm on it!"

Boyle stood, facing the guns in the magistrate's office in defiance. "You'll pay for this! By God you will!" Uncle Bob had tied a rope around a hitching post and with his powerful back and arms pulled it out of the ground. He lifted the post up on his shoulders and looked fiercely at Boyle, waiting for orders. Boyle dropped his pistol, and with his bloody arm unsheathed his sword. "Chaaaarge!

The men of the *Chasseur* filled the road with their bodies and their bloodcurdling screams, chasing after their captain.

Boyle was in a fury, his eyes gaping wide and full of vergence, his black cape streaming on the wind in his wake. To a man, the raiding party ran straight for the two story structure before them; the cape they followed as black as their minds, intent on spilling British blood.

Musket fire pealed from the windows of the magistrate's building. Several of the marines were cut down. The Americans stopped, aimed their guns well, and poured a shower of balls into the windows.

Boyle urged his men forward waving his sword in the air. He reached the fence in front of the building and leaped. Uncle Bob, at Boyle's heel, kicked in the fence with his boot and then charged the great oak door of the magistrate's, the heavy post he bore, ripping into his shoulders. He screamed and rammed the door, every ounce of his sinew bent on its destruction. With one mighty blow, the door tore from its hinges, cracking and crashing to the ground.

The Americans let out a cheer and tumbled into the building. Boyle ran for the window where he saw the puff of smoke that sent his steward down. Uncle Bob was right behind him, still carrying the post. Boyle kicked open the magistrate's officedoor and raced into the room brandishing his sword. Shots rang out. Boyle was hit again in the same arm, balls shredded his clothing. A dozen men, in militia uniform rushed him. Uncle Bob pressed the post over his head and hurled it, over his captain, at the attacking militiamen. One officer took the post directly on his head, cracking his skull wide open. Boyle raised his sword with his left arm and hacked violently, repeatedly, at the uniforms before him. The room filled with Americans. There was no time, no chance, for the king's men to surrender. In minutes, they were all dead.

Chapter 17

Da

The curraghs didn't go out with their nets the day after the battle. No one, not even the fishermen were allowed out of Falcarragh and its surroundings. Liam saw to that. Still, there was work to be done. Over the winter months seaweed had been strewn across the potato fields for fertilizer and had long since dried. The fields were ready for spades and seed. Men could be seen digging the soil, making their ridges; their wives beneath them planting the seeds. Old men were busy mending torn nets and talking about the "grand rush" of the magistrate's office.

Dr. Williams had been busy all night with the wounded. The dead had been cleared from the magistrate's, that was used as a hospital. Dr. Williams was standing over a table where Boyle was lying. There was blood on the doctor's apron and on his hands, even on the coffee cup he had sipped on through the evening. Captain Boyle was the doctor's last patient. Boyle had insisted that the others be treated before him.

"Make your report, doctor, if you please."

"Of the *Chasseur's* company: six dead, six wounded. All the British are dead, except for the magistrate. The one on the horse?" Boyle nodded. "He's in the next room with a broken leg and a bruised pride. He's demanding to see you."

"How's the boy?" Boyle asked. Williams stopped bandaging his captain's arm.

"He'll live. I'm going back to the ship as soon as I've finished here."

"His leg. Can you save his leg?"

"That depends. I'll know more when I get back. You've lost a lot of blood, Tom. I want you to take it easy for a while. See the magistrate later. He's a bit vexed and a complete English snob. I don't want him to rile your temper." Boyle winced and sat up on the table. "Tom! I said take it easy."

"We've just taken a town in Ireland. The plan's just beginning. There's no time to take it easy. Tell Ken Russell I need to talk to him when you return to the ship, and send word on David's condition. I'll need another steward, for the time being. Another boy, ah - Michael, the young Dooley. Have him bring some wine." Doctor Williams had seen Boyle like this before, he knew he couldn't reason with him.

"I'll send word with Michael," Williams said, reluctantly, while putting the captain's arm in a sling, "and I'll send your best Madeira. But, you must promise me not to take your arm out of this until I tell you." Boyle rose from the table, grimacing. He put his left arm around his physician's shoulders and grinned.

"I promise, but only if it's not a choice between my arm or my neck, Doctor Williams."

Williams' diagnosis of the magistrate was correct. For twenty-three years, Duncan Willowby, has been the magistrate in Falcarragh. Assuming the post upon the death of his father. He was an esteemed member of the Orange Order and respected for his family connections with the Lord-Lieutenant of Ireland, and his hatred of papists. People, generally, attempted to stay on his good side, not only because he had power, but also because he possessed a talent for administrative organization and the audacity to do exactly what he said he would do. At this point, he could do nothing, hence his vexation.

"Your honor? May I come in?" Boyle was leaning against the doorway, nursing his arm in its sling. He had endeavored to clean himself up before attending to the magistrate, but the blood-stained bandages and his tired and unshaven face prohibited him from looking the part of the dashing captain that had come to be his trademark. Still, he had managed to swing a finely woven coat over his shoulders. The handsome cut of his waistline against his well-tailored pants, and the polish of his riding boots suggested to Willowby that this was a gentleman. The magistrate also remembered the gallant way in which the

American captain had charged the office, sword in hand, no regard for personal safety. Willowby detested dealing with rabble, but, a gentleman, especially a gallant one, was entitled to his most courtly manners.

"How do you do, sir. Pardon me for not getting up."

"Of course. Pardon me if I must sit down." Boyle found a chair and sat near the chaise upon which the magistrate was propped, his broken leg lying on a pillow.

Willowby studied Boyle's face. He noted a scar under one cheekbone. Another across the strong, square jaw. He noticed determination in the brown eyes, and a flash of pain as the American sat down. Boyle's jacket opened, revealing an athletic chest and stomach. The blood from the bandages on his right arm was also visible. Willowby was no stranger to battle. He had fought against the Americans with General Borgoyne, at Saratoga. He had dreamed of a military career as a young boy, and had reached the rank of colonel before his father determined that he should come home and take his proper place as magistrate. Willowby hated Falcarragh for that; hated all Ireland because of it. Even though he had lost to this striking American, as General Borgoyne had to Arnold at Saratoga so many years before, he felt no animosity. Suddenly, he resigned himself to the situation, and his vexation left him.

"After all," he thought, "it's not going to last long, and there's no shame in being overwhelmed by superior numbers. He's only an American. In the end I shall get what I want from him."

"I regret to inform your honor..."

"Willowby. Colonel Willowby." Boyle nodded and looked directly into the magistrate's cool, blue eyes.

"Colonel Willowby, I must tell you that none of your men survived. They were all killed in the assault." Boyle saw that his statement had no effect. The truth was the colonel's men had followed his instructions to the last. This pleased the colonel, greatly. It never occurred to him that higher authorities would later look upon his actions as cowardly. He thought it quite proper that he should ride to get reinforcements, while his men kept the enemy at bay. He was the best horseman in Donegal.

To the colonel's way of thinking, the British should have repelled the attack for a few days until a column could relieve the town. But he had never bargained on such brazen Americans, privateers no less, storming a well-armed establishment without regard for themselves. And for what purpose? These Americans weren't regular army, or even regular navy. They were fortune hunters. But there was no fortune in Falcarragh. Why had they come? Boyle continued:

"I hope your leg doesn't pain you that much, colonel?"

"Oh, no, Captain - ah - what shall I call you, or is that a secret?" Boyle laughed.

"I have no secrets, colonel. My name is Boyle. Captain Thomas Boyle, American Privateer Schooner *Chasseur*, sixteen guns, out of Baltimore." Willowby knitted his brows.

"Baltimore? That's in Maryland. I thought it to be under the strictest blockade?" Boyle shrugged, and winced from the pain it caused his arm.

"You've been misinformed, colonel. We Americans must have a different definition for what constitutes a strict blockade."

"May I see your commission?"

"At the earliest opportunity. I'll send for it. But, I wouldn't lie to you, suh." Willowby waved his hand.

"Tut, tut, captain. In your good time, please. Only a formality, I assure you." He smiled. "May I ask what your intentions are?"

"Of course. We will be needing your hospitality for only a short time. I intend to use your town as a base of operations for a few days, maybe a week, no longer."

"Operations?" Willowby couldn't help but to admire Boyle's audacity, much like his own, he thought.

"Yes, colonel. We plan to take quite a few prizes in these waters."

"Prizes!" Willowby chuckled, "Captain, you surprise me, how many prizes do you think to bag around here?" Boyle didn't answer him. He only showed his white teeth in a grin. "It isn't the commerce around here that your interested in, is it, captain? It's the trade between England and Ireland. Scotland, too. Now I'm beginning to see your strategy. It's because of your schooner. There are no vessels here that look like that ship of yours. Why, you could take another ship, outfit it with your armament, and use it for a privateer. Exchange that one, if it pleases you, and use another. No one will know it's the *Chasseur*. Even if they send a frigate, or a fast sloop to stop you, they won't know what to look for. You'll be adopting the persona of a different ship each time you go out. Brilliant, Captain Boyle, brilliant. Why you could stay holed up here for a month and no one would be the wiser. Capture millions in goods." Boyle shook his head.

"You take me for a fool, colonel?"

"Not after you stormed this office. That wasn't folly; that was leadership. But, if that isn't your plan, then..."

"Adopting a new ship and making continuous raids under a 'different persona' might be a fine idea for a pirate," Boyle said, cutting him short. "But, I am not a pirate. In the first place, I answer to the owners of the *Chasseur* and am held liable for the safe conduct of my ship. Secondly, this is not the Caribbean or the Mediterranean. There are no islands to establish a base with fellow pirates and prey on local trade, sinking ships and murdering prisoners so that no soul would live to point a finger at you. This is an honorable enterprise. A service to my country in a time of war. Third, I can out sail anything on the water in the *Chasseur*, why should I abandon her and chase prizes on a slow and clumsy brig or ship? Lastly, I would never attempt to hold Falcarragh for a month - even a week is stretching it. Communications, the mails, have been disrupted. It won't take long for the local militia to get wind of our doings. But, even if I can stop that, I'd expect a visit from one of His Majesty's ships of the Royal Navy to visit us soon enough. Why, I couldn't even take this town without word of my movements reaching you before I landed." Willowby was taken aback. He laughed, ingenuously.

"Come, Captain Boyle. We barely had time to make a defense."

"You had time to gather more than twenty men - uniformed men - who would have held out for days if I had been a more timid man."

"But, I only had time to get a mount. You know that. It was your giant of a man who took down my horse in the street, not a hundred yards from this office." Boyle pressed down his brows and peered at the colonel with intense, brown eyes.

"That was of secondary consideration to you, suh. Your primary aim was to defend the King's property, or has the Union between Ireland and England been dissolved since I've put to sea? You fully expected to get by my 'giant,' as you say, and gallop to get reserves, and them lead them to victory after you assessed the problem properly."

Willowby's expression changed drastically. There was no longer mirth, or even civility on his face. He realized that he hadn't gained anything from talking to the Captain of the *Chasseur*. Not one piece of valuable information. He knew he had been beaten at his own game. But, his genuine admiration for the man in the well groomed, black mustache could only increase. "By God, he is brilliant," Willowby thought, "and I haven't a clue as to what his real intentions are." He decided to change tactics.

"Of course, you're right, captain. My primary function is the preservation of the King's property. I used the little time I had to set up an adequate defense. My intentions were exactly as you describe. And, yes, I have my informer. You are new to Ireland, captain. Informers are almost a way of life, here - on both sides, for the right amount of money. It's just that we have much more money." Boyle had gotten what he wanted. He didn't know for sure if there was an informant, or if a loyalist had spotted them landing on the strand. He also changed tactics and showed his fine set of white teeth.

"My dear colonel, let us not have words. You are a soldier, and as such you know your duty. Please know that I know mine as well. I shall see to it that your officers and men are buried with full ceremony. Will tomorrow be all right?"

Mr. Leib gave Doctor Williams a hand over the railing. He was tired and it showed on his pale face.

"Rough going, Doctor?" Mr. Leib inquired. "I know we've took the town, one of the locals informed us."

"Yes, Mr. Leib, the town is ours, for the time being, but not without cost."

"How many, sir?" There was immediate silence. Ears on deck and above, on the tops and yards, strained to hear the fate of their shipmates. Williams was aware of this. He looked around at the crew. At one time or another he had healed every single one of them: setting broken bones from a fall, stitching up cuts from the swipe of a sword or the thrust of a pike, digging out musket balls, not to mention the usual fevers and infections.

"Six of us are gone, all marines: Keller, Blake, Fitzpatrick, McGinness, Cawley, and Clark. Six are down, but will recover: Laftey, O'Brien, Murphy, Donahue, McGurren, and McKavanaugh." The ship was still silent when Dr. Williams went below.

Jessica was holding David's hand. She had stayed with him through the night, placing cold compresses on his feverish head and applying fresh bandages over the wound on his thigh. Michael was standing next to her, his arm across her shoulder, squeezing her tightly when she became emotional and her body shook, holding back tears that a master's mate could not let go. Doctor Williams opened the door. Michael quickly pulled down his arm, but it was too late, the doctor had seen them. Strangely, he said nothing, but went straight to work, examining David's wound, checking his temperature.

"Has he woken, at all?"

"Yes," Jessica replied. "For a few moments. I gave him the draft you prescribed and he went right to sleep again. Will he be all right, doctor?" Williams glanced up at Jessica and took note of the tears in her swollen eyes.

"I - I don't know. He's in a critical period. The next forty-eight hours will determine whether or not he keeps his leg. I'll relieve you Mr. Henry, or whatever your name really is, you look like you could use some sleep, girl." Jessica bit her lip and looked at Michael.

"Did Captain Boyle tell you, doctor?" Michael asked.

"Son, I've been in medicine for over thirty years. During that time I've come to know the difference between the sexes. Besides, I saw your arm over her shoulder as I came in the door, and, Miss?" Jessica looked at him with questioning eyes, "you're still holding the boy's hand. That's something even the closest shipmates don't do." She withdrew her hand. David let out a sigh. Doctor Williams took Jessica by the arm.

"My advice to you is to be careful, very careful, not to act like anything but a young master's mate. That means you can't allow anyone to put his arm around you, and no matter how you feel, handholding simply won't do. But don't worry. Your secret is safe. I'm relieved, however, to know that the captain is aware of the situation. It would be my duty to tell him if he was not. Why you're on this ship is none of my business. But the health of the crew is very much my business and there are men on this ship who have no scruples, whatsoever, no sense of self-control. If they know that you're a girl, they will try to have their way with you - force you to have relations with them. Do you understand?" Jessica shook her head. "Good. Now go to your cabin, girl, and fetch Captain Ken, tell him the captain wishes to see him on shore, immediately." Jessica gazed down at David. "Go. I'll let you know if there are any changes."

Williams turned his attention to Michael. "You are to report ashore, as well. You are to be the captain's steward until David recovers."

That night a boat set out from Falcarragh making its way to Inishbofin. In it were Captain Boyle, Uncle Bob, Liam, Dan

Donovon, and the captain's new steward. After unloading cannon, to be used at key points in defense of the town, the *Chasseur* set sail with the tide. Captain Ken was in command. Liam had provided the schooner with another pilot. Ken's orders were to take and sink as many ships as possible in seventy-two hours. The object of this mission was to create as much general havoc as possible. "Stir up some noise," as Boyle had put it. Prizes that were taken were to be divested of valuables and transferred to the hold of the schooner. Prisoners were to be chained in the hold, as well. Then, the prizes were to be set afire.

It was a critical decision. But Boyle was convinced that no word of their arrival had made its way outside of Falcarragh. He was anxious to begin the operation and decided no to wait for Liam's intelligence on the enemy's strength in Londonderry. It was a bold move. Everyone knew that the party ashore could be trapped there. But there was another reason for Boyle to set his plans in motion before getting the news from Londonderry: the informer. Every moment lost before finding out his identity placed the *Chasseur* in increasing jeopardy.

The boat landed on Inishbofin at the same location where Uncle Bob and Dan had arrived to recruit a pilot. A stretcher was rigged for Liam, Uncle Bob and Dan Donovon carried the litter for and aft, and the party set out down the road to the village. Liam had the proprietor, Jimmy, close his pub earlier that usual. The party walked in through the unlocked door and sat on barrels alongside the long table. Boyle ordered porter and poitín for the group. Uncle Bob ordered a cup of tea for Michael.

"I brought you out here at Captain O'Brien's suggestion," Boyle began. "Somehow the magistrate was tipped off to our arrival. Falcarragh isn't safe to talk in until he's found out. That's why I sent the *Chasseur* out earlier than planned. We can't wait for the intelligence. If word reaches Londonderry, we'll have, at the most two days before we can expect a frigate's guns down our throats." Stares were exchanged over the rims of hoisted pints. Uncle Bob cleared his throat.

"Captain darlin', didn't you order Ken out fer seventy two hours?"

"That was my expressed order, yes. He needs that time to cause as much damage as possible. My hope is that, if there is a Royal Navy presence in Londonderry, they'll hear about the *Chasseur* before they do about us, and sail out after her. That's why I've ordered Captain Russell to go into Lough Foyle as far as he dares, keeping enough sea room to maneuver, and then shoot out to the east. If they follow him out they'll be further away from us, you see?"

"But won't dat put yer ship in danger?" It was Liam who interjected this time.

"Danger? A privateer is always in danger, suh. But as long as it's in the water the odds are on the *Chasseur's* side. She sails faster than anything in the world, and Captain Russell can handle her as well, maybe even better, than I can." Boyle took a long drink from his pint. "Ahhh, dear God that's good. We'll have to take some of this with us when we leave, hey Captain Dooley?"

"I've already seen ta dat, sir. But I don't understand how we can leave if, let's say, a frigate does sail in ta Falcarragh, or a column of lobster backs come marchin' up, an' we gotta go inta' hidin'."

"I was just getting to that," Boyle explained. "Captain O'Brien. You have a man posted on Horn Head, correct?"

"Aye, sir. Jerry it tis, sir, on the point."

"If the British come here, before the *Chasseur* returns, have him sling a light where it can be seen. I've told Captain Russell to sail by the point and look for that warning. If he sees it, he'll know to come to a small island, the one directly northwest of Inishbofin, and not sail into Falcarragh." Boyle broke out a map and spread it on the table. He looked at Uncle Bob. "Order some more of this delicious brew, would you Captain Dooley?"

"Barkeep!" Uncle Bob screamed, "more porter!" Jimmy quickly came to the table, with a pitcher. He refilled their pints with fresh porter.

Boyle pointed to an island off the coast of Inishbofin. "Here - in Tory Sound. Ironic name, isn't it? This is where Captain Russell will pick us up if there's trouble. At precisely midnight of the third day, and each subsequent day for an entire week, just in case we are delayed and cannot make the rendezvous." Boyle took a sip of the poitín and coughed. "My God, bartender, I could light the lamps on my ship with this."

"Aye, sir," Jimmy said with a smile, "its good fer cleanin' tar off yer clothes. It'll clean yer pistols nicely, too."

It was after midnight when the party made its way out of the village. They placed Liam in the boat, pushed it into the sea, and climbed on board - all but one. Dan Donovon was left behind. He quietly made his way in the darkness back to the village, keeping off the road. He waited on the docks, hiding in an old curragh. The crescent of the moon, and the stars that had shone brightly in the crisp, cold air were now cloaked with grey-black clouds. There would be a soft rain at first light. A man was struggling with his skiff on the opposite side of the docks. Dan could hear the banging of an oar, and an array of curses. The man had banged his shin in his hurry to step a small mast in his boat. The man cast off the ropes, still cursing, and headed southwest. Dan made his way down the dock to a curragh that was left in the water for him. He took the oars and placed them, gently, into the pinholes. The oars were wrapped with cloth to muffle the sound as Dan pulled through the water, pacing himself to keep within range of the man in the skiff.

An hour later, Uncle Bob, Liam, and Michael sat in Callahan's pub, directly across the street from the magistrate's office.

"I want t'thank ya, Callahan, fer keepin' queer hours tonight," Liam said to his old friend. "There's the devil's work t'do dis night. A man needs a pint t'stand him up for it." Liam was sitting on a stool at the bar. Uncle Bob and Michael were looking out the window.

"What sort of man are we looking for, uncle?"

"Da worst sort, boyo. A man who'd slice his own mudder's t'roat."

They sat at the window, on a broad sill, in silence, watching the door of the office. Uncle Bob was sipping porter from a tankard. Michael looked on him with curiosity.

"How does it feel to be home, in Ireland?" Bob reached out with his huge paw of a hand and patted his nephew on the head.

"It feels good, boyo. I remember dis place so very well. Me mudder used ta take me fer walks around da town when she came here ta visit in da summers."

"What was she like?" Bob thought for a moment.

"Like an Irish summer. Warm an' bright an' friendly. She had da same color hair as I do. An' da curls! God, dey were gorgeous. She used ta brush t'ose curls fer an hour before bed, she was dat proud of them." He took a long pull on his tankard. "She died when I was quite young, just like Teresa, God bless dere souls." Bob smiled. "I wonder what t'ose two are talkin' about in heaven."

"About us," Michael stated, with conviction. " About how they can help us, I bet. Do you believe in heaven, then, uncle?"

"Believe in heaven? Of course I believe in heaven," Bob said, indignantly. "I'm not a church goer, Michael, but I'm not a bloody heathen either." They sat without saying anything for a while. Bob went to the bar to refresh his tankard. Callahan grinned as Bob's massive frame approached him.

"Ah, little Bobby. It's good t'see you after all these years. Lord, how long has it been, then?' Callahan looked him over, up and down, as if he was buying a horse. "You've grown up, lad." Bob stared at him in disbelief. The last time he saw Mr. Callahan was when he would fetch ale for his father in a bucket and bring it back to the O'Brien cottage, just outside of town. Callahan was smiling, then, too. He always smiled. The creases from a constant smile had been etched into his ruddy face.

"Mr. Callahan, it's been almost forty years since I left home. A man tends ta grow up in dat span of time." Bob gulped his porter and thought back to the Falcarragh of his youth. There was the O'Brien cottage, with its thatched roof and white washed walls. The great, grey mountain of Errigal rising up into white clouds, seemingly within reach from the back window. In front of the mountain were lush, kelly green fields, and to the left of the fields, the deep blue of the blustery, whitecapped Atlantic. Uncle Bob saw all this in his mind, the mind of a six-year-old boy.

"Wake up, lad," Liam said, tapping him on the shoulder.

"Huh? Oh, sorry. I was just t'inkin' on da cottage. Is it still dere?"

"Aye. Dat it tis. Like your mother never left it. Now, tell me what happened to yer brother." Bob slammed his tankard onto the bar.

"Dey took 'em. Da bastards. He was impressed before da war. God only knows where he is now, t'ough Captain Ken t'inks he's tryin' ta make his way ta Canada, where he can sneak t'rough da lines. I don't know. We shipped wit' Captain Boyle rather dan sit on our hands an' do nothin' while dis war drags on." Liam withdrew the pipe he had in his mouth.

"Sounds like you should have shipped ta Canada. Didn't I hear dat all the fightin's goin on up there?" Bob took another tug of his brew.

"Maybe we will, uncle, maybe dat's exactly what we'll do. After we blockade Britain an' ruin dere trade. I like takin' English money. 'Specially after what dey did ta me da." Liam stared down at his pint.

"By the time I heard about yer father, it was too late. Bastards. He had a nice shop. Built it up all by himself, from the trade he learned from his father. Robert was a good man and a fine cooper. A man of the code." Bob's face turned grim.

"He was a Catholic! Dat was his only crime! An' because of dat - jest because of dat - he was..." Michael was listening to every word. Now, he saw his uncle reduced to tears. Bob

Dooley's great shoulders shuddering in torrents of emotion. Feelings that he had buried for decades, that had only showed themselves in battle, in his hate filled eyes and crazed mind as he quenched his thirst for English blood. But the blood never satisfied, not fully. He had resigned himself to a life with no peace. Only hatred and gnawing memories of his father swinging from an English rope. Liam shook his head.

"I'm sorry, Bobby, I shoulda been there fer ya. But Cork is a long way from Donegal. We didn't know about it until it was all over." Callahan stopped smiling, the sadness coming over him.

"Hung fer treason, wasn't it?"

"Aye." Liam thought back to the trial. "It was all a set up. Rumors had been goin' around dat the French were ta invade through Cork. I don't know if there was any truth ta it. Anyway, Bobby's da was selected ta take a fall fer somebody, or the other coopers devised a way t'get rid of Catholic competition. It's an old story. They dat control the law use it on those who don't. They planted a map, a French map, in one of Robert's barrels. Said it was found on a ship bound fer France. Dat Robert had sketched it. What absurdity! Robert didn't know French. An' he couldn't draw a straight line. It was all a set up."

Uncle Bob had sunk down into a chair at one of the tables. He was still trying to control his tears. Michael walked from the window and put his arms around his uncle.

"Dat's why I dropped da code, boyo. I couldn't t'ink on what was right an' wrong like yer fadder could. He didn't see. He wasn't dere da morning dey hung me da." With the comfort of his dear nephew's arms around him and the truth of his pain revealed, Bob felt something akin to peace.

"Oh - oh - da - da. I'm sorry, I'm so sorry. I fergot da code an' I let ya down." Bob put his head in his hands. He whispered to himself, but in the quiet of the pub, everyone heard him. "Know what ya ought ta believe; know what ya ought ta desire; know what ya ought ta do."

A long minute later, the front door of the pub burst in. Dan Donovon leaned his shoulder against the frame, panting.

"I outran 'em...he didn't see me...the bloody bastard will be here any minute." Liam turned to Uncle Bob and nodded.

"Use the knife. Make sure ya slit his bloody t'roat, all the way around." Bob took Michael into his arms and pressed his body to him.

"I've got ta go now boyo. I got ta do somethin' fer our people. When ya have laws ya can do it da right way. But da Irish have no law. An' people will die unless this man is stopped an' made an example of." He shoved Michael back from him and looked him in the eyes. "I can't leaved dis ta da Defenders. Somebody will have ta take a fall. It might as well be me. Dey can blame it all on me. Courage, boyo. Everythin's gonna be all right. We can talk, now. We'll talk about da code, boyo. From now on we'll talk about it. T'anks ta you." Bob stumbled out the door after Dan Donovon.

Colonel Willowby was propped on his chaise enjoying a glass of red wine. One of his spies had informed him of a meeting between the Americans and the volunteers on Inishbofin. He waited now for the details of that meeting from a new informant. It had cost him a great amount of gold, but it was worth it. He needed only to get that information to Londonderry and then take credit for spoiling the plans of the American raiders. Getting the information out wouldn't be that much of a problem. He had his network of agents ready. Tonight, with the information from that meeting and the name of the captain of the Defenders that had eluded him all these years, he would turn the fall of Falcarragh into a stunning victory. The colonel adjusted a pillow beneath his broken leg and thought about the medal he would receive from the Lord-Lieutenant. Maybe even a title. A trip to London - Westminster Castle. "Lord Willowby," he said with a grin.

The informant walked up to the magistrate's office in the dead of night feeling a deadness in his soul. He never thought he would ever do a thing like this. He stumbled on a rock and fell to the ground. He was still drunk from the bottle he had brought with him on his boat. Drunk to hide the guilt that enveloped him. He hit the ground with his fist and got up. He had no wife and no children. He only had the Defenders. Now, he was all alone.

"Can't pay me damned taxes...shut my place down...starve t'death in this cold...no...no....no...who cares?...it's all over now anyway...they'll never be another rising...Catholic an' Prod forever at each other's t'roats...every man fer himself...to Spain...America...I could be a king with all that money."

He tumbled across the lawn to the office, to a small window where a light was still shining. He tapped, quietly, on the pane. Willowby winced getting off the chaise.

"Ah," the colonel whispered to himself, "my salvation is at the window." That afternoon, at the same window, another man had slipped Willowby the gold he had requested. He had hidden the bag under the cushion of the chaise and now, unsteadily, he carried it to his informer. He walked slowly, very slowly and painfully. Willowby unlocked the latch on the window and looked out. No one was there. He looked down. Jimmy, the barkeep, lay on the ground. His throat sliced clean around. A knife was stuck in his chest. Attached to it read a note that read "BASTARD INFORMER."

Chapter 18

THE BLOCKADE

There was no light at the point on Horn Head, so Captain Ken sailed the *Chasseur* into Falcarragh with Liam's pilot at the helm. The old man's seventy-two hour sortie had been successful. He had sailed right into Lough Foyle taking six prizes before a frigate came up from Londonderry to stop him. *Chasseur* easily out sailed the enemy, even though the schooner had come to be deep in the water, carrying as she was fifty prisoners and a wealth of Anglo-Irish trade. Jerry, the Defender, who was the look out on Horn Head, sent a signal that the American privateer was coming in. Down the coastline, mirrors were hoisted relaying the signal, since the sun was full in an unusually cloudless Irish sky. Upon receipt of the signal, Boyle called for a final meeting at Callahan's.

The pub was decked out in the finest array a town the size of Falcarragh could proffer. Boyle insisted upon paying for everything and Uncle Bob took great pains to see that the celebration was done in fine style. Dancers were brought in dressed in traditional costume and a band was in the midst of a foot-tapping reel as Ken Russell came in the doorway. At Liam's order, the men of the *Chasseur* removed the magistrate from his office and had him carted outside of town, along with the prisoners that had been taken by the schooner. This made the townspeople feel more at ease. The Defenders knew, of course, that Duncan Willowby's wrath would be taken out on them, but they had weathered the colonel's anger before and would do so again. It was worth it to them to feel, even if it was for just a few hours, the joy of not being under the conqueror's boot. Not a precious moment was lost. Whole families took holiday from the drudgery of work in the fields to feast and party at the American captain's gala sendoff.

Captain Ken made his way through the crowded pub, a crowd that had spilled out onto the street and around the magistrate's office. Every crewmember of the *Chasseur* receiving a countless chorus of "God bless ya, son", pumping of hands, kisses and hugs. Ken saw Boyle at a make shift head table. One of the schooner's American flags had been sent from the ship and was hung, proudly, from the rafters over top the table. Boyle was enjoying the dancing of one particular lass. She was performing a traditional step dance and whirled around the head table, back straight, legs kicking high into the air, a pleasant smile upon her face. Uncle Bob leaned over and shouted in his ear

"She's gorgeous! Isn't she captain, darlin'!" Through the din Boyle could only show his white teeth in a broad smile and nod. He fixed his attention back to the girl. Her skirt flayed up to the tops of her thighs as she kicked her legs to the beat of the music. She had bright red hair that hung in curls and bounced to the music as well. Uncle Bob was at his ear again:

"She wants ta come ta America, sir. Wouldn't it be nice ta have such a talent on our long voyage? An' such a pair of legs da Point has never seen! I'm goin' ta propose ta her."

It was obvious, to Boyle, that his Captain of Marine was drunk. This didn't bother Boyle too much. The party was for the *Chasseur's* men, except the unlucky swabs who were on watch, as well as the townspeople. But, Boyle had known Uncle Bob to be a confirmed bachelor and this sudden bent toward matrimony astonished him. He looked, incredulously, at Bob Dooley.

"Aye, sir. I'm takin' back da code of me fathers an' am goin' ta settle down. Dis lass seems as good as any."

"They'll be no woman aboard my ship, Captain Dooley!" Boyle screamed above the music. "Send for her after the war, when you've regained your senses and your sobriety." Uncle Bob pointed in the girl's direction and was about to protest, to say something about the dancer sharing a cabin with Mr. Henry, but thought better of it and sat back down. Ken walked toward the head table and Boyle stood up. Liam, who was also seated at the table, put a stop to the music and shushed the crowd.

"It's good to see you well, suh," Boyle said coming out and around the table. "Are the prisoners secured?"

"Aye, cap'n. I understand the're all holed up in a cave somewhere until we're off on the tide, Cap'n O'Brien's orders, sir."

"Yes, a sound idea. They'll all be released after we've weighed anchor. A cave is much more comforting than what the English would have prepared for us. Your report then."

"Six prizes, cap'n. Enough valuables to buy a new ship, and twenty thousand pounds in specie." The crowd murmured in delight. Boyle motioned for the band to resume their reel. Then he bent close to Captain Ken, explaining something to him in private. Uncle Bob immediately became suspicious. He swung his trunk like legs over the head table and listened to his captain's commands:

"Then, follow these orders, Ken. Half of the provisions, commodities of value in these parts, and half the specie to be given to the good people of Falcarragh and Inishbofin before we leave." Uncle Bob raised and shook his hands in front of him in a pleading manner.

"No! Don't be doin' dis, captain, please!" Boyle shot a glance at him with angry eyes. "Oh, forgive me, captain, please I know dese people. If you tell dem your gonna give dem money, dey will argue da details fer years, generations, even." Boyle brought his hand to an end of his mustache and rolled it in his fingers.

"All right, Captain Dooley, what do you suggest?" Uncle Bob looked around to make sure no one was eavesdropping.

"Dis is a lot of money, captain. More money dan da people here have seen in dere whole lives. Dere isn't a way fer it ta be divided up without argumentation. It's - it's in da blood, sir."

"Then how can I show them my appreciation?" Bob thought for a moment, then raised his finger with an idea.

"Give half ta da priest, God bless 'em, an' half ta da Defenders. But, under no circumstances, let anybody know ya gave the money." Boyle nodded and then took Ken by the shoulder.

"Take Captain O'Brien with you. Find Mr. Hollingsworth and get everything into the boats as soon as possible." Ken looked at his captain with surprise. "Don't worry, old friend. I and I alone will answer to the owners of the *Chasseur*. Everything will be accounted for in my logs. We couldn't have succeeded in this operation unless the Defenders were with us. By God, this was an extraordinary accomplishment. People will be talking about the *Chasseur* for years after we've gone."

Liam had the Defenders lift him onto the table. The crowd quieted, in expectation of the old man's words. Hands were raised fore and aft to steady him as he struggled to make his bending, aching knees support his frame. He raised his pint, solemnly.

"To the President of the United States!" Uncle Bob put an unsteady boot on the table and rose with his tankard waving in the air and his eyes full of tears.

"Raise your glasses, lads! C'mon, dat's right." He shot his tankard upwards, in preparation for a toast, spilling half it's contents onto the crowd. "Ta da Defenders of our countries, be they Amer'can or Irish. Ta Wolf Tone an' Wash'ton!"

That evening, Uncle Bob stood in the waist, leaning over the weather rail. A land breeze came up after the sun had finally set. Michael was standing at his side. They stared back at the coast of Donegal. Neither one of them wanting for words. Captain Ken approached them and put his squatty arms over their shoulders.

"Well, Bob, I understand you've decided to take on a bride." Michael turned his eyes and looked up at his uncle in shock.

"A bride? You? Why, that's incredible, uncle. You used to tell my mother that you could never marry, since she had already been taken and no other woman in the world could match her." Bob looked forlorn.

"Aye, boyo, dat's true. I got caught up in da celebratin'. Da drink goes ta yer head an' makes ya do queer t'ings." Bob saw the look of disappointment in his nephew's eyes. "Not dat I haven't decided ta take da plunge. A man of da code knows what he ought ta desire. But, Captain Boyle set me sh'traight," he sighed. "Still, Ken, dat was a fine girl, dat dancer."

"You could be her grandfather," Ken chastised him. "You should be ashamed, you old coot."

"Ashamed, is it? An' who was leerin' from da doorway at her fer da longest time before ya finally made yer report ta da captain." Captain Ken whisked his arm away from Bob's shoulders.

"That, Robert Dooley, was a different kind of look. One ye wouldn't know bout. I've been in mournin' fer my 'Lizbeth these last thirty years. Ye know that!" Bob rolled his eyes in shame.

"Oh, mush-a-mush, Ken I didn't mean it dat way. Truly, I didn't. I know dat when a man gets attached ta a girl, I mean really attached, nothin', not years, nor space, nor death, can separate him from her. Just like Mike fer Teresa. It's just dat I always wanted dat fer meself. Dat kind of love fer a woman." Ken, once again, put his arms around his friend.

"Love that time nor tide, nor heaven, by God, kin come between ye. Truer words were never spoken, Bob - 'little Bobby' - hey, hey." Ken and Michael laughed together.

Uncle Bob was about to take offense at this, but the day and the porter and the music of his homeland were still with him. So were the thighs of the redhead, step dancing to a jubilant reel. Jessica came up the companionway and joined them.

"How's David?" Michael asked, a tenderness in his voice that made Uncle Bob and Captain Ken uneasy. This was the plan, of course, Father John's plan: to keep Michael and Jessica together. The dying wish of Teresa. But, nobody thought of the consequences once they did fall in love with each other. Uncle

Bob frowned as he checked to see no one was listening. Jessica's face was beaming.

"Doctor Williams says he'll not have to amputate. David's fever has gone down and the wound is draining nicely, although, David might have some trouble walking from now on. Still, isn't it wonderful!" Uncle Bob stopped frowning and patted Jessica on the head.

"Aye, dat it tis, St. Patrick himself has been wit' us on dis journey. Praise be, da boy will live on wit' two legs, da way God intended.

They all gazed out over the railing at the coastline, as the ship passed Horn Head. A light appeared in the grayness of the point.

It's Jerry, by heaven," Bob exclaimed. "What does it say Ken?" Captain Ken's blue eyes read the signal, and then drooped down, blinking. This was the first time Bob Dooley had ever seen Ken become emotional.

"It says," and then in a lower voice, "it says, 'in God's name'."

Michael found a bucket on deck and tied a rope around the handle. He dipped the bucket into the ocean and brought it up to the railing. He smiled at Jessica, Uncle Bob, and Captain Ken. Then, very deliberately, he dipped his forefinger and middle finger into the briny water and blessed himself. They all did.

Luck and Thomas Boyle were never apart for any stretch of time. Especially when he took advantage of a stiff, northwest breeze and sailed the schooner into the North Channel, towards the Isle of Man, and into the Irish Sea. With the sailing ability of the *Chasseur*, the experience of her crew, and the ingenuity and bravado of her captain, nothing since, perhaps, John Paul Jones and the *Bonhomme Richard*, had ever gotten so much attention from the Royal Navy. Four man-of-war brigs were sent out to catch the sleek, Baltimore schooner.

The *Chasseur* sailed on defiantly, taking prizes by the score. The fastest and best prizes were lightly manned and sent to safe ports in France, or home to an American port, where the owners of the *Chasseur* had secured business agents and banking houses to see that the ships and cargoes were sold at a good price.

Insurance rates soared for Anglo-Irish shipping. Merchants cried out for protection. Lloyd's of London, the best-known insurer of shipping, hesitated on insuring any ship at all. Meetings were called in Milford, Glasgow, and Bristol to draw up resolutions demanding that the Royal Navy do something about the American privateers. The *Chasseur* was joined in English waters by many privateers. Some American captains were almost as daring and successful as Boyle himself. There was *Young Wasp*, of Philadelphia, *Harpy*, of Baltimore, *Leo*, of Boston, and the *Siren*, *Mammoth*, *Sabine*, *Surprise*, and the *Governor Tompkins*, which burned fourteen merchant vessels in succession in the British Channel. And, next to the *Chasseur*, the most audacious privateer in the Irish Sea: the *Prince of Neufchatel*, of New York. Uncle Bob was right, the British press carried stories of American privateers choking the commerce of the kingdom. The public became infuriated with accounts of American raiding and prize taking. "And," the press asked, "where was the Royal Navy, with her thousand ships? The little United States of America, previously held in contempt, mocked and laughed at, now blockading Britain, and with a private navy!" Even the London *Times* had once looked at the Americans as a joke. As early as 1807, the *Times* had stated that the Americans couldn't even cross over to Staten Island without British permission.

Now, all that had changed. Boyle was sitting in his cabin, leather boot resting on a footstool, laughing at a copy of a resolution he had obtained from *Carlbury*, of London, bound for Curacao, via Jamaica. Captain Ken was seated across from him, sipping strong coffee.

"Will you listen to this, Ken." Boyle stood up and held the document up to a light that was rocking sideways with the motion of the ship. " 'Be it resolved; that the number of American privateers with which our channels have been infested, the audacity with which they have approached our coasts, and the success with which their enterprise has been attended, have proved injurious to our commerce, humbling to our pride, and discreditable to the directors of the naval power of the British nation, whose flag till of late waved over every sea and triumphed over every rival...'

"Ha! Wait! This is the best part." Boyle could hardly control himself. "'...Whose maritime strength we have hitherto impolitically held in contempt.'! Good God! Impolitically! Hell! I'd say it was impolitic to hold us in contempt! Damned impolite, as well." Ken enjoyed seeing Boyle having so much fun.

"Ye did it, Tom. The whole world is talkin' 'bout us privateerin' men. But, that's a heap of words fer somebody who wants ta say: 'look, we made a big mistake and would like ta carry on our business without peerin' down the muzzle of a gun, and givin' over everythin' we have cause we don't mean ta be impolitikin' anymore.'"

Boyle sat back down in a state of giddiness. Ken picked up a newspaper and cleared his throat. "I got this here one from the captain's cabin of the *Amicus*. It's from the *Times*, dated two weeks ago: 'The American cruisers daily enter in among our convoys, seize prizes in sight of those that should afford protection, and if pursued, put on their sea-wings and laugh at the clumsy English pursuers. To what is this owin'? Cannot we build ships? It must be encouragin' to Mr. Madison to read the logs of his cruisers. If they fight, they are sure to conquer; if they fly, they are sure to escape.' " Ken dropped the newspaper to his lap, a puzzled look on his old face. "Tom, I don't git it."

"Get what? It's perfectly obvious, my friend. They're confused. They don't unda'stand what happened. They can take on old Boney and a million French soldiers in the field, despite the respect they have for Napoleon and the French on land, but they can't stop us." Boyle sighed and giggled at the same time. "But, they're an intelligent people. One of these days, after the war is over, they'll realize that Americans are good sailors and even better ship makers."

"No, Tom, that's not what I meant. We did it before. In the First War of Independence. We outfitted privateers and sailed them over and sent their insurance rates up somethin' awful. What I can't git is how come they don't remember?" Boyle's giddiness left him. He played with the end of his mustache and shook his head.

"I'm not sure. Perhaps it's because they never really saw Yorktown as the end of the war. To them the war never ended, this is just the second phase. And without a break in their thinking, they never took the time to properly assess what they did wrong the last time around. Maybe I can't blame them. They've been almost constantly at war with France for so long they haven't had time to think about America. About how we've grown - as a nation, I mean."

"But they see us as divided," Ken said, "not as one nation. That's why they went down the St. Lawrence and Champlain in the last war, ta split us up - New England from the rest of the country. And they'll do it again, by God, they will."

"But all that's changing, now," Boyle insisted. "We seamen never cared which state we were from, we've been flying the national flag since the beginning, and are quite proud of it. That's why our success has been at sea. Both in our navy and with us privateers. We know what this war is about. We've shared the humility of impressed shipmates and of not being able to trade freely on the world's oceans because of European wars. And that feeling - that feeling of oneness under one flag is contagious. Why, people in Boston cheered as hard and as long as people in Fells Point did when the news of *Constitution* over *Java* was heard. In every town in America the news was cheered. Nobody asked what state the *Constitution* was from, everyone recognized it as a national victory. This is a subtle change, I admit. But, it's a change in the way we view ourselves in relation to the whole." Ken waved his hands in disgust.

"No disrespect, Tom. But those militia boys in New York refused to cross the border into Canada, 'cause they only joined ta fight fer New York. No, I don't see it. Why, practical all of New England is agin' this war. There was talk of secession when we put ta sea. Our people are very different. The South doesn't even see their blacks as people, let alone Americans." They both reflected on what Ken just said.

"I know it's a long way off, Ken. Maybe - maybe we aren't ready to see ourselves as one people. These things take time. But we have the right vessel to take us there."

"A vessel? Waddaya mean, a ship?"

"Yes and no," Boyle said with uncertainty. "Maybe that's why it was the *Constitution* that secured our first victory. In the Constitution, our national Constitution, lie the answers we're looking for. Perhaps not today, nor tomorrow, but soon, one day, soon."

Boyle rubbed his tired eyes. The deep nature of their conversation had mixed with a long day's work and his mind began to drift. He slapped a hand onto his knee to bring him back to the business of captaining his ship. "Have we finished unloading the *Amicus*?"

"Aye, Tom. What do ya want us ta do with her?"

"Send her back with the prisoners, she's a rum sailor, and we have no more prize crews to take her into port. How many men do we have left?"

"Not more than sixty. A dozen ta fifteen prime hands is all we got left."

"Just enough to get us back home. I'll set a course. Is the master of the *Amicus* aboard?"

"Coolin' his heels ta see ya. But why send the brig back at all? Why don't we burn her up?"

"You'll see in a minute, suh. I want to do one more thing before we leave these waters and go back home. Pass the word for the Master of the brig."

The Sailing Master of the *Amicus* was Nathan Campbell. A worthy old salt who saw his crew run below decks when the

Chasseur fired a bow chaser and ordered her to come into the wind. Without a crew to defend his ship and fire its compliment of six guns, he had no choice but to comply. Being a stubborn Scotsman, he would have preferred giving the privateer at least a broadside before hauling down his colors. Boyle had been looking forward to this moment for some time.

"Good evening, Captain Campbell."

"Nay, sir, tis nothing of the kind, not for me."

"It will be, suh, I assure you. Prey, have a seat at the desk. I wish you to write a proclamation for me and to deliver it in person to Lloyd's of London. In return, I won't burn your ship, nor take any prisoners. May I have your word, suh, as a gentleman, that you will do me this service?" Campbell was as much shocked with Boyle's offer as Captain Ken, who had stayed in the cabin upon seeing that devilish look in Boyle's brown eyes, and was determined to see what mischief his captain had in mind.

"I - well - you are very gracious, sir. It is, indeed, a bonny offer. Of course, I'd do anything, short of treason ta keep ma'ship. But I can no unda'stand your reasoning for such a display of generosity, especially on the part of an American."

"Here is a quill Captain Campbell. Just write what I tell you, if you will be so kind." Campbell shrugged his shoulders.

"Aye, laddy. Today's date?"

"Yes." Boyle began pacing the cabin's deck. "Whereas, it has been customary with the admirals of Great Britain commanding the small forces on the coast of the United States, particularly with Sir John Borlaise Warren and Sir Alexander Cochrane to declare the coast of the said United States in a state of strict and rigorous blockade, without possessing the power to justify such a declaration or stationing an adequate force to maintain such blockade;

"I do, therefore, by virtue of the power and authority in me vested, possessing sufficient force, declare all the ports, harbors, bays, creeks, rivers, inlets, outlets, islands, and sea coast of the

United Kingdom of Great Britain and Ireland in a state of strict and rigorous blockade.

"And I do further declare, that I consider the force under my command adequate to maintain, strictly, rigorously, and effectually, the said blockade.

"And I do hereby require the respective officers, whether Captains, Commanders, or Commanding Officers under my command, employed or to be employed on the coast of England, Ireland, and Scotland, to pay strict attention to this my Proclamation.

"And I do hereby caution and forbid the ships and vessels of all and every nation in amity and peace with the United States from entering or attempting to enter, or from forming or attempting to come out of any of the said ports, harbours, bays creeks, rivers inlets, outlets, islands, or sea coasts, on or under any pretense whatsoever.

"And that no person may plead ignorance of this my proclamation, I have ordered the same to be made public in England.

"Given under my hand on board the *Chausser*; day and date as above."

Campbell lifted the proclamation up to the light so that Boyle could examine it.

"Very well, suh. You may proceed to your ship," Boyle said. Before he left the cabin, escorted by Captain Ken, Campbell offered his hand to Boyle.

"It pleases me highly ta do business with you, sir. I'll put this where every broker kin see it, on the front door of Lloyds Coffee House." They clasped hands and smiled at each other. "My conscious forces me ta tell you, Captain Boyle, that they'll be a great deal of noise when this is posted. Many a gentlemen will call fer your head on a silver platter."

"It's the only way heads should be served, Captain Campbell," Boyle replied. The Scotsman turned and followed Ken up the ladder to the deck. In the waning light of day, Campbell looked, once more, at Boyle's Proclamation. "Lawyers and insurance men, their all bastards any way, laddy," he muttered to Captain Ken.

Happy George was in the fighting top, scanning the horizon. "On deck! Sail off the starboard beam!" Ken cupped his hands to his eyes. The sun was just at the horizon and his blue eyes were blinded by the golden light reflecting off the chop of the channel. Michael was at the starboard railing squinting his eyes, along with many of what was left of the crew.

"Michael!" Ken shouted in his high pitched voice, "inform the captain at once." Campbell was being rowed over to the *Amicus* in the Captain's gig, and had heard the topman's sighting.

"What is she, laddy! Kin you make her out?" Boyle arrived on deck and quickly mounted the main shrouds. He yelled down to Mr. Leib, who was in the gig with Campbell.

"Look sharp there! Get that boat to the *Amicus* and back again, quickly!"

"On deck! It's a brig! A man-of-war brig!" Happy screamed. Boyle looked down at Captain Ken on the quarterdeck.

"I smell a rat, Captain Russell. She's snuck up on us using the *Amicus* and the dusk to steal her from view.

"On deck!" It was Happy again, pointing off the stern. "Another sail - another brig off the larboard quarter!"

"I knew it!" Boyle exclaimed. "Captain Russell! All hands prepare to make sail!"

"Aye, captain, all hands it is."

"Captain Dooley! Marines to the clewlines and reef tackle. Lieutenant Donovon! Ease the inner and outer buntlines."

The *Chasseur* crew was in a fury of sound and movement. Orders barked out and repeated, men scurrying up the rat lines and over the yards loosening sail, waisters and marines removing lines from the belaying pins, manning some, letting others run free.

"Hurry, Mr. Leib! For God's sake, hurry!" Boyle shouted in the direction of the *Amicus*.

It was a trap. While the *Chasseur* was taking the *Amicus*, the brig to starboard stood off until the second brig, off the larboard quarter, could close in. Had Happy not spotted the faint silhouette in the setting sun, the fate of the *Chasseur* would have been sealed. As it was, Boyle had time to get the schooner under way, but the British were already nearly within firing range. The gig was hoisted onto the schooner as her sails bellowed in the wind. A shot rang out from starboard. The ball went cleanly through the fore topsail and splashed in the water off the larboard bow. Jessica noticed Captain Boyle smiling, at the wheel, but she couldn't understand why.

"We've been hit. Will they take us, sir."

"We'll take a few more hits like that any day, Mr. Henry. Whether we're taken depends on a number of things. In the meantime, you and Captain Russell fix the position of those brigs. Estimate their speed and at what point they'll intersect our course. Then tell me what rate of speed the *Chasseur* will need to make sure they don't intersect our course at all, unda'stand?"

"Yes, sir. Estimate intersection and needed speed."

Boyle already knew that the speed the *Chasseur* needed was to clap on every rag of sail and run her on their present course until they were temporarily out of danger. Temporarily, because the schooner's present course brought her father away from the brig off starboard, but nearer to the brig coming up from behind to larboard. He had no choice. Soon, there would be other things to do, but for now the hunter was the hunted, and he thought it best to keep the young girl occupied with mathematics, rather than worry about capture.

The captain of the man-of-war to starboard knew he was losing his range. He brought his ship into the wind and gambled on losing time in catching the privateer with the chance of knocking down a spar or two with his broadside. The man-of-war's battery hit the *Chasseur* simultaneously, shaking the deck and knocking down men as it did so. Boyle was still at the wheel, but he could see the broadside hit his foremast. It cracked like thunder as it was ripped from the ship and hurled into the water. Screams were heard from below deck. Mr. Conner raced to the quarterdeck.

"The forem'st was shot clear away, sir! About twelve feet up." Boyle became agitated.

"Don't just stand there, Mr. Conner, put axes to those lines and clear the rigging. Fish a new mast and jury-rig it. Move!" Uncle Bob was on his knees in the waist and shouted up to Boyle.

"A ball struck da gunwale of port number five, tore away all da sill and plank shear, dismounted da gun and went t'rough da deck. It wounded t'ree of me marines. Henry Watson's leg is pretty near torn off, sir."

"Thank you, Captain Dooley, have Doctor Williams set up sick bay in my cabin. Make the men as comfortable as possible."

"Aye, sir. Hospital in yer cabin." Jessica appeared on the quarterdeck. She had been in the stern with the log line checking the speed of the schooner and estimating the speed of the brigs.

"We've lost two knots with the forem'st gone, captain. The brig to starboard is out of range and is just now coming up on four knots. We're running at seven. The brig to larboard is gaining, not from speed she's only doing seven knots as well, but from our course." Boyle laughed.

"By God, Mr. Henry are you advising me to change course?" Jessica blushed.

"To - to - cut the angle to the brig to larboard, sir. Um, yes, sir."

"Well, then. Change of course it is! Ha! Ha! The captain who fired his broadside won't have a commission after today! He should have been more patient. They'll be no intersection, now, Mr. Henry. When the foremast is repaired, I'll run with the wind on my quarter and nothing afloat will catch us. Until then, we've got to endure that infernal brig on the other side. What would you suggest, Mr. Henry?" Jessica took a deep breath.

"Take her six points to starboard, captain. Show the brig our stern and hope to God that we can repair the forem'st before she gets within range, which will be any minute now." Boyle laughed again. Jessica saw a look of wild enthusiasm on his face.

"I'll take your advice, my young master's mate. But I'll be damned if we're going to let that brig take aim with her bow chasers. Pass the word for Mr. Lugger."

"Mr. Lugger, yes sir." Jessica shouted forward for the bosun, and as she did so, he appeared before her, staring at her with a smirk on his face. He brushed by her, still staring with his awful, magnetic eyes.

"Mr. Lugger, I want you to have every other gun thrown over and any spare yards. Also, start releasing the water. Have the carpenter come aft and take away the stern rail, and move *Slingshot* into the stern." Jessica went back to her log line as Mr. Lugger directed the carpenter and a crew of men to remove the railing and bring the other long nine aft. The men tore their shirts off, their bodies glistening with sweat while they hoisted the gun and moved it from bow to stern.

James Darymple barked orders to his gun crew as he sighted *Slingshot* on the pursuing brig. Michael took his place behind the gun, glancing, nervously, at Jessica. With the railing gone, the two long nines would have plenty of play when the man-of-war was astern the *Chasseur*. Jessica noticed the ship's speed picking up immediately as the guns and water were thrown over the side. She tried hard to keep her eyes and her mind on her work, but Lugger was there beside her, brushing up against her, staring at her. Michael noticed it too, but there was nothing he could do.

The British opened fire with their bow chaser. The shots came over the stern, hurling down into the waist, crashing onto the deck. Chain shot wrapped around the main mast and went bouncing and careening off the bulwark, taking off arms and breaking legs and heads. Mr. Connor worked the second long nine in the stern, but his shots went wide of the brig, whose gun crew worked furiously, pounding the *Chasseur*, raking her without mercy. Jessica now hid beneath the railing. She looked back in horror upon the murderous path the British fire had taken on the deck of the schooner. She wanted to scream. To warn Michael to lie down. To tell him to run away. But the sight of so much blood paralyzed her.

Michael's body shook with fear and rage. He looked at Jessica curled up in a ball. For a moment, they found each other's eyes. Suddenly, both of them were chilled. Emptiness swept over their spirit as if this would be the last time they would see each other.

"James!" Boyle shouted. James trained *Slingshot's* sights on the massive bow of the oncoming brig. He waited, patiently, though the whirl of chain shot whizzed over his head, for the crest of a wave. Michael crouched beside him, lighted match in his shaking hand. James grabbed the match and yanked it from Michael's tight grip. He thrust the match to the touchhole.

"Fire in da hole!" James screamed. *Slingshot* exploded and whipped back on her carriage, straining tackle and blocks. It sent its ball on a true line across to the bow of the brig. The ball smashed into one of the bow chasers as it was ready to fire, igniting its gun powder while swinging the gun carriage astern. Jessica stood up and peeked over the railing to see if James had hit his mark. The British bow chaser fired into her own ship, raking it. Chain shot, meant for the Americans, killed with impunity the powder monkey, captain, first lieutenant, and boson's mate of the brig. British blood ran through the scuppers and emptied into the channel.

Then, *Chasseur* simply flew over the sea. Her foremast had been repaired, and with the weight of cannon and water over the side, the schooner nearly soared. The distance spread as nightfall came.

Boyle yawned.

"Mr. Henry." Jessica slowly made her way to the captain's side. "Tell Mr. Conner to stand down and set up the watch. Get the cook to fix something hearty for the men. It's been a long day." He looked at Jessica with a father's eye. Her face was white, her eyes dull. She had seen chain and ball rip into mens' bodies. She had seen *Slingshot's* ball hit the British bow chaser. She saw the enemy's powder monkey a second before he was hit, disappear in a belch of smoke and flame. Boyle knew the look. It was the same with men everywhere who first taste battle. He decided to bring her mind on another tack. "Oh, and well done, Mr. Henry! I've never seen anyone faster at figures than you. Well done, indeed."

"Thank you, captain," she stated, dryly, not feeling any pride. "Mr. Conner it is." She shouted foreword and Mr. Conner came up directly. She turned to Boyle with questioning eyes. "Where to now, sir?"

"To? Oh, yes. Good question, Mr. Henry. We have precious little men to fight with. Boarding would be impossible. I believe our cruise is coming to an end, Mr. Henry."

Boyle stood aside and let his second mate take the wheel. "Steer due South, Mr. Conner, for the present. We'll go down to the Canary Islands, reprovision, and make the crossing with the northeast trade winds."

Chapter 19

INTUITION

Ships have been following the Northeast trade winds to the New World since Columbus mistakenly named the West Indies. These strong winds are usually reliable, but as a ship sails further north, the wind becomes fickle and begins to vary, sometimes vanishing completely. Unhappily, the *Chasseur* found itself in this doldrum like state. The schooner was now wallowing in little to light airs. The sailors, who were not needed to go aloft during these windless days and nights, and the marines who were always bored without the prospect of a fight, became restless. The heat and stench building up below kept most of the crew on the gun deck, huddling around what little comfort could be found from makeshift canvas stretched over the lower yards and providing a modicum of shade. Michael and Uncle Bob used this inactivity to provide a private forum for their discussions on the code of Aquinas.

Michael understood, now, fully. Ever since he received the code from Father John, Michael suspected some strange occurrence had befallen his uncle that forced him to swear off the code of their ancestors. That night at Callahan's uncovered the burden Bob Dooley had borne in his aching heart these many years. As far as the code was concerned, there was a lot of catching up to do on Uncle Bob's part, and both uncle and nephew had questions that only a true man of the code could answer. But, Mike Dooley was far from the small deck of the *Chasseur*. So, Michael and Uncle Bob tried to sort things out as best they could.

The young Dooley talked as much as his uncle during these long, undisturbed conversations. Undisturbed, because the rest of the ship's company had rather talk about the portion of prize money they expected to receive or the amount of credit that would be afforded them from loan sharks like the "King" on the Point.

It was on one of these occasions Michael realized his uncle had truly decided to take the code to heart, albeit by a different route than any Dooley in history. They were up in the bow, as usual, gazing, lazily, at the blue water.

"Haven't had a drop dese many weeks, boyo," Bob Dooley said with amazement. "Don't feel anythin' like I did on the way over." They both peered at the horizon. The sameness of water and sun that frustrated the ship's company, had an opposite effect on the Dooley's. A closeness had established itself over them. Just as men who have fought in battle and survived feel an unspoken bond, so too did uncle and nephew experience a commonality, A shared respect that was understood. This camaraderie that was felt with quiet joy. Water and sun, and a motionless ship which rocked gently on what was left of the equatorial current, served to add closure to the pain both had felt in their hearts. Michael's, for the death of his mother and the absence of his father. Uncle Bob's, for the execution of his da before his very eyes.

"Have you sworn off the drink, then?" Michael asked, breaking the silence of the calm sea. Bob Dooley shuffled his feet.

"Maybe it's..." the giant Irishmen hesitated, searching within himself for the answer "...maybe it's too late fer me. I have a weakness, ya see. I'm not used ta usin' da code all me life like yer fadder, God help 'im. I t'ink it's goin' ta take time ta have it enter me soul an' make da decisions fer me. Mike doesn't even have ta t'ink on da code anymore. Da code t'inks fer 'im." Michael picked his head up, questions in his brown eyes.

"What are you saying? Does the code take over your mind?" Bob glanced down at his nephew and shrugged his huge shoulders.

"In a manner of speakin', it does dat very t'ing. Look, I haven't had a conscience in da last fifty years. I've done whatever I pleased, whenever I pleased, ya see? It's goin' ta take time wit' me, dat's all." Bob could see the disappointment on Michael's face. "Oh, don't be worrin', boyo, it's all right. Or it's goin' ta be soon." Bob sighed and put both of his massive hands on the railing, gripping the wood with thick fingers. " 'Know what ya ought ta believe; know what ya ought ta desire; know what ya ought ta do.'" He shook his head, red curls falling about his eyes. "Simple words. Simple words. Words dat can change ya over a lifetime. But, me lifetime's mostly behind me. I wonder if it's too late fer me? In the meantime, I've a stash of lovely Madeira. It's true I don't feel anxious fer da drink. Not like I used ta. When yer young it's different. Ya can put da code ta work in yer life early. Ya can check what you do, da decisions ya face, wit' da meanin' of da code. Ya know. T'ink on it at night when ya have a moment of da soul an' can't sleep a wink; or talk it over wit' yer da, as I did when I first got it from him. But, dat was half a century ago, boyo. A lot of water under da bridge - dirty water fer me, mixed wit' whiskey an' gin. I'll not be embarrassin' ya anymore, t'ough, boyo. I'll try ta stay sober an' remember da code." Bob poked his head out from the shade of the canvas and winced at the blistering sun. "But, if one of t'ose hurricanes comes dis way, I'll not be responsible fer breakin' anybody's code - not in dis world anyway."

Michael didn't mind Uncle Bob talking this way. He knew his uncle was speaking the truth. Not attempting to fool anyone, let alone himself. That was refreshing. A side of his uncle he would always cherish. They looked at the expanse of sea before them and fell quiet for a moment.

"Tell me, uncle. Once you've taken the code, and I mean anyone - not just you and I - do you use it to make important decisions just with your mind, or can you do it with your - umm - with your feelings?"

"Whadda ya mean, yer feelins'?"

"Well, when Father John asked me to think on the code before I decided to sail on the *Chasseur*, I made that decision with my mind. I thought about it, and prayed on it, and saw it -

thought it - to be something I ought to do. But, before we landed in Donegal, when I realized how much Jessica meant to me and how badly I had treated her, I didn't think of the code. It just happened. It was a feeling, uncle. A feeling that she is what I *ought* to desire. But, it felt like the code - like I was using the code with my heart." Bob crouched back under the canvas and put a hand over Michael's mouth.

"Watch da 'J' word, boyo. Dere's lads here who are doin' dere own desirin' an' aren't particular about who dey do it wit'. Let's have none of dat talk 'till we're below."

"Sorry. But, that's something I've got to talk to you about, too."

"Later, boyo, later. Fer God's sake. Now, as fer feelin' da code, dat's only natural. Yer mudder, Teresa, God bless her soul, had as strong a feelin's as any woman. Mike has strong feelin's, too. Not everythin' has ta be run t'rough yer head first. But ya have ta watch yerself. Remember when I wanted ta take dat dancer back ta America wit' us?" Michael nodded and rolled his eyes. "Not bein' a strong man of da code, an' feelin' no pain, as it were, I desired da wrong t'ing. Usin' da code ta pick a mate fer life is probably da most important t'ing ya can do. Somehow, I get da feelin' da code an' da drink don't work well together. But, I can remember how yer dear mudder felt about t'ings, especially when it concerned you and... well, we'll talk about dat later. It's not somethin' we *ought* ta do. Not now, anyway."

Clouds swept over the *Chasseur's* wake until they engulfed the sky from horizon to horizon. With the gray clouds came a fresh breeze, and the marines celebrated the cool motion of the ship, now skimming over the water with her sails billowing out to the northeast. But, the sailors knew better. For with the wind, came news the glass in the captain's cabin had dropped, dropped significantly. Seamen chanted warnings, fore and aft, about a change in weather. Chanted them repeatedly. Their dread voices singing out in unison:

First rise after low,

foretells stronger blow.

Uncle Bob and the rest of the marines shot each other nervous sideglances. The strange ways of the seamen had always bothered them, and when the sailors climbed the standing rigging and reefed sail singing more ditties, the marines were as spooked as if Davy Jones had come out of his locker. This only served to please the sailors. Happy George couldn't have been more happy. He sat on his top and bellowed down ditty after foreboding ditty. His favorite had his mates pinching themselves in order not to laugh:

With rising wind and falling glass,
soundly sleeps the silly ass.

The *Chasseur* was popping up and down on a perfect bow wave, with the northeast wind pushing against her white, cotton sails. Everyone came up to the gun deck to feel the breeze chase the heat from their bodies. David's face was as pale as his duck trousers as he came up the companionway. He managed to take a daily walk on deck nursing both his wounded thigh and his sensitive heart. Jessica hadn't been at the side of his bunk these last few months. When she was sure of his recovery, Jessica thought it best to keep her distance, not demonstrating too much feminine care. She had to think of how Michael felt as well. It wasn't too long ago that she had almost fallen in love with David. But, that was all changed. Now, Michael took every safe chance he could to dart her a knowing look, or secretly squeeze her hand. Jessica reciprocated, carefully parting her lips, miming the words "I love you."

David had accepted the fact that Michael and Jessica were in love with each other. Love and David were strangers most of his life. His mother, a prostitute in New York, abandoned him when he was eight years old. But, by that time, he was already inured to the hard life of a harbor town, and was able to do enough begging and stealing to see him from one day to the next. David was a survivor, and this latest setback in love was something he knew he would get over. Still, he felt a pang in his chest every once in awhile. He felt one now, as he found Jessica in the stern, doing some figures on her slate. Months had passed since the battle in the English Channel between the *Chasseur* and the English brigs. Jessica had recovered from seeing the men she had known, and the powder monkey she had not, die from the chain shot. Still, she dreamt of it from time to time, always seeing Michael as the powder monkey, always waking up in a cold sweat. But, the early October sun, warm as always in these latitudes, and the joy of seeing Michael rallied her spirits.

David noticed she had grown since he had first seen her. Her shirt tugged slightly against developing breasts that were easier to conceal under a heavy woolen coat in the North Atlantic, but becoming a daily difficulty in the heat of 20 degrees latitude. Her face had tanned, adding even more of a sparkle to her blue eyes and providing definition to her high cheekbones. Her lips were full and red, especially after she licked them when they were dry from the heat. The trousers she used to cuff on the crossing now hung about her slight shins and over top delicate ankles and toes. David noticed these things with want and trepidation. He thought it was about time to convince Jessica of the danger she faced. The schooner was still a week out of a friendly French port in the Leeward Islands. The men, who were agitated after spending day and night with no wind to bend even a candle's flame, had been long enough out of port to do just about anything to quell their desires. Men, who David knew had unmasked Jessica's identity. David hobbled into the stern supported by a crutch. His thigh had healed ever so slowly, but the shot had severed enough of the muscle on his quadriceps to hamper his ability to walk without a little pain.

"One day ya gotta teach me." Jessica picked her head up.

"It's about time you dragged yourself on deck today. I was beginning to worry you had taken ill, David, you're so pale. Teach you what?"

"Figurin'. On a slate, like you do."

"I'd love to," Jessica said, smiling, her white teeth contrasting against tanned skin and red lips. David propped his crutch against the railing and leaned over the bow. The *Chasseur* was gliding over the turquoise water, bobbing her bow at an ever-increasing rate this last hour.

"We're makin' some speed. It's good to feel the ship movin' over the water again."

"Six knots. I just checked. But, you're right. It feels grand to move! Ahh!" she sighed, as she whisked off her hat and let the wind from the quarter blow through her black hair. Hair that had grown longer in the long months since they had left the Point. "It was so hot I thought I would die. This feels soooo good..."

"Put your hat on you fool," David scolded in a whisper. Jessica tucked her hair under the bear skin hat that was part of her disguise and frowned.

"A steward isn't supposed to yell at a master's mate. What will the men think?"

"They'll think you're a woman and, after that, God knows what else. It's time to turn in Mr. Henry's sextant and come under the protection of Cap'n Boyle." Jessica's eyes turned sapphire blue.

"You want me to spend the rest of this cursed cruise chained to my cabin? Coming onto the deck with a guard once a day like a prisoner? Do you have any idea what that would have been like when we were without the wind, just sitting on the water like a duck on a pond, with the heat down there like it was a furnace?"

"The cap'n will know what to do. He'll explain somethin' to the crew. Somethin' they'll understand and respect. Ain't no use pretendin' anymore. You're practically a grown woman. I've seen how you've grown since the snow in the Chesapeake. Others have seen, too. 'Sides, I have a funny feelin' that somethin's goin' to happen. Don't ask me how. I've always had a feelin' before somethin' bad happens."

"I thought only women had intuition like that?"

"Don't be smart. I don't know what intu... whatever is. I just know somethin's goin' to happen. Knew it when my ma left me to fend fer myself. Knew it every time I was goin' to get beat fer not stealin' enough to keep my old boss in the drink."

"What about when you got shot in the leg? You never told me about any such feeling. We spent a good deal of time talking to each other before Ireland, if you recall."

"I recall." David felt another pang inside his chest. "But I didn't feel a thing - not about somethin' goin' wrong, that is. Not then. Not down here, anyway." He pointed to the pit of his stomach. "But, that wasn't bad, that was good. I know I can't walk much now, but you were with me the whole time I was lyin' with the fever. Even after. Nursin' me while I was sick. Wasn't you?" Jessica dropped her head in her lap.

"I - I - do care about you, David. Honestly. But Michael and I were born for each other. Born *for* each other. A saintly woman told me that once. I knew it the moment she said it. Knew it to be fact. Felt it in my heart. I - I - guess I forgot for a time on the crossing. Forgive me."

"Who was it. This woman that told you. Who was it?"

"His mom. Teresa. I can't help feelin' the way I do about Michael deep inside. Do you - can't you understand?" David stared into her eyes. The severity of the saphires had been extinguished. Now, she gazed on him with a supple, light blue.

"Yeah. It's the same way I feel right now. But I'll be all right. Always have. Besides, Michael's got dibs. I understand. You and him practically growin' up together and all. I ain't nobody to stand in his ma's way. Or your's, if that what you're feelin'." Tears welled into Jessica's eyes. She pretended to write something on her slate.

"Thank you," she said, softly.

"You'll thank me a lot more if you go to the cap'n. Tell him you know that at least two men, two dangerous men, know who and what you are. He'll take good care of you, Jessica. Please, if I ever meant anything to you, please, do this for me." Jessica didn't look at him. She kept her head down over the slate.

"And if I don't?"

The foamy waters that the *Chasseur's* bow cut through and the darkening horizon to the east were portents of a blow that Captain Ken knew would be coming from the aching in his ancient joints. The entire crew had been ordered to prepare the ship for a gale. Storm sail was set, cannon were seized fore and aft to the bulwark, and lifelines were strung. Uncle Bob, himself, made sure the apple barrels below were lashed down tightly. Both watches were ready for long hours, knowing they would sleep in their hammocks, when they could sleep, wearing the very drenched clothes they would have on for days, battling the onrushing tempest.

There was a long line to the head. Every jack tar and marine wanted to use the humble facilities before the storm hit. Venturing on deck, and attempting a trip to the necessary in the bow of a ship whose deck would be swamped with a surging sea was asking for an inglorious end. But, the line wasn't moving. Brian Burdick, one of the ship's caulkers, came limping from the head, barely holding up his trousers.

"Me arse is cut clean through, as if there was sharks nippin' at me bum from below." The crowd of men stood off to the rail to let Burdick by. They gasped as the caulker passed them. The seat of Burdick's trousers was soaked with blood. "Take care mates," Burdick cautioned, making his way to Doctor William's cabin, "there's glass all over the head. Somebody must'a passed a bottle, God help him."

The storm hit with a wicked wind, driving rain so hard it hurt as it flayed down on seamens' backs, even with the protection of Sou'westers and tarpaulin jackets. Jessica had not yet told Captain Boyle that two members of his crew knew her identity. David went to Michael and explained the ill feeling in the pit of his stomach. Michael agreed: Jessica must be put under the captain's protection before something happened. They slowly made their way to Captain Ken's cabin. Michael assisted David, who could not walk because the schooner was being tossed to and fro in the teeth of the mighty gale.

Jessica convinced them that it wasn't the right time. The captain had better things to do, with the storm threatening the ship, than to worry about an attack on his master's mate. They agreed to tell Boyle after the storm had abated. The two boys left, but only after Jessica agreed to lock herself in the cabin. Michael went below, to take his turn at the pumps, while David stood guard outside the cabin door. The ship lurched violently. David managed to endure the increasing and piercing stab running down his leg. His feeble body was knocked, back and forth, along the passageway. Finally, he slid his back down against Captain Ken's door and plopped to the floor, grabbing his thigh.

The little schooner was thrown about mercilessly. Captains Boyle and Ken took trick after trick at the wheel, desperately trying to keep the nose of the ship from coming into the wind. The storm did not subside. Into the second watch, when hopes were running high that the worst was certainly over, it grew in strength: hurling sheets of water from the coal, black sky, wind whipping the Atlantic in cross seas that swept over the *Chasseur's* deck knocking down men who bobbed in and out of water and were saved only by the ropes tied tightly about their waists and attached to the life lines running from mast to mast. No one slept. Happy George, a veteran of many a storm at sea, blessed himself constantly, whispering prayer after prayer for his Peggy and their six children in Philadelphia. Cursing himself for having taunted the marines with his diddies.

The marines, who felt death with every lurch of the bow, gazed at each other in horror. When they saw the sailors frightened, chills quivered up their spines. But Captain Boyle had taken every precaution: top masts were struck, reducing the weight aloft; additional ballast, in the way of cannon, was brought below and centered amidships and further astern to allow the bow to come up faster after dipping into the trough of a wave. Captain Ken kept the wind two or three points off the stern, so the ship could absorb the onrushing waves at an angle instead of full astern. The *Chasseur* scudded madly before the wind under double-reefed foresail alone, all her other poles bare. Two men, now, were assigned to the wheel, should the ship take a blow from the sea directly on her rudder, breaking it off and taking control of the helm. Another hour, and another, and still the storm raged. Men lashed themselves with cordage to anything that appeared immovable.

Captain Ken took a breather below. He had seen gales like this before. Had sailed safely through hurricanes in the Antilles. He knew the *Chasseur* to be a weatherly ship. Properly manned and captained, he was certain the schooner would survive. Yet, there was an undercurrent of dread that seemed pervasive among the crew, and epidemic among the landlubbers. He saw men huddling into corners, whispering. Ken knew the ways of men and ships. He knew something was wrong. Seasoned, skillful seamen acted as if the ship were to be broached at any moment. It was as if the *Chasseur* was already pooped and sinking. There was no immediate reason for the sailors to feel that way, he thought. The men were talking - a rumor had swept the ship that foretold its destruction as if it had been written in stone. But the men knew this ship, too. They, to a man, knew her to be sound, had seen the proof of it with their own eyes in the crossing. Yes, the gale was a whopper. But that should only serve conditioned sailors to look sharp and ride out the tempest working in unison. The *Chasseur* had already earned the reputation as "The Pride of Baltimore." Her sailing qualities were legendary in the seafaring community. The men knew this. For some reason, imagined and not real, they had forgotten it - lost confidence in their vessel. Nothing could be worse. Ken could guess at only one reason for this to occur: the talk of a Jonah. Only the whispers of a Jonah, among superstitious sailors and ignorant marines, would elicit this kind of panic.

But why? Why would someone spread the rumor of a Jonah, and who was the Jonah in the first place? Ken didn't like the leers of the sailors that followed his every move. He knew the sailors were too far gone. Once a tar was convinced of the existence of a Jonah, nothing could persuade him otherwise. It was simply a matter of life and death. And the men obviously couldn't talk to him about it. They watched him closely, but took pains to stay out of his way. Ken knew he had to move quickly. He drew Bob Dooley out of earshot.

"I want ya to git yer men back on an even keel." Uncle Bob leveled an angry stare into the old man's sharp, blue eyes.

"Tis a queer t'ing, you talkin' about an even keel at a time like dis."

"Listen, Bob. Yer men and the sailors are spreadin' rumors that we're by the lee, that we can't make it outta this here storm."

"An' da truth is?" Captain Ken snatched hold of Dooley's wide shoulders and pulled him down, bringing them face to face.

"There's no truth in it unless we believe it ta be the truth." Bob drew back. He was going to accuse the sailors of spreading rumors. Of incessant talk of a curse aboard the ship. That it was the sailors who infected the marines with talk of a dark curse, and that no one would talk to him, either. The men went out of their way not to talk to him. Then, he calmed himself.

"Know what you *ought* ta believe," Bob stated, plainly.

"That's right. We're gonna make it, Bob. I'd never lie ta ye, not bout life and death. But somebody's spreadin' lies. Somebody's got the crew inta an evil mood." Ken looked around to make certain no one else was listening. "I've seen this before. Once mens' minds are certain their gonna die they usually do. Seen ships abandoned, only ta be picked up later, comin' through a storm without a scratch. The men all drowned tryin' ta make it in the boats. Lord, they'll do anythin' iffin' we don't put a stop ta this nonsense right now." Bob shrugged his shoulders.

"So what if dey moan an' groan. The captain will never allow da men ta abandon da ship. Would he?"

"They won't ask the cap'n. Any of us cap'ns. We'll be dead." Bob suddenly realized what Ken was referring to.

"Mutiny," he whispered, "so dat's what da Federalist bastards are talkin' about, all chumy like, in dark corners." He darted his eyes, furtively, around the ship. "But how can we be sure it's come ta mutiny?"

"Bob, ya darned fool. It's me who's tellin' ya. I know a mutiny when I smells one, and I smells one right now." Bob felt in his pocket for the keys to the armory. They were gone.

"Oh, Lord. I'm a stupid ass. Me keys ta da gun room. Dey've fleeced me pockets. Captain Boyle will kill me, if he's still alive, poor soul." Bob's face took on a painful, pathetic expression. "I've failed ya. Everyone. Never shoulda drank da bottle before da storm. An' poor Burdick wit' da stitches in his rump. When will I ever learn. I promised ta come back ta da code. But I haven't da bloodiest idea what ta do - what I *ought* ta do!" Ken grabbed him again.

"I do! Now listen ya big bullox..."

Straining their muscles, a group of men struggled out of the forehatch and proceeded, hand over hand, along the lifeline. Captain Ken was in the lead, followed by Bob Dooley, Dan Donavon, Michael, Happy George, and James Darymple. Mr. Leib was about to lift his voice above the wind, reminding the men not to come on deck through the forehatch and endanger the ship by allowing the sea to fall into the bow. It was critical to lighten the bow, not have it wieghed down with seawater. But Captain Ken signaled him to keep silent. The group made their way aft, onto the quarterdeck. Boyle knew something was wrong when he spied their grim, drenched faces.

"By God, suhs!. What is the meanin' of this?" Ken grabbed Boyle by the arm and shouted in his ear over the screaming wind of the gale.

"There's mutiny aboard, cap'n! Talk of a Jonah! It's too far gone! Can't be stopped!" Boyle dropped his jaw. He stared at the group of men he knew to be loyal, disbelieving so few would remain so.

"The weapons! Ken! Have you secured the weapons!"

"We've retaken the armory! They were at it already! Killed Mr. Hollingsworth, sir! Mr. Conner has the blunderbuss and has the armory secured! He'll send to hell anyone who comes within twenty yards!" Boyle nodded, he was satisfied, at least, that Mr. Conner and Mr. Hollingsworth did their duty. But there was no time to grieve over the death of his supercargoe.

"We must act quickly! Take the helm! Leave Captain Dooley to guard the hatches! See that no one comes up! They can't take the ship from below! Whoever steers this wheel is in control!" Ken nodded in assent. Uncle Bob drew his long knife from its sheathe and put it into his mouth, clenching the blade with his teeth. Boyle seethed with anger. "As God is my judge, suh, I'll go down with this ship, lay it down by the beam, before we give in to this scum!" The captain quickly led the rest of the group foreward, leaving Ken and Uncle Bob on deck. Before they went below, Boyle shouted at Michael. "Where's David! He can't be with them?" Michael shook his head.

"He's guarding Jessica! Some of the men know who she is!" Suddenly, Boyle's eyes bulged. He knew, now, who the Jonah was, and why the men turned against him. Boy or no boy, Mr. Henry was an officer of the ship. The men knew Boyle would never have gotten rid of his master's mate, not for all the talk in the world about Jonahs. He turned to James Darymple. The gunner was perplexed. He didn't understand this talk of a woman aboard ship.

"Get to Captain Russell's cabin! Mr. Henry's in danger. Don't let those bastards near her! We'll join Mr. Conner at the armory and work our way forward." James went ahead of them and scurried below.

David was massaging his thigh. The pain had been so intense that he had tears in his eyes. Tears that blinded him from the shadow and the lookout that fell on him from both sides. The pain in David's leg ceased when, suddenly, he felt nothing. Lugger, the shadow, had pistol-whipped him across the forehead. The lookout, Cyrus Bently, kicked David out from the doorway and smiled at Mr. Lugger, the shadow.

"We'll take the ship. Our men have seen to that. But first I've got paybacks to make. That little girl will know it was a mistake to tell me how to steer a ship by the time I'm through with her!" Lugger grabbed Bently, swinging him around.

"No! I'll be in charge from here on in! I'll take her first. You do what you want after. I don't care. Boyle and the rest will be dead in minutes, and the storm will not last long now. Our timing has been perfect. Everyone will think we survived because we got rid of the little Jonah, and with the treasure on this ship we'll be richer than we can ever hope to be! We have the weapons. We have enough men and arms to take the ship. They can't stand against our numbers. You can steer this ship to a French port. And then we can split everything up and live like kings!" Shots rang out. Lugger smiled. "That's our men. Boyle and Dooley weren't armed. I hope Dooley's only wounded. I'd like to finish him myself. In the meantime, I've some business with our master's mate." Lugger stared at Bently, and the lookout backed away from the door. The bosun's eyes frightened him. They bespoke of something not like lust, not like greed. They were glazed over with a strange vacancy. A predator's eyes before a kill. Unfeeling. Blank. Merciless.

Lugger kicked the door in. Jessica was crouched in a corner of her bunk. She had heard desperate voices outside the door but couldn't make them out over the wind screaming above deck. There was no light in the cabin. Jessica had extinguished her candle, hoping whoever was outside the cabin wouldn't see a light under the doorway and would just go away. She heard the gunfire and thought immediately of the feeling in the pit of David's stomach. Lugger stepped in. She screamed out in terror. She sensed the presense of the man she dreaded most. She knew it to be him even though she could only see his silhouette in the doorway. Lugger laughed.

"Well. So the master's mate is a little coward, hey? Scream if you like. No one can hear you over the gale, my dear. And even if they could, they couldn't help you. You see, I had them all killed." Jessica's complexion changed from one of a little girl frighted, to one of a woman prepared to meet her fate. Her eyes turned sapphire blue. If they were dead. If what he said was true, then it didn't matter - not without Michael.

"Do what you must."

"What I must? Oh, I'll do what I must, my dear Mr. Henry. I'm afraid someone's been spreading terrible rumors about you. They say you're a Jonah. That you threaten the ship because your a girl disguised as a - as a what? A boy? But we both know better. I saw you that night. Talking with that infernal old man and the cooper's boy. Of course, I knew it from the first. But the night you took young Dooley's hand confirmed it. To tell you the truth I didn't care if you were a boy or not. It doesn't matter to me. Yet, I was so taken with the old man's story. Romantic, wasn't it?" Jessica saw another silhouette in the doorway, behind the bosun. It was tall and thin and graceful. Lugger took a step toward her, clutching her blanket and ripping it from her arms. "Care to do a little stargazing with your boson, Mr. Henry? I'm so sorry. But, I'm the last star you'll ever see."

Jessica winced as the blade of a knife swept across Lugger's throat. She blinked as blood gushed out into her eyes and onto her bedding. James let Lugger fall to the deck with a thud. Outside the door, the lookout had met a similiar fate.

"Are you all right, mame, I mean Mr. Henry?" James asked, holding his hand out to her. Jessica took the outstreched hand and looked down at the bloody body of the bosun. James felt her hand shaking. Jessica let out a muffled cry and embraced the gunner, sobbing uncontrollably. "It's all right, now, girl," James said, soothingly, patting her head with his large right hand. "It's all right." More gunfire, closer this time, echoed through the ship. Jessica raised her head.

"What's - what's going on, James? Where's Michael?"

"Don't worry, missy. Cap'n Russell was on to them befoh they could take the ship. Talk of a Jonah, it was, that put 'em to mutiny. Foolish talk 'bout you bein' a Jonah. Michael and the others are on their way. I gotta go now. See to da boy, outside. He's hurt, bad."

James turned to go, but Michael met him at the door, followed by Dan Donavon, and Happy. Michael took Jessica in his arms. He wept as he held her. They both wept.

"It was James, Michael. He saved my life," Jessica managed to say through her tears. But then she suddenly pulled away. "David!" Jessica ran outside the cabin, Michael, James, and Happy followed.

Boyle was kneeling. He had David's body cradled in his arms. Tears were streaming down his face. Jessica put her hands to her head and dropped to her knees.

"Captain - oh captain - David, is he... Boyle wiped the blood from David's face. The lookout had slit David's throat seconds before James got there.

Boyle rocked David's body gently in his arms. "My boy. My boy. My poor, poor boy.

George J. Galloway

Chapter 20

MACDONOUGH

Napoleon was vanquished. The Corsican emperor was no longer a threat to the peace of the world. Now, England had only one war to fight: the contemptible little war in North America. Thousands of battle hardened British troops, who fought under the Duke of Wellington, were getting ready for an American invasion. Captain Ken was right. The British planned to take the Champlain Valley and march down on New York, severing New England from the rest of the country. In the Revolutionary War, New England was the hot bed of patriotic fervor. But, in December of 1813, it was New Englanders who protested the prosecution of war against Great Britain. They called it, mockingly, "Mr. Madison's War." England, who strove to divide the colonies in the Revolution in order to halt the poison of New England treason, now looked to those states to stop Madison and Henry Clay, and split the new United States of America.

To effect this, Britain would send thousands of troops down the St. Lawrence River. Fifteen thousand crack, British regulars to stand against timid militiamen from New York. After taking Lake Champlain, the British would drive through to the Hudson River. If Britain succeeded - if she could sustain an army in the heart of New York, she could sue for a separate peace with the New England states.

No one was more aware of this than a young navy lieutenant from Delaware whose job it was to keep the British off Lake Champlain. Thomas Macdonough knew he held the future of his country in his hands. Somehow, he had to keep control of the lake. His problem was men. Seasoned tars were a commodity in a lake bordered by Vermont and upstate New York.

But, Macdonough had time. Lake Champlain freezes over in the winter. The lieutenant decided to take a trip to New York City and recruit the men he needed to man his small fleet and make a last defense against the English juggernaut.

****

As Mr. Lugger had predicted, the gale that brought so much misery to the Chasseur and her crew subsided quickly after the mutiny. The dead were thrown over the railing. Captain Boyle performed a simple ceremony for his steward. Reading from John, he stated, emotionally, "'Greater love hath no one than this, that he lay down his life for his friends.'" Jessica personally sewed David's and Mr. Hollingsworth's bodies into seamen's caskets of white canvas. Before the last stitch on David's was sewn, she slipped in the delicate cup David used to bring on deck filled with piping hot coffee during the cold nights of the crossing. The bodies were draped with Stars and Stripes. As James, the gunner, sang a Negro spiritual in a deep baritone, Mr. Hollingsworth's body was lifted by Uncle Bob and Captain Ken. They let the body slip out from under the flag and into the sea. Michael and Captain Boyle carried David on a litter, to the taff rail. Everyone touched the steward, through the canvas, one last time. James had "Slingshot" primed and ready, and as they slipped David over the side, before Jessica could hear the splash of his body, the cannon boomed.

Most of the mutineers had been killed, but there was still a half dozen that remained in chains below decks. Boyle decided to make for New Orleans, where they could be charged and tried. By the time a jury found the mutineers guilty and a judge sentenced them to the gallows, everyone was anxious to get home. Boyle knew the strength of the British blockade of Southern ports would necessitate sailing North. He remanned the *Chasseur* with eager sailors in New Orleans and plotted a course for New York.

The British stood on and off Hudson's Lower Bay, but because of American batteries at Fort Richmond, which commanded the Narrows from the high ground on Staten Island, they wouldn't dare cross into the bay. American gunboats did a good job harassing the British and keeping them from totally restricting commerce. To prevent a combined land and sea invasion, a fort was built on Liberty Island, and a circular battery with heavy gun emplacements was constructed on Ellis Island. Shore batteries, arsenals, and earthworks were constructed on Lower Manhattan, Governors Island, and at Fort Lafayette. Still, blockade running was a tricky business. Boyle decided to out flank the blockade and take his ship around Long Island. This was risky, because it meant coming in through the channel at Hell Gate. But, Captain Ken had successfully negotiated the channel on numerous occasions and he promised Boyle to pilot the ship in without a scratch. On Christmas Eve, exactly one year to the day the *Chasseur* escaped a frigate's broadside escaping out of the Chesapeake, Boyle and his crew headed into Long Island Sound.

Michael and Jessica were in the bow, huddled under Captain Ken's great coat, sharing the warmth of each other's bodies. Her disguise as a boy was behind her now. She was no longer an inexperienced, academic sailor, but a seasoned mate who had earned the respect of the crew. To Jessica's delight, Boyle insisted she remain an officer of the ship. The men marveled at how quickly she could work figures on her slate.

Jessica grabbed the back of Michael's seaman-like tail and yanked it.

"Ouch! What did you do that for?" She giggled and wrapped her arms around him tightly.

"You were thinking about something instead of talking to me. What were you thinking about, sweetheart?" Michael pressed his lips together, uncertain about how Jessica would take what was on his mind.

"About my father. Captain Ken said he would try to make it to the interior lakes. He said the British would get together an army and invade from Canada down to New York. I was just wondering if us comin' to New York wasn't a sign."

"A sign?"

"Yea. I mean, is it just a coincidence that Captain Boyle chose New York? He could have taken the ship into another port. And, now, here we are, sailing past Long Island into New York."

"But, New York is one of the easiest places to dodge the blockade. The *Chasseur* is a fast ship with little draft. No frigate can follow us into shallow waters and we can outrun or outfight anything smaller they send against us. New York was the perfect choice, especially with Captain Ken piloting the ship past Hell Gate." Michael turned his head toward her and smiled.

"Oh, go on with ya, Jess. I forgot I was talkin' to an officer." Jessica laughed, a small, light laugh that Michael had come to love.

"I'm sorry," she said, sincerely, "you were going to say something about a coincidence."

"Yea. New York might be a sensible place to run the blockade, but don't you find it strange that my father might be..." Michael stopped short and gazed out onto the dark water. Boyle had waited for a cloudy night to make his approach, with no light from moon and stars. That it happened to be Christmas Eve, when lookouts on blockading ships might pay less attention to their duty was even better. "...might be on the border, right now. I - I was just thinkin' that - that - well..." Jessica pressed herself against him.

"That we should go north?" She placed her head gently on his shoulder. They didn't say anything for a time. A feeling of melancholy swept over them. Michael was thinking on the code and what he ought to do. He thought about what Uncle Bob had said when they were discussing feelings - using your heart, sometimes, instead of your head. Letting the code work through your heart, like his mother had done. He wanted to go up north, but he had a responsibility, now, to Jessica. He couldn't bear leaving her, not after everything that had happened.

Off into the distance, the muffled clang of a church bell struck twelve. Michael lifted Jessica's head and stared into her eyes.

"Merry Christmas, Jess." Before she could return the sentiment, Michael gently pressed his lips to hers.

The *Chasseur* slid safely into New York, proudly flying her American colors. She saluted the city with a broadside and the city welcomed her with a parade and a formal dinner. News of the privateer's arrival was printed in the city's papers. People flocked to the docks to gaze at "The Pride of Baltimore." Credit was arranged for the ship's company with bankers familiar with the *Chasseur's* owners. Testimonial after testimonial, toast after toast, was poured on the schooner's captain and crew.

Before leaving New Orleans, Boyle had seen to it that Jessica was dressed in the latest French fashions. Seamstresses and designers created stunning gowns for the orphan waif from Fell's Point. There was nothing of an orphan look about her as she entered the mayor's house under Michael's arm. Jessica wore a rose colored gown, trimmed in ermine. It was made to show off as much of her elegant neck and shoulders as was tasteful for a girl her age. Her black hair hung in ringlets about her shoulders, and, dangling from her neck was a sizable, sparkling sapphire to match her eyes.

Michael had purchased a handsome shirt with laced cuffs, a black coat with wide shoulders, over which hung his tail decorated with blue ribbon, a pair of black leather shoes with silver buckles, hat and gloves, of course, and, to Jessica's delight, a black cape that billowed in the wind.

They entered the grand ballroom after being formally announced. Captain Boyle arranged to have her announced as Master's Mate Jessica Farmer. Every head turned. Every neck strained to take in the dazzling young girl from Baltimore. A girl who had actually fought with America's foremost privateer and was an officer on a commissioned ship of war. Some said it was grand, others romantic, a few older women expressed their sympathy over such a pretty girl having to live in such a small ship for so long a time. Invitations were sent immediately for her to stay at the city's best homes and hotels. Regardless of what they said, she was the talk and toast of New York.

"I wish Desiree Pechin was here right now," Jessica whispered to Michael.

Uncle Bob was announced as Captain of the Marine. He too, did a little shopping in New Orleans and was bedecked in an elaborate uniform: a seven inch leather shako hat, with a three inch visor, gold cords and tassels, and a silver plate with an eagle flying above an etching of the *Chasseur*; a dark green coatee, with short tails, red cuffs, and a high collar that extended to his ear lobes, and, over his broad shoulders, gold epaulettes; his trousers were of green wool that tucked into fancy, polished leather riding boots; he carried a gold hilted sword and set the whole thing off with a crimson silk sash around his enormous waist. It was the worst statement in fashion New York would ever see.

Happy and the other sailors were gaily dressed in bleached white duck trousers, red striped shirts, red ribbons on newly greased tails, and deep, blue hats that had *Chasseur* stitched in white and trimmed in red. Captain Ken wore a conservative black jacket and knickers. On formal occasions, he still wore the same suit he wore when he buried his wife thirty years before. Captain Boyle was dressed in his usual finery, and acting the part of the flamboyant sea captain.

The affair went off smoothly, except when Bob Dooley rose on a table to toast "George Wash'ton" in a slurry, tearful, yet booming voice. Newspapermen surrounded them to get their stories and draw a quick sketch. Uncle Bob was quoted as saying that it would be better if America and England would send their armies and navies home and just let him sail to London and fight it out with the King, one on one. Michael darted a chastising glance his way, and Bob took pains to behave himself for the rest of the evening.

At the head table, seated at the end, was a young naval lieutenant with bright red hair, stunning blue eyes, fair skin, aquiline nose, and a manly jaw. No one paid the least bit of attention to him, which pleased him greatly. He had been invited, as an afterthought, when it was known he was in the city, recruiting seamen to join his small fleet on Lake Champlain. Owing to the blockade, he was able to sign on some seamen, but not the sailors with the kind of fight he was looking for; the kind of daring and nerve that had earned him a reputation as a promising naval officer. A reputation that he and a number of young naval officers had attained in the Tripolitan war. He gazed at the crew of the *Chasseur* with eager eyes. These were the sort he'd been after all along. Slowly, he worked his way through the crowd to Captain Boyle. The mayor was chatting away about his exploits as a boy sailing a catboat up the Hudson. Boyle looked bored.

"Pardon me, your honor. Captain Boyle?"

"Yes lieutenant. How may I serve you," Boyle said, with a wide grin, happy to escape from the mayor's childhood.

"Oh, yes," the mayor said, taken aback by the interruption. "Captain Thomas Boyle may I present, ahm - present Lieutenant, ahm..." the mayor looked around for assistance.

"Thomas Macdonough, a great privilege Captain Boyle," the lieutenant said, showing deep set dimples in his smile. "I wonder if I may have a word with you?"

"A pleasure, lieutenant. Shall we refresh our glasses? Would you excuse us, your honor?"

Boyle led Macdonough a safe distance away from the mayor. "Thank you, suh. By God, I was being suffocated." He raised his hand to get the attention of a waiter. Handing the waiter his glass of champagne, he ordered a bottle of bourbon. Boyle offered Lieutenant Macdonough a cigar and they sat down at a table.

"May I ask you a favor, Captain Boyle?"

"As much as it is in my power." Macdonough leaned close to Boyle and spoke with great sincerity in his boyish, blue eyes.

"I would like to address your men." Boyle smiled.

"Is it your intention to recruit my men for service in the navy, sir?"

"It is," Macdonough said, matter of factly.

"My dear, lieutenant. These men have money fallin' out of their pockets. We had a very successful cruise, you know." Macdonough's face reddened. Boyle liked him from the start. He had an honest face and a humble manner. There was no pretension in his voice.

"I know and admire your work, Captain Boyle. But I need men. I desperately need men. The kind of men you have on the *Chasseur*. Men who know how to fight. May I have your permission, sir?"

"For what service?"

"Lake Champlain." Boyle, who had just begun taking a sip from his glass, sprayed bourbon on to the table.

"A lake? You mean to take my men on a lake? Why they have salt - salt, suh - in their every vein. Do you think you'll have any luck offering professional sailors work on a lake?" Macdonough didn't blink an eye.

"The only kind of work worth speaking about, captain. Work that will make men proud and a nation grateful." Boyle admired the crispness and sincerity in his answer. He raised his hands in surrender.

"Very well, lieutenant. Drunk or sober, you'll have their undivided attention." Boyle walked to the center of the great room and put his hands in the air. "Ladies and gentlemen! May I beg your indulgence for just a moment!" He motioned for Macdonough to join him. "There is an officer of the navy here, who would like to speak to my men!" The crowd at the mayor's ball hushed. They saw the sheepish, boy-lieutenant march into the middle of the room, underneath a glistening, crystal chandelier. The light from the chandelier gave a glow to his pale skin, setting off a remarkable contrast to his wavy, orange hair. He smiled, showing his dimples, a look of humble deference to the elite in the throng, and bowed, exquisitely. But, then he raised his chin. A different look entirely. The humility was gone. He appeared strong, almost defiant. He directed his gaze on the crew of the *Chasseur* who had assembled in front of the head table.

"During the Tripolitan War, I had the honor of serving under Captain Isaac Hull. Together, we witnessed the brutality of English impressment. Tonight, I want to tell you about that brutal practice. I thank Captain Boyle for allowing me this opportunity, for no other subject is nearer to my heart." His eyes softened and he lowered his head for a moment, collecting his thoughts.

"After the war with Tripoli, I was sent to Liverpool to deliver some dispatches. I had already gained my promotion from ensign to lieutenant, and like most young men who are proud of their country's uniform, I took every penny I had, and spent it on a beautifully altered coat. Alterations were in order, since it was second hand." Men in the crowd, who were familiar with the low salary of a naval lieutenant, smiled. Such a candid statement in a room representing the wealth of the city was admirable. "Still, I had a few shillings in my pocket, and I decided to celebrate my good fortune with simple fare at the hotel where I was lodging. After a bottle," he cocked his head here and smiled, "or two. Possibly three?" The guests at the ball, and especially the men of the *Chasseur* laughed. He was winning them over with his charming dimples and simple style.

"Nothin' of the high hat 'bout this bloke," Happy George commented to his mates.

"Anyway, I was in good spirits. And why not? It was just desserts for the service we had seen against the pirates of Tripoli. I decided to take a stroll, to enjoy the moment as it were, when I was met outside my hotel by a band of brigands the English know as a press gang. They forced me - in my uniform - onto an English ship. Put me under guard and informed me that I was to begin service in the king's navy." Macdonough paused and swallowed, his face becoming red under the light of the chandelier, anger swelling into his blue eyes.

"The king's navy! An officer of the United States taken in public view and impressed into the king's navy! Then, and only then, did the issue of impressment ring true in my heart.

"I was placed under the guard of a corporal of marine below decks. There the swift events of the evening unfurled in my mind. The wine had worn away and my thoughts ran clear. I decided my impressment represented more than just myself. It was a representation of an evil practice on the whole of America!

"I was determined to save the honor of my uniform. Second hand or no, it was the uniform of the United States Navy. I feigned sickness, drawing the corporal near and bashed him across the jaw. I stripped and put on the corporal's uniform, while hiding my own in a bundle. Then, sneaking through the ship, I made it up on deck. A sentry was nearby, but he failed to see me in the shadows. I noticed a boat anchored off the bow. Hurriedly stepping from the shadows, I startled the sentry by telling him that I thought there to be rum on board the boat." Macdonough smiled, his blue eyes twinkling in the light. "Of course, the sentry having enough salt in his veins, promptly ordered me to investigate." More laughter now. Michael and Jessica grinned at each other. The fair lieutenant's dimples mesmerized women throughout the ballroom.

"Just then, the corporal I had bashed came running up the hatchway, screaming the alarm. I pushed him backwards, took a well-aimed swing at the sentry and leaped over the railing. Somehow, by the grace of God, I managed to get ashore and escape. But, that night, sitting by a fire, I swore to the Almighty that this evil must end. American sailors, to a man, must end this evil. Men taken and never seen again! Whipped with the cat, beaten with the cane! Wives and children left destitute!" Macdonough paused, catching his breath. Every eye was upon him, every ear straining, no one wanting to miss the strength of his oratory.

"Gentlemen. You have just completed, with all honor and glory, a great and successful cruise. Captain Boyle and the rest of America's privateers, our great private navy, have dealt a mighty blow to England. On behalf of the American Navy, I congratulate you. You have bested England in her own waters, have grabbed the lion by the tail, destroyed or captured her ships and commerce. But, now the beast is mad with rage. Now, England plans to retaliate. In one last attempt, England will amass such force as has never been seen on this continent. Already it's begun. My correspondence, and this is no secret for all of Canada is talking about it, has informed me that thousands of battle trained troops are to be amassed on the border of New York." The crowd murmured. Newspaper reporters sent messengers flying out the door. Macdonough spoke quickly, now.

"When the spring arrives, their campaign will begin in earnest. The same invasion of New York we repelled in the War for Independence, that was won at Saratoga, is to be relived! Only this time - this time - the British will move swiftly. They won't make the same mistakes this time around." He shook his head, a look of foreboding on his fair face. "These will be Wellington's men. The victors over Napoleon!" The lieutenant walked slowly, deliberately, towards the men of the *Chasseur*.

"And what is to stop them? Our poorly trained militia? No. No. They need the water to transport such a force. The lake - Lake Champlain - is the key, the door to the destruction of our nation!" Macdonough drew his sword from its scabbard and placed it on the floor. He took several steps back.

"I have contracted, on behalf of the Secretary of the Navy, William Jones, to build a ship and add it to my meager fleet. That ship, my flagship, is to be constructed under the direction of two of the world's greatest ship builders, Aaron and Noah Brown." Macdonough pointed to one of the tables. The Brown brothers, New York City's premier ship builders, stood and bowed to the men of the *Chasseur*. Macdonough set his blue eyes firmly on the faces of Boyle's crew. The men were sobered at the unmistakeable sincerity, passion, and courage in those eyes.

"But, I need men! Men who will fight! Men who know, firsthand, from mates who have been impressed, from the tears of their wives and children, their mothers and fathers - their sweethearts - that England! - England! - must! - be! - stopped!" The ballroom burst into wild cheers.

Michael led Jessica across the floor. He glanced at her before they stepped over Macdonough's sword.

"Let's do what we *ought* to do," she said. Again, the room exploded in delight. The little girl who had captured the heart of New York - the master's mate of the *Chasseur*, and the cooper's son from Fells Point, were the first to stand by Macdonough's side. Captain Ken and Uncle Bob quickly followed. In the span of a solitary minute, Boyle had lost most of his crew.

Macdonough spied Thomas Boyle across the room. Boyle clenched a cigar in his grinning mouth, and a glass of bourbon in his hand. The captain raised his glass high into the air.

"To the crew of the United States Privateer *Chasseur*! And fresh water sailing!"

Chapter 21

CAPTAIN MOONLIGHT

By March, Boyle and the *Chasseur* were in the West Indies on another cruise. But the schooner was short thirty men: men who were overcome by Macdonough's plea to save Champlain against the expected British invasion. Happy George, James Darymple, and Dan Donovon, joined Michael, Jessica, Uncle Bob, and Captain Ken with Lieutenant Macdonough at his shipyard in Vengennes, Vermont. Aaron and Noah Brown quickly set to work building a ship large enough to dominate the lake and foil Captain Ping, Macdonough's counterpart in the Royal Navy, whose larger fleet kept Champlain in British hands. For the moment, Ping enjoyed sailing up and down the lake with impunity, harassing local towns, capturing provisions, and seeing that the illegal trade between Canada and the northern frontier of the United States continued as if there was no war at all.

Trading with the enemy was lucrative for Americans. In Boston, and throughout New England, the Royal Navy gave American ship captains special licenses to safely sail in and out of ports under blockade. Licenses were openly sold without the threat of penalty from the federal government, and without the slightest pang of conscience. On Champlain, barges regularly made their way into Canada selling essential provisions to the British army and navy. To Uncle Bob this seemed incredulous.

"Here we are workin' an' slavin' ta get dis ship built, an' da damned federalists are in cohoots wit' da Limeys. Dey t'ink they can go about dis business wit'out nobody sayin' nothin', like dey was still Brits an' da revolution never happened." Bob and Michael were employed laying the keel of Macdonough's ship off the banks of Otter Creek. Macdonough had chosen a safe place to build his fleet. Vengennes was a small village, not numbering a thousand inhabitants, but to the skilled eyes of the Brown brothers it was heaven sent. Vengennes had a waterfall for power, unlimited timber, iron deposits, eight different forges, air furnaces, rolling mills, a wire factory, and grist, saw, and fulling mills; everything the Browns needed to do the job. The creek, a river really, was deep enough to float a large ship out onto the lake. But, that meant that an enemy ship could also come into the river and destroy the shipyard before Macdonough's fleet was ready. To eliminate that threat, Macdonough borrowed army engineers and men from General Macomb and built Fort Cassin at the mouth of the river. The British would have to take the fort if they wanted to keep control of the lake. Michael and Uncle Bob were working up a sweat operating a two-man saw. Michael motioned for his uncle to stop so he could catch his breath.

"You're going to do something about the illegal trade, aren't you?"

"Wadda ya mean, boyo? Of course I'm goin' ta do somethin' about it. Ya t'ink I can stand by while t'ose federalists make money an' we're here laborin' from dawn ta dusk?" Michael shook his head as they put the saw to work on the ship's beam again.

"You had better tell me, uncle," Michael shouted over the scratch of the saw, "what you're planning to do. Did you use the code?"

"I did. Indeed, I did, boyo. Ya know, yerself, wit' all dis physical labor an' healt'y north air I've led a productive life of da code. No, bordellos here ta git a man inta trouble, praise be."

"Uncle!" Michael shouted, emphatically. "You go to the tavern every night till it closes!" They both stopped sawing. Bob put his hand to his chest feigning innocence.

"But dat's headquarters, boyo. It's dere I meet wit' me spies."

"What spies?"

"Da lads from da army. Scouts dey call them. Indian scouts. Dere leader is a lad by da name of Elizer Williams, he's a half breed."

"Why should the scouts work for you?"

"A queer custom in dese parts says dat an Injun can't be served liquor. Can you imagine dat? So, I persuaded da innkeeper ta be a bit more like a patriot an' t'ose Indian boys love me fer it."

"You threatened the innkeeper?"

"I did nothin' of da kind. I merely brought it ta his attention dat scouts are regular army personnel, an' as such should be treated wit' respect. He saw me point, immediately. But, dey can only have a taste when I'm at da tavern. So, ya see, I gotta be dere." Noah Brown noticed the Dooley's were talking, not working.

"Look sharp, there! Lay into it, boys, there's no time for conversation." The Brown brothers had promised to have the ship ready in sixty days. They had three teams of men working around the clock. Michael and Bob redoubled their efforts until their cut was made.

"What are your plans, uncle?"

"Da Irish know how ta handle such traitors. Uncle Liam would have called it 'Captain Moonlight.' It's da old way of lettin' da landlord know he's gone too far. A visit from some of da lads in da dead of night an' some power of persuasion is all dat's needed. Pity dese Vermonters don't know nothin' about how ta stop smugglin'. Dey coulda put a stop ta dis nonsense long ago. But, whaddaya expect from people who don't know how ta cross a border."

That evening, Michael and Jessica joined each other for dinner at the tavern. Jessica had hired herself to work for Mrs. Macdonough, cooking and cleaning. The Macdonough's had rented a small cottage in the village. In return for her service, Jessica was paid a small sum and room and board. The tavern was warm and friendly, especially since Uncle Bob had persuaded the innkeeper to serve his fare to his Indian patrons with a smile. The innkeeper was nervously smiling now as Uncle Bob, Elizer Williams, Dan Donovon, and Happy George raised their tankards in a toast to "dear Jamie." Michael was also smiling. He had not seen Jessica for almost a week. After working at the shipyard during the day, he volunteered for duty at Fort Cassin, working the cannon as a powder monkey.

"How's everything going at the commodore's?" Michael referred to Macdonough as a commodore because he was in charge of a fleet. The title was purely honorary, as the American navy had not yet established such a rank. Jessica blew on her spoon and hungrily swallowed a mouthful of rabbit stew.

"She's a dear, Michael, you'd love her. She reminds me a great deal of your mother. She went wild over the gowns and jewelry Captain Boyle bought me in New Orleans. And the work is easy, just the two of them. But, I'm afraid I've some bad news for you - for us, really."

"News? What news?"

"I've told her all about us. She thought it was so romantic, falling in love on board the *Chasseur*. But, she's laying down some rules as far as when we can see each other." Michael had been dipping a slice of his ham steak into the yolk of an egg, but dropped his fork into the egg when Jessica mentioned the word "rules."

"What do you mean she laying down rules?"

"Well, she's right, Michael. A young lady should be courted properly." Michael became indignant.

"Courtin'! Are we courtin'?"

"Why, yes, silly, of course we are." Jessica waved her hand at Captain Ken, who entered the door with the Brown brothers. Ken was consulting the builders on the type and weight of armament the ship would carry.

"Hold on Jess, you mean I can't come and see you when I got some free time? You know I'm working day and night. This isn't Fells Point. It's not like I can send a note and ask to call at so and so an hour for tea." Jessica raised sapphire-blue eyes from the bowl of rabbit stew and gave him a withering stare.

"And why not? You did for Desiree Pechin. Do I deserve less than that? Or do you still look on me as your servant girl?"

"Jeeze, Jess, Don't look at me that way. I'm only sayin' - I'm sayin' - for cryin' out loud, Jess, we're at war!"

Uncle Bob overheard Michael's voice and stuck his elbow in Happy's ribs. "Now, isn't dat lovely. Dere first spat. T'ough callin' it a war is goin' a little too far. I'll have ta speak ta him." Happy smiled, knowingly.

"Aye, Captain Dooley. A regular spit in your eye married conversation. Just like me and my Peggy. What a wonderful pair of turtle doves. Just look at 'im. Ain't nothin' like a good argument ta get the juices flowin'. I'd wager they make up and kiss before dessert." Uncle Bob motioned for Captain Ken to come up to the bar. Ken excused himself from the Brown's table.

"Listen, Ken," Bob whispered into the old man's ear, "Elizer, here, has some news. He says da Brits know 'bout Macdonough layin' da keel down on da ship. Word is, da Brits are sailin' down from Plattsburg ta storm Otter creek." Ken glanced at Elizer.

"Is that Injun trustworthy?" Bob looked shocked.

"I'd trust him wit' me own mudder." Ken wasn't impressed.

"Then why is he blabberin' intelligence to an ex Captain of the Marine, now a common laborer at a shipyard, and, of all places, in a public tavern with a tankard in his fist?" Bob pouted his lips and then drained his glass.

"Ya know how ta cut a man ta da quick when he's down, don'tcha ya ol' Hollander."

"I'm not Dutch, my people are Norwegian. Tom Boyle called me a Dutchman too. Why does everybody git that mixed up?"

"Same t'ing. Your all a bunch of no good Vikin' raiders." Ken rolled his eyes.

"All right, all right, ya big dope. What have you been up ta these last few weeks that the head of the army scouts is tellin' you about military secrets."

"He's part of me network of spies. Dere's Federalists here dat fergot dere was a war on. We have plans ta help dem remember."

"Uncle Liam style, I suppose? Oh, never mind, sounds a bit like the Sons of Liberty to me. Anyway, Macdonough's ready for the English. He has two emplacements at the mouth of the river. Even if the British fleet wants to, they'll not come within a mile and a half of the river. The batteries onshore are too heavy. They'd have ta land marines and take us from behind. When and if this Injun hears somethin' worthwhile hearin', tell me, or tell Macdonough. Now, I've got work ta do." Bob grabbed Ken by the arm. Ken Russell was startled. In all the years they had known each other, dating back to the Revolution, the Irishman had never forced himself on him, physically.

"Dere's more. Ya t'ink I didn't know 'bout da gun emplacements? Me, who's been slavin' ta build yer precious ship?" Ken studied the fierceness in Dooley's eyes.

"Okay, Bob. For God's sake, what is it?"

"Elizer, here, is on a special mission fer me. He has his people, Indian people, lookin' out fer t'ings at da Brits' base on da Richelieu River, just up on da Canadian side of da border." Bob popped his head up to see if anyone was paying attention.

"Dere's a t'ousand or more Vermont militia stationed around Vengennes. Da Brits can't fit dat many marines on their ships an' take us from behind, an' dey can't bloody well march 'im down from Canada until dere ready ta start dere invasion. More of da lobster backs dat served wit' Wellington in Spain are bein' shipped down da St. Lawrence, but dey won't have da strength ta mount an invasion until around September. Dat gives us six months. Da Brits know dat if Macdonough gets his ship built, da lake will be in American hands. Dere plan is ta try ta blow up our emplacements on da river, cause dere Brits an' t'ink dere superior gunners and sailors. Dey just t'ink dat will work. But, even if it doesn't work, dey have plans ta build a bigger ship on da Richelieu. Just in time fer dere invasion in September. Now, how's dat fer intelligence?" Ken bowed his head.

"I'm sorry, Bob. I shoulda figur'd you'd be up ta yer neck in the real spyin' goin' on around here. But, those Browns have got me in a tizzy. They think they can build that ship in less than sixty days - much less. And I've got ta make sure she's seaworthy. But, that's my problem. You should be doin' what ya do best, and not wastin' yer time acting the role of a carpenter. Yer more valuable to us gettin' the information we need. Let me speak ta Macdonough and have ya transferred to the scouts full time. A kinda naval intelligence officer wit' the army." Ken thought Dooley would be pleased with this offer, but the fierceness was still in Bob's eyes.

"Dere's one more t'ing, Ken." Dooley bent down close to Captain Ken's ear and whispered something. Ken's eyes bulged.

"Mike! My God, Bob. Mike. Is there word? Is yer brother up there on the Richelieu?"

"Dat he is. Dey brought a bunch of carpenters down da St. Lawrence from Halifax. Elizer says one of dem works in chains. Dey fear he'll desert. Scuttlebut is, he made an attempt ta escape already. He speaks wit' a brogue. It's got ta be him. Ken!" the intensity in Bob's eyes melted into tears, "me brudder. He's not a hundred miles from dis very spot."

Mrs. Macdonough had waited six long years before she married her naval officer. "But," she insisted to Jessica that night, "it was worth every day. A man and a woman must first become friends - life long friends - before they marry. It's the civilized thing to do. Love, the kind of love that will last, isn't hurried. It's like a building, or a ship that's completed over time, with careful consideration. If we take our time with such material things, how much more time should we take building a relationship we expect to last for a lifetime? If a man truly loves you, he will take the time to come to know you. To be your friend in good times and in bad, well before a ring is placed on your finger."

Jessica and Michael had made up that night. They kissed over their gingerbread cake, as Happy had predicted. Michael had escorted Jessica back to the Macdonough's and kissed her again at the doorstep. Now, Mrs. Macdonough and Jessica were sipping tea in front of a warm and comforting fire in the parlor.

"You are still quite young," Mrs. Macdonough continued. "Passions must be controlled. That is what courting is all about. You and Michael have much to do before you can settle down together and raise a family."

"I feel we've already gone through so much together," Jessica said, sighing. "Michael's taken this so hard. If he only knew how hard it is for me. I love him so much. We're used to being with each other all the time. I've grown to rely upon it. As if it were like the very air that I breathe. I never want to be separated from him - Father John insisted that we shouldn't be separated. Michael's mother wanted us to be together, always." Lucy Ann Macdonough patted Jessica on the knee.

"I'm sure Father John would agree with me. And Mrs. Dooley, bless her memory. I confess, I am ignorant of your religion. In Middletown, Connecticut, where I was born, the Episcopal Church was the only faith I was exposed to. But, I'll write to Father John and inform him of your arrival here and my plans for you and Michael. You've told me so much about Teresa Dooley, my dear. I pray I can give you the same guidance and love that she did. Your Father John will approve."

Jessica was in bed by the time Uncle Bob, Elizer Williams, Dan Donovon, James Darymple, Happy George, and Michael had donned black masks over their heads and rode out to visit some of the houses of distinguished Vermont citizens who lacked the conscious not to trade with the enemy. Bob Dooley had insisted that Michael be brought along, claiming Michael had the duty to learn the way of his ancestors.

The ride under a moonlit sky wasn't easy. Vermont, in the spring, is one giant quagmire of mud. As the earth and water, frozen in the bitter cold of the northern weather thaws, a soupy mess of mud is a constant companion until the ground hardens once more in June. Despite the mud, the party made their way to the homes of several trade runners. Riding up to the doors of these houses, Michael felt something was wrong. This isn't the way lawful people should conduct themselves, he thought. He was glad Uncle Bob had asked him to go, but, now, he found it unsettling. He repeated the code over and over in his mind, trying to justify what they were going to do. These Americans were blatantly ignoring their patriotic duty, he thought. They were trading with the enemy. Providing them with essential food that would keep an invading army and navy strong, and war materials that would only inflict damage on American soldiers and sailors. Despite that, was this what they *ought* to do?

Uncle Bob noticed Michael's silence as the group made their way through the mud of the countryside.

"What's on yer mind, boyo? Yer as quiet as a church mouse. Is it da code yer thinkin' on, den?" Michael had been riding along staring at his saddle horn for the last two miles.

"Why do we have to take the law into our own hands, uncle? That makes us vigilantes, doesn't it?"

"Vigilwho?"

"A Committee of Vigilance. That's what Mr. Pechin called the Deptford Hundred and everyone else who went after Mr. Hanson and stormed the *American*." Bob Dooley felt a tinge of guilt go up his spine.

"Well, as fer dat I - well, I..."

"That was wrong, wasn't it, uncle?"

"Yes, boyo. Dat was wrong. It was da damned drink. Poor Joe Durkin. I'll caution ya again, Michael, me lad, stay off da drink. It steals yer soul."

"And how is this different from that?"

"Because da practice of tradin' wit' da enemy is to widespread in dese parts. Da government can't stop it, boyo. But we can. It's our duty ta stop it. How many good men have ta die before Americans realize dere duty? If dere wasn't a war, well, dat would be different. But, we took an oath ta defend da country when we joined da Commodore, didn't we? Don't be worryin', lad. We're not goin' ta kill anybody tonight, praise be.

It isn't like the case of Jimmy da barkeep. No, dese people only need gentle persuadin'. T'ink on it, boyo."

As they rode along Michael finally, slowly, saw this as a good thing. In his heart, he was able to justify it through the code. It was something they ought to do. Something that had to be done.

Uncle Bob was in his glory. Their last stop was a farmhouse just outside of Vengennes. The group gathered in front of the house and remained in their saddles as Uncle Bob dismounted. The house was dark, and a dog yelped uncontrollably until the farmer lit a lantern inside. Bob unfurled a whip as the door creaked open.

"What's this!" the farmer demanded, pointing a gun. "How dare you trespass on my land!" The farmer's sleepy eyes made out the black masks of the horsemen. His angry scow now changed to one of fear. The dog stood on his hind legs in front of his master, barking fiercely. Bob cracked his whip and the dog retreated back into the house, whimpering. "Who are you! What do you want!" the farmer shouted.

"I am Captain Moonlight," Uncle Bob said slowly. "An' you - are a no good, limey lovin' son of a bitch!"

"Zachery!" the farmer's wife, armed with a broom and dressed in her nightgown, pushed her husband out the door. "Who are these demons, Zachery? Tell them to get off our land. Do you hear me? This very instant!"

The farmer was confused over Bob Dooley's accent. "I think Irish bandits are on our land, mother." Uncle Bob laughed and cracked his whip again.

"D'ya hear dat, boyos!"

"E's off 'es rocker, 'at's what, Captain Moonlight. Why, e's 'ead is as thick as 'es plough." Happy declared through his mask.

"English!" the farmer gasped.

"White men have short memories," Elizer said, in a forboding voice. "They think they own land forever. They forget the Tory and how the patriot chased him back to his England or north to his British brother in Canada."

"And Indians, mother!" the farmer exclaimed to his wife, pointing at Elizer.

"Dis white man fohgets what side he's on, Cap'n Moonlight," James chimed in. "Why don't you jest tell him plain, what happens to folks who fohget."

"Lord, mother, Negroes!"

"Americans!" Bob screamed, indignantly. "Americans, ya bloody heathen Tory traitor! Don't you remember what happened ta da Tories in da last war? Do ya t'ink people will just forget dat you were makin' money tradin' wit' da Brits when dis war is over?"

"We don't have anything to do with Madison's war!" the farmer's wife protested.

"Dat's right! Ya don't have anythin' ta do wit' it any more." Bob cracked his whip and then pointed it at the farmer and his wife. "If good patriots hear of anyone tradin' wit' da Brits they call on me, Captain Moonlight! An' I'll make sure dat traitors like you pay fer dere crimes. I'll hound you from yer land! I'll chase you back to yer bloody king!" The farmer pushed his stubborn wife into the house and shut the door.

"Please. Please, gentlemen. The land is all I have. Please leave us be." he pleaded.

"Swear allegiance ta da United States of America!"

"I swear! Please, gentlemen, I swear by the Lord!"

Uncle Bob was right. Every single house they visited that night, and for seven straight nights after that, swore their allegiance to the United States. The illegal trade with the British was abated, at least within the vicinity of Captain Moonlight.

Captain Pring sailed his fleet past Burlington, down to Otter Creek and weighed anchor. An alarm was sent out and Michael made his way with James Darymple to their gun among the batteries, at Fort Cassin. Captain Boyle had sent cannon, including his pride and joy "Slingshot" to Macdonough as a present. It took sixty teams of horses for the cannon and munitions to travel from Albany to Vengennes; the mud was that thick. But now "Slingshot" was cleaned and primed and ready. The magazine, where Michael ran to get the powder was some thirty yards away from the guns. Michael had to run, downhill, from the cannon to the bunker where the magazine was housed, and back uphill to James in less than two minutes.

Pring, cautiously, crept his fleet closer to the Fort, hoping in vain to clear the cannon from the ridge so he could sail down the river and destroy Macdonough's ship. But James and "Slingshot" stopped them with pinpoint accuracy, putting shot after shot within feet of Pring's ships, driving them back. The British attempt was futile. After two hours of trading cannon fire, Pring set sail back to Canada, knowing he would lose control of the lake the minute the Americans put their ship in the water. Macdonough, personally, congratulated James' gun crew for their heroic marksmanship. "I've never seen anyone sight a cannon with such consistent accuracy!" James smiled at Michael, who was lying on the ground soaked in sweat, out of breath, and clutching the stitch of pain he had endured in his side for the duration of the contest. Michael had dashed to and from the magazine a total of thirty three times in the first hour alone.

"Thank ya Commodore. But the boy here deserves the credit. He done run his fool head off!" James bent down and extended his bear like hand to Michael, lifting him off the ground with ease.

"No, James... The Commodore is right... You were marvelous! Just like in the bow of the *Chasseur...* Those Britishers didn't stand a chance," Michael panted.

"He's right Seaman Darymple," Macdonough insisted, "never before have I seen such a mighty display." James laughed, heartily.

"Why Commodore, ya knows yurself that the ground is a whole lot better to fire from than the bow of a ship. This here ground don't move like a ship does. Ain't nuttin' easier than primin' an' sightin' Slingshot on a steady deck like this here fort." Macdonough shook the hands of the gun crew and then saluted James.

"Seaman Darymple, for your heroism today, I am promoting you to gunner on my flagship, *Saratoga*, the very ship you've saved today. You will assume the rank of warrant officer and act as gunner of the ship. Congratulations," Macdonough said, showing his dimples and saluting again. They all returned the salute. James broke down in tears.

"An offisah! If that don't beat all! An offisah!"

The brothers Brown were more than true to their word. *Saratoga* was launched within forty days from the start of her construction. Mrs. Macdonough had the honor of christening the ship. From the moment *Saratoga* sailed onto the lake, she commanded it. The British took their fleet up the Richelieu to their base at Isle-aux-Noix. More redcoats arrived throughout the summer. The British were busy building *Confiance*, a ship slightly larger than Macdonough's flag ship, and making plans for invasion. Uncle Bob was right. It wasn't until September that the English were prepared to attack.

Elizer Williams, himself, had seen, what looked like, Mike Dooley working on the *Confiance*, but he couldn't get within three hundred yards of the ship. The British needed the ship to take on the American fleet or the invasion would have to be called off. Everything depended on this. The British army couldn't march their soldiers down into the Champlain Valley, they needed the lake to sail them down. Moreover, the lessons of Saratoga in the last war were heeded in London. England knew they had to have a protected supply line. They would never send an army down into New York or Vermont without control of the lake, for the lake could supply an army with reserves and munitions from Halifax via the St. Lawrence. Without the lake, the British would be overextended in enemy territory, repeating the embarrassment of the Battle of Saratoga.

Day after day, Pring received communications from the army urging him to put *Confiance* into the water. The army was ready and their battle summer was slipping by. Finally, Pring, who through no fault of his own couldn't get the materials and naval man power to finish the ship to the satisfaction of the army, was relieved of command. Captain George Downie took *Confiance* with his carpenters still working on the ship, down the Richelieu on the seventh of September.

Uncle Bob, who had been given special assignment scouting with the army, received news of the British carpenters' departure from Elizer Williams the day after the *Confiance* sailed. Bob was stationed in Plattsburgh, New York, where the army, under General Macomb, had constructed several forts. Plattsburgh, a small town snuggled underneath Cumberland Head, was headquarters for the small American army.

The British had a three-fold plan. General Robert Ross sailed into Chesapeake Bay with a fleet and four thousand seasoned troops. Ross attacked Washington, burning the White House in retaliation for the burning of the government house in Toronto by American troops the year before. Ross then turned his attention to Baltimore, where he prepared to attack the city and make it pay for being home to the nest of privateers that had done so much damage to English commerce. Second, a later attack on the city of New Orleans was planned. This was intended to stretch the American defenses across the breadth of the country, so that the invasion from Canada, the third and most important part of the plan, could succeed without opposing a concentrated enemy force. Years later, the Dooley's would appreciate the irony of fighting on the northern frontier while thier beloved Fells Point faced direct attack.

Except for *Confiance*, everything was ready. The British juggernaut had begun.

Chapter 22

"WHAT WE *OUGHT* TO DO"

The *Saratoga* sailed proudly up Lake Champlain with a crew of two hundred and ten men, and boasting twenty-six guns. The rest of the American fleet followed her. Lieutenant Stephen Cassin commanded the schooner *Ticonderoga*, with one hundred and ten men, including Captain Ken as sailing master, and seventeen guns. Lieutenant Robert Henley captained the brig *Eagle*, one hundred and twenty men, and twenty guns. The sloop, *Preble,* was in the hands of Lieutenant Charles Budd, carrying thirty men, and seven cannon. To the rear struggled ten gunboats with a total compliment of five hundred and eighty men, and a combined armament of sixteen guns. The fleet's destination was Plattsburgh. General Macomb had sent word that he intended to make an initial defense of the town. He was well supplied for a long siege with his forts on the high ground facing the town and the Saranac River, and his right flank facing Plattsburgh Bay. It was Macdonough's job to protect Macomb's rear. Macomb had nearly twenty nine hundred men to defend his forts, but, sadly, dysentery, diarrhea, and typhus were running rampant throughout his command and a thousand of his regulars were on the sick list.

Michael was with James in the bow of the *Saratoga*. He saw Valcour Island off to starboard and remembered Captain Ken telling him about the battle that was fought under the lee of the island during the Revolution. The Americans had lost that battle, but as Ken Russell would claim, if it were not for Benedict Arnold, who had command of the American fleet on the lake, and who fought side by side with Captain Ken, the Revolution would have ended in defeat. It was Arnold, who snuck his sinking fleet past the victorious British ships in the dead of night, saving them, ostensibly, to fight another day that postponed the British invasion of New York. That foiled the British timetable and the postponement allowed the Americans to muster an army strong enough to defeat General Burgoyne at Saratoga.

Michael wondered if Macdonough could muster the same spirit in his men that Arnold had done. He also wondered if he, himself, had the courage and fortitude to, once again, stand in the bow with James and the gun crew of *Slingshot* and stand up to ball and chain shot. Finally, he thought of his father. Was he in Lower Canada now?

Uncle Bob had never told his nephew that he thought Mike Dooley to be a carpenter on *Confiance*. Bob couldn't bring himself to let the boy know. Not until a time when Mike could be rescued and brought safely through to the American lines. Uncle Bob knew Michael would not be able to stand the constant strain of knowing where his father was and not being able to do anything about it. Bob Dooley could barely stand it himself. He worked the problem over and over in his mind, desperately trying to find a way to get his brother off the *Confiance*. But, it was to no avail. Any attempt to save Mike Dooley would only serve to kill him. The ship was too well guarded. Hundreds of sailors and marines combed over her decks. Thousands of redcoats, now pouring into New York, stood between the two brothers.

The American fleet anchored in Plattsburgh bay. Immediately, Macdonough went to join Macomb for a council of war. Michael obtained permission to visit his uncle.

The British invasion force was commanded by Lt. General Sir George Prevost. He was the civil and military chief, as well as the Governor General for Great Britain in Canada. Since the onset of hostilities, he had beaten back American attempts to invade his domain. It earned him the title "Savior of Canada." Now, it was his turn. He sent out a message to the people of New York assuring the populace of "kind usage and generous treatment." But, Prevost left no doubt as to who his real enemies were: "It is against the government of the United States, by whom this unjust and unprovoked war has been declared, and against those who support it, either openly or secretly, that the arms of his majesty are directed." What he wanted was to tear the United States apart, appealing to the federalists who were against the war from the beginning, to turn their back on their own government and quit the war.

But, men who were too timid to cross the border and attack Canada proved to be stout hearted in their nation's defense. It's one thing to ask a man to charge into his neighbor's country and claim it as his own, and quite another to defend his homeland, wife, and family. All over Northern New York, militia came running to Plattsburg's defense.

Still, the numbers of redcoats crossing the border were astonishing. Macdonough and Macomb met with Elizer Williams and Uncle Bob at a Council of War on September second. Michael waited outside Macomb's office.

"My staff has urged me to retreat," Macomb stated, flatly. "There isn't an officer on my staff who thinks we can withstand a siege. They want me to move south. Wait until more militia can bolster our numbers." The general walked out from behind his desk, his hands clasped behind his back. "Elizer, what intelligence have you these past few hours?" The scout smiled.

"There is war spirit over the militia. General Mooers has led the militia from Essex, Clinton, and Franklin counties to the Chazy road. They behave well. Like men. They will run, of course, when they see the red coat. That is what militia do. But not before firing their guns, putting holes in the English lines." Macomb seemed pleased. He sent for his orderly, hurriedly scratched orders for Mooers, and turned to Uncle Bob.

"Captain Dooley, isn't it?"

"At yer service, gen'ral."

"What of the *Confiance*? I know you have a personal as well as a professional stake in all this." Bob turned to Elizer, who nodded his head. The chief scout kept nothing from his general and had told Macomb all about Mike Dooley.

"Last reports tell us she's on da lake. But da Britishers are still workin' on her. She isn't ready, not by a long shot." Macomb rubbed his hands in joy.

The general glanced at Macdonough. The commodore shared the general's joy and was showing his dimples from ear to ear.

"I'll not move my fleet, general. By the Almighty, I'll not move. When the British fleet arrives, they'll have to sail around Cumberland head to engage us. With the wind out of the northwest, as it always is this time of year, Pring will have to sail into the wind to come into the bay. At least, I hope he comes into the bay. He doesn't have to. He has a frigate's armament: twenty-seven long guns. Together, the *Confiance* and the *Linnet* have as many long-range weapons as my entire fleet. They can stand off and bear their long guns on us until we are forced to come out and meet them. But, I'm banking on the fact that Prevost has ordered an attack, not a bombardment. Besides, you know the Royal Navy. Their arrogance will compel them into the bay. And when they do come in I'll poor fire and brimstone into them." Uncle Bob cleared his throat.

"You have something to add, Captain Dooley?" Macomb asked.

"It's not Pring, sir. He's not commandin' da Britisher's fleet anymore. Dey got a new guy, sir. Captain George Downie, sir. Prevost got rid of Pring 'cause he couldn't get da *Confiance* ready in time. Prevost is livid. Word is he won't attack yer position until Downie brings da fleet down ta Plattsburgh. Pring is on da *Linnet* now."

"By God! What luck! Everyday we buy from their floundering gives us a better chance. My hope is that more militia will arrive everyday. I've already put out calls to the governors of New York and Vermont to send as many men as possible. The longer we hold here, the more time those militia have to come up. It's our only chance. To quit here now will mean the British will pick off the militiamen piecemeal. We must give them time to concentrate. How much time do I have,

Captain Dooley?" Uncle Bob scratched the stubble of beard on his chin.

"Sir, ya got a week, maybe more. I've a feelin' me brodder's done a little harm ta da Britishers on dat ship, ta delay a few t'ings, here an' dere. Ya know, sir, accidents happin'. Mike's a good one fer t'inkin' up ways ta make it look like t'ings are gettin' done, when da opposite is closer ta da truth. I taught him dat."

"You must introduce us when we make them haul down their colors, Captain," Macdonough remarked.

"An honor, sir. He was impressed ya know, sir." Macdonough hung his head for a moment.

"I know. Captain Russell has told me. We'll make them pay for that mistake, Captain Dooley."

"It's decided, then," Macomb said with finality. "We'll make our stand here. If Prevost waits for his fleet before laying siege in earnest, that means everything will rest with Commodore Macdonough. They'll have to sail into the bay and defeat his fleet first, before they can overwhelm my position. I hate to put it this way, Tom," Macomb said, firmly, to Macdonough, "but this entire battle, the last stand against the invasion of our country, and, perhaps the last battle of this war, rests squarely on your shoulders. Defeat them in the bay and they'll go home. May God be with you, sir."

Michael met Uncle Bob as he came through the door of Macomb's office. He didn't like the look on his uncle's face.

"C'mere, boyo, wouldja?" Bob took Michael by the arm and led him away from the busy atmosphere of Macomb's headquarters. News had already filtered out that the command was going to sit tight until the bitter end. Officers and men scurried about. Michael noticed nervous expressions. They were the faces of men who had to reconcile themselves to the fact they were hopelessly outnumbered. Uncle Bob drew Michael outside.

"Ahhh! Would ya breathe dis nice, clean air, boyo! Not like da Point wit' its stinkin' backwash dis time of year." Michael peeled his uncle's fingers from his arm.

"What's going on? How come you took me outta there in such a hurry?"

"Now, boyo, don't be gettin' yer Irish up. I just have ta explain sometin' to you is all. I'm sorry if I hurt yer arm, but I t'ought it would be better if we were alone. Ya know, like we were when we were talkin' over da complications of da code on da deck of da *Chasseur* not too long ago."

"Please, uncle, don't treat me like a child. Tell me what's goin' on!"

"An' me not seein' ya dese past weeks? Can't I at least inquire how Jessica's is doin', da dear lass?" Michael sighed.

"You know she nearly killed me when I told her she couldn't come to Plattsburgh. Thank God for Mrs. Macdonough, she agreed with me and demanded that Jess stay with her in Burlington until the outcome. Mrs. Macdonough's really takin' over. Made up a whole bunch of rules, it was terrible." Michael lowered his eyes, not wanting to show any emotion. "The truth is I miss her, terribly. I have this ache in my stomach. I can't eat. I can't even think straight."

"Dat's love fer ya, boyo. Makes a man feel just awful."

"But, we've been through so much together. All the way from Fells Point. We were always together. You, me, Jess, and Captain Ken. Even James, Dan Donovon, and Happy. All of a sudden I wish she was here." Uncle Bob raised his forefinger.

"Ya did da only t'ing ya could do, boyo. Dis is no place fer a girl, even if she is da best master's mate in da bloody fleet. Soon terrible t'ings are goin' ta happen. Which is why I'm sendin' ya back ta Jessica." Michael's face reddened as his temper flared up. He took a step away from his uncle.

"No! No you don't! I've signed onto this fleet like every other sailor here. You can't - and you won't - take me outta this. I have just as much a right to be here as you do!"

"An' I admire dat kind of spunk, Michael, darlin'. Ya wouldn't be a Dooley if ya didn't feel any udder way. But. Michael. There's sometin' I have ta tell ya dat yer not goin' ta like. But, it's da only way."

"None of your tricks, uncle. What is it?" Bob looked down at his shuffling feet.

"It's about yer fadder."

"My pa! You know something about my pa?"

"Known it fer quite some time, boyo."

"And you didn't tell me?"

"Couldn't, boyo. Didn't have da guts fer tellin' ya. Yer fadder is on da Britisher's flagship. Has been dese many months. I couldn't tell ya, boyo. Not in good conscious. I worked da code over an' over, an' I decided ta keep it from ya soes ya can sleep at night. God knows, I've gotten little sleep meself, tryin' ta come up wit' a way ta get yer fadder out of dere. But, it was no use, boyo. As God is me judge, 'twas no use a'tall."

"But, what does my pa bein' on the Britisher's flag ship got to do with me stayin' here?"

"Don't ya see, boyo? Why, yer fadder would kill me if I let ya go t'rough dis battle dat's comin'. An' it's comin', lad. Da whole British army is on its way here. Everythin' depends on Macdonough. If he can beat da Britisher's fleet an' keep control of da lake, den da Brits have ta march home wit' dere tail between dere legs."

"So, what's that have to do with me? I'm a powder monkey aboard the *Saratoga*, and it's my job to get powder to *Slingshot*. If you take me out of this battle some other kid will have to take my place. No, uncle, you can't justify that with the code. It's what I *ought* to do - what we *ought* to do!" Bob Dooley knelt down on the ground in front of his nephew. He took Michael's hands and placed them in his.

"If ya work da cannon on dat ship yer gonna be firin' balls at yer own fadder. It stands ta reason da *Confiance* will take on da *Saratoga*. Dere both ships of equal size an' guns. Boyo, how can ya do dat? In God's name, how can da code tell ya ta shoot at yer own fadder?" Michael took a few steps away with his head down.

"Know what you *ought* to believe; know what you *ought* to desire; know what you *ought* to do," he said out loud. Suddenly, he turned his determined face up to his uncle. "If I kill my own pa I'll never know it. James will have those guns firin' so fast that there won't be time to think or see anything. No, uncle. My place is with my ship. I couldn't call myself a Dooley, or a man of the code, or anything respectable if I don't get myself back aboard the *Saratoga* and do my job." Uncle Bob's face was contorted with pain.

"Den, da blood of me brudder be on me own soul, an' not his son's. An', God help us, da blood of da son be on me own soul, an' not da fadder's."

It took eleven days for Captain Downie to ready *Confiance*. In that time, General Macomb was able to strengthen his forts and welcome newly arriving militia. The hospital was burned to the ground and the sick transported to Crab Island, which lay Southeast of Plattsburgh, directly opposite Cumberland Head in the bay. On September fifth, a small battery was set up on the island, manned by convalescents.

Prevost had his columns advance into Plattsburgh. The British took control of most of the town, but the American forts were well defended. Still, Macomb would have no choice but to surrender if the American fleet was defeated. General Macomb gathered his entire force around the forts south of Plattsburgh. There were three forts. They were built in the shape of a peak facing the Saranac River. Fort Moreau, the largest, was in the center of the American position, jutting out and forming the peak. Fort Brown held the left flank, and Fort Scott the right flank, close to the bay. They were earthen fortifications, dug so the enemy would have to come up a steep slope, directly in the path of American forty-two pound cannon.

Macdonough placed his ships in a line of battle across the bay, protecting Macomb's forts. The commodore put *Eagle* at the North end of the bay, parallel with the mouth of the Saranac River. The line stretched south, and the *Eagle* was followed by *Saratoga*, *Ticonderoga*, and *Preble*, which lie close to Crab Island. Three gunboats were positioned north of *Eagle*, three between *Eagle* and *Saratoga*, and four between *Saratoga* and *Ticonderoga*. It was a nice, tight line.

On land, the British outnumbered Macomb's army by four to one. The redcoats who were prepared to take the American forts were the same battle hardened troops that had defeated Napoleon. The Americans had little or no taste of battle, be they army or navy. General Mooers' militia had fired their volleys and ran. But, not all of them kept on running. Many of them took positions adjacent to the British line of march and poured a harassing sniper fire on the enemy. Still, redcoats by the thousands marched into Plattsburgh.

Captain Downie finally sent word that the *Confiance* was ready. He dispatched a boat with all the carpenters, save one, to Cumberland Head. Mike Dooley had no choice but to enter Plattsburgh Bay on a British ship of war against his chosen country.

Now that the British fleet was in tact and prepared for battle, the officers of the Royal navy gathered for an elegant dinner on the evening of September tenth. The English were certain the next day would be theirs.

English men and women in fine array, picnicked in small boats as Downie tacked into Plattsburgh Bay on the eleventh of September. But, Macdonough was more than ready for the British fleet. He had each of his ships anchored both at the bow and the stern. Then, he had springs, or hawsers, attached to both anchors so that by hauling on these lines, he could turn his ships at will, without the necessity of wind, bringing fresh broadsides to bear on the enemy if his cannon were damaged and out of action.

On seeing the English ships come into Plattsburgh Bay, Macdonough knelt down on his gun deck and led his men in prayer. He had a flag hoisted below his pennant that read: "For free trade and seamen's rights."

Michael was stationed in the bow of Macdonough's flagship, behind *Slingshot*. Happy George was in his fighting foretop, constantly bellowing the progress of the enemy to the officers below. Dan Donovon was with Bob Dooley in the waist of the ship. The marines had manned the lines of the hawsers, ready to turn the ship at a moment's notice. Slowly, the English ships crept into the bay against the wind. Macdonough positioned himself behind one of the starboard guns. He waited, patiently, for all the British ships to come into the bay.

At that moment, a small boat lay along the *Saratoga*. Someone quickly climbed over the larboard railing.

Eagle fired the first shot. Macdonough fired the second from one his long nines. The ball raked the *Confiance*, killing one seaman, wounding several others, and knocking out the wheel of the English flagship.

Downie's battle plan called for his eleven-gun sloop, *Finch*, to sail towards Crab Island and engage *Preble*. Then he sent Captain Pring with the sixteen-gun brig, *Linnet*, and sloop, *Chub*, with eleven guns, against *Eagle*. Downie then split his thirteen gunboats to attack both *Preble* and *Ticonderoga*. The *Saratoga,* Downie wanted all by himself with the *Confiance*. It was a masterful plan. But, there were two difficulties that Macdonough had counted on and Downie thought he could overcome. The first was the wind. As the British came into the bay they had to sail against a very uncooperative wind. Macdonough's ships were already anchored and waiting for the enemy. The American commodore had plenty of time to prepare. Downie had to make those preparations while sailing into the bay. His men were performing two functions simultaneously. The second, was the fact that Macdonough had more short distance carronades than the British. At close range, they would be more effective, almost like the difference between using a shotgun and a rifle. Owning to the narrow geography of the bay, the advantage swung to short range weaponry. Regardless, Downie came on into the maelstrom, positioning his ships as best he could under a withering fire from the Americans.

Michael turned to a tap on his shoulder.

"My God in heaven. Sweetheart what..." Jessica hugged and kissed him. James turned to see the sweet exchange

"Lord, Almighty. Honey, we's 'bout ta git what foh from da English. Ain't no time foh kissin' mah powder monkey, now." Michael broke their hold and looked, sternly, into her eyes.

"Why? I've missed ya so, but why?" Jessica's eyes were afire with sapphire.

"I can't leave you now! Everything I told you about the roof of the church is a lie! I came on the *Chasseur* because Father John promised your mother that we wouldn't be separated. You talk about a code, about knowing what you ought to do. Well, I know what I *ought* to do! I can't leave you now. On an oath to Teresa Dooley, I can't leave you!" Michael took her into his arms.

"Thank you, Jess. You're meant to be here, just like I am. The code works wonders, things we can't understand. But, once we've taken it to heart, it does the thinking for us. Jess, my pa is on the *Confiance*."

"Oh, Michael!"

"We're all meant to be here. I don't know why. But, we're all meant to be here." Uncle Bob came storming up from the waist after seeing Jessica at the bow chaser.

"Dis is madness, boyo. We're gonna lose half our number in dis battle. Mike will kill me. Dat bloody priest will kill me. What on earth are ya doin' on dis ship, lass?"

A shot rang out from *Confiance*. It hit a chicken coop in the waist of the ship. One of the roosters flew up to the mainmast and started to flap its wings and crow. The crew of the *Saratoga* thought it to be a good omen of things to come. Dan Donovon led the entire ship's company in three cheers. Michael put Jessica's hand into Uncle Bob's.

"Get her below. She can work with the surgeon. She's my girl, uncle. A few of the men have their wives with them on board. Look at Patrick Rourke over there. His wife wouldn't leave either. She's the gun's powder monkey. Take Jessica to the surgeon, uncle. There's plenty she can do there." Bob Dooley shook his head in disbelief and then quickly pulled Jessica across the deck and below.

The *Confiance* was now in position. She fired all her larboard cannon, seemingly, at the same instant. It was a broadside, double shotted over smooth water, fired from long twenty-four pounders. It struck *Saratoga* like a thunderbolt. Forty of her crew were immediately cut down. Splinters flew in every direction.

Michael was paralyzed. It took him several seconds to recognize the fact that he was completely naked. Like the other men working the cannon, he had taken off his shirt. But, now, every stitch of clothing he wore was ripped from his body. Splinters had shred his clothing and left it in tattered bits on the deck of the ship. Miraculously, Michael was not injured. He gazed at others not as forutnate. Men lay in agony in every direction. Seamen slipped on blood that gushed onto the deck from dismembered bodies. James' great black hand whipped across Michael's face, forcing him back to reality.

"I said moh powder! Now move!" James shoved Michael aft. Somehow, Michael found the power to move his legs. He jumped over the bleeding and crippled forms of his shipmates and disappeared below deck.

On the northern side of the line, the *Chub* took a crippling broadside from the *Eagle* and drifted, helplessly, toward the Americans. Everything stopped as she struck her colors. Not a gun could be fired from either side until the *Chub* was out of danger and clear of the American line. Macdonough quickly sent one of his midshipmen to take possession of her and tow her inshore. Nearly half of the *Chub's* compliment had been killed or wounded in the opening minutes of battle. Then, the fighting renewed with even more ferocity. James had the guns of the

Saratoga firing at such a rate that the men of the gun crews fell down out of shear exhaustion.

At the other end of the line, the British sloop *Finch* was driven from her position by constant fire from *Ticonderoga. Finch* drifted upon the shoal at Crab Island and surrendered after the American invalids from the hospital, who had manned the battery, compelled her to do so. The British gunboats redoubled their efforts, furiously attacking *Preble.* The American schooner was so cut up that she had to sever her cables and drift inshore, leaving the engagement entirely. With *Preble* out of action, the British gunboats swarmed around *Ticonderoga.*

As the northwest wind carried smoke from the cannon fire towards him, Michael could barely see the action on the right flank of the American line. In between running below decks to fetch powder for *Slingshot,* naked still, but completely indifferent to it, he caught a glimpse of *Ticonderoga* with her marines pouring musket on the British gun boats, not two or three feet away from boarding her. Through the smoke, Michael saw Captain Ken standing on the bow, straddling a forestay line, pistol in hand, firing into the attacking gun boats, urging his men to their duty. He saw Captain Ken double over, clutching his stomach, and fall into the water. He knew Ken Russell was dead. Michael felt as if he himself had been hit with the musket ball. Hit in his own heart. He staggered back to *Slingshot.*

On the northern side of the line, cannon fire lessened. Each side had succeeded in displacing almost every single gun of their opponent. The *Saratoga* had only one gun still in operation. The gun captain was Patrick Rourke. He was one of the men whose wife had insisted on staying with him through the engagement. The *Confiance* fired one of her long nines directly at that cannon. The ball severed Rourke's head and sent it hurling towards the quarterdeck. Unbelievably, it slammed into Macdonough's chest with a loud thud. Rourke's head struck the commodore with such force that it rendered him unconscious. Uncle Bob quickly doused Macdonough with a bucket of water.

"Twas' a mighty blow, commodore! Does ya have yer wits, sir? It's time to turn da ship," Bob urged the captain. Macdonough was stunned.

"My Lord, Captain Dooley, what was it that hit me?"

"Rourke's head, sir. But, for da love of God, it could have been dat cannon ball. Get up now, sir! It's time ta do da turnin'."

Michael saw Rourke's wife come up from the companionway. She moved her husband's body aside and took control over the cannon. There was no time to think. No time to consider whether this was the right thing to do. It was just done.

Macdonough composed himself and commanded the winding of his ship. He ordered his men to leave go the stern anchor and cut the bow cable. Then he turned to Uncle Bob and ordered him and his twenty marines to pull the line and turn the ship. Bob positioned himself at the end of the rope and tied it around his massive chest.

"Heave lads! Heave!" Bob screamed. Without wind, using only cables and anchors alone, *Saratoga* slowly began to swing around. At that moment, the *Confiance* was desperately attempting the same maneuver. The battle hinged on which side could complete the turn first. Uncle Bob, Dan Donavan, and their marines strained every muscle. *Saratoga* groaned as she inched into the turn, mimicking the pitiful moans of the dying men on her decks, as if the ship itself were in pain.

On both sides, guns were silent, but a frenzy seized the men who jumped to the cables, realizing that eveything depended on this deadly race. Screaming oaths of British officers could be heard even on the *Saratoga*, as the *Confiance* lost hold of her anchor and the British, to a man, realized that they couldn't turn their ship. English faces popped up over the railing to see an omnimous American larboard battery. Many immediately resigned themselves to death.

James already had his gun crews prime their cannons. Not one American took pleasure in what they had to do. Michael fell down to his knees, begging the Almighty to spare his father.

James, slow match smoking in his hand, stared intently at Macdonough, waiting for the signal.

"Fire!"

Within seconds the *Saratoga* poured on such a tremendous cannonade that the *Confiance* was forced to strike her colors. The battle was over. Not a sail on any ship of either fleet was left in its rigging.

Upon hearing of the English defeat on the lake, Sir George Prevost ordered his army home. The British invasion had been turned back. Macdonough sent a dispatch to Secretary Jones: "The Almighty has been pleased to grant us a signal victory on Lake Champlain, in the capture of one frigate, one brig, and two sloops of war of the enemy."

Michael was still in a state of shock. The arms and limbs and heads of his shipmates lay strewn about the deck. Their blood ran down the scuppers into Plattsburgh Bay.

Jessica came up on deck weeping. She had blood dripping from her apron. She took Michael into her arms, covering him with the apron.

Uncle Bob came racing towards them, pointing to the *Confiance.*

"She's sinkin', boyo. We've got ta get on her before she goes down." Uncle Bob ordered a boat into the water. He yelled for Dan Donovon, James, and Happy to jump in. Michael grabbed Uncle Bob.

"Uncle! Captain Ken! I saw him, uncle. I saw..." Bob shook his head vehemetly.

"Don't say it, boyo. I don't want ta know. God help us. I don't want ta know." Michael squeezed Jessica close to him.

"He died a hero's death, Jess," Michael whispered. "Captain Ken is a hero."

"God bless his soul," Jessica whispered back. They didn't cry. There was no time to cry.

They rowed across to the *Confiance* expecting the worst. She was so cut up, not a sail or line of running rigging was left on her broken masts, and shot through her hull so badly that only supreme effort could save her from floundering. As Uncle Bob came over the railing, he cringed at the sight of broken bodies everywhere. Michael followed his uncle up the side of the ship and ran across the deck.

"Pa!" he shouted, "Pa!" Uncle Bob checked the dead lying in a row on the gun deck. Dan Donovon, Happy, and James ran down to work the pumps, working side by side with their English enemies to keep the ship afloat.

Jessica chased after Michael. She found him kneeling beside one of the wounded. Mike Dooley was lying on the gun deck. He had been hit in the right arm. He gazed, increduously, at his son. The fact that Michael was dressed only in an apron about his waist never registered in their minds.

"I don't know why or what you're doing here. But, I'm so glad that you are," Mike said, breathing heavily. He clutched his son with his left arm and brought him close. "How? How did you come to be here?"

Finally, they were face to face, kissing, hugging, happy. Michael looked upon his father, tears pouring down his dirty face. Jessica held her hands to her cheeks. Her body shaking from sheer joy.

Michael inhaled deeply and shouted in a broken and emotional voice to his father: "Know what you *ought* to believe; know what you *ought* to desire; know what you *ought* to do."

With James, Dan Donovon, and Happy working the pumps, and both English and American sailors straining every muscle, *Confiance* managed to swim and not sink in Plattsburg Bay. Jessica, Michael, and Mike Dooley embraced each other as Uncle Bob joined them. Bob picked his brother off of the deck. Mike and Bob looked down at Michael and Jessica, who were embracing each other. Then Bob did likewise, bringing Mike to his bearlike chest.

"It's Teresa dat's done it. An' da code of Aquinas." Mike shook his head.

"Bob. You've changed. You changed your mind about da code. It's true isn't it?"

"Aye, brudder. Tis true. My mind. And my heart." With tears streaming down his face, Bob Dooley carried his brother across the bloody deck. At the railing, they stopped, all of them, to gaze over the bay upon the *Saratoga* and the Stars and Stripes that waved majestically over her masthead. "It's time, Mike," Bob said in a whisper. "It's time ta go home."

About the Author

George J. Galloway is active in his community, especially in his parish, and is the founder of the Bucks County St. Patrick's Day Parade. A former aide to a Pennsylvania state senator, Mr. Galloway pursued a career in public life before turning back to his love of history and has been teaching history for the past five years in secondary schools. He has traveled extensively doing research on sailing ships, the history of Baltimore, and the War of 1812. He lives with his wife and three children in Fallsington, Pennsylvania. The *Powder Monkey* is his first novel.

9 780759 604773